PRAISE FOR CAROLYN HAINES

"A writer of exceptional talent."

—*Milwaukee Journal Sentinel* on *Them Bones*

"Southern storytelling is indeed a very special art form."

—*New York Times Book Review* on *The Darkling*

"Written with a languid sensuality, this rich and complex work features quirky, fully developed characters involved in an unpredictable story, with Mattie's long-awaited revenge providing a bittersweet but satisfying coda."

—*Publishers Weekly* on *Touched*

"So vivid, so energetic, so poignant that it seems to move on reels rather than pages."

—*Chicago Tribune* on *Touched*

"Like the heat of a Deep South summer, Ms. Haines's novel has an undeniable intensity; it's impossible to shake its brooding atmosphere."

—*New York Times Book Review* on *Touched*

OTHER NOVELS BY CAROLYN HAINES

Deception
Summer of the Redeemers
Touched
Judas Burning
Penumbra

Fever Moon
Revenant
Skin Dancer
Shop Talk

Pluto's Snitch Mysteries

The Book of Beloved

Sarah Booth Delaney Mysteries

Them Bones
Buried Bones
Splintered Bones
Crossed Bones
Hallowed Bones
Bones to Pick
Ham Bones
Wishbones
Greedy Bones

Bones Appétit
Bones of a Feather
Bonefire of the Vanities
Smarty Bones
Booty Bones
Bone to Be Wild
Rock-a-Bye Bones
Sticks and Bones

Writing as R. B. Chesterton

The Darkling
The Seeker

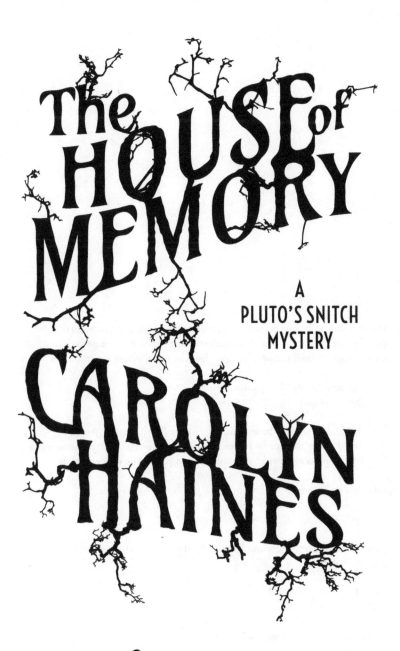

THE HOUSE OF MEMORY

A
PLUTO'S SNITCH
MYSTERY

CAROLYN HAINES

THOMAS & MERCER

Text copyright © 2017 by Carolyn Haines

Published by Thomas & Mercer, Seattle

www.apub.com

Amazon, the Amazon logo, and Thomas & Mercer are trademarks of Amazon.com, Inc., or its affiliates.

ISBN-13: 9781477819937
ISBN-10: 1477819932

Cover design by Cyanotype Book Architects

Printed in the United States of America

Life ends with a snap of small bones, a head cracked from its stem, and a spirit unmoored.

—*Sarah Kernochan*

CHAPTER ONE

The bow of the steamboat *Miss Vandy* cut through the dark water of the Alabama River as we moved north against the current. We'd left the subtropics of the delta behind and motored past the landing and boatyard at Saint Stephens, steadily progressing toward Montgomery. Impenetrable forests marked each bank of the broad river, and even in the daylight, it seemed as if the woods were filled with the spirits of the long-departed. Indians, trappers, French and Spanish explorers, the ravaged soldiers of the Union and Confederacy. The Alabama River had provided transportation for all of them. And, for many, a watery grave.

I stood on the deck, reveling in the fitful breeze, thankful that the July sun was on the decline. Night would bring the bloodsuckers out, but the harsh sun's glare would be gone. My first adventure in travel by steamboat had proven exciting and tedious, with tedium taking the greater balance. The paddle-wheeler, though well appointed, had only so much space where a passenger could stroll, and many of the landings were nothing more than primitive docks for loading and unloading goods. The river towns, where settlements had managed to thrive, were delightful and a pleasure to explore while *Miss Vandy* took on wood for fuel and supplies.

I stood on the boiler deck outside my first-class room. Reginald Proctor, my partner in our spanking-new private-investigation agency, remained in the saloon playing cards with two Montgomery businessmen who had no idea of Reginald's talents. I'd watched my partner fleece the men for half an hour, until the heat in the saloon and the repetition of the businessmen's foolish desire to hurl their money into Reginald's pocket had driven me outside. Besides, I had an appointment to keep. Gossip among the crew had given me an avenue of interest to pursue.

At last the young man I'd been waiting for came to stand beside me. "Mrs. Raissa James? I'm Kerry McBride, ma'am. The captain said you wished to speak with me."

He was maybe eighteen, lean and muscled from the hard work on the ship. Although I was only in my early twenties, I was a school-teacher, a widow, and now an investigator into the spirit world—older, if not wiser, than my age indicated. I had questions for the deckhand, but I didn't want to make him uncomfortable. I opened the conversation with the mundane details of the steamboat business. My uncle had told me the boat carried sugar, cloth, furniture, and an illegal supply of rum upriver to Montgomery, where it would be off-loaded. On the trip back downriver, the paddle-wheeler would pick up passengers and merchandise to sell in Mobile.

The young man confirmed the details in monosyllables. He was shy and couldn't hide his discomfort. His duties called, but he also knew I was the shipowner's niece, leaving him caught between duty and expediency.

"Kerry's an interesting name. How do you come by it?" I asked.

"Named for the county in western Ireland where my grandda was born. He came to America to work." He shifted and looked pointedly at the men on the lower deck moving cargo about.

"I won't keep you long," I said. "The captain tells me you've had a number of unusual experiences." Captain Abner Blythe had, in fact, told me that young Kerry had the ability to see spirits. Since I shared the ability to some extent, I was curious to know what he actually saw.

His restlessness stopped, and he looked chagrined. "It's just some foolishness to entertain the crew when we're docked and waiting."

"I write stories. Ghost stories." That won Kerry's full attention. "I wanted to talk to you about some of the things you've seen."

"Like I said, it's just old yarns my grandda told us kids. The men like a chill of an evening when we're havin' a sip of rum."

"But you don't see spirits?"

"Miss, I'd better get to my work."

I tried once more. "I see spirits, too." I pointed to the riverbank. "Do you see the woman there?" She stood just behind the first growth of trees. Her gingham dress blended with the gray-and-brown trunks of the trees, and her blonde hair blew in the wind. She watched us with an unbearable sadness.

"You see her?" he asked, amazed.

"I do. You share my gift."

"Gift?" He looked at me. "Likely more a curse."

"Maybe you won't feel the same when we've finished talking."

He looked back to the water and pointed. "See that wooden chute?"

We'd come upon another of the makeshift docks that stood empty. A narrow wooden chute clung to the bluff.

"I do."

"There's a cotton gin atop that bluff," Kerry said. "When the cotton crop is picked come September and October, the planters'll gin it and bale it."

"I've seen the bales on the docks in Savannah ready to be shipped to England," I said.

"We'll stop at the dock on our downriver trips and pick up the bales. They'll slide them down the chute to the stevedores, who'll load 'em up on the ship."

"I wouldn't want to be the person at the bottom of the chute," I said. It was a tremendous drop, and the weight of a cotton bale could easily crush a man.

"Back before the war, the slaves worked the top, and we Irish worked the bottom. The top workers were called rolladores. Slaves were too valuable to risk at the bottom, so it was the micks who took the job. My grandda was crushed at a chute like that."

"I'm sorry." I wasn't prepared for the sense of loss that swept over me.

"He died at Wigham Bluff. That's just upriver from here. Sometimes when we pass that landing, he'll be there wavin' at me."

"Are you afraid of him?"

Kerry smiled at last. "Not as long as he stays on the landing and I stay on the ship. If he starts to walk across the water, though, I'm swimmin' to the other shore."

He had an easy smile, and if he relaxed, he'd be a great storyteller. "Would you mind sharing some of your stories with me before we dock at Montgomery?"

"Later this evening, when the work is done, I'd be happy to tell you a yarn or two. On one condition."

"What's that?"

"You tell me if you see my grandda on the dock when we pass Wigham Bluff."

"Agreed." I held out my hand, and we shook on it. "My uncle Brett tells me the *Miss Vandy* is haunted. Could you tell me anything about that?"

He nodded. "I will, but I'd best get on with my work now or the captain will think I'm a loafer."

"Thank you, Kerry."

He doffed his hat and strode away.

We left the chute behind us and paddled upriver, following the bends and crooks of the waterway. Reginald and I were answering a call for help from a young woman in Montgomery who'd recently seized the nation's imagination. Southern belle Zelda Sayre had married the highly regarded novelist F. Scott Fitzgerald, and the pair had almost single-handedly launched the Jazz Age in America. I was on my way to consult with Mrs. Fitzgerald about a friend of hers she believed to be possessed. She'd learned about Pluto's Snitch Agency from a friend of my uncle's and had sent a desperate letter to Uncle Brett's home in Mobile, requesting Reginald's and my help. Reginald and I had just founded Pluto's Snitch, a private-investigation agency specializing in the occult, and we'd agreed to look into the troubles of Camilla Granger, a young woman whose sudden violent behavior had landed her in a mental institution. The threat of extreme therapy now hung over the young woman's head, and time was running out.

The deck door for Reginald's cabin opened, and he stepped out. "Shall I butt you?" he asked, offering the cigarettes.

I shook my head. I smoked occasionally but hadn't really acquired the habit. "Another two days to Montgomery," I said with a sigh. "I'm not a sailor, I guess. I'm eager for land under my feet."

"Thank your lucky stars we haven't run aground or hit a snag. Your uncle knows how to run a boating company. And these boats of his are racehorses compared to other fleets."

"I'm sure Uncle Brett would glow with your praise."

"You're worried about the case, aren't you?" He lit up, and the smell of burning tobacco was a bit of comfort.

"I am. Camilla Granger's only seventeen, and Mrs. Fitzgerald sounded desperate. She said something about dire medical treatment. I wonder what that means."

"We'll know in two days. No point getting the cart before the horse."

He was right, and it was one reason I liked him so much. Reginald had come into my life only weeks before as an assistant to the world-famous medium Madam Madelyn Petalungro. At her suggestion, Reginald had returned to Mobile with my uncle to help us resolve the haunting of Caoin House, my uncle's estate.

In the course of our work to help the spirits of Caoin House move along, I'd come to discover that Reginald wasn't truly a medium. Instead he was an astute observer of human nature who knew every trick of the spiritualist's trade. As such, he made a perfect partner in Pluto's Snitch. After resolving several tragedies—both past and present—at Caoin House, we'd embarked on our first paid case.

"Once we see the lay of the land, we'll figure it out," Reginald said.

"We'll certainly do our best." I lacked the confidence Reginald came by so naturally. He was a handsome man with an olive complexion and straight, white teeth—some would say a cake-eater—who'd made his way from an orphanage into the front parlors of some of the wealthiest people in New Orleans. Hardship had taught him composure and comportment. And how to hide his deepest secrets.

"Oh, come now, Raissa. You have a talent. Stop selling yourself short. If this young woman is bedeviled by a spirit, we'll figure it out and set her free."

I reached over and took the cigarette from his lips and inhaled lightly. "Yes, we will."

"That's my girl." He took his cigarette back.

"You're every bit as talented as I am, you know," I told him.

"Hardly." He threw the butt over the railing and into the dark water of the river. "I really would like to see spirits . . ."

"I know. We'll practice."

"Do you really think it's something I can learn?"

"I don't know. I saw them as a child, and apparently my mother saw them, as does Uncle Brett, to some degree. But growing up I somehow taught myself *not* to see them. I believe it was my husband's death that awakened me to the supernatural world again. Maybe all people have the ability when they're young, but most never turn it back on."

With the breeze cooling us, the ride upriver was pleasant. The sun was slipping behind the trees on the riverbank, and soon the evening temperatures would drop enough so that dinner would be served in the saloon.

"When we get to Wigham Bluff," I told Reginald, "you can help me look for a crew member's grandfather. He died, crushed by a cotton bale that came down one of the chutes. The young man sees him every time he passes."

Reginald smiled. "Do you think you will?"

"I don't know. But we can only look. I haven't figured out why I can see some spirits and not others."

"Madam believes the spirits have to use extraordinary energy to manifest. Perhaps we see only the ones who have that kind of energy." He nudged my arm. "I know you want to see your parents."

"I do." I missed my mother and father, a longing that overtook me at strange moments. "And Alex." My husband had been killed in the Great War. He'd died a hero, which gave me no comfort.

"Have you ever considered that maybe your dead don't want you pining for them? Maybe that's why they don't show up."

It wasn't a thought that had occurred to me, but I liked it. "So they don't appear, lest I seek the company of the dead instead of the living?"

He shrugged. "It's possible."

"Thank you." Reginald was a kind man, though he tried to hide it.

"My pleasure."

"How much did you take those gentlemen for in the card game?"

"Enough to pinch but not enough to holler."

I laughed out loud. "And that would be how much, in dollars?"

"Twenty each, roughly."

That did indeed pinch. Reginald was a sharp. "I hope they aren't sore losers."

"Not in the least, and I'll buy you the fanciest dinner in Montgomery when we arrive."

"And I'll hold you to it," I said, putting my arm through his. "Ill-gotten gains should be spent only on pleasurable activities."

CHAPTER TWO

The next two days passed in conversation and the kind of drowsy heat that makes an afternoon nap irresistible. The motion of the boat and the July weather sent me into my stateroom not long after lunch. I returned to the world of the living at night, much like the villain of Bram Stoker's horrific tale. I'd thrilled my students with the Irish author's gothic story of the living dead who fed on the blood of innocent maidens. The students weren't the only ones affected by Mr. Stoker's prose. I'd given myself more than a few chill bumps.

I'd managed two additional conversations with Kerry McBride and learned more about his gift. I had no doubt that, before long, he'd blunt that ability. And who was I to discourage him from doing so? To see things that others couldn't wasn't always easy. But tonight we were due to come upon Wigham Bluff, and I'd promised the young man I'd look for the spirit of his grandfather.

When I slipped out of the saloon and onto the deck, Reginald was deep in conversation with a young lawyer. I'd call him when the landing approached. If he wanted to practice seeing spirits, this would be a perfect opportunity. A full moon slipped in and out of clouds as I stargazed in the bedazzled sky. I'd heard the sailors predicting rain, but it wasn't supposed to start until we docked at Montgomery.

On either side of the river, the land looked untouched by humans. Growing up in Savannah, I hadn't fully anticipated the wildness of the state of Alabama. The Georgia and South Carolina coasts were populated with estates of the wealthy, but Alabama was different. Before the Civil War, vast acreage had been cultivated for cotton and crops, but there were also stretches of forest that were virtually unexplored. Moving along the river at night, the isolation touched me.

I'd come to love living at Caoin House in Mobile with my uncle. I'd never thought I'd leave Savannah, but Uncle Brett had sent men to pack my belongings and bring them to Mobile. At first I'd resisted, but finally I'd given in. I had been so alone in Savannah. I would miss teaching my students, but now I would have time to pursue my own writing. My first story would be published in October in the *Saturday Evening Post*. If I missed teaching too much, I could always seek a position in the Chickasaw school near Caoin House.

Up ahead a ghostly gray landing jutted into the river. I looked down on the lower deck and saw Kerry. He signaled to me, and I waved back. I dashed into the saloon and dragged Reginald out of a conversation with hastily murmured apologies. If he was going to be a ghost hunter, he needed to apply himself.

Reginald stepped onto the deck with a frown. "What couldn't wait?"

At last it occurred to me that Reginald's interest in lawyer Gerald Colson might have been more than merely conversational. There had been something between them, perhaps.

"I'm sorry. I didn't think." I pointed upriver, where the small dock was only a few hundred yards away. "It's Wigham Bluff. The ghost."

"Oh." He was instantly over his pique and hurried to the boat's railing to lean out. "I don't see anything."

"Neither do I." Which was something of a relief. Kerry looked up. I shook my head and motioned for him to join us on the upper deck. He disappeared as he went to find the stairs.

I eased beside Reginald as the boat drew closer to the roughly constructed wooden dock that jutted out into the river. The long wooden chute rose up the riverbank seventy feet or more. A cotton bale weighed five hundred pounds. It would hurtle down that height with the velocity of a locomotive. I could only hope Kerry's grandfather's death had been instantaneous. If his spirit still lingered and decided to show itself, I'd know soon enough.

Kerry came to stand beside me as the steamboat drew alongside the landing. For a moment I saw nothing. The wooden platform was just large enough to load and unload the cotton and hold a wooden shed some twenty-by-twenty feet. Because the cotton crop was still at least two months away from picking, the platform was empty. We moved abreast, and I was relieved that no one waited there for us.

"I guess he's shy tonight," Kerry said.

"Damn." Reginald brought out his cigarettes and offered, but both Kerry and I declined. "I was hoping to see a spirit."

And then he was there. I pointed at the man, not old as I'd anticipated, but young and strong, his chest wide and braces holding up his pants. He strode to the edge of the platform and nodded at us as we passed. He looked a lot like the young man standing beside me.

"Grandda," Kerry said softly and waved.

"I don't see him." Reginald was disappointed. "I sense something, but there's nothing to be seen."

"Maybe you're trying too hard," I said. When I looked again, the dock was empty.

"Why won't he leave?" Kerry asked me. "It's wrong that he waits there. He should go to . . . wherever he's going."

"His death was sudden. It's possible he can't accept that he died. He doesn't seem distressed or angry or . . ." I let the sentence die. I'd meant to say *malevolent*, but there was no need to put such things in Kerry's mind. "From the little I've experienced, sometimes spirits are confused. Time isn't the same for them as it is for us."

"Poor Grandda," Kerry sighed. "I wish I could send him on his way."

I brightened. "Maybe you can. I'll ask the captain to stop at the landing on the return trip. If he can give you a few moments alone on the dock, talk to your grandfather. Tell him what happened. Maybe once he understands, he'll know what to do."

"That might work," Reginald agreed. "Madam Petalungro says that once spirits accept their deaths, they often move on."

We'd seen that happen at Caoin House. But I couldn't guarantee anything. My work with spirits was raw and unproved. My only guidance came from Reginald and what he'd learned from Madam Petalungro.

"I was happy to see your grandfather as a healthy young man," I said.

"Aye, he was brawn and muscle. A handsome devil, like me."

"Indeed." He felt better about what he could see, and I was glad.

"You both saw him. I saw nothing," Reginald said.

"If I could give you my ability, I would," Kerry said. "But I don't think you'd want it. At least not all the time." He took a step back. "Ma'am, sir, I have work to do."

"Thank you, Kerry. I hope you're able to help your relative."

"Thanks." And he was gone, hustling across the deck until he disappeared. He was a good worker and someone I would call to my uncle's attention.

"We should retire," I said. The heat had taken all the energy out of me. By the end of the day, although I'd done nothing in the way of labor or even walking, I felt tired. "We'll be in Montgomery in the morning."

Reginald nodded. "My two card-playing friends have given up the game, at least for this river trip."

11

"You won too much of their money." I had to give Reginald credit. Gambling might be a vice, but it was gainful employment from his perspective. "How do you do it?" I asked. "Do you count the cards? I've heard some people do that."

Reginald thought for a moment. "No, I don't count. I watch the other players. There's really no such thing as a poker face. There's always a tell. Most people, if they're holding a winning hand, show it in their posture or their faces. I fold then."

"And if you're holding the winning hand?" I asked.

"I hesitate with my bets. I play for time and pretend that I'm trying to decide what to do."

"In other words, you deceive them."

"Ah, look, you've caught me."

"Don't you see? *That* skill is as much a talent as ghost sighting. And your ability to read the emotions of the living is vital to our work. I think you'll learn to see the spirits if we keep practicing, but never feel what you do isn't equally important to our success."

"You're a kind, dear woman." He kissed my hand, his little caterpillar of a mustache tickling my skin.

"Be careful with your affections or you'll ruin my reputation. After all, we are traveling together."

"If only they knew the truth." And he kissed my hand again before we both called it a night and headed to our rooms.

Tomorrow promised to be exciting. Zelda Fitzgerald would meet us at the docks and drive us into the bustling city of Montgomery.

CHAPTER THREE

Excitement took hold of me as the steamboat docked at Montgomery. Mobile and Montgomery shared the heat and suffocating humidity, but not much else. Unlike Mobile, the state capital of Alabama was an inland city on a bluff. The port's docks had none of the exotic flavor of the port of Mobile. The soft twang and slower manner of speech of rural Alabama predominated as we passed the stevedores off-loading the supplies the *Miss Vandy* had brought upriver. The sun showed no mercy. Reginald and I hurried off the dock to where a fashionable—and provocative—Zelda Sayre Fitzgerald waited beside a handsome sports coupe.

I hadn't expected the woman who'd scandalized New York with her drunken, flamboyant honeymoon parties to be so petite, but her winsome beauty had not been exaggerated. Uncle Brett and his romantic companion, Isabelle Brown, had filled me in on all the gossip about the young woman, who'd been labeled an icon of the flapper age. Rather than run from scandal, Uncle Brett would have given his eyeteeth to tag along. In fact, he'd ordered me to write him all the details. As much as he loved a good party, Uncle Brett loved adventure and people who flouted convention with style more.

Zelda's dark-gold curls were tucked beneath a wide-brimmed straw hat, and she wore a summer dress, sleeveless and banded at the hip. The skirt was short, showing off elegant legs. I'd heard she loved to dance—particularly in public and on the steps of the state capitol. Those legs were a testament to her athletic pursuits. When she saw us and realized who we were, she waved and came forward in a long, swinging stride. I liked her instantly; she was a woman who owned the ground she stood on.

"Porter, bring their bags here," Zelda called. She grasped my hands. "Thank you. Thank you for coming." She assessed Reginald and then put a hand on his arm. "And you, too, Mr. Proctor. I can't thank you enough."

There was an urgency in her grip, in the intensity of her blue eyes. "I'll tell you all about poor Camilla as soon as I get you home. I know you must be exhausted. A quick tour, then a bath and a stiff drink. That's what's called for." She hurried to direct the porter to load our baggage onto the rear of the car. "Scott bought this sports coupe with his first check from the publisher. He wanted a red Stutz, of course, but I love this car."

As soon as we were seated, Zelda set the vehicle in motion. "I'll run you around Montgomery. It won't take long," she said. "I have a bit of a reputation here, as does my friend Tallulah, who'll join us for breakfast. Pay the gossips no mind. It's a love-hate relationship, as I tell my father. The upright citizens of Montgomery love that I scandalize them so that they can pretend to be shocked. They're only jealous that I do what they're afraid to."

I'd heard stories of the flesh-colored swimsuits that made her appear to be nude, frolics in the public fountain in downtown Montgomery, and the tribute to Greek goddesses she and actress Tallulah Bankhead had performed in front of the courthouse. It was hard for me to believe that this publicity-seeking paragon of public misconduct was only twenty. She'd just married F. Scott Fitzgerald in April, and here she was, home to help her friend three months later.

Zelda gave us a whizbang tour, talking with great animation as she drove. The main street of Montgomery was filled with the bustle of a small city. When we passed a trolley car, I pointed with delight.

"Montgomery has twenty-nine miles of electric trolley track," Zelda said. "I can give you a tour of the statehouse, the courthouse, the city. I was a city hostess for the Montgomery Tintagil Club . . . until they lost their nerve and completely did away with the city hostesses. I think they were afraid of what Tallulah and I would get up to."

The look she cut over at me told me how much she enjoyed her notoriety.

The city of forty-four thousand still bore the scars of new roads cut into the red clay, raw lumber, and a sense of good prospects. Zelda made a turn around the business center before heading out of town again. She relayed a wealth of information as she drove. Montgomery had been the first seat of the Confederacy, but the lack of railroad connections had made travel difficult, so the Confederate capital had been moved to Richmond, Virginia. Since the 1860s, though, the railroad network had been vastly improved, and the city on the banks of the Alabama River had thrived.

"Daddy says Montgomery is on the brink of a boom," Zelda said with a doubtful shrug.

She drove through a wooded section of hardwoods mixed with pines and turned into a neighborhood of large, shaded lawns and two-story homes. Reginald and I were staying at the Sayre house as guests of Judge Anthony and Minnie Sayre. I knew only that Judge Sayre was a respected jurist who sat on the Alabama Supreme Court. I suspected he was not the fun-loving man my uncle was, and Zelda's expression when she spoke of her father told me I'd guessed accurately.

"Tell us about Camilla," Reginald gently probed when we'd turned down a quiet neighborhood street.

"She's a peach," Zelda said. Her tone changed, and her driving slowed. "She's not violent. Not in the least. She's a tender girl. There's no explanation except a spirit of some kind has taken control of her."

"Tell us from the beginning," Reginald said, leaning forward in the backseat. "Remember, we know only that your friend is in trouble. We have none of the details."

Zelda dived into the story. "Camilla Granger loves David Simpson, and she wants to marry him. More than anything she wants to be his wife. But first she wanted a summer to be free. To be"—she sighed heavily—"to be her own person instead of a wife." A shadow fell across her face. "I shouldn't have encouraged her."

I had no idea how Camilla's desire for independence might have played into her current plight.

"Why don't you tell us about Camilla and her problems *before* we get to your parents' home," I suggested.

A big sycamore shaded a portion of the street, and Zelda stopped beneath it. "I've known Camilla most of my life, though she's two years younger than I am. Before I ran off to New York City and married Scott, Camilla and Tallulah and I began to socialize." Her gaze focused on something in the distance. "I never wanted to stay in Alabama. Never. Tallulah loves the stage. She'll leave Alabama, too. We shouldn't have filled Camilla's head with dreams. She can't leave Montgomery. Not really. She just wanted a chance to be a woman before she became a wife. Just a few short months."

"Okay," Reginald said. "I can see why that might upset her parents or her fiancé, but it isn't like she robbed a bank."

"Oh, you don't know Maude Granger. She is a dragon. David is the best catch in Montgomery. He has family and money. Mrs. Granger insisted that Camilla plan her wedding without delay. Since David proposed, there have been endless engagement parties, bridal showers, china patterns selected, a whirlwind of nuptial business. The dragon wanted to be sure there was no backing out of the wedding by either bride or groom. To do so would mean social ruin."

"But if Camilla loved David—"

"It wasn't about David. Not really." Zelda looked miserable. "Mrs. Granger had her thumb on Camilla, and she kept pressing harder and harder until . . ." Her knuckles on the steering wheel whitened. "Camilla seemed to snap. She tried to stab David."

I didn't know what to say. This didn't sound like a haunting.

"Was Camilla charged with a crime?" Reginald asked.

"No. David hushed it up. He would never bring charges against her. No one knows about it except a few close friends. Our family physician, Dr. Abbott, secured a place at Bryce Hospital for Camilla in the hopes the doctors there could diagnose her and find a cure." She tapped the steering wheel with her painted fingernails. "Mrs. Granger's told everyone that Camilla has gone to a finishing school in preparation for becoming David's wife."

"Surely they've postponed the wedding?" I couldn't believe a mother would continue to push her daughter toward a marriage if her mental health was at risk.

"Mrs. Granger isn't going to let this opportunity slip away. And David still wants to marry her. If only he could wed her now, he'd be in charge of her fate, which is the best option—believe me. He'd elope with her, but Mrs. Granger is insisting on all the formalities and a huge wedding."

Across the street, a young mother pushing a baby pram walked out the front door of a two-story brick home. She stared at us, then walked in the opposite direction.

"Why do you think we can help your friend?" Reginald asked.

"Camilla had another episode after the first one. It's only David she tries to harm. Only David. That's why I think she's possessed. These things only happen when she's with David, as if he triggers something."

"Has she had an episode since she was institutionalized?" I asked.

"No. At Bryce she's docile as a lamb. The old Camilla."

"And where is David Simpson?"

"At Roswell, the house he bought and has been renovating for her. It's magnificent."

"What does he believe?" Reginald asked.

"He thinks she's possessed, too."

"Have you spoken with a priest?"

Zelda released her tight grip on the steering wheel. "It's not a matter for a priest. And we don't have time for all that mumbo jumbo. Incense and Latin aren't going to help Camilla. Mrs. Granger's decided that Camilla needs a new treatment, and a priest isn't going to change her mind. It's a surgical experiment." She shifted so she could see both of us. "It's supposed to make people submissive."

After receiving Zelda's letter, I'd researched the latest psychosurgical tactics some doctors were performing. A portion of the skull was removed, and the "white matter" of the front of the brain was severed or destroyed by an alcohol injection. Although the results were mixed, the procedure was still in use.

Reginald stiffened. "From what I've heard, it's ghastly and the results are unreliable."

"Dear God." I touched my forehead instinctively. "Her *mother* wants this done to her?"

"She's demanding it. It's the only way she thinks she can make Camilla obedient enough to marry David. She also claims that Dr. Perkins has made improvements to the surgery. A technique developed in Europe that isn't so disfiguring."

"And what does David say?"

"He's opposed. But he would marry Camilla in any condition to get her away from her mother."

"Surely Camilla can object to this procedure."

"She's willing to do whatever is necessary to prevent another episode of violence toward David. Her mother and Dr. Perkins have convinced her this is the answer." Zelda composed herself. "My father has tried to reason with the Grangers, but Maude Granger won't hear of it. She blames me for Camilla's illness. I'm forbidden from seeing her."

"Will we be able to visit Camilla at the hospital?" I wasn't certain what latitude we'd have with a minor.

"Absolutely. Dr. Abbott has agreed to help me, though he's skeptical that Camilla's suffering from a spiritual illness. Well, a bit more than skeptical about what you can accomplish."

"What does he believe is wrong with her?"

"That she has a mental disorder. He disagrees with the psychosurgery. He says it hasn't been proven to be effective, and the chances for damaging the brain are too great." She lifted her chin. "Do you think you can help her?"

"I don't know," Reginald said. "We can assess the situation and see. Why do you believe she's possessed?"

"My husband is a Catholic, something my family disdains. He believes that Satan or an evil spirit can possess a human vessel. It's the only explanation for what happened to Camilla. She's sweet and tender and caring. She wouldn't harm anyone, much less David."

I met Reginald's gaze; though I was no mind reader, it was clear what he was thinking. "We will try," I said. "We cannot promise a result, because this isn't something we know about. If this is a ghost or spirit, we might have an effect. But we make no promises."

Zelda grasped Reginald's hand on the backseat and my shoulder. "Thank you. Now, Mother's planned a party to introduce you to the town. Tomorrow I want you to meet David and the Grangers." She gave us a conspiratorial look. "Here's how I've set up your visit: Reginald owns a company developing new pharmaceuticals, and you're a writer helping him get the word out about his medicines. If you play your cards right, Maude will believe you can help her daughter and give you complete access to Camilla. We'll travel by train to Tuscaloosa to see her. It's only a short ride."

I knew where Tuscaloosa was on the map but nothing else about it. Nevertheless, we'd travel where the case took us, even if it meant going to a mental institution.

CHAPTER FOUR

The Sayre home was no match in size for Caoin House, my uncle's Mobile estate, but the six columns across the front created a graceful exterior and a shady gallery for the spillover of guests from the welcome party that Minnie Sayre had arranged for Reginald and me.

Though Judge Sayre was a prominent member of the judiciary, he was no teetotaler. Prohibition had been voted into effect in January, but those with money could find rum, gin, vodka, or whiskey. Backwoods bootleggers did a booming business. Booze might have been illegal, but it certainly wasn't invisible.

At the Sayre home, champagne and wine flowed, and Montgomery society indulged its taste for the juice of the grape. It was a festive party with beverages iced in tubs in the sunroom, where black men in white jackets served with quiet efficiency. The dining table was laden with meats, breads, delicious olives imported from Spain, soft cheeses that spread over the pumpernickel bread, and pies and cakes.

The women of Montgomery were as fashionable and attractive as any I'd seen in Savannah and Mobile. Minnie Sayre's grace was unrivaled. Her friends were flawless in their manners. They greeted me as if I were a celebrity.

Several young women—obviously schoolmates of Zelda, though more conservatively dressed—livened up the party with laughter. I knew Zelda hadn't told anyone except her parents about our true purpose here, but word of my writing had clearly gotten out.

"I understand you'll have a ghost story published soon," Sherrilyn Wells said. "I love the tales of Edgar Allan Poe."

"Tell us," Bettie McComb said with some urgency. "Do you really see ghosts?"

And also word of my special talent, it seemed. "I . . . have, on occasion, seen the spirits of departed people."

"How does it work? Can you call forth whomever you want? Like Czar Nicholas II? I'm fascinated by the execution of him and his family," a pretty blonde girl said. "Can you ask him about it?"

"You are morbid, Francesca," her friend exclaimed in a shrill voice. "Morbid!" She looked to me. "*Can* you call up the czar?"

"No, I can't call up specific spirits. It doesn't work that way."

"Francesca, Luann," said Zelda, "don't be a goof. Raissa can't just dial up the big boneyard in the sky and speak to anyone. By the way, I saw Malcolm Newberry in the library. I didn't know he was stepping out with Hattie Sanderson." Zelda pinched me lightly on the wrist as Francesca and Luann screamed their alarm.

"He can't date that gold digger. We'll save him," Luanne declared. They hustled toward the library.

Zelda took my arm and steered me toward the dining room. "Hurry, let's find Mother. She'll protect you."

When we found Minnie, Zelda quickly turned me over to her tender mercies.

My natural shyness was an obstacle as Minnie took me from group to group of partiers, making introductions. Never great at remembering names, I soon gave up. This was another of Reginald's talents, and I admired his social ease from across the room as he moved among five dozen strangers, making jokes, complimenting women, and including men in asides that made them guffaw as if he'd known them all his life. In this setting, he was the sleek racehorse, and I was the donkey.

I liked Minnie immensely, and her love for Zelda made me ache with longing for my own mother. Judge Sayre was a stern man who was reputed to be the best jurist in the region. Not a single one of his rulings had ever been reversed on appeal. He had found a corner of the library and sat in a circle of club chairs, speaking with the older men in attendance.

Minnie and I moved through the room, a glass of gin sweating in my grip. I had no time to sip it as I greeted the social elite of Montgomery. "This is Dr. Fred Abbott, our family physician," Minnie said. "He's a wonderful doctor, a man of science and art."

"Dr. Abbott," I said, eager for a word with the tall, distinguished-looking physician. "If you could spare a moment." I was in the middle of fabricating an excuse when I was saved from lying by Zelda's arrival.

"Come out on the porch for some air," she said to the doctor. "Tallulah can't make it tonight. She's coming home on the late train from Birmingham." She put a hand on his arm. "He adores Tallulah."

"I can't wait to meet her," I said, happy to follow them outside.

Several men gathered on the west side of the porch, but Zelda led us into the side yard, away from the chatter of the party. When Dr. Abbott began to protest, she shushed him. "We need a word."

"About what?" He looked back at the glowing lights of the house. Around us the heavy scent of roses teased a gentle wind.

"Raissa's here to help Camilla."

"I told you I would try to help Camilla, but I don't see what these people can do."

Enough light filtered into the yard from the house that I could see the worry in his face.

"She and Mr. Proctor are detectives. Very special detectives. They're going to figure out what happened to Camilla and put it to right."

I started to protest her declarations, but she stopped me. "Dr. Abbott, please tell her about Camilla."

The doctor stepped back. "I can't do that."

"But you must. I've hired Raissa and her friend to help. They need to know your diagnosis. You've examined Camilla. Do you believe the procedure Mrs. Granger is insisting on will help her?"

"No. I'm not in favor of that invasive technique, but I'm no longer her doctor, and I have no say-so in her treatment."

"You can help Camilla by talking to Raissa. Please, just talk to her." Zelda had potent appeal when she put her heart into it. "You know Camilla. She isn't violent or cruel. Something has happened to her from the outside. She has no one willing to help her except me and Tallulah, and now Raissa and Reginald. You might think me mad, but I believe Camilla may be haunted."

Dr. Abbott stepped back as if he'd been slapped. "You're not serious."

"I understand your reluctance to entertain the idea," I told the doctor calmly. "Science and the supernatural often seem at odds, but they really aren't. If you believe in a soul, then think of a haunting as a troubled soul. And if you can't believe in that, please consider that the treatment Reginald and I offer is not permanently damaging or potentially deadly like brain surgery. Give us a chance."

Zelda said, "Please, Dr. Abbott. Once Camilla's brain is surgically altered, there's no going back."

"What do you want to know?" Abbott asked.

"Can you tell me what you witnessed when you treated Miss Granger?" I spoke firmly but in a quiet voice. "If I had even that small bit of information, it would help. Did she say or do anything unusual?"

"Aside from the fact she went after the man she loves with a butcher knife and threatened to cut off his head?" Abbott sighed heavily. "I'm sorry. That was unnecessary."

"I know you're distressed." Reginald stepped from the shadows like a man materializing out of thin air. He startled even me. "You're frustrated that you can't help Camilla, that she's out of your reach. You're worried for her. Believe me—we only want to help. If the supernatural isn't involved here, we won't harm her."

I thought for a moment Reginald had overstepped himself, but Dr. Abbott slumped in defeat. "I fear the treatment Mrs. Granger is proposing. I've told her of my concerns, but she's determined to 'break this rebellious streak,' as she puts it. She believes Camilla is acting insane to have her own way, and this mental break is nothing more than a charade. She's willing to have her daughter destroyed to prove her point."

Dragon was not nearly harsh enough to label this mother; *monster* was more like it.

"Could you describe her symptoms, as you witnessed them?" My little notepad and pencil were inside the house, but I would commit what he said to memory.

"It was half an hour after the episode before I saw her," Abbott said. "I didn't witness any violent actions on her part, but I did put five stitches in David's forearm where she struck him with a blade."

A chill passed over me, even though the night was hot and humid. "Please, tell us from the beginning. Reginald and I aren't aware of any of the events. The smallest detail might prove helpful."

Zelda began the story. "David took Camilla to Roswell House to show her the renovations. He'd bought the place with the idea of holding their wedding there and making it their home."

"Had she seen the house before?" Reginald asked.

"We'd all gone there on high school larks," Zelda explained. "The place was abandoned, but the gardens were still exotic and lovely. It's an incredibly Southern place, the typical antebellum mansion with the columns and galleries all around."

"High school kids used to go there to neck." Dr. Abbot's tone had only a hint of disapproval.

"And more, after a swig of gin," Zelda added cheekily. "Those who dared. Everyone said it was haunted."

"But Camilla hadn't seen the house since David started the renovations?" Reginald put the conversation back on track.

"Correct. The house was a surprise gift. He hadn't told anyone except the men he'd hired to do the work."

David Simpson sounded like a pretty good guy to me, but one thing I'd learned in my brief tenure as a detective was not to jump to conclusions—good or bad—about a person. Sometimes men who did all the right things, said all the right words, and professed all the best intentions could be liars. I knew that only too well from personal experience.

"The attack against Mr. Simpson took place at Roswell." Reginald was quick to put the pieces together. "He and Camilla were alone there?"

"Yes."

"So we have only his word for what occurred?"

"That is true," Dr. Abbott said. "Miss Camilla was unconscious when I saw her. Mr. Simpson said she collapsed, and he took her straight home. Mr. Granger called me to attend her. I went as quickly as I could. She was unresponsive, lying fully clothed in her bedroom when I arrived."

Reginald's face told me his suspicions—David had been alone with Camilla. It was possible he'd initiated the attack or fabricated the whole event. "Did Camilla say or do anything?" I asked.

"When I was finally able to rouse her, she was delusional and babbling."

"It would be helpful if we knew what she said."

Dr. Abbott gazed at the ground. "I'm uncomfortable saying any more."

"Please," Zelda begged him. "For Camilla's sake. In order to save her, we need all the information we can find."

"Very well," the doctor finally agreed. "When I tried to rouse her from her stupor, she became agitated and fought me. She said, 'I'd do it again. For him.'"

"And that upsets you? Why?" Reginald asked.

"It wasn't *what* she said. But *how* she said it. She didn't speak in Camilla's voice. This voice was deeper, huskier . . . prouder."

The doctor's words silenced us all. Again my skin danced with a chill beneath the hot July moon. A breeze kicked up, and the fluttering of the large, stiff leaves in a magnolia tree made me start.

"Her agitation ended as suddenly as it began, and she didn't remember any of it," Dr. Abbott continued after a moment. "She had no idea how she'd gotten home or that she'd done anything harmful to David." He cleared his throat. "I treated her for a fever, though her temperature wasn't elevated. David convinced me to keep quiet about the incident. She returned to normal by that evening, and everyone agreed to put the bizarre behavior behind them."

"How did she end up at Bryce Hospital?" I asked.

Zelda answered my question. "There was a second episode. She tried to cut David again. When we told her what she'd done, she *asked* to be taken to the mental hospital. Now she says she'll do whatever's necessary to be cured. She knows her mother is pushing for the experimental surgery, and she says she won't fight it." Zelda had lost the edge of energy and spunk. "She'll let them do the operation if we don't stop her. She loves David that much."

"Perhaps," said Reginald, "Camilla was exposed to something—a plant or drink or substance . . ." He let the sentence run down.

The doctor raised his eyebrows. "You're thinking she may have taken opium or something of that nature, which produced vivid dreams, delusions."

Reginald shrugged. "Perhaps unintentionally. I think it's worth looking into."

"I agree," Dr. Abbott said. "I've known Camilla all her life, and it never occurred to me that someone else may have given her something. This is a possibility. Will you keep me informed? It's possible I can be of help."

"Of course we will," I said. "If we find anything at all, we'll be in touch with you."

"Then we should return to the party," Zelda said. Minnie Sayre opened the back door and peered into the yard. "Mother's looking for me."

I wondered how many times Minnie had anxiously waited for her daughter to return home. Zelda would have been a trial on any mother's nerves. Her brains and her beauty give her a license that could easily lead to trouble.

"Give your parents my regards," Dr. Abbott said. "I need to make rounds at the hospital."

"Thank you for coming." Zelda impulsively gave the doctor a hug.

He looked to Reginald and me. "I pray you're successful. The girl faces a terrible future otherwise." He walked away into the night.

"Zelda!" Minnie called from the stoop. "Come inside."

"Yes, Mother," Zelda sang out and ran to the back door, leaving Reginald and me to make our way to the front and enter without fuss. An hour later, I left Reginald gabbing with a handful of party malingerers, mostly young people. The house had cleared, and Judge Sayre and Minnie had retired. The long day had taken a toll on me, too, and I slipped away to my room. I wanted to jot down the things I'd witnessed and heard regarding Camilla Granger before I went to sleep.

The maid had turned down my bed, and I shrugged out of my clothes and into a nightgown, then slid between the crisp sheets. As I picked up my journal and pen, I realized how much I missed my typewriter. And to think I'd almost thrown it out. Uncle Brett's cooler head had prevailed, thank goodness. When I got home, I could type up my scattered notes into a more comprehensible form. For now the ink pen would have to do.

Outside my window, a mockingbird and a crow bickered. The normal sounds of a Southern night calmed me, and I put my pen aside and pulled up the light sheet. The night was hot. The earlier breeze had abandoned Montgomery, leaving a stillness that felt like a heavy hand pressed upon my forehead. The heat was like a drug, tugging me under the tide of sleep.

A noise outside my window dragged me back from the void of slumber. I forced my eyelids open, only to close them again and slide back toward unconsciousness.

"Help me."

I sat up, fully awake.

The crow ruled the night, cawing in a pecan tree only a few feet from my bedroom, but it wasn't the crow that had awakened me.

"Help me, please." The words, so desperate and afraid, came from outside.

I threw back the sheet and rushed to the window. The moon cast enough light to make shadows, and I searched among them for a female. She had to be close to the house—I heard her clearly.

Shadow upon shadow slumped in the night, but the yard was empty. I *must* have been dreaming. I was turning away when I saw her. She stood beside a large camellia. Moonlight glistened off the waxy greenness of the dense leaves. She stepped forward, aware that I could see her. There was something terribly wrong with her head, as if a hank of hair had been yanked out by the roots. One eye wandered.

"Please," she said, "help me."

I couldn't move. My limbs felt paralyzed. I was helpless as she came closer, not walking but floating across the lawn. When she reached a pool of moonlight, I realized she was transparent. Blood dripped down her face, sliding down her bosom and dripping on the ground. Bruises bloomed on her neck, dark and angry.

"Who are you?" I asked. There was no point trying to run.

"Help me," she said in a voice so hopeless I wanted to cry.

"I will. Tell me who you are."

Horror struck her pale features. "He's coming. He's coming. I—" And she was gone. The yard was silent. Not even the crow disturbed the night.

I waited for a long time, wondering if she'd return. She didn't, and I finally went back to bed, sleepless for most of the night.

CHAPTER FIVE

The Sayre dining table was set with a full service of gold-rimmed Devonshire bone china in a violet pattern and Waterford pitchers of fresh-squeezed orange and grapefruit juice. The drama of my nocturnal visitor had faded with the morning sun, and although I intended to tell Reginald, I was in no rush.

Reginald and I found our seats moments before the front door opened and a tall, slender beauty entered the room. She ran to our hostess and grabbed her. "Miss Minnie, I'm finally back from that ghastly trip Father insisted I take."

"Your father has only your best interests at heart." Minnie kissed the young woman's cheek.

"Tallulah!" Zelda ran into the room, squealing with pleasure, and hugged her friend. "Thank God you're home. Another day in Montgomery without you and I'd have to dance naked on Main Street just to stir up some gossip. This is Raissa and Reginald."

"So pleased to meet you." Tallulah had the poise of royalty, but her smile sparkled with pure devilment. I could see where Zelda and Tallulah together would be more than Montgomery's old, polite society could tolerate. Uncle Brett would have adored them.

Judge Sayre stood and nodded. "You're late, Tallulah. Please be seated so we can start breakfast." Before he could even sit, the maid brought platters of bacon, pancakes, scrambled eggs, fresh fruit, steaming biscuits, and sliced ham. There was enough food for four dozen hungry men.

"Sorry, Judge," Tallulah said, demonstrating not one iota of remorse as she slipped into a chair and put her napkin in her lap. "Oh, Minnie, you made biscuits. They are divine. I hope you've said the blessing because I have no intention of waiting." She bit into a biscuit and sighed with pleasure.

"We have a busy day planned," Zelda told her father.

"I hope it doesn't include any of your scandalous stunts."

"Not today." She grinned at her mother. "Besides, I'm a married woman, and I've put away such childish conduct."

"Dear heavens," Tallulah said. "Minnie, I think Zelda is running a fever. The day she wants to behave is the day we'll put her in the grave."

"I just have to ask myself, 'What would Scott want me to do?'"

"And the answer to that is whatever causes the most uproar." Tallulah buttered another biscuit and bit into it.

"We have guests," Minnie said gently.

"And we promise to show them a good time," Zelda said. "They're visiting the old dragon herself this morning."

Judge Sayre put his napkin beside his plate and stood. "Marriage hasn't done a thing to settle you down. I pray for your husband." He left the room on peals of Zelda's and Tallulah's laughter, but he got only as far as the front door. A loud knock stopped him.

"Who's here at such an hour of the morning?" he grumbled as he opened the door.

"Judge Sayre, another girl is missing," a male voice said.

Zelda left the table, and we followed, stopping at the foyer and peeking around the door frame. Judge Sayre spoke with a Montgomery police officer, who remained on the front porch. A handsome man sat behind the wheel of a magnificent teal Duesenberg at the street.

"Who is that?" I asked.

"A private investigator, just like you." Zelda shrugged. "Jason Kuddle. He used to be a policeman here, but he gave up the uniform to do private work. The Ralston family hired him last year when their daughter Julie went missing. He found her in Nashville, Tennessee, with a guitar picker and a bun in the oven. Now *that* was a scandal. She came home pregnant and unmarried."

"Why didn't you hire him to help Camilla?" I asked.

"Because he only pursues living, breathing villains, darling," Tallulah said. "If Camilla is haunted, we need your special services."

"Hush," Zelda whispered. "I can't hear what Father is talking about."

"It's another missing-persons case," Reginald said. "A girl went missing yesterday after school."

"Are you psychic?" Tallulah asked.

"Not at all." Reginald was amused. I'd have to ask him later if lip-reading was among his other talents.

Judge Sayre closed the door and turned to find us snooping. "Zelda, take your friends back to the dining room. This is bad business, and it would seem you have a plateful of trouble already."

"Yes, Father," she said, herding us all away. "He loves me," Zelda says. "He just wishes I'd been born a boy."

"It's a disease among our families," Tallulah said, rolling her eyes. "Boys can defy society, and no one worries about tainted reputations. Girls must behave or we reflect poorly on our families."

"Who cares about the delicate sensibilities of a few bluestockings?" Zelda said. "It's time to go," she told Reginald and me. "Your audience with the dragon awaits. Tallulah and I will drop you off—Maude Granger can't stand us. We'll pick you up in an hour. Remember, Reginald, you're doing groundbreaking work with your pharmaceutical company and think you might be able to cure, or at least control, Camilla's symptoms. If Maude sniffs a rat, we're done for."

⁕━━━⌄━━━⁕

The Granger house was a two-story clapboard with a curved wrap-around porch and intricate gingerbread trim. The house had a pleasant demeanor and lots of shade trees. They were oaks, but Reginald told me the climate was too cold for the live oaks that graced the lawn of Caoin House. These were white oaks, a taller, more upright cousin of the Southern oak that I loved so much.

I walked up the steps to the porch with some trepidation. Much depended on winning Mrs. Granger's permission to visit her daughter at Bryce Hospital.

A maid in a starched uniform opened the door with downcast eyes. She bade us wait in the foyer while she announced us to Mrs. Granger "for an audience."

"Bit of a royal, isn't she?" Reginald whispered, almost making me laugh.

I composed myself just in time as we were ushered into a lovely room shaded by pink-and-green floral draperies, antique furnishings, and a welcome electric fan. Mrs. Granger sat in a high-backed wicker chair with chintz cushions that reminded me of an early-spring morning. The effect of the room was an explosion at a flower market. She might be a dragon, but she surrounded herself with the most ladylike accoutrements. And while time and temperament had coarsened her looks, I could see that once she had been an extraordinary beauty.

"Mrs. Granger," I said, walking forward and extending my hand.

She ignored my offer of a shake. "Understand that I did not seek this meeting. Judge Sayre asked me to speak with you. I have no idea why. A writer and a chemist of some sort, according to the judge? I have no use for either. If that hoyden Zelda is behind any of this, I *will* be angry."

I started stumbling into the cover story that Zelda had prepared; then Reginald stepped forward. He took her hand and kissed it. "It's such a pleasure, Mrs. Granger. Reginald Proctor, at your service. We're thrilled to meet you, and we're hopeful that some of the work my pharmaceutical company is engaged in might prove helpful to your daughter. Ms. James is a writer working with me. She is to be a published author in her own right soon, and I have been fortunate enough to employ her to help me document my important work."

"Pharmaceuticals?" She was hooked. "What do you mean?"

"New treatments for many disorders are in the final stages of development at my company. I heard of the difficulties your daughter is experiencing, and I'm hopeful modern medicine may offer a solution."

"You want my daughter for a test subject?" Mrs. Granger was sharp as a tack.

"First we need to examine the patient, and then I'll stop by and talk with you. It's pointless to discuss treatments and possibilities until I determine if Miss Camilla is a suitable candidate for a trial."

I had to hand it to Reginald. He knew how to pitch a lie so that the batter couldn't help but take a swing.

"Can you tell us about Camilla?" I asked. "Childhood illnesses, any unusual episodes that might be a precursor to her current situation?"

"She was a perfectly average girl until she took up with those flappers Zelda Sayre and Tallulah Bankhead. I hold them responsible for her . . . problems."

"But weren't they in New York when she had her first episode?"

"They put ideas in her head. They told her to be independent, to travel to New York and experience the city life, to aspire to be more than a wife and a mother. These thoughts confused her, and that confusion led to mental instability and, finally, calamity."

I started to speak, but Reginald must have read my belligerent expression and was quicker. "Tell us about Camilla. What are her hobbies? What does she like?"

"She loves needlework," Mrs. Granger said. "And piano. She plays . . . she used to play at the First Presbyterian Church before she took up with that godless duo of misconduct." She snapped open a fan and sent tiny tendrils of still-luxurious hair fluttering. "The maid is teaching her to cook, because a lady must know enough about cooking to make sure the help isn't robbing her blind."

A middle-aged Negro who'd been standing in the doorway stepped back and disappeared. Obviously Mrs. Granger had no concerns about how her words might cut, or else she assumed, like so many others, that "the help" lost the ability to hear when they took a job.

"Is your daughter a good student?" I asked, trying to keep my voice even.

"Yes. She made good marks in everything except mathematics, but that's of no significance. A girl doesn't need arithmetic or book smarts to run a household. This idea of educating females is having a tremendous negative effect on families. Women demanding the vote, jobs, and their own bank accounts!" She snapped the fan angrily. "Her husband will handle the finances. She will raise the children and run the household."

"What are Camilla's greatest accomplishments, by your standards?" Reginald asked quickly, cutting off anything I might have said.

"She's a talented hostess and a lovely bridge player. An accomplished pianist. I've seen to that. She can plan and organize a party and will be a social benefit to her husband. A helpmate, as the Bible dictates."

"I understand Camilla is engaged," I said.

"If she doesn't frighten David away with her behavior, she'll make the best catch in town." She lifted her chin. "Every young woman in Montgomery has tried to snare him, but it is Camilla he settled upon. David has money, a profession, a family name, and connections.

Everything a young woman could ask. I will not allow her to destroy her chances for a good marriage."

"I'm sure he understands that she isn't well," Reginald said.

"He may, but I don't." She spoke with anger. "The girl has had everything. The world at her feet, and she can't control herself? I don't believe for a minute that she's mentally ill. She's willful. Determined that I let her go to New York with that hussy Zelda, but I will not. She will stay in Alabama. If she continues to defy me with her attempts at drama, then I'll do what's necessary to bring her into line."

"You don't believe she could be mentally ill?" I asked, appalled at her lack of compassion for her own child.

"She is no more mentally ill than I am a jackrabbit," Mrs. Granger said. "She's willful and defiant, and she will learn that those are expensive habits to nurture. She will suffer the consequences of her defiance."

I'd thought Dr. Abbott might have exaggerated Mrs. Granger's attitude about punishing her daughter for being "defiant." He had not.

"I'd like to visit Camilla, if I may," Reginald said smoothly. I could only admire his ability to maintain his composure. "If she is merely willful, I believe that my company may have something that will . . . modify that behavior. Something that's not as risky as a surgical procedure but that will leave her docile and loving and perfectly able to perform all her duties as wife and mother."

Calculations raced across Mrs. Granger's face. "That sounds too good to be true. If you have such a drug, all the men in Alabama will be purchasing it for their wives and daughters."

"Don't think the possibilities are lost on me or my company," Reginald said, sharing a wink with her. "For those females who have lost the true meaning of femininity and decorum, my pharmaceutical might be a welcome medication."

"Is the drug available now?" She fanned herself again.

"For a trial."

She waved Reginald away. "I don't have time for a trial. Dr. Perkins, one of the leading authorities on treating the mentally ill, concurs with me that if Camilla refuses to fall in line, unorthodox measures will have to be taken."

"With my medication, the dose can be manipulated to produce the exact response. That isn't true of surgery," Reginald said. "With the procedure you're considering, there have been adverse results in Europe. Some patients become little more than large toddlers, drooling and unable even to retain bathroom training. The procedure hasn't been studied here in the United States."

Mrs. Granger snapped her fan shut. "Dr. Perkins said the medical association is coming around to accept the benefits of brain surgery. Poor results were true only in the early stages of the surgery. He has . . . refined the result."

"I'd still like an opportunity to evaluate Miss Granger," Reginald said. "Consider it a kindness to me and possibly patients in the future."

Mrs. Granger looked away from us. "I'll speak with my husband."

"And I'd be delighted to meet Mr. Granger and explain," Reginald offered.

"There's no need. I can convey your request. Jefferson trusts my judgment implicitly."

More likely, he was afraid if he disagreed, she'd set *him* up for brain surgery.

Reginald stood, and I followed suit. "Then may I call you this evening?" he asked.

"That would be acceptable."

"I hope your day is as pleasant as your personality," Reginald said with a smile. "I look forward to our next encounter."

Mrs. Granger offered her hand for Reginald to squeeze. She didn't bother to acknowledge me. "Florence, see them out."

When Florence showed us out of the house, her face was as blank as an empty page. We made it down the steps and through the yard to the sidewalk before Reginald grasped my arm and walked me around the corner of the block. "She is a nightmare," he said, pulling out his cigarette case. When he offered, I accepted.

"We don't have to have her permission to visit Camilla, do we?"

"It will make things easier. A lot easier."

I inhaled the cigarette and coughed.

Reginald patted my back, took the cigarette from my hand, and crushed it with his foot. "If I have to, I'll visit her again this evening. Without you."

I nodded. "She acted as if I weren't there. A mere woman isn't worth her focus. You'll do better on your own. Now it's time to meet the groom. I wonder what role he plays in all this."

Reginald took a last drag on his cigarette, then tossed it on the hot sidewalk. "I can't wait to find out."

CHAPTER SIX

Lunch with David Simpson had been planned at the Elite Restaurant, a place, Zelda assured us, that emulated the class and atmosphere of the finest New York eateries. A tuxedoed waiter showed us to the table where David waited. He rose swiftly when he saw us. I took him in—a handsome young man, clean-shaven, tall, broad-shouldered, and slender. Like the other male diners, he wore a suit and tie. His pale gaze was haunted with hope when he assessed Reginald and me. "Thank you for coming." He turned to Zelda and Tallulah. "I owe you two a great deal. You're good friends to my fiancée and to me."

We took our seats, and the waiter asked if we'd like drinks with our meal. The 1,520 Volstead Act enforcers patrolling the nation's drinkers evidently didn't view Alabama as a serious problem. Liquor could be had by all who tipped generously. David ordered bourbon for Reginald and himself and sherry for us women.

"There's no need to thank us. Camilla is our friend," Zelda said. "I also feel some responsibility. We enticed her to some mischief and fun that upset her mother."

"We should slay the dragon." Tallulah made a slashing motion with her dinner knife. "Behead the beast. Camilla's problem is her mother and nothing else."

"Can you help Camilla?" David asked.

If the sincerity he projected was false, I couldn't see it. Besides, David had nothing to gain from accusing his fiancée of attempted murder. Nor did Mrs. Granger. If someone was tampering with Camilla's perception by giving her drugs or some other agent of delusion, it made no sense that it would be those who benefited from the marriage.

"I don't know that we can help," I said, not wanting to create false expectations. "If she is mentally ill, we don't have any experience in that area."

David hummed with tension. "And if she is possessed?"

"If it's a haunting, as we hope, we'll do everything we can. If it's something darker, a priest would be your best bet," Reginald said. "We work with departed spirits of the living. I don't know if I believe in satanic demons, but if there are such things, we aren't equipped to exorcise them."

"I understand," David said solemnly. "I have a hard time thinking Camilla is possessed by a ghost or under the influence of some supernatural element. Especially not a demon. She is the kindest, sweetest woman alive. There's never been a hint of any darkness in her spirit. Yet I can't accept that she's mentally defective."

"Camilla certainly is *not* mentally defective," Tallulah said. "Her mother, that two-legged tarantula, has pressured her to the point of snapping. If we could get her away from Mrs. Granger, she would be back to herself in no time. Even when you visited her at Bryce, she hasn't had another single episode." She pulled out a gold cigarette case. Reginald had a light ready for her before she could blink. She gave him a look through her heavily mascaraed lashes. "You, darling, are indispensable. I like that in a man."

"Mrs. Granger says she believes Camilla is defying her, and Maude Granger has no intention of losing a battle of wills." I wanted everyone to know the score. "That makes the proposed surgery a form of punishment for deliberate disobedience."

"That woman's off her nut," Zelda said.

"What do *you* think has happened to Camilla?" Reginald asked David.

"I don't know. She was fine, ebullient even. In March we set the October 7 wedding date. Camilla had chosen a seamstress to make her gown. Her bridal attendants' gowns would mimic the fall colors. My parents had accepted my choice of a wife. Everything was falling into place."

"Tell me about the day she first attacked you." Reginald brought out his cigarette case and offered it around the table.

David signaled the waiter for another drink and lit a cigarette. "The first time she had an episode was in late April. I'd taken her to see her wedding gift, Roswell House. I'd kept it a surprise because I wanted her to know that she would always have a place of her own. The deed to the house was to be her wedding gift." He took a long swallow of his drink. "Camilla was elated. She ran inside and went from room to room, exclaiming about the things she loved. I've never seen her so happy."

"And what happened?" I asked.

"She ran into the kitchen talking about the dinner parties we'd have, the dances, the lawn parties. She was . . . so happy. I was in the library checking the shelving the carpenter had finished. I heard something like a scuffle. Then Camilla cried out, 'No, no! Help! Stay away.' I ran to the kitchen as quickly as I could and found her staring out the window as if she were in a trance. There was nothing outside, just the overgrown gardens. When I spoke her name, she didn't answer. I grasped her shoulders, intending to help her. She spun around, and she had a butcher knife in her hand. She slashed at me without warning."

By the time he finished, he was almost panting. He took a large swallow of his new drink, draining the glass. "The look on her face was pure hatred. I have no doubt she would have killed me if she'd been faster."

"And there was nothing in the house or yard to provoke this reaction?" I asked. "You didn't sense anything?"

"Nothing I could see. One minute she was delighted with the house, and then suddenly she was furious and dangerous. The blade actually cut through my coat and shirt and into my skin. I was lucky the wound wasn't deep. Had I gone to the hospital, the police might have become involved."

"Did she eat or drink anything in the house?" I shifted the focus a bit so David could collect himself. The memory of Camilla's startling transformation from happy young fiancée to angry attacker had clearly distressed him.

"No. We didn't bring food with us, and the plumbing isn't completed yet, so water must be brought in from the well. There was nothing to eat or drink in the house."

"Did she say anything when she attacked?"

He shook his head, holding up his glass to gain the waiter's attention. "She was savage. Animalistic. When she swung the blade at me, she was . . . grunting with exertion. I've never seen anything like it."

I had a few theories. I'd read stories of possession by dark influences, creatures more beast than human. Not demons but something not human either. And stories of malevolent spirits. Henry James's *The Turn of the Screw* was a favorite. Amelia B. Edwards's tale *Was It an Illusion?* walked the edges of the twists of a brain caught between rationalism and superstition. My favorite authors speculated on such things, and I hoped someday to explore that terrain with my own writing.

"How did you escape her?" I asked.

"I ran out of the house. She followed and then collapsed in the yard. I couldn't rouse her, so I drove her home, and the doctor was called."

"Dr. Abbott," I said.

"Yes. When Camilla came back to herself, she had no memory of the events."

"And there were other occurrences?"

"One more."

"And both times were you alone with Camilla?" Reginald spoke as gently as he could, but the implication couldn't be ignored.

"I was, but you have to believe I'd never do anything to harm Camilla. I love her, and I *will* marry her and care for her, no matter what."

The waiter delivered David's drink, and Zelda stopped him with a flirtatious hand on his arm before he could leave the table. "I'll have a drink. Make mine a gin fizz, please." When she focused on David, all signs of the coquette were gone. "Don't you dare tell the dragon that you'll marry Camilla no matter what state she's in, or Maude will send her back to you like an imbecile capable of incubating your children and little else."

David looked stricken at the harsh image Zelda painted, but I didn't think she was overstating the situation. The waiter returned to take our orders, and Tallulah and I deferred to Zelda's recommendation of beef over a bed of rice and fresh mushrooms. Reginald and Scott ordered steaks. When the waiter had gone, Reginald continued his questions.

"Please, tell us about the second episode."

"Weeks had passed without incident, and we'd all been lulled into the belief that Camilla was fine. We'd convinced ourselves that she'd eaten something tainted or been stung by something that produced an adverse reaction. The wedding plans continued, and finally last month Camilla and I went back to Roswell to outline the wedding decorations. Her mother was to meet us. It was similar to the first event, except that

Camilla was in the upstairs ballroom, planning where the musicians would be, and I was measuring the parlor floor for a Turkish rug. I heard what sounded like a struggle upstairs. I called out to Camilla, and I heard her cry as if someone were hurting her. I rushed upstairs. She came at me again with a knife. She must have taken the knife upstairs with her. I ran outside again, and she came after me. Luckily the same thing happened. She fell down, unconscious."

"When did Mrs. Granger arrive?"

"I was trying to revive Camilla when Mrs. Granger's driver pulled up. We took Camilla home, and Dr. Abbott came immediately. It was then that Mrs. Granger decided to have Camilla put in Bryce Hospital. She convinced Camilla to go voluntarily. She said it was our only hope. Now she's been there for four weeks, and each time I see her she's more eager to come home." David rubbed the side of his face. "But she refuses to come home with me until she's assured she's not a danger."

"Why not pick her up at the hospital, drive off to a justice of the peace, and marry her?" I asked David. "She'd be your wife. You could take care of her."

He drew in a ragged breath. "Because I fear I'm the trigger that sends her into violence. It only happens when we're alone together. What if I'm . . . bad for her?"

Silence fell over the table. Three waiters arrived with the food we'd ordered. The dishes were delicious, but the will to eat had fled. The others ate slowly and in silence.

"Did you object to Camilla spending some time in New York City with Zelda and Tallulah?" I had to ask David this. If he had somehow manipulated Camilla to prevent her from pursuing her dream of a brief respite of independence, I wanted to know.

"I would have worried about her. My family is from New York, and we have banking concerns there. I've spent enough time in the city to be aware of the dangers, but I didn't oppose her desire to taste freedom. I have great faith in our love for each other. Besides, shouldn't we all, men and women, know a life of independence before we agree to a partnership?"

It was the perfect answer. David Simpson was either a remarkably progressive man or a very clever manipulator.

"Do your parents approve of Camilla?" Reginald asked David.

"How could they not?" Zelda responded.

"They would have preferred that I marry into one of the banking families," David said. "Ideally a family they knew. It's how alliances are created. But I told Mother and Father I intended to marry for love or not at all."

"Are they aware of Camilla's problems?"

"No. I haven't told them, but I can't keep the truth from them much longer. The wedding is set for October 7. They'll be arriving here in Montgomery in September, and they'll expect to spend time with their future daughter-in-law. I can't very well take them to a mental hospital."

"They aren't gonna like it if she's a dim bulb." Zelda pushed her plate away. She'd barely touched her food, and she signaled for another drink. "I talked to Scott last night. He said Southern women are suffocated by the past. We live in the shadow of the fallen South, a burden the women carry more so than the men."

"Slow down on that gin, darling, or you'll give Scott all of your best lines," Tallulah said as she lit one of Zelda's cigarettes.

David kept his attention on Reginald and me. "My parents will adore Camilla when she's herself. A kinder, sweeter young woman has never been created. I will not allow her to be butchered. If you can't help her, I'll take necessary action."

"Which is?" I asked.

"Exactly what you said: pick her up in the hospital, take her to a justice of the peace, and marry her. With or without her parents' permission. Once she's my wife, I can make sure she receives the proper help."

"And if she tries to kill you?" Reginald asked softly.

"I'll find a way to help her. I can take her to New York or Europe. There are other treatments safer than Dr. Perkins's barbaric surgery. If I have to, I'll set her free to live as she chooses in New York or anywhere else. If she's my wife, Mrs. Granger will have no say."

He was right about that. I'd known of young girls who ran away and married. Some were underage. Once the wedding night was over, there was little the parents could do to return the girl to a state of virginity, so the marriage was accepted. Of course, the Grangers could disown Camilla, and I didn't doubt the dragon's power to make that happen.

"I'd like to see Roswell House," I said. "Would that be possible?"

"Yes, I can give you a key. There are workmen there on some days. Because I believe Camilla will be well again, I've continued with the renovations."

I nodded. "Could you accompany us?"

"Of course. But it will be three days. I have to travel to Birmingham in the morning."

"And we're scheduled to visit Camilla at Bryce Hospital tomorrow," Zelda reminded me. "We can't disappoint her. I don't believe her parents have been to see her at all. You can tour Roswell House when we return."

"David, how was she when you visited?" I asked.

"She was . . . normal. We walked the grounds, under the ever-watchful eye of two aides, but we spent an afternoon together. Nothing untoward occurred. I believe she's beyond the worst of whatever affliction she had."

"She does seem jolly when she sees David," Tallulah said. "I visited her a week ago. She asked for chocolate, which I happily smuggled in to her. If I'd had a flask, I would have given it to her, but I gather she isn't much for cocktails. Chocolate and David are the only things she asked about."

"Not her parents?" Reginald asked.

Tallulah shook her head. "You can hardly blame her. Mrs. Granger would cannibalize her young if she thought it would make her more socially desirable. Camilla realized long ago she was a weapon to her mother, something to be used to pry open the door of polite society. The terrible thing, darlings, is that Camilla would have been accepted anywhere on her own dime. No matter how much money she acquires, the dragon never will. Camilla is her only possible ticket into the world she believes she deserves."

"When we return from Bryce Hospital, I'll be in touch," I told David. We thanked him for our lunch and left.

Outside the restaurant, Tallulah firmly took the keys from a weaving Zelda. Relief washed over me that Zelda wouldn't be behind the wheel. Not that there was much traffic to contend with in residential Montgomery. But there were plenty of trees.

CHAPTER SEVEN

"Would it be possible to ride the trolley?" I asked before we climbed into the car. The sun was hot in the early afternoon and throbbed off the newly laid asphalt of the road. "Uncle Brett would be so disappointed if I didn't give the electric vehicles a try and return with a full report."

"Darling, why would you want to ride the trolley when we have a perfectly good car?" Tallulah asked.

"The trolley might be cooler," I suggested.

"Oh, take her for a ride." Zelda did a pirouette. "Let a girl live a little."

I had to laugh. She was tipsy but generous of heart. "Thank you."

We sauntered slowly to the trolley stop, and, within a minute or two, the electric car arrived. Reginald was amused by my interest in electric transportation. New Orleans boasted a trolley system, so he was familiar with the contraptions. I'd never been aboard one.

Once we were moving, the breeze made the heat much more tolerable. I'd taken a bench at the front, and a folded newspaper left on the seat caught my eye. KLAN HOLDS RALLY IN SELMA was the front-page headline. The story was illustrated with a photograph of men wearing robes and pointed hats that covered their faces as they cheered around a burning cross. The photograph brought back the lynching death of a young Mobile man I'd known and the abduction of my uncle. The horror of those events remained all too close in memory.

Reginald must have seen my pale countenance, so he picked up the paper to move it. "Bad people are everywhere," he said softly. "The past is over."

"I know." I reached for the paper because I wanted to read the story later, alone in my room at the Sayre home. When I folded it to slip under my arm, another story caught my eye: TEENAGE GIRL MISSING.

My visitor from the night before came back to my mind. The girl, begging for help. I scanned the narrow column of type, which gave only the barest of details. A young girl who lived in the county northwest of Montgomery had disappeared while walking home from town. This was the girl the police officer had been talking about when he came to speak to Judge Sayre. From what I'd overheard, she was not the first young woman to disappear in the area.

According to the article, Autauga County law enforcement was asking for volunteers to search the rural area. They needed mounted men and searchers on foot.

I don't know why the story hit me with such power. The details about the missing girl were scant. Her name was Pamela DuMond, and she was sixteen. She lived with her mother in the small community of Autaugaville, which had a population of slightly more than two hundred. She walked home every school day, a distance of less than a mile. She'd gone into town to meet a friend for an afternoon of teenage chatter.

"Raissa?" Zelda had come to sit across the trolley aisle from me. "Are you okay?"

"I am. It's the missing girl the officer was talking to your father about." I showed her the headline.

"How terrible. Do you . . . sense her ghost?"

It shouldn't have been an unexpected question, but it caught me flat-footed. "I don't, I'm afraid. Maybe she's still alive." I didn't want to mention the girl I'd seen—or dreamed about—the night before. She'd been so afraid, so lonely. And I knew beyond a doubt she was dead.

"I'll ask my father to find out what he can." In an obvious effort to distract me, Zelda pointed to a raised white house on a shady lot. "Look, there's the first White House of the Confederacy. Jefferson Davis lived there for three months before the Confederate capital was moved to Richmond, Virginia."

The Italianate design of the clapboard house was pleasing and serene. Magnolia trees provided a shady lawn, and I was glad it had survived the shells and torches that had been the fate of so many lovely homes.

"Mrs. Davis hosted lots of galas," Zelda said. "The cream of the Confederacy attended. My grandmother spoke of the parties and socials."

"Can you imagine wearing those dreadful laced corsets?" Tallulah joined in the conversation. "Add in all those petticoats, pantaloons, and floor-length skirts? I would have been driven to homicide. And no one would have blamed me."

"We would have stripped naked and danced on the lawn," Zelda agreed. "Why have women allowed men to set the rules for their attire, hairstyles, and choices?" She fingered her short curls. "Not to mention voting. Are you fighting for the right to vote?" she asked me. "We need one more state for ratification."

"I have protested and signed petitions," I said, though I had never been in the forefront of the suffragette movement. "My husband was a lawyer, and he assisted the Savannah suffragettes with legal advice before he went to war. He believed, and so do I, that the Nineteenth Amendment must be ratified."

"Hopefully next month," Tallulah said, and for a moment she no longer seemed like a bored, sophisticated vamp but rather a young woman with a cause. "There's talk that Tennessee will ratify."

"And Alabama?" I asked.

"Hopeless." Zelda's mouth took on a grim set. "Which is why I'll live in New York. And Tallulah, too. She'll be queen of the Broadway stage, and I'll be on the invitation list for every party of any importance in the city. Scott is in demand, and I've begun to develop my own following of devotees."

"Oh, those naughty vixens." Tallulah's laugh was low and throaty. "Zelda will lead the vanguard of scandalous women who refuse to be quiet or demur or be well behaved or *managed*." She put a hand on her friend's shoulder. "Your work is about a lot more than upsetting a few high hats." The sly grin returned. "But I promise you—before we leave town we'll make Maude Granger have a blue-faced fit."

When Zelda noticed that another passenger on the trolley, a young man in a business suit, was more interested in our conversation than anything else, she put a finger to her lips. "Enough of that talk. Look, there's the high court where Daddy's a judge."

As we continued through the heart of Montgomery, Zelda and Tallulah pointed out the sights. By the time we hopped off at the stop near the parked car, I felt I knew a bit about the state capital, and I had to agree with Judge Sayre's assessment that Montgomery was a booming young town.

We returned to the Sayre house, and I could barely suppress a series of yawns. The big meal, two glasses of sherry, and July heat had wilted me into a puddle of uselessness. I excused myself for a nap and fell on the bed in the guest room, where a breeze stirred the lace curtains at the open window. Outside songbirds called to one another, lulling me into a light sleep.

When I woke up, I realized something was off. My eyes refused to open. It felt as if the muscles no longer worked. Panic bloomed in my chest. I didn't need my sight to know someone else was in my room. It took a few moments for me to remember where I was. At last I forced my eyes open and felt the air leave my lungs. A young girl stood at the foot of my bed. Her curly blonde hair fell about her shoulders, and her china-blue eyes regarded me with deep sadness.

"I'll be good," she said. Blood slowly leaked from her head, tracing down the side of her nose and finally dripping off her chin. "I'll be good. Please don't hurt me."

The nightmare closed around me, paralyzing my body. At last I sat up in bed, my heart thrumming. I looked around my empty bedroom. Could my brain have somehow combined the horror of Camilla's potential surgery and the missing girl from Autaugaville into a dream that depicted the horror of both young women?

I washed my face in the basin on the dressing table, straightened my clothes and hair, and hurried into the parlor in the hopes of finding a companion. Until I shook off the desperation of my dream, I didn't want to be alone.

Judge Sayre dropped us at Union Station the next morning as dawn cracked the sky. Zelda sat on the depot bench, her eyes closed and her forehead gripped in both hands. "The heat here is intolerable. I can't wait to return to New York and Scott." For the first time since I'd met her, she sounded small and lonely.

I didn't blame her. Scott Fitzgerald was a handsome pilot, a man who'd been stationed at nearby Fort Sheridan during the war. I'd read his novel, a gift from my uncle, before I left Mobile. The world he'd created between the pages made me long for a glamorous life I'd never experienced, and I had no doubt that Beatrice O'Hara shared more than a few of Zelda's character traits.

I sat beside Zelda, recalling the very public story of her romance with the writer. While I tended to shield my private moments, Zelda and Scott sought the limelight, living their golden romance and showering spectators with wild behavior. Scott had met Zelda at a Montgomery dance, the pair igniting a flame that threatened to burn them and the whole city down. Zelda, in true belle form, refused to marry Scott until he could support her in the manner she'd become accustomed. His answer had been a book, *This Side of Paradise*, that had rocketed him to fame. It had been published March 26, and he and Zelda had married on April 3 at Saint Patrick's Cathedral in New York City.

"When will you return to the city?" I asked.

She lifted her head and stared at the empty train tracks. "As soon as I can. I'll make the introductions with Camilla, and then I'm returning to Montgomery on the evening train. Scott will call me, and I must talk to him." She stood up and stretched, avoiding eye contact. "You'll think me a coward, but I can't stay at Bryce Hospital for long. I feel like I'm trapped there, unable to get away. Like I might die there."

My body reacted with a chill. I'd pushed the idea of actually spending time at a mental facility far, far into the back of my thoughts. I'd seen newspaper photographs of some asylums, and the complete desperation, the sense of humans lost in their own misery, was staggering.

Once upon a time, according to Uncle Brett, Bryce Hospital had been the exception. It was built on the Kirkbride Plan, incorporating "moral architecture," and was considered to be in the top tier of psychiatric hospitals around the world. In the years since the Civil War, though, state funding for the facility had dried up, and Uncle Brett had warned me the hospital was overcrowded and understaffed. Would I be able to handle what I might see?

"Reginald and I can manage on our own," I told her. "Once Camilla's aware we've come to help her, there's no reason for you to remain."

There was no point in telling Zelda that I, too, was a coward.

CHAPTER EIGHT

As Zelda's hired car drove through a shady lane of trees, Bryce Hospital came into view. The beauty of the building was unexpected. The Italianate edifice stood dead center at the end of the driveway, a white central building with a rotunda flanked on either side by three wards, staggered for maximum privacy. The hospital, which was a self-sufficient community, ran off the labor of the patients, and it was set amid a large acreage that offered beauty and serenity, land for farming, and untamed areas for the enjoyment of nature—all elements of a design that had been promoted by Dorothea Dix.

A social reformer of the nineteenth century, Dix was a woman I greatly admired. I regretted that she had not lived to see the suffragette movement she'd championed come so near to ratification. Her work for the insane had made life better for hundreds of thousands of patients. As I'd learned from several trips to the Mobile Public Library, the Alabama Hospital for the Insane, later renamed for Dr. Bryce, was perhaps the facility that had, at one time, most closely followed the plan that Dix and Thomas Story Kirkbride had created to achieve the maximum help for the mentally ill.

When we pulled up beside the fountain featuring a young woman pouring water, I inhaled several times to calm my jittery nerves. Zelda asked the driver to wait for her. It was obvious the asylum made her nervous. She practically leaped from the hired car. She, Reginald, and I walked across the limestone rocks to the front door and entered.

The facility was open and airy and graciously designed, but peeling paint and the odor of damp and mildew spoke of neglect. The young nurse who greeted us knew Zelda, who carried more than a little weight at the hospital. I wondered if it was because of her father or because of her own notoriety. Nurse Mahala chatted as she led us to the patient. "Camilla isn't unhappy here, but I think she's lonely," she said. "She doesn't trust herself to go home, though she desperately wants to."

"Is she eating?" Zelda asked.

"Not enough." The nurse walked beside Zelda while Reginald and I followed. "Head Nurse Brady has threatened to force-feed her if her appetite doesn't pick up."

"I say, is that necessary?" Reginald asked. "It's a rather brutal tactic."

The nurse shot a look over her shoulder. "We can't allow a patient to starve to death here."

"I'll speak with her," Zelda said. "Force-feeding won't be necessary—I assure you."

We turned down a wide hallway, and I dropped back to look out some windows onto a rose garden in desperate need of weeding and pruning. Once it must have been magnificent, a place of respite for the troubled patients.

The footfalls of Zelda, the nurse, and Reginald moved down the hallway as I stared outside. The whole institution seemed buried under sadness. Beyond the rose garden a woman, presumably a patient, walked in circles. Other patients sat in the shade, unmoving. They were not dead, but neither did they seem fully alive.

A young brunette woman, really just a girl, moved through a copse of slender poplar trees some fifty yards in the distance. I caught a glimpse of her, and then she was gone, leaving me to wonder if she'd been a real patient or a ghost. Bryce Hospital was clearly a haunted place, and the energy of the departed could gather in the dark corners of the hallways and various rooms. They wouldn't likely materialize, as the spirits at Caoin House had done. These, I perceived, were fragments of people who'd once been. Residual energy, unable to fully incarnate and unable to let go. They were as trapped as the patients whose mental disabilities kept them from a normal life, but I didn't sense violence or danger.

The hallway was empty, and I hurried to catch up with my party. Sunlight struck something shiny on the floor, and I bent to pick up an earbob made of black jet. I clutched it in my hand as I ran lightly down the hall until I'd fallen back in step with Reginald.

"Is Camilla improving?" Reginald asked the nurse. "Since she hasn't had another episode and she hasn't been diagnosed with a treatable illness, perhaps it's time for her to return to Montgomery. It might be best to see what happens."

"You'll have to speak to Dr. Perkins about her condition." Mahala kept walking. "He isn't available today. You can make an appointment for next week."

Lucky for us that Dr. Winston Perkins was away for a few more days, delivering a talk on his experimental surgical procedure in Vienna. That was the time frame we had to work within. Either we could help Camilla, or, upon the doctor's return, we would lose the chance.

Zelda was as good as her word. She found Camilla in the dayroom, introduced us, kissed her friend, and left.

We were seated in a sunny room with a piano, several sofas, a few rocking chairs, and bookshelves. Camilla wore a cool lawn dress, an older style. Her long hair had been pulled up into a bun, a look more suited to her mother's generation than her own. I couldn't tell if she was trying to conform or if she simply hadn't thought about her appearance.

The nurse left us with a long, speculative look. When she was gone, we drew two chairs close to Camilla. She was a beautiful young woman with large brown eyes and lush, dark hair. With her milky complexion and air of calm containment, she reminded me of one of Jane Austen's heroines.

"Don't think poorly of Zelda for leaving like that," Camilla said. "She's brave in so many ways, but illness terrifies her. She said that you wanted to help me. How do you plan to do that?"

Her directness set me back, but it also made me like her. "We're not certain, exactly," I said. "First we need to find out from you what happened."

"I tried to kill the man I love," she said, her gaze never wavering from mine. "I don't know if I'm crazy or a monster of some kind."

"Perhaps neither," Reginald said softly. "There are other possibilities, you know."

"Such as?" She leaned forward. "For the past three weeks, I've done nothing but think of other possibilities and come up empty-handed. Either I am mentally unstable or there is a buried part of me that is angry and ugly and wants to harm people. Either way I can't risk returning to Montgomery."

"But you've attacked only your fiancé," I pointed out, electing for the blunt approach myself. "Has he harmed you in any way?"

"David?" She laughed. "He's one of the kindest people you'd ever hope to meet."

"A nice dodge," I said. I didn't know this woman, but I couldn't waste days of my life and Zelda's money. "Answer my question."

"He's never harmed me," she said. "But *I've* tried to cut his throat."

"Tell us what you remember," Reginald prompted.

"I've told it so many times already." She seemed to withdraw a little.

"Please tell us again," he said. "We haven't much time, Miss Camilla. Your doctor is away, and I lied to your mother about why we came to see you. When she finds out the truth, I'll be thrown out of here on my ear. So please, please help us to help you."

She nodded. "The first time anything strange happened, David and I had gone to the house he'd purchased for us to live in. Workmen were renovating, but no one was there that day but us. I didn't know about the house. I'd never dreamed that I would live in our own estate, and such a beautiful place. It was built before the Civil War, at a time when crown molding made from plaster and horsehair was shaped in hand-carved forms of original design. The paneling is tiger oak, and the floors are three-quarter-inch planks. I'd always dreamed of such a home, and David had bought it for us."

"We hope to see Roswell House in a day or so," I mentioned.

"I think about going back there as David's wife." She swallowed and blinked back tears. "I cling to those dreams."

"Wouldn't you rather go to New York? To be independent for a little while?"

Camilla's smile was the saddest thing I'd ever seen. "A month ago, I wanted to be independent, just for a few weeks. My mother is . . . very controlling. She's told me what to say, what to think, what to wear, what to eat, how to eat it. I wanted, for a few weeks, to be my own person. Zelda and Tallulah would have watched over me. Mama almost cast a kitten." She smiled. "See, I was learning the proper slang."

What struck me was the lack of agitation in Camilla's voice. She'd been relentlessly pressed and shaped into a package, yet she didn't sound angry. "We met your mother."

"Then you can understand. I wasn't going to do anything wild or wanton, just laugh and go to some Broadway shows, get dressed up and walk down the street, window-shopping."

Reginald exchanged a look with me. We were both thinking what a true innocent Camilla was.

"But your mother refused," Reginald said.

"Of course. She went insane when I proposed the trip, though David wanted me to go. He has relatives in the city, and he offered to make an introduction."

"So you truly want to marry David?"

"More than anything." She leaned forward in her chair. "I don't care all that much about going to New York anymore. I just want to be David's wife. One thing about spending nearly a month in a place like this, where so many patients don't have the freedom to walk outside. It puts a completely different perspective on what's important."

"Why don't you speak with your mother about returning to Montgomery and Dr. Abbott's treatment?" I asked. "Reginald and I will work with you to figure out what happened to you, but you don't have to stay here." The hospital was one of the most depressing places I'd ever been, and if Camilla's problems stemmed from a haunting at Roswell House, we'd need to address it there with her.

"No. I'll go home cured, or I won't go home at all." Her voice broke, and she brushed a single tear away. "I could have killed David, and I have no memory at all of my actions."

"He wasn't hurt," Reginald pointed out.

"Only because he moved quickly and avoided the knife. From what he told me, I changed into someone else. Some*thing* else."

Camilla was shaken to the core of her being by what she'd done. What David Simpson told her she'd done, I amended.

"Both instances occurred when you were alone with David." Reginald took her hand as he talked. "Correct?"

She sighed. "And both times we were at Roswell House, my new home. *If* I marry David."

She'd marry the banker if Maude Granger had her way, even if Camilla had been reduced to the mental awareness of a rutabaga. I couldn't tell her that, though. Not yet. She had enough to contend with.

"Zelda told you we work with spirits?" I didn't want to give her false hope, but I had to get a sense of her willingness to work with us. "We're looking into Roswell House. If your behavior stems from a location, an angry spirit remaining there, we may truly be able to help."

"I'm not sure my troubles come from a haunting."

"We're not sure either," I said. "But we intend to find out. We have until your doctor returns from his presentation. Will you work with us?"

"Absolutely." She had no hesitation.

"Then we'll begin."

CHAPTER NINE

The afternoon sun slanted through the window, falling just short of the chair where Camilla sat, her hands folded in her lap. "When David took me to Roswell House, it was a complete shock. He'd refused to say where we were going, only that it was a surprise."

"What was your first reaction?" I asked.

"We turned down the drive, which was overgrown with volunteer scrub oaks and pines. Some of the shrubs had grown to mammoth proportions and almost blocked the driveway. I couldn't imagine where David was taking me, but he was laughing and had this air of adventure, so I didn't care. We were together, and that was all that mattered."

"And the house?" Reginald asked.

"When I first saw it, I realized where we were. It was a place we came as schoolchildren, daring one another to run up the porch and knock on the door. It had been abandoned for at least a decade then and said to be haunted. My first reaction was to be a little afraid."

"Why was the house left to sit empty?" I asked.

"The Roswell family died out, I guess." Camilla was unsure. "The Roswells were once powerful and acquired thousands of acres of land, some said by pressuring people into selling."

"Did you know the family?"

"No, Roswell House has been empty as long as I can remember. I know a bit about the house because David told me."

I nodded for her to continue.

"Back before the war, Ramsey Roswell acquired a fortune selling timber to the steamboats and railroad for fuel. With his money and what is said to be brutal and unethical tactics, Ramsey bought a large tract of land. He was betting big that the city of Montgomery would be built on his land. It didn't happen that way, though. Montgomery was located to the north." She fell silent.

I gently encouraged her to continue. "Uncle Brett says land speculation is a gambler's delight."

Camilla's fingers plucked at the material of her dress. "Ramsey wasn't a man to accept defeat. He realized that the land he'd bought had access to a valuable resource, a navigable creek. He built the original Roswell House near Tonka Creek and began raiding and robbing both Rebel and Union stockpiles, hiding his stolen spoils up Tonka Creek and sailing them downriver to Mobile for a handy profit. Soon after building his big house there, he learned that the creek was prone to flooding. The higher ground next to his plot of land had been purchased by a family that lived out of state. Ramsey couldn't bribe or threaten them into selling. It wasn't until after the war, after the Yankees burned Ramsey's house to the ground, that the Peebles family, who owned the high ground, arrived in Alabama to homestead. Like so many others, they had hard luck, and Wick Roswell, Ramsey's young son, bought the land from them and built the current Roswell House."

"I can't wait to see it."

"It's one of the best examples of Greek Revival architecture built during the postbellum period. Most Southerners were near starvation, but the Roswells had great wealth. Some say Wick was obsessed with restoring what the Yankees had destroyed. He bragged that his house and his wife were of impeccable lineage." One corner of her mouth tilted up. "He spared no expense in materials or furnishings, and the house was considered one of the finest homes in the Southeast."

Camilla had learned the details of the house admirably. While she could recite all the facts, they didn't seem to resonate emotionally with her. She seemed unattached to the house or its history. It was the first hopeful thing I'd come across.

"So David took you to the house and told you it was to be your new home when you were married. What did you think?"

"I was overwhelmed, and then I thought how much Mama would love it that I had my own antebellum mansion. She'd lord it over everyone she could."

Reginald's lips twitched into a smile, and then he laughed aloud. "You have Maude Granger pegged."

"She's my mother, but I am aware of her pettiness."

"And what of the house? Did you connect with it?" I thought of my attachment to Caoin House, my bedroom overlooking the beautiful oaks, the library. Even the cemetery. There was so much I loved about my uncle's estate.

"Roswell House is magnificent."

Despite her claim, something felt off. I couldn't put my finger on it. "And?" I hated to press, but it was important.

"There's a cantilevered staircase in the house that floats. It circles the foyer and reaches to the second floor as if supported by air."

I'd heard of such staircases, but I'd never seen one. "Was there a room you loved?"

"The ballroom." She inhaled sharply. "There's a sense that one could dance there all night long. I could almost hear the music."

My pulse increased. Aural manifestations were clues to a haunting, according to Madam Petalungro and much of the literature I'd read. "Did you imagine the parties, the men and women dressed for the evening, moving about the dance floor? Could you see it?"

She tilted her head, and for the first time, her smile was relaxed. "You want to know if I imagined other people in the house or if the house is haunted."

"I do." There was no point in denying it. If Camilla had sensed someone else there, it might help us figure out what, or who, might be influencing her.

"It was my imagination. Nothing more."

"Camilla, two times you've changed personality so radically that you attempted to harm the person you love. Both times you were alone with David and at Roswell House. If David himself and/or Roswell House are the source of your . . . illness, we have to know." Reginald leaned forward and patted her hand. "We want to help, but you must tell us everything you remember."

"I guess it's a little late to worry that people will think I'm crazy." She tried to shrug it off, but it was clear she was hurting.

"This is what we do," I said. "I've had my own experience with departed spirits. I've lost people I cared about because of it. I don't want that to be your experience."

She nodded sharply. "The first time I . . . changed, I was in the kitchen at Roswell House. I was so thrilled at what David had done, buying the house and property, renovating it, planning to put the house in a trust for me so that I always have my own place, away from Mama."

"What happened?" I asked.

"I don't know. I was exploring the cupboards, arranging the kitchen in my mind. David had samples of countertops and cabinets for me to pick from. I was going to have things my way. For the first time in my life, I was allowed to make decisions." She withdrew her hand from Reginald's. "I was so happy. Then I became aware I was acutely cold, and then hot, burning hot. I couldn't see. It felt as if I'd been pushed deep down inside my body. Like I was trapped. I could feel my legs moving, walking, my hand finding the butcher knife . . . I could feel my fingers grasping it, but I couldn't see or move or speak."

Reginald and I were riveted, not daring to interrupt.

"I was overwhelmed with an urge to kill David. To slice his throat or take his head." She ignored the tears that streaked her cheeks. "The next thing I knew, I was lying in the grass outside the house. David was beside me, bleeding where I'd cut him."

Reginald and I exchanged looks. I knew nothing about such intense hauntings. I hoped he had some experience.

"Did you notice anything else unusual before you felt the cold?" Reginald asked. "A smell or odor? Maybe a change in the light or a heaviness of atmosphere?"

She shook her head and finally wiped the tears away.

"Did you see anything? A shadow? Or maybe sense a presence?" I followed up.

"One minute I was so happy and excited. The next I was freezing, then burning up. Then I wanted to murder the man I love."

"Why did David buy Roswell House? You said it had been abandoned. Why not build a new house?"

"When I first met David, I mentioned the house to him. I said that I wanted a house just like Roswell, with the beautiful columns and the porches and balconies. He wanted to give me my dream. I think the lavish, glamorous history of the property also appealed to David. He wasn't from here, but he could buy a part of the past."

"What happened to the Roswell family? Yellow fever? Financial disaster? Or something worse?" A murder could account for a haunting.

"I only know the family died out, except for one heir who was born up north and never even came to Alabama. I don't think he ever saw the house. David tracked him down and made an offer."

"You mentioned the house was reputed to be haunted," Reginald began.

"Schoolgirl foolishness. You know, a place to go and pet with the thrill of a possible ghost lurking about. Nothing like a little trill of fear to push a girl into a boy's arms."

She was right about that. "But you never saw anything there."

"We'd scare ourselves by seeing something pass in front of a window. Or we'd see someone in the rose garden or in the shadows of a tree. Fluttering dresses or tree leaves, who can say? You know how the imagination conjures up images on a dark night."

Oh, I knew it well. I also knew that it wasn't always the imagination. Spirits did roam. Roswell House, with a past not unlike my uncle's home, might reasonably be expected to have some danglers, as Madam Petalungro called the spirits caught between life and death.

"But you never sense anything . . . sinister?" I asked.

"Nothing like that. Ever."

"Thank you, Camilla." I felt the young woman had told us everything she knew.

Camilla's body tensed, as if she dreaded our leaving. "Before you go, can I ask you something? How is David? Really? I haven't seen him for days. Mama's left word with the nurses that he shouldn't be allowed to visit me again. She says I'll frighten him into canceling the engagement. No man wants to be tied to a maniac. That's what she says."

If Maude Granger had stood before me, and if I'd had a butcher knife in my hand, I might have been tempted to cut off her head, or at least slice out her tongue.

"Your mother has a remarkable talent for brutality," Reginald said. He offered Camilla his arm and assisted her to her feet. "Let's walk. I'd like to see more of the hospital. I'm particularly interested in the area where Dr. Perkins conducts his studies."

Three abreast, we left the sunny room and headed down a corridor that wasn't well lit. I realized that the day had slipped away from us. Night was still a long way off, but the angle of the sun had shifted, and this hallway obviously received morning light.

Ahead of us, the sound of something skittering across the floor stopped us in our tracks. Reginald walked forward and quickly bent over. When he returned, he held out a jet earbob, a perfect match to the one in my pocket. I drew it out and held it beside the one he'd found.

"Those are Joanne's," Camilla said.

"Joanne?" I asked. "A nurse?"

"No, she's my friend. She doesn't want to be here. She says she doesn't belong with the deranged."

The earbobs looked expensive, and I was curious as to why a young woman would bring jewelry to a mental hospital, where it could easily be stolen. "They're lovely." I put them in Camilla's hand.

"She'll be happy to have them back. She puts a high value on them. Her brother gave them to her before he left for the war." She looked down at the floor. "He didn't come back."

A chill touched my neck and back. I had no doubt the placement of the jewelry was deliberate.

What game, I wondered, was this Joanne playing that she left them in the hallways for us to find?

CHAPTER TEN

Bryce Hospital had been designed to house fewer than five hundred patients, but the population had swelled to the point that facilities, staff, and services were strained to bursting. Camilla had a private room, but the wards were bunk to bunk with patients in all states of mental anguish. The sounds of that distress bruised my heart.

We passed a male who stood in the corridor banging his head against the wall over and over.

"Can we help him?" I asked Reginald. It was almost more than I could tolerate, watching a man harm himself. I'd thought Zelda a coward for turning tail and running. Now I understood her actions and wanted only to follow suit.

"They'll give him medicine to make him quiet," Camilla said. "His name is Tobias. Dr. Perkins is going to perform the new brain surgery on him when he returns from his meeting. I'm after Tobias."

I tried my best to master the fear that surged at Camilla's casual mention of the surgery that had been proposed as treatment for her. "You're agreeable to having them cut into your brain?"

"I want to go home. I want to marry David and be his wife and the mother of his children. I can't do that if I'm afraid I'll kill him. I have to be cured."

"At any cost?" Reginald asked.

"What do you mean?"

"Surgery should be the last alternative," I said. "I hope Reginald and I can find a reason for your outbursts and that surgery can be avoided." As much as I wanted to terrify Camilla with the details of what Dr. Perkins had planned for her, it wasn't my place to do so.

"Miss Granger!" The two words cracked down the hallway like artillery fire.

We all turned to find a broad-hipped nurse striding toward us, fire in her eyes.

"Who are these people, and what are they doing in the ward?" the nurse demanded.

Camilla calmly made introductions. "Head Nurse Margaret Brady, this is Raissa James, a writer, and Reginald Proctor, a chemist for Proctor Pharmaceuticals." She smoothly used the cover story Zelda had devised for us. "My mother sent them for a consultation."

Nurse Brady eyed us with dark suspicion. "You should have checked in at the front desk and obtained permission to tour the wards."

"I apologize." Reginald stepped up. "Miss Granger was telling us how hard the nurses here work. And that poor patient"—he indicated Tobias, who'd finally stopped banging his head as he watched Nurse Brady—"needs attention. I was on my way to find someone."

"Return to your room," Nurse Brady said to Camilla. "I'll be there shortly."

"Yes, ma'am." Camilla said her good-byes and excused herself. I wouldn't have dared disobey the nurse either.

"Tobias, return to your bed, please." She spoke with some gentleness to the man, whose hands were now bloody from rubbing his bleeding forehead.

"Yes, ma'am." He shambled away, now calm.

The nurse rounded on us. "I don't care that Maude Granger sent you here. She doesn't have the authority to grant you access to my patients." Margaret Brady drew herself up to her full height of nearly six feet. She was physically sound and obviously able to handle most patients if force proved necessary. "You must leave."

Reginald motioned the head nurse aside, leaving me to stand in the corridor. I watched him work his charm, and, after a few moments, he had her nodding at whatever he said. For a man who had no real interest in women, Reginald certainly knew how to manage them.

Nurse Brady approached me. "I understand you're a writer working with Mr. Proctor to report the effects of his new drugs."

"Yes," I said. Better not to embellish a lie.

"His company's using the powdered root of a shrub grown in India?" She watched me sharply.

I refused to look at Reginald for confirmation. "I've only seen the capsules, so I can't say how the substance is obtained. If I'm to truly document this remarkable medical breakthrough, I'll have to probe more deeply into the process he's using." I gave him a look. "Like many other inventors, Mr. Proctor is very secretive."

"Mrs. Brady, I don't wish to make trouble for you." Reginald showed no irritation. "The state mental institution in Whitefield, Mississippi, has agreed to work with me. I came to Bryce Hospital because of Dr. Perkins's reputation. He is a daring physician and surgeon who is willing to try new techniques to help his patients. But I don't want to cause any problems. I'll take my trial—"

"Dr. Perkins will return next week." Nurse Brady's tone had softened. "I don't see the harm in showing you around the hospital, but our involvement with your drug trial will be up to him."

"Of course," Reginald said, smiling. "His endorsement is what I came to get. His work is well known, and a word of approval from him will smooth the way for Proctor Pharmaceuticals. Now, if you have a few moments, perhaps you could show me around."

Unbelievable. Nurse Brady was no one's fool, yet Reginald had charmed her into doing exactly as he wanted.

"I'd like to return to my interview with Miss Granger," I said. I had no desire to see the operating theater where brains were cut into and disabled.

"I'm not sure Dr. Perkins would approve of an interview." Nurse Brady might have yielded to Reginald, but she hadn't warmed to me.

Reginald stepped in. "It's merely a statement of how she feels, how the rages come over her. These will help with the initial dose of medicine, if Dr. Perkins decides that he wants to work with me and if Miss Granger chooses to participate."

"I am wary of writers." Nurse Brady eyed me.

"I write in the service of Mr. Proctor," I said. "I'm not a reporter. I'm merely trying to get as clear a picture of Miss Granger's illness before and after. It will help draw financial backers for Proctor Pharmaceuticals. The development of a new drug is an expensive proposition." I was talking through my hat, but I employed Reginald's absolute self-assurance. Amazingly, it worked.

"Of course." Nurse Brady wasn't happy, but her complaints subsided.

"Mr. Proctor, shall I meet you in the front lobby in . . . half an hour?" I asked.

"Give us an hour," Nurse Brady said. "There is much to see. Dr. Perkins is a pioneer, and I'd like Mr. Proctor to understand the scope of his work."

"Of course." I turned and walked away. When I was out of sight, I slowed my pace and began to explore the hospital. The high ceilings offered as much ventilation as possible, but the day was hot and humid. The heat worked on me, and I could only imagine how it must be in the wards, where dozens and dozens of patients were stacked so close together.

Some of the patients were serene, seemingly at peace with their surroundings, but others were agitated. Some were tied to chairs. The nursing staff was thin, and they hustled about. What was it like to work in a place where the possibility of recovery was slim? What about the patients' families? Camilla's parents had not visited, I reminded myself. Only David, Zelda, and Tallulah.

I came to the lobby—obviously I'd lost my way—and stepped outside for a moment to compose my thoughts. The grounds had the potential for great loveliness, but gardening and landscaping came with a price tag. The fountain of Hygeia, the goddess of healing, was forlorn. Mold stained her face, giving her the look of black tears. It was a distressing thought, and I turned to go back inside. My time with Camilla was limited, and I needed to make the most of it.

Around the corner of the main building, I caught a glimpse of the young dark-haired girl I'd seen before, in the trees beyond the rose garden. She looked even younger from this distance. Surely she wasn't an inmate. She looked to be no older than fifteen or sixteen, at most.

I started after her, compelled by curiosity, and then a growing sense of dread. Something wasn't right about this girl.

I made the corner of a building and saw her disappearing behind a bank of shrubs. She wasn't running, but she covered the ground quickly. A chill traced along my back as I ran after her. There was no one else about on the front grounds, and fear drove me forward. Fear of what? I couldn't name it, but it squeezed my lungs in a tight grip.

When I made it to the shrub, I saw her standing in the shade of a tree. She looked directly at me. The sun caught her brown curls, and I realized she was a beautiful girl, angelic in visage.

"What's your name?" I had to speak loudly as I walked slowly toward her.

She didn't answer.

She wore a yellow frock, a shift, still in the style of a young girl, though I could see she'd begun her womanly development. A yellow ribbon tied back her hair.

"What's your name?" I asked again. "I'm Raissa."

Instead of answering, she cut and ran, her thin legs churning. She disappeared behind a cistern, and I stopped. Chasing her might damage her. If she was a patient, I didn't want to terrify her. I would ask Camilla who she might be.

I returned to the front, avoiding the sad Hygeia as she poured her water. The lobby had filled with vacant-eyed patients who sat passively, watching me walk by. No one attempted to talk to me, though several looked as if they might cry. I couldn't allow myself to imagine what they were thinking or feeling.

I passed by a table of four women, their hair a fright, their nightgowns dingy. I forced a smile. "Hello." I nodded politely and walked past.

"Help her." One of the women spoke just as I'd left them behind. I stopped and turned to face the table. They stared into space, not seeming to notice me at all. Yet one had spoken.

"Help who?" I asked, stepping closer. "Tell me and I'll try."

They didn't move or acknowledge my presence. Out of the corner of my eye, I saw the brunette girl standing at the corridor. Before I could react, she disappeared down the hallway. When I got to the corridor, there was no trace of her. Though I listened for footsteps, I heard nothing as I found my way back to Camilla.

CHAPTER ELEVEN

Camilla sat in a straight-backed chair in the small cubicle that was her room. She'd returned there, just as Nurse Brady had ordered, to wait patiently. I found it difficult to believe this young woman had ever defied her mother or anyone else in authority. She wasn't a flapper by any definition I'd ever heard.

I told her about the young girl who flitted about the hospital.

"That's Connie Shelton," she said. "I've been looking for her, but they told me she went home."

"Connie's a patient?"

"Was. She went home."

What was the proper phrasing to ask what mental illness someone suffered from? "How did Connie come to be at Bryce?"

"Her parents were killed in a fire, and a neighbor accused her of setting it. A few days later she tried to set the neighbor on fire."

"Oh." It was a pathetically weak response.

"There's more to the story," Camilla said softly. "Connie's father died when she was a child. Her stepfather forced her to . . . do things."

I knew exactly what she meant. "That poor girl."

"It gets worse," Camilla warned. "The neighbor knew what was happening in that house and refused to help Connie. He held the common belief that women are chattel, meant to serve the needs of the man."

I nearly staggered, then sat, trying to conceal the murderous rage I felt. The young girl I saw, barely coming into her maturity, had been used by the people who should have protected her. I didn't want to think about such a thing. My childhood had been so safe and secure. It had given me the strength to endure loss and heartbreak.

"The court sent Connie here. They view her as dangerous, but she was only trying to survive. The neighbor told the court she could stay with him, and so they sent her there. She has no other relatives willing to take her. Well, her room and board came with a price tag."

"Did she set the fire that killed her mother and stepfather?"

"She doesn't remember doing it. The neighbor told the law officers that he saw her do it, but he could be lying. He could have done it. He told the court she acted like she was in a trance." Camilla scoffed. "I have some sympathy for her in that regard."

My interest was immediately stirred. "I'd like to talk with her."

"They let her out yesterday."

"But I just saw her." If it was the same girl. "She was wearing a yellow dress, and she had long, dark-brown hair. She was outside behind the rose garden and then in the front of the administration building. I tried, but I couldn't catch up with her."

"That sounds like her, but she left yesterday morning. I saw them leave. I was looking out the window." She went to the window and pulled back the drapes, revealing the bars across the opening. This was a hospital, but it was also a kind of prison.

"If she has no relatives, who came for her?"

"Nurse Brady said her uncle had finally agreed to take her in and provide medical care for her. I couldn't find out if she'll be tried for the death of her parents or not. Maybe they decided she wasn't responsible because she is ill." She returned to her chair. "I wonder who you saw. Most of the patients are older than I am. Not many younger girls here."

"I'll ask at the desk," I said. "Now, tell me a little about David. I met him yesterday, and he seems completely devoted to you."

Camilla's body relaxed, and she smiled. "He's a good man. I love him with all my heart. He's nothing like Mama. He wants me to be safe, of course, but he also respects that I can do things on my own."

"Like visit Zelda in New York City?"

She nodded. "He knows I want to work in the bank before I start a family, and he agrees. He wants me to share that part of his life, like true partners."

I was surprised. Most men of David Simpson's social standing wouldn't consider having a wife who worked. Women were the domestic helpmates, to use Maude Granger's word. Men worked, controlled the finances and all decisions about the family. The exceptions were the women like Maude, who'd terrorized their husbands into compliance. And now the modern women who wanted to shoulder responsibility and have a say in what happened in their homes and families and the workplace. The Great War had taken my husband, a man I missed every day of my life, but it had also given women the impetus to demand equality.

"Do you think you can help me?" Camilla asked.

"We'll certainly try." Camilla looked drained, and I wanted to explore Bryce a bit. "I have to find Reginald, but we'll return tomorrow," I told her as I picked up my clutch.

Camilla put a hand on my arm to stop me. "Do you sense anything? Wrong with me, I mean?" Her confidence faltered. "Like a dark spirit or demon inside me?"

"Not at all," I assured her. "I don't sense anything untoward or dangerous in the least."

"Thank you." She came to me and hugged me tightly.

Camilla was petite, and I put my arms around her, feeling more protective than ever. If David Simpson were somehow playing her false, I'd make him sorry.

I left her standing in the middle of her stark room, so small and so alone. She held her shoulders back and stood erect and lifted her hand in farewell. She was strong. Maybe stronger than I was. I hurried down the hallway, my leather-soled shoes clacking along the wooden boards.

When I reached the lobby, Reginald was there, still under the watchful eye of Nurse Brady. He thanked her profusely for her assistance in the tour, and we started out the front door. Reginald had called a car to drive us into Tuscaloosa, where we'd booked a hotel room for the night.

"I need a moment," I said to Reginald when I felt certain Nurse Brady had gone about her duties. "Please hold the car when it arrives."

"What are you up to?" he asked.

"Checking on another patient. Connie Shelton. I saw her today, but Camilla insists she left with her uncle yesterday morning."

"I'll hold the car," Reginald said.

A few minutes later I was in the business office, wearing a smile. "Can you tell me how to get in touch with Connie Shelton? She was friends with Camilla, who asked me to deliver a letter. If I had Connie's address, I could mail it."

The clerk barely looked up. She went to a file cabinet and riffled through some tabs before she pulled up a manila folder. "Says here Connie Shelton left with her uncle, James Patrickson of Decatur, Alabama."

"Is there an address?" I asked, notebook and pencil in hand.

She gave me the address; there was no phone number, which wasn't uncommon for rural areas.

"Connie left with him yesterday?" I had doubts about this good-hearted uncle's miraculous appearance.

"Yes, he signed her out. He had a form from the Montgomery police chief saying it was okay to release her to her uncle's custody and care." She handed the form to me.

"Yes, of course. It's good a relative came to help her." I'd believe it when I checked it out.

"We get fire starters sometimes," the woman confided. "The doctors say it's a compulsion that can't be controlled. Except with surgery. But the law said to turn her loose, so we did it. She'll be back after she chars a few more people."

So Connie was another candidate for Dr. Perkins's knife. "I see. Thank you." I returned the folder and hurried outside before Nurse Brady discovered me poking into files.

Reginald waited beside the hired car and helped me into the backseat. "Did you find the information you wanted?"

"I did, and I'm afraid Connie Shelton may be dead. What did you discover?"

"Dr. Perkins has free rein at the hospital to conduct his surgeries. The board governing the hospital believes he's on the verge of finding a cure for mental illness so that the residents at Bryce Hospital can be returned to their communities, docile and no longer a danger to themselves or others. He's developed a less invasive procedure that doesn't require removal of the top of the skull. It's very hush-hush. A miracle treatment, or so Nurse Brady believes."

"Docile and no longer able to care for themselves or make a decision or work. If their families won't care for them, what will happen to them?"

"They'll live on the streets or wherever they can find shelter, but they won't be a drain on the state budget."

The car pulled down the long lane of trees and turned toward the river town of Tuscaloosa. A breeze blew through the open windows of the car. The day was fading into a beautiful sunset. I glanced behind us and viewed Bryce Hospital. A young woman, barely older than a girl, stood beside the fountain of Hygiea. The wind ruffled the skirt of her yellow dress and her brunette curls. She lifted a hand in farewell, turned, and was lost from view.

CHAPTER TWELVE

The Burchfield Hotel was a Tuscaloosa highlight, a three-story brick building on the corner of Third Street and Greensboro Avenue near the train depot. It was well known for its fine dining. Zelda had arranged our rooms, and our bags were at the front desk, waiting to be delivered. For the sake of propriety, Reginald's room and mine were separated by a long hall. An independent woman, even a widow, was not above suspicion when traveling with a man. It amused me that hotel management felt it was its duty to protect my honor.

I tipped the bellboy when he put my bag down and waited until the door clicked behind him. I fell across the bed, exhausted. I hadn't realized how tense I'd been. Relaxing into the soft mattress, I took in the room. The floral wallpaper was cheerful, and the sturdy furniture serviceable and clean. The dresser and highboy were well crafted, but they were poor imitations of the antique pieces at Caoin House. Still, the room was comfortable and pleasant.

After dinner with Reginald, I intended to come back to this room, take a hot bath, and crawl into bed. Tomorrow we had to go back to Bryce Hospital. It would be another grueling day.

A light tap at my door told me Reginald was ready to go down to dinner. I forced myself off the bed and met him in the hallway. The long corridor that led to an elevator was dark, though electric lights helped dispel the gloom. Cherry wainscoting covered the lower portion of the hall with red-and-gold-patterned wallpaper on the upper portion.

"I'm starving," Reginald said as he offered his arm. "Shall we eat in the hotel dining room or venture out?"

"I'm happy to stay here." I had no desire to leave the hotel. In fact, room service sounded like heaven. Were it not for leaving Reginald alone in a strange city, I would have gladly gone without dinner for the chance to sleep.

We took the elevator down to the first floor, and I stepped off the creaking contraption with some relief. I wanted to learn about all the modern conveniences of city life, but riding three floors above the ground in a box held by cables and wires made me anxious. Stairs were perfectly adequate for my needs.

The hotel dining room, lit by beautiful crystal chandeliers, bustled with waiting staff. Hotel guests and locals sat at white-linen-covered tables as Negro men brought drinks and menus, served the food, and cleared the tables. White waiters took the orders. The maître d' showed us to a table in the back of the dining room with an excellent view of the entire room. Tired though I was, I enjoyed people watching. Folks who were out of town—whether for business or pleasure—had a tendency to feel anonymous. The proper behavior imposed by neighbors and community went out the window.

My gaze fell on a young woman at a table with an older man. She looked to be about sixteen, but it was impossible to tell because of the heavy makeup and provocative dress she wore. Her V-neck plunged low, and a long strand of pearls enticed the eye to her cleavage. Her kohled eyes were languid, suggestive, sensual. Her dark hair was cut short, and the marcel waves showed time and expense. Judging by her behavior, she was old enough to know the ways of men.

The tablecloth had been pulled back by the gentleman's girth, and I could clearly see her foot, free of a shoe, rubbing his leg. Her painted toes crept higher and higher. He liked it very much, judging from the way he leaned toward her. His hand moved beneath the table, and he ran his fingers up her thigh.

Reginald raised his eyebrows. "Learning some new maneuvers?"

"I admire a woman who knows how to get her way," I whispered. "Though she doesn't look much older than a girl. I wonder why her parents let her marry a man so much older."

Reginald sighed. "Oh, she'll get everything she wants from him before the night is over, plus some hard cash. Youth is an asset when it comes to selling flesh. In New Orleans the young prostitutes, male and female, are easy to find. Some no older than twelve. They do what's necessary to survive."

"She's a prostitute?"

"The oldest profession, or so they say."

My impulse was to rise and . . . what? Intervene? What help could I offer the young woman?

"Should we call the police?"

"The cops would arrest the girl and let the man go. Do you really want to punish her? I suspect her life is hard enough."

Without being obvious, I studied the girl. She hadn't touched her food, but the portly man was wolfing down a thick steak and potatoes. He hadn't noticed that she wasn't eating, only drinking. Fury at his cavalier attitude toward the young woman made me want to walk over to his table and slap him as hard as I could.

"Don't do it." Reginald put his fork down. "Don't."

"Do what?" I clenched my jaw so hard I had to force the words out.

"Don't go over there and slug him. You'll be the one in trouble. If you break this up, he'll find another girl. You know that."

"He's a swine."

"He is." Reginald nudged my wineglass toward me. "Take a sip."

I did as he ordered.

"Raissa, the world is unfair. For women. For men like me. For the poor. For the Negroes. For so many. When you can make a difference, by God, intervene. This isn't an instance where you can make a difference."

"It bothers me." I thought about the women I'd seen at Carlton McKay's private club in Mobile. I hadn't gone 'round the bend with anger over them. They were a different kettle of fish, the difference being that they were grown women. They had a sense of contentment, even enjoyment, about their lives. The girl across the room with the fat man looked . . . dead. The idea of moving beneath that man would take the joy out of life, but I couldn't see that she was being forced. It was her choice, yet it seemed so wrong.

"Much in life bothers me, but I don't run around punching people in the face. By the way, if you *do* go over there and start a fight, kick him in the balls. Hard. I'll go your bail for the pleasure of watching."

Reginald signaled a waiter. When the man arrived, Reginald whispered in his ear. He pulled the forty dollars he'd made gambling on the paddle-wheel out of his billfold and slipped it to the waiter, who left with a curt nod.

"Zelda has covered our meals and expenses," I reminded him.

"That was for the floor show."

I frowned, but he nodded toward the waiter he'd just tipped, who came from the bar carrying a trayful of drinks. Just as he approached the table where the young prostitute sat, he stumbled. He tried to regain his feet but failed, plunging headlong into the table. The drinks flew across the expanse of linen directly into the man's face. A wedge of lime rested on one shoulder, and broken crystal cluttered the floor around the soaked diner's chair.

"Oh, sir, I am so sorry." The waiter dabbed at various stains on the man's chest. "I apologize, Mr. Wilton. Let me help you to your room, and I'll take your suit to be cleaned immediately."

For a moment Mr. Wilton refused to move. He sat as still as stone, then pushed back his chair so vehemently that it fell over. All conversation in the dining room had stopped.

"I'll have your job," Mr. Wilton said to the waiter. "You clumsy baboon. You won't work here again."

"Please, sir, it was an accident. I tripped." The waiter gathered more napkins to dab at Mr. Wilton's dripping front. "Let me help you to your room. I'll have these clothes cleaned and back to you by tomorrow morning."

"Get out of my sight."

The waiter hurried away. Wilton turned on the young girl. "Don't just sit there. Get up and help me."

The girl sat at the table, her gaze on her untouched plate. Her hands gripped the edges of her chair.

The maître d' rushed over and spoke soothingly to Mr. Wilton. "This will all be taken care of. We apologize. I saw what happened, and Burton tripped. It was a terrible accident. Your meal is, of course, on the hotel. I'll have something else prepared and sent to your room while your clothes are being cleaned." He led Mr. Wilton away.

Burton stopped at the table and spoke to the young woman, who finally looked up at him. Whatever he said made her smile. A moment later, she left the dining room.

"We can't change her life for her," Reginald said, "but we did change tonight. The waiter gave her the money I paid him."

"That was kind."

"If you women and the Negroes ever banded up together, you could take over this country."

We both laughed, and it was much needed. "What a day," I said at last.

"Indeed. And you weren't touring the chamber of horrors with Dr. Perkins's most devoted follower."

"Nurse Brady's a true believer, eh? Despite the dangers?"

"You have to crack a few eggs to make an omelet. That's the way she looks at it."

"I don't want Camilla to be one of those eggs."

"Neither do I. So we'd better figure out what's going on with her. In watching and listening to her, I found her believable. She makes eye contact. She isn't evasive or sly. She doesn't remember trying to harm David or why she did it. There's something outside Camilla at play here. Any ideas?"

I tried to clear my mind and let random thoughts float up. What I was attempting had no scientific formula or easy way to get to the truth. I had to allow my sixth sense, my intuition, free rein. Madam Petalungro assured Reginald, and me, that this would become easier the more I practiced. I visualized Camilla sitting in her chair. As I focused on the image, I was aware of the room darkening, as if a cloud had blotted out the sun. Or an entity had seeped into the space.

"There's something not right about her. A darkness around her." I hesitated. "But I don't think she's haunted. Not as in a ghost who takes charge of her."

"This darkness. Can you tell me the source?"

"I wish I could. To some degree, I think Camilla's aware of it. She could leave Bryce Hospital whenever she chooses. But she stays. She's *that* afraid of harming David Simpson."

Reginald tilted his head. "You think she knows more than she's letting on?"

I didn't want to say that. "I don't know. I'd like to get her out of the building and on the grounds tomorrow. I want to see her outside, away from the watchers. If you keep Nurse Brady busy, I'll manage it."

"I don't like you going off with Camilla alone. What if she becomes violent?"

"She won't. It's not about me." I couldn't say why I was so certain, but the darkness that gathered around Camilla was for her alone.

CHAPTER THIRTEEN

The waiter finally came back to our table, and we ordered a light meal. The day's heat was fading, but it was still hot and breathless in the dining room. The oscillating ceiling fans helped, but it was July, inland, in Alabama. For a split second, I longed for the breezes of Savannah, but my life there was done, a closed chapter. In Savannah I'd been a daughter, a bride, and a wife, in turn. I felt Alex's hand holding mine as we stood on the shore of Tybee Island, our faces turned into the salty breeze off the Atlantic. I'd wanted nothing more than to make Alex happy, to have a family, and to grow old together. I'd been denied that by German bullets in a war across the ocean.

"Where have you gone, Raissa?"

"Woolgathering off Tybee Island." Lies were unnecessary with Reginald. "I was longing for Alex."

He reached across the table and squeezed my hand. "I'm sorry."

"Me, too." I was beyond the surges of grief that had once overwhelmed me. Sadness, though, was never far. "Alex and I postponed our honeymoon. When he returned from the war, we'd planned to go to Adam's Cove in the Poconos. We'd have our honeymoon, along with the other soldiers who wanted solitude and serenity. While Alex was overseas, I spent a lot of time planning that trip. I thought if I made the future real in my mind, I would keep him safe."

"And now you find yourself in a hotel with another man."

Despite the melancholy that surrounded me, I smiled. "And a scandalous man at that."

"Men have little use except as scandalous partners and train robbers."

"You've been studying the attitudes of the famous outlaw, the Sundance Kid." I'd found Reginald reading one of the dime novels about the outlaw on board the steamboat.

"Had I not become a snitch with you, I would have made an excellent outlaw."

"I think not." I realized then that he'd successfully diverted me from my doldrums. "You'd have to sweat and hide out in dirty places, sleeping in barns, and eating beans from a can. You're too much of a dandy to live like that."

"Perhaps you're right." He was about to say something else when he stopped. "The private investigator who came by Judge Sayre's home. That's him."

I turned slightly to follow his gaze. Jason Kuddle sat in earnest conversation with a uniformed police officer at a table by the window. "He was working on the case of that girl who disappeared north of Montgomery. I wonder if they've made any progress."

"I'll ask." Reginald folded his napkin and stood. He crossed the dining room and stopped at Kuddle's table. A moment later he was shaking hands with Kuddle and the policeman. They chatted a moment, and then the men turned to me and nodded.

I wanted badly to go over and join the conversation, but it would have been too forward. Besides, I had no idea what story Reginald was telling Kuddle about who we were and what we were doing in Tuscaloosa.

The waiter stopped at the table and refilled my wineglass. Five minutes later he came out with our food. Reginald returned with a crooked smile. "Kuddle's here on another case. He was surprised that I knew him."

"And the officer?"

"Michael Driggs. He worked in Montgomery with Kuddle. Eat something or they'll know we're talking about them."

The chicken cordon bleu was excellent. Midway through Reginald caught my attention. "Don't look now, but Kuddle's coming over. He was too curious about you not to." Reginald stood. "Mr. Kuddle. How good of you to come and speak to Mrs. James."

"I understand you're a writer," he said, winking at Reginald. Kuddle was a handsome man with blue eyes and longish, light-brown hair. He dressed well, and he was alert. His gaze didn't linger but moved across me, my food, the wine. He paid attention to the details, which would be a useful habit for a gumshoe. "What do you write?"

"Different things. Mostly short stories."

"Don't be modest, Raissa. Tell him about your ghost stories." Reginald turned to Kuddle. "Her first story will be published in October in the *Saturday Evening Post*. It's quite the chilling tale."

"I'll pick up a copy. I like a good yarn." Kuddle looked around. His companion had left. "So you're staying here in the hotel?"

"Yes. It's lovely, isn't it?" Reginald was smooth.

"The food's good. I won't be staying. I have to travel over to Mississippi on the late train, but I'll be back in a few days."

"Are you working on a case?" I couldn't stop myself.

"Yes." He didn't offer anything else.

"You know writers are so curious," I said. "Can you share some details? A missing person? Maybe a cheating husband?" I laughed softly. "I suppose I've read too many novels where mysteries are resolved by a brilliant character seeking answers. Are you familiar with Wilkie Collins's *The Woman in White*?"

"I'll have to pick up a copy," Kuddle said again, making it clear he had no intention of doing so.

"It's thrilling. And *The Moonstone*, too. And, of course, there's Poe and Dickens and Doyle's brilliant Sherlock Holmes. Any private investigator would aspire to the genius of Holmes's rational deduction." I blathered on, giving the impression of a bookwormish woman who lived in tall tales.

Kuddle's gaze flicked from me to Reginald, then about the room. He was not a reader—that much I could tell. "Facts, the here and now, that's how I butter my bread. Books are nice, and meaning no disrespect, but they're stories made up."

"Raissa is very enthusiastic about her writing," Reginald said. "Perhaps you could share some stories about your cases." He indicated a chair at our table. "You might inspire a masterpiece."

Kuddle checked his watch, a fine bracelet timepiece that transcended the more feminine models designed as jewelry for affluent women. "Sure, I'll sit for a spell."

"Tell us about your work," I said, pulling out my notebook. "This will help me so much. Do you mind if I take notes?" I wasn't stretching the truth. Kuddle was a real gumshoe. Reginald and I had our talents, but neither of us had worked as policemen or trained to solve crimes. Any tips would be useful.

"When we were at Judge Sayre's house, we couldn't help overhearing the conversation with the judge. What about the young girl from Autaugaville?" Reginald asked. "Any leads?"

"An interestin' case." Kuddle seemed to have relaxed and decided to enjoy himself. "Pretty girl, Pamela DuMond, with no history of giving her family trouble. Her teachers said she was a good student, a bit weak in the higher concepts of math they've just begun to teach." He laughed. "Girls need to learn to cook and clean. Math's a waste."

I swallowed a gulp of wine to keep from speaking.

"So no one thinks she ran off?" Reginald kept the conversation going.

"Her family says no. Her friends say no. They say she was reliable, a good girl." He tilted his head quickly. "I say maybe. Relatives see what they want to see."

"Was there evidence she ran away?" I asked.

"Her best dress and new shoes are missing. That indicates to me she was planning to wear her finery somewhere."

"And how did she leave? She couldn't have walked. Autaugaville is miles from anywhere, and if she'd tried to cross the river on the ferry, they would have seen her."

Kuddle grinned. "You're a pretty smart tootsie."

"Either someone picked her up, or she's injured between the school and her house."

"Unless her family's involved."

Kuddle's words made me think of poor, abused Connie Shelton, whose desperation had led to deadly arson. "Was there something going on in the DuMond family? Did you find evidence of abuse?"

"No evidence, but the family's . . . different."

"How so?"

"Off-kilter, wrong." Kuddle pursed his lips. "Somethin' ain't right, if you get my angle. The father was tore up about the missing girl, but the mother, she was more afraid."

That did sound suspicious. "Did the neighbors have any information?"

"The girl lived on an isolated farm, and from what the family said, she was a hard worker in the garden and with the livestock. No one outside the family knew much about her. She went to school every day. She made good marks. She was shy and didn't make friends."

That didn't sound like any sixteen-year-old girl I knew. Friends were everything in that adolescent world. Then again, for a child being abused, friends could be dangerous. "There wasn't anyone she called a friend?"

"There was a girl named Hope, but her mother said she couldn't speak with me."

"Hope who?"

"Harrington. Upper-crust family. Didn't want to be involved. Mr. Harrington's a big wheel in the county. Seems like the whole community knows something they aren't tellin'."

"Surely if you pressed them . . . I'm sorry. I don't mean to be presumptuous."

"I get what you're hittin' on, Mrs. James. The thing is, I'm not a copper anymore. I can't make people talk. I can ask, but that's the limit of my authority. If they don't want to talk, they tell me to beat it."

"I understand." But I was still frustrated.

"And I understand your concern. I'm worried, too. Could be she ran off to the city, tired of hoeing weeds and diggin' taters. Or it could be a lot worse."

"Could you tell us what happened before she disappeared?" Reginald asked.

"She went into town to get alum for puttin' up pickles. She was gonna spend the afternoon with a girlfriend. She made her purchase and left the grocery store. She was seen walkin' home, just like she did all the time. When she wasn't home by four o'clock, her mama sent an older sister to look for her. The older girl found the grocery bag on the side of the road, no trace of Pamela. Vanished."

It didn't sound good. Not at all. Girls didn't vanish off the side of a dirt road unless someone took them. "You said some of her things were missing?"

"Seems like she may have met up with someone and left. Either she took the clothes with her when she walked to town—except no one remembers seeing her carrying anything except a grocery sack. My guess is she planned this out and left her good clothes hidden in the woods."

I couldn't imagine running away from home, but not all families were like mine. I was lucky, and I knew it. My parents had been quiet and loving. My father was a professor, and my mother gave private lessons in Latin and piano. They'd shared a great love and a quiet life; I had been a child of privilege. Not in money, but in love and education. They had died in an accident, and I missed them every day.

"A girl can't simply vanish," I said.

"They can and do. Every day." Kuddle leaned back in his chair. "I alerted the law in eight counties. I figured she'd head to Montgomery, and if not there, maybe Birmingham, if she can hitch a ride."

"If she's still alive."

"I've put out the word and posters. Not much else we can do. The DuMond family doesn't have the money to hire me for long. After I'm off the case, she'll be forgotten."

"It shouldn't be that way." I might as well have smacked my head into the wall, like the poor patient I'd seen at Bryce.

"I don't disagree, Mrs. James. But I can't change how things are. Pamela DuMond's gone. From the photo I got from her mama, she's a pretty young woman. I'm afraid that isn't a good thing in this case."

CHAPTER FOURTEEN

Kuddle left us, and with him he took the last of my fading energy. We finished our meal in quiet companionship, and I realized Reginald was exhausted, too. The things he'd seen in Dr. Perkins's operating theater—I didn't want to know.

We parted at the elevator on the third floor. Reginald's room, 303, was at the end of the corridor. Mine, 317, was at the opposite end of the hall. "Sleep well," he called to me.

"As soon as I climb into bed, I'll be a goner." I gave him a wave far perkier than I felt as he disappeared inside his room. A few moments later, I'd used the heavy key to open my door. The maid had turned the bed linens back and opened a window. The curtains flitted on a gentle breeze, and I stopped for a moment to explore the view of the train station and a now-sleepy downtown. I was too tired for a bath, but I brushed my teeth and put my clothes away.

The minute I slipped beneath the sheets, I was asleep. I skidded into unconsciousness, barely aware of the soft bed or the sound of a train stopping at the depot. I was back in Savannah, sitting on the porch with Alex. Our chairs side by side in the gloaming of a summer evening, we both read. Our bare feet touched on a wicker hassock. I looked over at him and felt my heart rent asunder, a physical pain, with the power of my love.

"I love you." I reached across and touched his cheek, the lightest stubble scruffing my palm.

"I love you more," he said.

"Impossible." I closed my book. "I love you more than anyone has ever been loved."

"You'll love again," he said. "You have much love to give."

"Only you." I laughed at his foolishness. Some marriages lost the tender feelings, but we wouldn't be those people. We completed each other. "We're married, you know."

"Till death do us part." He wasn't smiling. "Let me go, Raissa. Find love again."

"What?" I couldn't believe what he was saying.

He shifted so the dimming light caught him full-on. His face was riddled with bullet holes. Blood bloomed through his white shirt.

A terrible pain in my chest made me gasp. I woke up struggling out of the darkness that suffocated me, then lay rigid on the bed, inhaling and exhaling, forcing my heart to calm. A dream or visitation, it didn't matter which. The conclusion was the same. Alex was dead.

I drank a glass of water and pulled the sheet over me. I didn't expect to sleep again, but I slipped back beneath the darkness and found myself in the hallway of a gloomy hotel. Behind one of the closed doors, I heard low moans, the rhythmic creaking of the bed springs, the sounds of sex.

In a cloudy mirror, I caught my own reflection. I wore my favorite dress, a sleeveless green shift banded at the hip. It was cool and roomy, allowing me to move freely.

Though I didn't know where I was, I somehow knew I was traveling and spending the night in a hotel. It was an adventure, and I walked down a long, dark corridor with electric lamps at regular intervals providing a gloomy sort of light. My room was at the end of the hall. As

I approached my door, I was aware of the echo of my footsteps. The sounds of lovemaking ceased. I was alone in the hotel.

Behind me shadows gathered, drawing closer. If I turned, the hallway would be empty. Wall sconces generated dim pools of light in the dark hallway. As I stepped forward, the nearest light fizzled and went out. All down the hallway the bulbs popped and died.

"Help me." A girl whispered the words, though I couldn't see her.

"Please don't hurt me." A different voice spoke, also young and female.

Out of the murkiness, two girls stepped forward. They wore the straight, short dresses with the fringe and beads of the flapper. Cloche hats, dark lipstick, and heavy mascara completed the image of the modern woman. As I stared at them, blood seeped from the corners of their right eyes, sliding past the corners of their lips and dripping onto the bodices of their dresses.

"Please don't hurt us," they said in unison. "We'll be good."

"Who are you?"

"Names no more." One nudged the other in the shoulder. "Names mean nothing."

I didn't understand, but the way they spoke together was unnerving. "Where do you live?"

"We're always with you." The dark-haired girl was in front of me before I could move. Her voice turned gravelly and mean. "No escape. Pretty is quiet."

"I'll help you if I can," I said. "Tell me your names."

The fairer girl joined her. Their eyes were dark and haunted in the illumination cast by the hallway lights, which had come back on. "Bad girl. Wicked tongue. You'll pay."

"Tell me your names," I said, my voice breaking.

They shook their heads slowly. Before I could ask another question, they began to struggle, clawing at their necks as if something, or someone, was strangling them. Blood, like crimson tears, began to leak from their eyes again. At last their heads were wrenched gruesomely to the side, the sound of the bones snapping.

And then they were gone.

When I came to my senses, I was standing in the middle of the Burchfield hallway in my flimsy nightgown and no wrap. Dread seeped through my bones, and my heart pounded. My brain couldn't comprehend my circumstances, but I focused on the pattern of gold sprigs in the dark-red wallpaper and at last calmed my breathing. I was alone. No other presence was near me. The hallway lights glowed dimly, exactly as they had in my dream. No remnants of my nocturnal visitors remained.

The night was stifling; the unventilated corridor felt close. Sweat dripped down my back. I wiped my face with my hand and couldn't resist checking to be sure I wasn't bleeding. The dream had been so intense, obviously inspired by my grave concerns for Camilla Granger. The dream girls had been her age, garbed in the flapper attire Camilla had wanted to wear for her brief independence in New York. Enforced silence was the rule they honored. The blood leaking from their eyes puzzled me, but I knew it was somehow connected to Camilla's illness. Simply thinking about it galvanized me to action.

I hurried back to my room and locked the door behind me. Walking around strange hotels in my nightgown qualified as dangerous conduct. Had anyone seen me, my reputation would be ruined. In an attempt to catch a breeze, I went to the window and looked out over the Tuscaloosa night. The downtown area was empty of traffic. The city slept, even if I didn't.

Too unsettled to go back to bed, I picked up my notebook. While the dream was fresh in my mind, I would start a new short story. I had an idea for a tale of ghosts living among the bold, modern women of a big city. These ghosts wanted life—they wanted what the living had.

And they meant to take it. "They Walk among Us" was the title that came to me, and I began with the words I'd heard in my dream.

We're always with you.

By the time I put my pen down, the sun was casting long shadows. I stood and stretched. I'd pay for the lack of sleep, but I'd had no other option. I bathed, dressed, and was ready for breakfast when Reginald knocked on my door.

"Are you ill?" he asked, stepping into my room to get a better look at me.

"Lack of sleep. I had a nightmare."

We stepped back into the hallway and walked to the elevator.

"I had strange dreams, too," he said. "It will come as no surprise that Valkyrie Brady was involved. She had me tied into a chair, and she came at me with a scalpel. She kept saying, 'It's just a close shave.'"

I had to laugh. If Reginald was pulling my leg, I didn't care. I needed a bit of mirth. "I dread going back to Bryce."

"Me, too. But this is our last chance to look around and make sure we haven't missed anything important."

I nodded. "I wish we could bring Camilla home with us." The dream girls, bleeding from their eyes, quickened my fear. "Dr. Perkins will return from his travels soon, and I have no doubt he'll push to operate on Camilla."

"It would be a feather in his cap to 'cure' someone like her, even if he reduces her to the state of a drooling child."

"*Cure* has different meanings for different people, doesn't it? Come on. Let's take the stairs." I wasn't in the mood for the creaking and moaning elevator.

We ate a quick, cold breakfast of biscuits and butter and were on the street just as the hired car arrived. The drive to the hospital was beautiful, but I couldn't shake the sense of depression that clung to me. I stepped onto the grounds of Bryce Hospital with some reluctance. My gaze went to the window I knew to be Camilla's, and I was surprised to see a young woman standing there. Not Camilla—someone close to her age but taller. She was gone before I got a clear image of her.

Soon I was walking the grounds with Camilla and two stout aides, who followed twenty paces behind. If Camilla was bothered by her guards, she didn't show it. She was courteous to them, as she was to the patients and the staff we encountered. I watched her closely for any hint that something dark lurked behind her gaze, but I saw nothing. The mist of darkness I'd perceived earlier was gone. Perhaps I'd only imagined it.

We walked beneath the shade of oaks and sycamores, ignoring the humidity and yellow flies, until we came to the south bank of the Black Warrior River that bounded the hospital grounds. "I love coming here," Camilla said. "Even with my keepers." She smiled at the two men. "The flow of the river is like life. It moves on, no matter how sad or happy I am. Life sweeps past. It reminds me to think of the good things."

True though it might be, I couldn't imagine that she truly wanted to remain at Bryce. "Come home with me, Camilla. Your mother said you came here voluntarily. Call her. Tell her you're ready to come home. Tell her you're ready to marry David, and give us a chance to figure out what's going on with you."

Hesitation and longing crossed her face.

"What if it's something at Roswell House?" I pressed. "What if you have the surgery only to discover that the problem was external? Think, Camilla. You've had trouble only at that house."

"That's true."

"We can pick you up in the morning," I urged. "You can stay at the Sayre house, I'm sure. Zelda is leaving for New York soon, but Minnie adores you. She spoke so highly of you when I was visiting there. It would give you a chance to recover in surroundings you know and love, and you would be right there to help us unravel why this is happening to you."

"Mama will demand I return home." Her face was now blank of any expression. It gave me a chill to think that might be her permanent demeanor if she allowed Dr. Perkins to operate on her.

"Once you're free of here, you don't have to obey your mother. You're almost eighteen."

"If I leave here, I have to do as Mama tells me. I'm not of age."

"You're old enough to fight for your future. If you don't want to get a room of your own, stay with the Sayres."

"Mama will make a scandal of it, and the Sayres will suffer."

I couldn't deny her statement, and I was about to suggest that she elope with David simply to escape the dragon when I saw a fleet of small boats coming down the river. They were flat-bottomed, two-man boats used for fishing near the banks and inlets. They drifted on the current, spread across the Black Warrior. Each boat contained a man with a paddle and another who pulled a rope dragging something.

"I wonder what they're fishing for," Camilla said. "Look, it's Deakon, one of the groundskeepers." She went to the edge of the river and waved at him. "Deakon!"

The black man looked away, ignoring her.

"What are you doing?" Camilla called out.

He didn't have to answer. Nurse Brady had come up behind us and startled me to the point that I actually jumped.

"They're dragging the river for a body," she said. "Now go back to the hospital. I've warned all of you about coming to the river. You could stumble into the swift current and drown. Dr. Perkins will have my head for this."

"I didn't come alone. I wasn't in any danger. I had Raissa and two aides. We—" Camilla's attempt to explain was cut short.

"Go back to the hospital. Now."

Camilla turned and walked away, an aide on either side of her. Margaret Brady gave me a long glare, but I merely absorbed it. She couldn't boss me. "Who's missing?" I asked, knowing it had to be one of the patients.

"I don't need you poking about here."

There was likely liability attached to a patient walking into the river and drowning, so I ignored her snappy attitude. "Probably not, but I am here, so you might as well tell me. Perhaps I can help."

She pushed a strand of hair from her face. "It's Cheryl, one of Dr. Perkins's success stories. I don't know how she got out of her room. The staff assures me the door was locked, but obviously it wasn't. Dr. Perkins will be furious if she's drowned."

"What makes you think she's drowned?"

"She disappeared last night—and no one called me. I would have had search parties out for her. A fisherman saw her wading into the river this morning. He tried to save her, but the current caught her and pulled her under. Now the most we can do is recover the body for an autopsy."

"Surely the current has taken her downriver."

"Possibly. Or she might have been caught up nearby. If she's stuck here, they'll find her with the grappling hooks."

I turned away, appalled at the picture she painted. "How could she have gotten out unnoticed?" I managed after a moment.

"You've been here for what, six hours, and you think you know everything? Would you prefer to have these patients chained to the wall? Maybe tied in bed or a chair? We don't have the staff to send an aide with every patient who wants to walk on the grounds. So it's either let them walk by themselves or tie them in their rooms or beds. Which sounds kinder to you?"

I swallowed. "Could she swim? Isn't there any chance she survived?"

"I doubt it," Nurse Brady said. "Cheryl was troubled. Dr. Perkins did what he could, but she never came out of it. She came here so angry she lashed out at everyone. She escaped repeatedly, only to be brought back. Her family didn't want her returned to them, but that's all she talked about. Going home. She slipped out of her bed all the time and walked the property. Punishment didn't stop her, so we quit disciplining her."

"What about her family?"

"They dropped her off and never came back. It happens more than you'd ever imagine."

"You're right. I don't know anything. I'm sorry if I came across that way."

"Believe it or not, I care about my patients, but I can't be soft. They need structure and routine. Some of the treatments are painful and unpleasant. But Dr. Perkins and I want to see these people returned to normal life, to live with their families able to work a job and contribute. We want to give them the simple things that so many take for granted."

My opinion of Nurse Brady had begun to shift. Her manner was gruff and aggressive, but she did seem to care.

"We got her!" One of the men in the boat stood up and waved.

As the boat moved to shore, the man in the stern began pulling in the rope he held. Something white bobbed up in the water and then submerged again.

CHAPTER FIFTEEN

The grappling hook had caught her just under the rib cage. The men pulled their boats up on a small sandbar and then waded into the river to grasp her arms and legs. They brought her out, her clothes molded to her thin form. I wanted to weep, though I didn't even know her.

"It's Cheryl Lawrence," one of the men yelled up to Nurse Brady.

"Damn." The nurse strode down the bank to the little patch of white sand where the men put the body. She knelt beside the girl, but it was no use. She was long dead, her skin a luminous lavender.

Clutching tree limbs and roots, I made my way down the bank and stopped. "Is there anything I can do to help?"

"No." Nurse Brady looked up at me. She brushed wet strands of hair from the dead girl's face. "After Dr. Perkins treated her, she became a sweet girl. Slow and prone to running away, but she wasn't bad."

She might once have been pretty, but it was impossible to tell. What held my gaze, though, was the scar and bald patch on her skull that showed the efforts of Dr. Perkins's surgery. "I'm sorry." I stepped back, intending to find Reginald. I had no idea where he might be since he wasn't with Nurse Brady.

"I'll have the body brought to the hospital," Nurse Brady said as she rose to her feet slowly. "Would you find Dr. Bentley and ask him to be on hand? I'd like to get the necessary documents signed and the body ready to be taken home. The water and the heat . . . she needs to be embalmed. Her family will have to take her, like it or not."

"Dr. Bentley? I wasn't aware another physician worked at the hospital."

"There are two others. Dr. Bentley is a superb alienist. Dr. French is an apprentice physician working under Dr. Bentley and Dr. Perkins. He's studied anatomy in France and was a field medic during the war."

"I'll find Dr. Bentley," I said as I scrambled back up the bank.

———◦———

Dr. Samuel Bentley and Dr. Millard French were making rounds, and I found the *Mutt and Jeff* duo with ease. Bentley was a short, round man with the demeanor of an ambulatory cadaver and a painful smile. French was something else. He was movie-star handsome, tall with broad shoulders. His slicked-back hair glistened, and he sported a thin mustache. He gave Reginald a run for his money in the looks department.

I relayed Nurse Brady's request, only to be met with Bentley's sour response. "I'll be in the west wing. She can find me there. I spend more time signing forms here than I do healing patients."

Dr. French smiled. "Tell her we're evaluating new patients. She'll know where to find us." He had sandy-blond hair and an easy smile. He was only a few years older than I, but he exuded confidence. I wanted to ask him about his experiences on the battlefield, but I didn't. Thinking of Alex and what he'd endured would only lead me down into melancholy, which would do little to help me do my job.

"Are you studying to be a psychiatrist?" I asked. "Nurse Brady said you had served as a medic in Europe."

"My chosen field is general surgeon. Bryce offers me a tremendous opportunity. There are a number of patients who need surgical care, but the state doesn't have the budget to pay for a surgeon. Under the guidance of Dr. Bentley and Dr. Perkins, I can operate and help the patients while also gaining invaluable experience. I come here two days a week. Dr. Bentley does most of the orthopedic operations, and I assist him. I handle the soft-tissue cases."

I suspected that Dr. French would have no dearth of female patients suffering ailments simply for a chance to see the handsome doctor. His ring finger was bare, and a prestigious doctor would be a fine catch.

"Millard, we have patients." Dr. Bentley stood five feet away, impatiently waiting.

"Of course." Dr. French gave a nod and a smile before he sauntered after the rotund Bentley and disappeared. Instead of going back to the river, I found an orderly and sent a message to Nurse Brady. My job was to find Reginald.

I heard his laughter before I found him in the third-floor records room. He was sitting on a young woman's desk, telling her stories of the New Orleans street musicians. I hung back, enjoying the way he offered a few titillating details. He had the young woman in the palm of his hand. Word of the tragedy at the river hadn't spread to the offices yet, but it wouldn't be long.

Reginald might have sensed me, because he looked at his pocket watch and made an annoyed face. "I have an appointment, Faith. I should go." He stood. "It's been a real pleasure talking with you."

"And you, Mr. Proctor. Will you be at the hospital for a few days? If you haven't found the best places to eat, I can make a list. I'd start with Carmichael's Catfish Cabin. Best fried catfish in the state. They bring them straight out of the river. It's close, too. Maybe, if you wanted, I could show you where it's at."

"I'd love that, but I have a dinner appointment. Work takes precedence over pleasure, I'm afraid. By the way, I'm working with Dr. Perkins on some new treatments for patients. Might I have a look at Camilla Granger's file? And her friend Connie Shelton's?"

"Those are surgery patients," she said, going to a file cabinet. "Here you go. Granger, Shelton, Lawrence, Wilkins, Hebert, Tanner, Welford, and Knight. They're all Dr. Perkins's surgery patients. Joanne Pence is to be evaluated."

"Did Connie Shelton have the surgery before she went home with her uncle?"

"I don't know. The file will tell you."

Reginald took the folders and indicated a chair. "Mind if I rest my posterior?"

"You go right ahead." She was pleased he'd decided to stay a little longer, even if it was only to look through the files.

I backed away, unwilling to disturb Reginald's quest for information, though I wondered what he hoped to find in the files. The hand on the back of my arm almost made me scream. When I whipped around, I found a young woman with dark hair and dark eyes grasping my arm. She wore the jet earbobs we'd found in the hall.

"Help me," she said in a whisper.

"Joanne?" I remembered Camilla calling her that.

She nodded. "I can't stay here anymore." She looked up and down the hall. "Can you help me leave?"

"I don't know." I answered honestly. There could be charges if I simply took her from hospital care. "Why are you here?"

She backed away. "I'm sick."

"You're here to be helped."

She turned and ran. She was small and thin, and her shoes barely made a sound on the hardwood floors. Someone else approached, and I ducked into a linen closet just as Dr. Bentley rounded the corner and headed into the records room. I couldn't see what was happening, but I could hear.

"What are you doing here?" Dr. Bentley asked.

"I was just leaving," Reginald said. "I want to be able to provide Dr. Perkins my best evaluation of which patients my pharmaceutical might help. I'm very eager for his return. Thank you for your help, Faith," Reginald said.

"You're welcome, Mr. Proctor. Good luck with your research. I'll just refile those records."

"Have a good day, Doctor, Faith." Reginald came out of the office and almost bumped into me before I dodged him.

"Let's go," Reginald whispered, hurrying me down the empty hall.

"Is it wrong to charm young girls into helping you?" I asked. I'd tell him about my strange encounter with Joanne later. The bigger news was the poor drowned woman.

"It might be, but I found out something interesting."

"What?" I didn't mind delaying my news.

"All of the patients who've received the benefits of having their skulls opened and their brains sliced have been discharged except for one. A Lawrence girl."

I nodded. "Cheryl Lawrence."

"How did you know?"

"She's dead. They just pulled her out of the river."

"Was it an accident or a suicide?" Reginald grasped my arm and eased me into the shadows. "Or was it murder?"

"Murder? Who would murder a mental patient?"

"A doctor who botched the job."

"But Dr. Perkins is in Europe. He couldn't have harmed her."

Reginald put his arm around my shoulders and moved me down the hall at a brisk pace. At the end of the hallway, there was a small alcove where cleaning supplies were stored. We stepped inside, listening for footsteps.

When we heard nothing, Reginald continued. "Men like Perkins pay others to do their dirty work. And he's got the perfect alibi."

"Do you really think he murdered his own patient?" I didn't want to believe it. This was the man in charge of Camilla's fate. "Why would he do such a thing?"

"I only glanced quickly at the file, but Cheryl Lawrence was diagnosed as 'feebleminded' *before* the surgical procedure. That's not what Nurse Brady said." Reginald peeked into the hallway and motioned for me to hold our position. "Perhaps she was a bad result. A living example of what could happen if the surgery failed. Which would be worth hiding, don't you think?"

I nodded. "Drowning would be the simplest way to murder her and leave no evidence. If she was simpleminded, then it's easy enough to make people believe she wandered away from the hospital, stepped into the river to cool off on a hot summer day, and drowned." I looked at him. "Camilla's in danger."

"You're not wrong about that."

Out of the corner of my eye, I saw a shadow moving down the wall of the hallway. I put my fingers on Reginald's mouth to silence him. "Someone's there."

We eased back against the wall with the mops and brooms and held our breath. Reginald's hand gripped my arm, giving me support. In a moment Dr. French passed the opening. He was in such a hurry he didn't even glance in the alcove. I couldn't account for the terror I felt. As a child I'd sometimes played hide-and-seek with other children, and I'd had the same unreasonable terror. I hated hiding and hoping not to be found. Helplessness and fear made my legs weak, and I trembled.

"Are you okay?" Reginald asked. The danger had passed, and he offered his arm as we left the small alcove.

"I've always hated hiding." I tried to brush it off with a laugh, but even to me the sound was pitiful. "The other children would laugh at me because I always volunteered to be 'it.' I wanted to hunt, not hide."

"No victim behavior for you." Reginald gently guided me down the hallway. "Did something happen to you? Maybe someone meant to hurt you and you had to hide?"

"No, nothing like that. No bad experiences. Just a character quirk." I felt so much better moving down the hall. We passed a window and looked out at the sunshine in the oak and sycamore trees. It was like a tonic.

"Madam would say this is something from a past life, an unreasonable fear or impulse that has no explanation in life experience."

"So I was in danger in a past life and hid, terrified of being found. What would I have been?" The discussion felt silly, but I didn't care. The act of walking and talking calmed me.

"Perhaps you were a thief, trapped in your victim's house. Or a battered wife. Or a spy."

"I like the idea that I was a spy. Perhaps in the Civil War."

"Or maybe in Athens or Sparta. Madam believes that our souls have been in existence since the beginning of time. We return to this reality to experience a physical life in an effort for our spirits to mature and grow."

"Do you believe this?" I asked Reginald.

"I don't disbelieve it. Your writer hero, Arthur Conan Doyle, has been taken through a rebirth of past lives through the use of hypnosis. It is called a regression."

"I've never heard of this."

Reginald explained. "In ancient Indian literature, some great religious men practiced exploring their incarnations through yoga and meditation. The idea is to unburden this life from past experiences. Mr. Doyle is a firm believer. He and Madam have delved deeply into the subject. Madam says this physical life teaches compassion, because we suffer so much loss and pain."

"Certainly that." We turned the corner to the hallway containing Camilla's room. I slowed my pace. I'd lost my parents and Alex, and I was only twenty-four years old. The time that stretched in front of me would bring more loss. "How can I discover my past life?"

"There are those trained in the technique. Before you ask, I am not."

He was correct that I wanted to try it.

"When we resolve this case, we'll travel to New Orleans and talk to Madam." Reginald looked straight ahead instead of at me.

"Promise?" I asked.

"If you still want to when we finish this case, I'll take you. Sometimes knowing too much isn't the right answer."

"Why would you say that?" I stopped so he faced me.

"Because it's true. We are here now. Whatever happened in the past is gone, as if it never happened. I believe it's best to leave that behind and simply try to live today as best we can."

"But what harm to explore?"

"People under hypnosis aren't always reliable. It isn't a science, Raissa."

"Were you regressed?"

He set off at a walk. "No. But I've seen it done."

I caught the sleeve of his jacket. "What happened?"

"The results were . . . tragic." He pointed toward Camilla's door. "We should be plotting a way to get her out of here."

"Wait. Tell me what happened. I'm not a child or a fool."

"The hypnotist regressed a young man to a life in Persia. He was a sex slave. And he liked it." Reginald's eyes were sharp and hot. "When he woke up and realized what he'd admitted to, he hanged himself that night. He couldn't bear the humiliation of being a male prostitute. Not even in a past life."

Reginald had grown up on the streets. He'd been in an orphanage. What had he endured?

"I'm sorry. I should have let it drop."

"No, you have a right to know, to learn. But this past-life regression isn't a party trick."

"The young man who took his own life—no one could prove that he was a sex slave two hundred years ago. He should have shrugged it off."

"Perhaps he killed himself because he was forced to confront his real feelings. Desires he couldn't even admit to himself. When people are unmasked and they aren't ready to face the truth, it can be devastating. Imagine your most shameful fantasy or desire being revealed to a group of your friends. Everyone has secrets, things they hide even from themselves."

"It would be difficult."

"Not a single one of us expected Jacob to take his own life. If he'd only talked to me, I might have helped him."

"Did Madam perform the regression?"

"No, her sessions are always private. To prevent something like this from happening."

"Does a present life always echo a past life?" I asked.

"Seldom, from my experience, but I'm a novice. It's dangerous, though, when an interest or behavior is revealed. As I said, none of us was prepared for what happened, especially not Jacob. And Malcolm, the hypnotist, was devastated."

"I'm so sorry, for all involved."

"Society isn't kind to those who differ from the accepted path. But who decides what's accepted? Isn't that the question we should be asking? Who decides that women are property? Or that the murder of a white man is punishable, but the murder of a black man is not important?"

Reginald had raised some issues I wanted to discuss, but not before we spoke to Camilla. If we were going to convince her to leave with us, we needed to do it right away.

CHAPTER SIXTEEN

"But I'm not cured."

Camilla sat in the straight-back chair beside the tiny desk in her room. Her pose was demure, but I'd struck a will of iron beneath the calm, pliant exterior. The progress I'd made on the riverbank convincing her to leave had faded to nothing.

"Dr. Abbott can care for you in Montgomery. He's agreed to do this. There's a hospital there. Just let us get you out of here." I knelt beside her and grasped her hands. "It's not safe here. Let us help you."

"I can't. I've thought about what you said, but I can't. Were I to go to the hospital in Montgomery and word got out that I had attempted to kill David, my family would be ruined. Our engagement would be broken. He could never marry a woman who tried to kill him—he would be a social outcast, and banking is about connections in society. David says he doesn't care, but I do. Even a whiff that I'm a madwoman is unacceptable. I can't risk that. I love David, and I want to be his wife."

"Then stay in your home or the Sayres' home." I refused to release her hands.

"No." She met my gaze full-on. "I will not. Mother won't have me, and she'll punish the Sayres if they get involved."

"Camilla, something's not right about Dr. Perkins." I hadn't wanted to tell her about Cheryl Lawrence's death. I didn't want to shock or upset her. I had no idea how tenuous her grasp on her calm logic might be. But I told her anyway. She had to know.

"Do you have proof Dr. Perkins had anything to do with her death? Or just suspicions? I've seen her walk to the river. Sometimes she was calm enough, but other times she was frantic. She talked about swimming across the river to get away from Bryce. Maybe she tried that and drowned. If you have evidence of foul play, tell me now."

"In this instance, suspicions are enough," Reginald said. "If the girl drowned herself because of what had been done to her—or if she was drowned by someone else because of it—in either instance, you could be in danger."

Our arguments weren't budging her. I tried a different tack. "What if I speak with your mother and convince her that it isn't safe for you here?" It would be a Herculean chore, but I was willing to try.

"She won't allow it. She made herself clear, and one thing you should know—Mama never backs down. If I want to return to Montgomery, I must be cured." At last she looked at us. "Or I must believe the source of my illness can be found and eradicated. Am I haunted? Can you say that positively? Can you promise that my behavior stems from Roswell House?"

"I don't know."

She shook her head. "If it's come to the place where being haunted by a dead spirit is preferable to all else, then I am lost," she said.

I'd failed her. I sensed nothing around her, and the only identifiable spirits I'd seen at Bryce had nothing to do with Camilla, except they seemed to point out the fate she might share with them.

She plucked at the fabric of her dress. "If I'm not haunted, then clearly I'm mad. To lose control of my body and commit such a terrible act—with no memory of doing it or explanation as to why I would—that is madness, and I won't subject my family to ridicule from my behavior. And I certainly won't risk David's life."

I stood. We would not sway her. If we meant to take her with us, we would have to abduct her against her will. I couldn't see that Reginald would agree to such an action. I wasn't certain I could, though I was worried enough about her welfare to consider it.

"We have to go now," I said. "We return to Montgomery tomorrow morning. After we've visited Roswell House, maybe we'll have some answers for you."

"I hope you find something. I sincerely do. I want to go home. I hope you know that. But I can't. I just can't." Tears pooled in the corners of her eyes, but she didn't allow them to fall. Her will was impressive.

"We'll do everything we can to find a way to help you and return you, undamaged, to your life." Reginald patted her shoulder. "For now we'll leave you to rest." He inclined his head toward the hall, and we left the room.

Reginald and I were silent as we traversed the hall. Sobs and moans came from some of the patient wards. The murmur of conversation buzzed like a distant hive. I wondered if the glassy-eyed patients we passed viewed us as ghosts of a life left behind. To them, the world we lived in was no more real than visitations from the dead.

While Reginald stopped in the lobby to call for a car to drive us, I went outside. The heat was so oppressive, and a sudden light-headedness made me stagger. As I sank to the steps to sit, a movement in my periphery vision compelled me to turn my head. Connie Shelton stood not a hundred yards away. She wore the same dress, and her hair lifted and fell on a breeze that only she could feel.

I knew for certain then. She was a ghost.

My heart hammered, and the sense of dizziness made me brace my palms on the steps to keep from falling over and cracking my head. For what felt like an eternity, I couldn't hear anything. It was as if a bell jar had been placed around me. When Reginald's shoes showed up beside me, I looked up at him, unable to communicate.

"Raissa! Are you sick?" He took my hands and helped me up. Sound returned, and I could speak.

"Connie Shelton didn't leave with her uncle, as the nurse told us. She's dead."

"How do you know?"

"She's standing right there, beside the camellia bush." Unladylike as it might be, I pointed. Connie Shelton stood beside the glossy forest-green leaves of a tall camellia. She turned slowly around, revealing the back of her dress ripped and shredded. Her back was a lacework of blood, as if she'd been flayed by something.

"Oh dear God." I stumbled, but Reginald held me upright. "She's been savagely abused."

"I can't see her."

"Be glad you can't. Someone beat her without mercy. Her spirit has returned here to Bryce, and she wouldn't be here if she were alive. She'd be with her uncle. If such a person even exists." Connie had left with someone purporting to be a relative. I knew better. The person she'd left with had killed her. "As soon as we get to Montgomery, we have to look into it. We have her uncle's address. We have to find out what happened to her. Maybe tomorrow we can examine her file."

"What the hell is going on here?" Reginald asked.

"I'm almost afraid to find out." I was still a bit woozy, and I leaned on his arm as he helped me into the hired car that had arrived.

"You need to eat something, and I want to explore some topics." He asked the driver if he knew how to reach the catfish restaurant Faith had told him about. A moment later, we were under way.

I looked back at the hospital. On the first floor, where the records office was, I saw a dim shadow standing in a window. It was male, and the man seemed to be watching us depart. By the time I called

Reginald's attention to the window, the figure was gone. Almost as if I'd imagined it.

A chill traced over me, and, despite the ninety-degree heat, I felt cold.

⸺⟨⟩⸺

Carmichael's Catfish Cabin boasted the decor of a gentleman's hunting and fishing camp. It catered to the Tuscaloosa elite who wanted to get away from the city for an evening of fresh fried catfish and a view of the beautiful Black Warrior River. It was set deep in the woods, a place both isolated and romantic as the sun descended. The drive had been winding and filled with hairpin curves, skirting cypress swamps and black-water sloughs.

The restaurant was situated on a bluff with a lovely view of the river below. I sat at a table along an open front porch and looked out. The river reminded me of Cheryl Lawrence, the poor young woman who'd drowned. Under suspicious circumstances.

Reginald ordered for us both, and the food was delicious. I'd thought I couldn't eat, but after one taste of the light cornmeal-dipped fish, I realized I was starving. Reginald ordered iced teas, a perfect complement to the crispy fish and tart coleslaw. As I ate and watched the sun set, my body relaxed, and I was able to laugh at Reginald's jokes.

"Thank goodness," he said, signaling for more tea. "You had me worried."

"Well, we clearly can't help Camilla by taking her out of Bryce. She refuses to leave." I sipped the cold, sweet beverage, glad the day was finally over. "So let's talk about what we *can* do."

"The way I see it," said Reginald, "we still don't have all the facts. I see three possibilities. She is insane, she is haunted, or she is being manipulated by someone, whether through chemicals or some method I don't know. My money is on a supernatural force."

I nodded. "We must examine Roswell House."

"Top of the list tomorrow," he agreed. "As soon as we get to Montgomery."

The waitress approached, and I was glad of the distraction. "We have fresh watermelon, pear tarts, or pound cake for dessert."

"I couldn't eat another bite, but the choices sound wonderful."

"I'm stuffed, too." Reginald slid folded bills toward her. "Keep the change. Can you call a car for us to get a ride back to Tuscaloosa?"

"There are some drivers waiting for fares. I'll let one know."

As we walked through the dining area, two men watched me. Their interest was so naked and intense that I stepped to the other side of Reginald.

"You caught their eye," he whispered.

"Unwanted attention. They don't look friendly."

They stood up and left before we passed the table. One man turned back, and his gaze drilled into my back as I went to the ladies' washroom. When we left the restaurant, I was relieved to see they were gone. A driver assisted Reginald and me into the backseat of a running car, and in another moment we were off. We'd be at the hotel in twenty minutes. I only had to sit up straight and act proper for a short time. Mostly I wanted to kick off my shoes, slump across the seat, and let Reginald take charge of getting us back to our rooms. The day—and my visions—had taken all the starch out of my spine.

CHAPTER SEVENTEEN

We traveled the same winding river road that had taken us to Carmichael's Catfish Cabin, only this time the sun had set and the trees felt crowded too closely to the red-clay road. Frogs chorused beside the road, a sound that traveled in waves. It would swell and fall away, only to pulse loudly fifty yards down the road. I'd never heard the amphibians so loud, almost ominous. Though I was tired, I was strangely tense. The car's headlights cut a path of light through the thick night, and the driver took his time, navigating carefully. Staying in the middle of the unpaved and narrow road, the driver took the hairpin turns with care.

The nature of the road hadn't troubled me in the daylight. Now, though, I found myself holding my breath and squeezing the edge of my seat as we spun around a curve, the headlights cutting over the shallow slough of cypress knees and green scum.

"The river's been up due to heavy rains the last few weeks," the driver explained. "At least the road's dry enough to navigate. Last week it was a different story. Several cars got stuck and had to be pulled out. Not good for business at Carmichael's."

Reginald chatted with the driver, who'd left the family farm north of Tuscaloosa to make his fortune in town. Driving hired cars was the first step in his plan to own his own car business. I liked his ambition and the careful way he kept his gaze on the road even as he talked.

"What brings you to Tuscaloosa?" he asked.

"We're investigators," Reginald said. "We're looking into the disappearance of several young women in this part of the state."

"I heard about those three girls missing from Marthasville. Not hide nor hair of them found. Like they walked off the edge of the earth."

"We're investigating a young woman from near Montgomery and one in this area. I wonder if these disappearances could be related to the missing girls you mention."

"Couldn't say. All I know is teenage girls were there one minute, and then they weren't. Pretty girls. Maybe sixteen or so. None of them known to be wild, but that's what the rumors are—that they took off to the city, lured by the idea of being a flapper."

"Thanks for the information. I'll check in with the local law enforcement and see if the cases might share a link."

"I heard—" The driver's sentence was cut short when headlights blinked on fewer than a hundred feet in front of us. The vehicle was in the middle of the road. It had been sitting with the lights off. The motor roared into life, and the car came at us at full speed.

The driver cried out and wrenched the wheel to the right. The road was too narrow, and the tires caught in the ruts. The driver threw his weight against the wheel in an effort to keep the car on the road, but it was too late. The vehicle swung first right, then left, the lighter back end fishtailing as it careened down the embankment and smashed into a big tree only a few feet from black water.

I was thrown out of the backseat and onto the floorboard of the car. I had no idea what had happened to Reginald or the driver. The only sounds were the hissing of the car's engine and the hum of mosquitoes that came at me like an invading army. And limbs snapping and crackling as someone came down the bank.

"Did it get 'em?" a male voice asked.

"They hit hard enough to push the tree over." There was satisfaction in the second male's voice. "Would ya look at the blood. They won't last the night, and nobody passing'll see the car down here."

"Maybe we should finish 'em off. You know, like he said. That woman don't look dead." Hands reached into the backseat, grabbed my ankle, and tugged, hard. "She's breathin', but she won't wake up. Musta hit her head. I say we get a stick and kill 'em."

"We tamper with them now, it'll be clear someone killed 'em. This way it looks like an accident. They ran off the road and died. Best to leave it alone and let nature take her course. Let's get out of here before another car comes along."

The sounds of the two men scrabbling up the bank encouraged me to remain perfectly still. In a moment a car motor revved to life, telling me they were leaving. I waited another moment and then pulled myself off the floorboard.

"Reginald?"

A moan was my only answer. The night was so black I might as well have been bundled in a spool of velvet cloth. I couldn't see anything. I reached over the seat and felt for Reginald, who was leaning against the dashboard. "Are you hurt?" I asked, trying to rouse him.

"What happened?" he asked.

"Someone ran us off the road. They were going to kill us, but they left."

A flick of a cigarette lighter illuminated a bloodbath in the front seat. The driver had split his forehead open on the steering wheel, and blood covered his legs and the seat. "He's really hurt," I said. "Are you injured?"

"No, I'm okay, I think. Just banged up a bit."

My knees were bleeding profusely, and my skirt was badly torn. One heel had broken off my shoe, but I had no serious injuries.

"Climb up on the road and flag down the first car that comes along." Reginald was out of the car and on the other side, trying to ascertain the driver's injuries. "Hurry, Raissa. This man is seriously hurt."

Using tree limbs and roots, I managed to get up the bank to the road. It seemed like hours before I saw vehicle headlights coming from the direction of the catfish restaurant. I had no idea which direction our attackers had gone, and I could only hope it was not them returning to the scene.

I stepped into the middle of the road and began waving my arms frantically. I'd picked out a spot to jump to in case the car didn't slow. To my great relief, the car slowed and finally stopped. The headlights blinded me, but I heard the door open and footsteps on the road. "Are you hurt?" a man asked.

"Yes," I said. "We were run off the road. Our driver is seriously injured. Could you find a telephone and call for a doctor and an ambulance?"

"Yeah, sure," the man said. "Johnny, give me the torch and then take the car back to the restaurant and call for an ambulance. I'll stay here and help these people." He put a gentle hand on my shoulder. "My name is Rupert."

"Thank you," I said. "Thank you so much." I wanted to cry, and I fought the emotion down.

"Show me." He took the light from his friend's hand and snapped it on. The yellow beam, much dimmer than the car's lights, cast about the woods, showing the damage to the earth and underbrush caused by the car's descent. "You can stay up here and wait for the ambulance," he said. "How many are down there?"

"Two. Reginald's okay, I think. It's the driver who was hurt." I didn't even know his name. I'd never asked.

Rupert started down the bank. When he heard me scrambling after him, he turned the light back on me. "Stay up on the road. There are snakes and alligators down here. Just stay up on the road and wave the ambulance down if it comes."

"Okay." I didn't have the heart to argue.

Rupert and Reginald discussed what to do. Since the driver would have to be brought to the road, they decided to do it. He was unconscious, but there was no guarantee his spine or brain wasn't critically injured. Leaving him at the bottom of the ravine wouldn't help him either.

Slowly the two men made their way to the road, carrying the driver's limp body. When they placed him on the narrow verge, I felt for a pulse and found a weak one. He was still alive. I used Reginald's shirt to press against a wound in his upper chest to stanch the flow of blood. And I silently cursed the ambulance for being slow.

Reginald told Rupert what had happened as the minutes slowly ticked by. I said nothing, but I thought of the two men in the restaurant and the steely way they'd looked at me and Reginald. Were they in the car that had wrecked us? I couldn't be positive, though I strongly suspected.

At last I heard the winding wail of the ambulance. Lights cut through the darkness, and the red light bounced off the thick tree trunks. Once they arrived, it was only a matter of minutes before the driver was loaded and the ambulance departed. The sheriff of Tuscaloosa County was another matter. For an hour he probed the wreck, examined the tire marks in the road, and grilled Reginald about what had happened. Once again my observations and thoughts were unwanted. Females were prone to hysteria and unreliable. The sheriff didn't have to say it; he showed it.

At last we were released to go back to town. Our rescuer and his friend had waited and kindly offered us a ride to the hotel. I was relieved when Reginald borrowed the phone at the front desk and called the hospital to check on the driver. He had been treated and taken to a room. His left arm and a set of ribs were broken, but it was the head injury that had the doctor concerned. Reginald was told to call back in the morning.

"Let's go to our rooms," Reginald said. "I'm dead on my feet."

"Me, too." I followed him to the elevator and this time didn't protest the creaky machine. I didn't have the energy to climb three flights of stairs. Once we were at his door, he pulled me inside.

"Let me get some things. I'll be down to stay in your room."

"Do you—"

He didn't let me get the question out. "Someone tried to kill us tonight. They sat in the road waiting for us to come along, and then they deliberately ran us off the road. You heard them say they expected us to die."

I nodded.

"You can either stay here with me, or I'll give you a chance to bathe and clean up and I'll come down to stay in your room."

I nodded again, still in something of a daze. "Thank you. Come down in half an hour."

"Your reputation may be ruined, but at least you'll be alive."

"I have no use of a reputation." I forced a smile. "I'm a writer. Scandal becomes me."

I left and hurried down the hall to my room. When I opened the door, I knew something was off immediately. My suitcase had been moved, the folded clothes slightly rearranged. It wasn't much of a change, and had we not been nearly killed, I might have attributed it to the maid tidying up. But someone had gone through my things. To what end, I couldn't say.

I locked the door, drew a hot bath, and allowed myself a soak. When some of the tension had left my body, I dressed and waited for Reginald's knock. Despite the awkwardness, I was glad for him to share the room with me.

He arrived dragging a bundle of bedclothes. He wore his slacks and undershirt, his hair still wet from his own nighttime routine. "I'm barely standing, but if you see something tonight, promise you'll wake me." He spread a blanket and pillows on the floor beside my bed.

"I'll step on you if I get up," I teased. "Thank you for staying with me."

"I wouldn't have it any other way." He reclined on the floor while I took the bed. I'd assumed awkwardness would keep us both awake, but I nodded off after only a few moments and found myself standing at the top of a stone stairway that went down, down, down below the surface of the earth into darkness. Far in the distance a single light burned.

With great reluctance, I stepped down into the darkness, my feet instinctively finding the steps, my hand tracing along the cool stone wall. I was compelled to descend. My legs trembled, and my breath was shallow and constricted, but still my feet moved step-by-step into the darkness. Above me hung a ceiling of arched beams and stones. When I finally came to the single, burning light, I was deep underground. In the glow of the light, I read the words engraved on a high arch: *Introieritis terram mortuorum. Caute procedere.*

I was entering the land of the dead and had been warned to proceed with caution.

CHAPTER EIGHTEEN

Latin and the mythology of the underworld were familiar to me. After all, I'd named my detective agency for the lord of the underworld. Pluto ruled the dead and also judged a man's sins. The dark god ruled the land across the River Styx guarded by Cerberus, the three-headed dog, who prevented the dead from leaving.

I'd learned the myths from my father in many a happy reading hour as I'd sat between my parents, drinking in their love of stories and knowledge. The capture of Persephone by Pluto/Hades had been one of my childhood favorites, because my parents had shaded the story toward romance and true love rather than rape and abduction. I knew that now, and I thanked them for their kindness.

Spring was Persephone's gift to the world, a promise of renewal, rebirth, and a season to grow and prosper to offset the sadness of death and winter. Life, death, life—the endless cycle.

As I stood at the portal to the land of the dead, I fully understood the terror of Persephone's abduction. To be dragged from light and life into this place of darkness and death would be the ultimate journey into fear. I wanted to turn back, but I couldn't. There was something here, in this terrible place, for me to learn.

I walked beneath the portal, the entrance to the underworld, and in the distance I heard the slow clanging of a chain. My literary friend, Mr. Dickens, and his ghost of Christmas past came to mind. Would I encounter a being with a litany of all my past mistakes? I inhaled raggedly and listened. Was it the chain that held Cerberus to his guard post?

What was coming to greet me, dragging chains?

A part of me knew I was in a dream, one I couldn't awaken from. But the sensations of dampness and entombment were so real I feared I might pass out or simply die of fright. If I wanted to probe the world of the dead, I could not let fear turn me into a craven coward.

I descended more steps. All noise faded away. I came to a corridor. Far in the distance, human figures moved about. I heard the rush of water, a fast-flowing stream. I had a choice. I could descend deeper, or I could walk toward the black-clad figures in robes and cowls to discover what manner of creature they were.

Turning from the stairs, I walked toward the figures. They scurried away, hiding in the shadows, as afraid of me as I was of them. Or so it seemed. The hallway cleared, leaving only the sound of water coursing by. When I came to the river, I stopped. The ebony waters were swift and treacherous, but a mossy stone bridge offered safe transport to the other side. If I crossed, could I return? Had I died without knowing it?

Those questions did little to bolster my courage.

I sensed a presence behind me and swiveled to find a hooded child. Or at least I assumed it was a child. His features were blank. No eyes or nose or mouth. "Who are you?"

"The future." Though he had no mouth, he spoke clearly. I could not look away from the terrible blankness where a face should have been.

"Why am I here?"

"To remind you of the journey."

I didn't understand, and a sense of panic made me want to flee, to go back the way I'd come before it was too late. If death was this eradication of the individual, a blank entity, doomed to a subterranean existence, I couldn't endure it. I wanted sunlight and flowers. I wanted paradise, not darkness.

"I am waiting for the future," the child said. "It is the spinning wheel of fortune. An ending, a new beginning. The goddess Fortuna rules here."

A clay vessel intricately carved with designs and filled with rods appeared at his side. He drew out a rod and unrolled a piece of parchment, which read: *Parvulus enim privilegium*. A child of privilege.

"And thus my journey begins again." He dropped the rod and stepped past me, walking the way I had come. Before he disappeared from sight, I started after him. I would not be trapped alone in the underworld.

He stayed ahead of me, and when I finally left the shadows behind and stepped back into the sunlight and the living, there was no sign of the child-shaped figure. Someone was tugging at my arm, though. Shaking me, calling my name.

I opened my eyes to see a worried Reginald standing over me. "You were struggling in your sleep."

I sat up, aware that I was in my hotel room. I took a deep breath, trying to shake off the strange dream that had wrapped around me so intensely that I'd felt buried alive.

"I'm okay." And I was. Just shaken. So much for sleep. "I'm sorry I woke you, too."

"What happened?"

I told him about my journey beneath the crust of the earth to the place of the dead. Instead of laughing, he sat on the edge of the bed, thinking. "A child with a blank face. Like an undeveloped child?"

I nodded. "A child waiting for . . . wanting a future."

"Do you suppose Camilla is suffering from some self-punishment?" Reginald danced around the question he wanted to ask. "Maybe the trip to New York was more than a lark. Maybe it was to see . . . another kind of doctor. The kind that can't be found in Montgomery."

I knew instantly what he meant. A formless child, a young woman so intensely under her mother's thumb she'd never admit to a mistake. Desperation drove people to madness. A trip to New York City with Zelda, where an anonymous doctor could be found, might have had an alternative purpose. Subconsciously, Camilla might blame the man she loved for such a tragic predicament. "We must ask David if Camilla's been pregnant."

"Yes, but until we get back to Montgomery and see him, let's catch another bit of sleep." Reginald yawned as he settled back on the floor. "If it wasn't a premonition, then it was just a nightmare. See what you remember in the morning." He reached up and grasped my hand. "I'm here for you."

It was only three o'clock. We didn't have to be up until six. I inched beneath the sheet, and Reginald continued to hold my hand. "Thank you."

"No more bad dreams."

I smiled and felt the weariness tugging me along. I let go and slept.

The next morning the fragments of the dream remained vivid, and I pondered them as Reginald returned to his room to pack and dress. We had a train to catch at eight o'clock, and I was eager to get back to Montgomery. Roswell House lured me like forbidden fruit. We had two possible leads—an unwanted pregnancy piled high with guilt and Roswell House. If the former proved true, then a compassionate doctor or a minister willing to perform a marriage might alleviate the source of the problem. If the house harbored ghosts, if it were the seed of Camilla's troubles, then Reginald and I might be able to effect a cure.

Reginald called the hospital to check on the driver while I ordered breakfast in the dining room. He returned with good news. The driver had sustained severe injuries, but he would survive with no permanent damage. Relief made the dewberry jam on my toast even sweeter.

In no time at all, we were on board the train and headed for Montgomery.

A vague sense of dread from the nightmare hung over me, and I found myself gazing out the window, watching the green, green, green of Alabama flash by and thinking of another train ride. One that had changed my life more than I'd ever dreamed possible.

I'd met a young man on the ride from Savannah down to Mobile and my uncle's Caoin House. Now Robert was dead. If I had to visit the underworld in my dreams, why couldn't I find Robert, or my husband, Alex, or my parents? Perhaps they were in Elysian Fields, the section of the underworld where bliss reigned. That gave me some comfort, to think they lived in beauty and abundance without truly tasting death.

"Are you worried? That something truly evil is in the house?"

"I hadn't really given the house a lot of thought. I suppose I should." After what we'd encountered in Caoin House, I had every right to be at least a little worried. If the house contained an entity strong enough to push a young woman to commit a violent act, I had to be careful.

"I hope it is the house," Reginald said. His tone let me know he was as concerned for Camilla as I was.

"Yes, a problem we can at least attempt to solve." I glanced out the train window and felt my heart seize. My reflection glared back at me, and my features were gone, replaced by a blank face. I cried out and pushed back.

"What is it?" Reginald leaned forward and grasped my upper arms. "What's wrong?"

I shook my head. I didn't want to return to that nightmare world, even to talk about it. "If the problem isn't Roswell House," I said, "do we have another plan?"

Reginald sighed. "No. But we'll think of something."

"You have such confidence in us."

"Not really. It's just that Camilla has no one else to help her."

CHAPTER NINETEEN

We returned to the Sayre house long enough to drop our bags, greet Minnie, and leave. David Simpson was still out of town and wouldn't return until the next day. He'd left Zelda a key to Roswell House so we could make an initial examination, and she drove us there straightaway while we filled her in on what had happened at Bryce Hospital and the attack on us that had resulted in our driver's injuries.

Clearly the car wreck upset her, and when we turned down an overgrown driveway, she stopped the car. "I'm not comfortable with you continuing," she said. "If the solution can't absolutely be found at Roswell, it might be best if you dropped this case. I have to consider your safety, too."

"Absolutely not," Reginald said. "That poor young woman is in dire circumstances. Whether you pay us or not, we'll continue."

I nodded. "This isn't the time to quit." I delicately broached the subject of an unwanted pregnancy to Zelda.

"Camilla? Pregnant? The pope would be caught with the Vatican full of harlots before that happened."

Relief and disappointment touched me. I was glad Camilla didn't have to live with regret, but a reason for her behavior would have given us a place to start for a cure. "There's not a chance?"

"Camilla told me everything. When she kissed David and got aroused, she called to confess to me. She was afraid she'd damaged herself." Zelda lit a cigarette. "Poor little schoolmarm. She's hopelessly proper."

A swarm of yellow flies had finally caught our scent and descended on the car. Zelda put the vehicle in gear and drove, the stinging flies in hot pursuit. What had once been planned landscaping of hydrangeas, camellias, and beautiful white oaks was now a jungle, and in places it encroached on the driveway to the extent that branches scraped the side of the car. Scuppernong and wisteria vines threaded through the shrubs and climbed the trees. Scrub oak and privet grew through some of the camellias and bridal wreath.

As we drew closer to the house, I saw a lawn crew hard at work. They used the two-man saws I'd seen applied to timbering as they cleared underbrush and removed the volunteer trees that had grown unchecked for more than a decade. It was backbreaking work in the summer heat.

"Wedding plans march forward," Reginald said.

"They do." Zelda was noncommittal. "You know, if Camilla had become pregnant, it might have solved all of our problems."

"Her mother would have killed her," I said.

"No, I don't think so. The old dragon would have secured a place in the Simpson family forever. She would be grandmother of the child, a blood link that could never be denied."

"What a twisted way of thinking." I got out of the car, my body already sticky in the heat and humidity.

"Twisted, but the mind-set of the successful predator. Never forget that Maude Granger is a predator. And we are all her prey." Zelda jumped out of the car and signaled us to follow her to the house. It was a short walk through a driveway clotted with felled trees and debris. When we broke into the cleared front lawn, I stopped.

Roswell House rose with such grace and beauty that it literally stole my breath. Fresh white paint glistened on the columns and the exterior walls. The windows were opened so that a cross breeze could blow through, and the sounds of carpenters came from the interior. The turpentine smell of paint thinner filled the air.

Zelda pocketed the key because the front door was wide-open. We stepped inside, and the temperature dropped at least ten degrees. I heaved a sigh of welcome relief. The house had been constructed for maximum cooling. It wasn't nearly as grand as Caoin House, but it was a jewel, a sparkling diamond of balance, grace, and charm. The foyer was huge and roomy with matching mirrors that gave back reflections of reflections—an illusion of depth that intrigued me.

The staircase, where I presumed the bride would descend for the wedding ceremony, did seem to float. I could imagine the banister and railings decorated in fall blooms wound with ivy, Camilla so beautiful in her white dress descending to her waiting groom. The bridesmaids would be waiting on one side, the groomsmen on the other.

Even the exquisite details of the room worked toward that image. The crown molding around the entrance hall was a cupid motif, obviously handcrafted for this home. The inlaid wooden floor created a starburst pattern of lighter and darker woods.

Hosting the nuptials here guaranteed one of the prettiest weddings ever. I understood completely Camilla's desire to have the ceremony here, to show off the fine home that was her future, to share the joy and beauty with those she loved.

If David Simpson was on the up-and-up, this house was a gift of adoration for his bride. But that was a big *if*. I leaned toward Reginald. "I don't know what I can pick up with all the workmen here." The hammering and calls of the carpenters made it difficult for me to sense anything that might lurk in the house.

"Zelda, do you think we could clear the house for an hour?" Reginald was a take-charge man.

"Hey, woodpecker," Zelda called out to a man who was hammering in the next room. "Knock it off for an hour. We need quiet."

Two men came out of the front parlor and spoke softly to Zelda. In a moment she had them laughing as they put their tools down and walked out the front door. Four other workmen followed with grins and tips of their hats. She had a way with men—that was for sure.

"Anything else?" she asked.

"No." I started up the stairs to the third-floor ballroom. I'd try there first.

"Shall I come with you?" Reginald asked.

"Maybe in a few minutes. Let me see what I sense." The house felt empty to me, as if any spirits that might have once dwelled there had left long ago.

The banister was smooth beneath my hand as I climbed the stairs to the third floor. The heat was more intense here, and I opened the large windows. The woodwork had been sanded and prepared for painting. The ballroom was not nearly as big or fine as the one at Caoin House, but it would be a lovely setting for the bride's first dance with her husband.

I walked to the center of the room and stopped, closing my eyes and letting my body sense the things around me—the slight breeze, the openness of the room, the smell of cut vegetation and summer easing in from outside. There was no hint of an unhappy spirit or ghost. I drew a total blank.

I walked the perimeter of the room, calming myself, opening up to the possibility of some other entity in that space. My mouth was dry, and my heart beat furiously—I was afraid. What dark entity might take hold of me? What if I wasn't strong enough to hold it out? My fear hindered me, but I tried nonetheless.

Minutes later I'd heard and sensed nothing. If a spirit was there, it was playing shy. Sometimes it took a bit of encouragement to bring a spirit forth. A séance might give me some answers, or at least a direction. Since my last attempt at holding a séance, in which I'd deliberately set out to manipulate the audience, I'd come to learn more about the procedure from Reginald. If I could not draw out a spirit without help, I'd propose that to Reginald.

The longer I stayed, the more collected I became. My confidence grew, but still I detected nothing. I went downstairs, my footsteps the only sound in the house. It was empty as far as I could tell.

I found Reginald in the library, examining the work of the carpenters. "They're doing a beautiful job," he said. "Anything?"

I shook my head, hiding my disappointment. "I'll try the kitchen. Why don't you go upstairs and see if you pick up on anything? It could be I'm holding the spirit at bay. Or that I'm not sensitive to . . . other things."

"Sure." He dusted off his hands and headed to the staircase.

I wasn't certain where Zelda had gone, but her presence wasn't necessary. She had such high energy that I wondered if she might emit a life force strong enough to repel spirits. An anti-ghost field. I'd have to share that with her for a laugh.

Construction in the kitchen was finished, and David had seen to all the modern conveniences, including a new Kelvinator refrigerator. Not even Uncle Brett had one of those—yet. The kitchen cabinets had been cleverly designed to match the wood of the refrigerator. The electric stove was also the newest thing. I'd never been much of a cook. The idea of tending a stove had made me set aside what little ambitions I'd had in the culinary arts. An electric stove would make all the difference.

I opened kitchen drawers and found a fine selection of new butcher knives. They were arranged on a satin cloth with indentations for each knife. One was missing—the second largest. These were professional tools, sharpened to a razor's edge. Great damage could be inflicted with one of the blades. What I couldn't imagine was dainty Camilla picking up a knife with the intention of harming anyone, especially David.

Shutting the drawer, I turned slightly, glancing out the open kitchen window as I shifted. I froze in place. Two young girls stood in the overgrown garden watching me. They wore matching pastel dresses, one of blue and the other green. The style was from the late 1800s, a calf-length skirt with ruffles, a pinafore, and matching bows in their long dark hair, much like the illustrations of Alice in Lewis Carroll's adventure tale. The girls were twins.

Holding hands, they moved toward me, not walking but floating over the tangled grass and weeds. I deduced their age to be about ten, still very young. Healthy, smiling, they were like children who'd died of fevers or some illness, for they didn't appear to have suffered any mistreatment.

"Save her." They spoke in unison, and a whisper of fear touched me. They were very close to the window now. The scent of wisteria came with them, a springtime perfume that was long past in the July heat. "Save her." Their brows furrowed, as if they were concentrating on some fact that eluded their grasp.

"Come inside," I suggested, knowing I didn't have to speak the words.

They shook their heads. "Afraid."

"Afraid to come inside?"

They nodded.

"Who are you?"

"Save her." Their happy little faces drew tight in frustration. "Butchery!" The word carried a blast of dark emotions.

Before I could respond, their heads toppled, and blood spurted from their necks. Their heads rolled into the weeds, but their bodies remained upright. "Save her," the heads said.

I didn't scream, but I stumbled backward, banging into the cabinets. Reginald heard the commotion and came instantly. "What's wrong?"

"Hurry." I grabbed his hand and dragged him through the pantry and out the back exit to the yard where I'd seen the girls. "They were here. Twin girls. They lost their heads. They were asking me to save someone—some female—and then their heads simply toppled into the grass as if they'd been beheaded."

"Come inside out of the heat." Reginald started toward the house, but I stopped him.

Reaching down into the grass, I picked up a tattered blue bow. A rusty stain had spattered over it. "They're here, the spirits of two little dead girls. But they aren't what's troubling Camilla. I'd say they might be protective of her."

"Then there is something else here in this house?" Reginald sounded excited.

"Yes. But I don't know who or what it is. I only know it's dangerous."

"We'll figure it out." He propelled me back into the cool depths of Roswell House. "We have to."

I passed the kitchen and forced Reginald to stop. The knife drawer was open, and all the dangerous blades had been withdrawn and were standing, stuck upright into the cabinet cutting board. "We have to leave." I couldn't explain my feelings, only that I knew I wasn't prepared to engage with whatever force controlled Roswell House. This entity, whether ghost or something else, was extremely powerful. And malevolent.

When Zelda returned from her examination of the work on the lawn, we were standing in the front gallery, waiting. She took one look. The play of emotions on her face went from concern to victory. "Hot damn! There's something here."

"I'm afraid there is," I said.

"Jump in the car. We'll leave this vale of tears behind."

Even as unnerved as I was, I had to laugh at Zelda's use of a biblical phrase. I'd never expected such to fall from her lips, and I said so.

"I was raised properly, Sunday school and church. It just didn't take."

As soon as Reginald closed his door, Zelda sped down the driveway. I looked back at Roswell House and felt a trill of fear. The two girls, heads in place, stood on the porch. Above them, in a second-story window, loomed a dark-haired woman. The atmosphere around her was thick with what looked like buzzing insects. Flies.

Zelda took a turn, and the house disappeared behind a dense glade of trees.

CHAPTER TWENTY

Reginald went straight for the bourbon when we arrived at the Sayre home, and a bracing drink was exactly what I needed. I managed to smoke part of a cigarette, but it only made my head swim, so I put it out. Zelda laughed at me. She and Reginald sat with me in the sunroom, begging for details of what I'd seen.

I told them everything.

With Zelda's permission to place a long-distance call, Reginald agreed to telephone Madam Petalungro. She was the only person we knew to turn to for help. Her experience in the spirit world was desperately needed. I had sensitivity to spirits but no experience. I was learning quickly—and with some trepidation—that more entities than ghosts roamed in the shadows. And even ghosts came with varying degrees of power and strength. The ghosts of Caoin House had been angry and malevolent, but I'd never felt such dark intent. The unwanted inhabitant of Roswell House was female, and she called to her the forces of darkness.

I told Reginald and Zelda of my dream about visiting the underworld. If it applied to this situation somehow, Madam might be able to tell me how, and I needed her help.

Reginald placed the call. As the phone rang in New Orleans, I sipped the bourbon and prayed for courage. Even false courage. What kind of investigator would I be if I was too afraid to investigate? A tiny little voice inside my head answered: *A live one.*

Reginald gave Madam Petalungro the basic details of what had occurred, while Zelda and I waited.

"I'll put Raissa on the phone." He handed the receiver to me.

"You must protect yourself," Madam told me. "This is no ordinary spirit."

"What is it?"

I heard only the buzzing of the open line for a moment. "I honestly can't say. If my health were better, I would come to help you. You must protect yourself. The flies you saw trouble me. They're a sign of . . . something that may never have been alive. A ghost is the energy, or some would say soul, of a human who has passed on. This thing that lurks in Roswell House concerns me."

She wouldn't say the word, and I didn't want to. But I had to. "Do you believe in demons?"

"Whatever you wish to call the darker spirits, you must protect yourself, Raissa."

"How?"

"Find the source of this entity. If you can discover what has drawn the darkness to Roswell House and this young woman you wish to help, you may be able to rid the premises of it. Just be careful."

"Do you know how I can do this?"

"I wish I had an answer. The spirit world is a complex place. There is something in that house. I reach for it, and it eludes me. It is powerful, filled with anger and betrayal and venom. The woman you saw in the window is dangerous."

"Could Camilla be possessed?" I had to know. "By a demon?"

"That is a distinct possibility, but the answer to that question is in Roswell House and Camilla's past. Be careful, Raissa. The longer this 'possession' continues—whether it is a demon or something else—the stronger the entity becomes. You aren't experienced. If you open the door to direct communication with this entity, you take a risk."

"What kind of risk?"

"The corruption of your soul. If you communicate directly with an agent of Satan, you have allowed a connection. That connection is a chain that binds you to the darkness. You may walk away and think you have won, and in this instance you might free Camilla. But you risk a recurrence when you least expect it. The devil will know your name. Evil will pull that chain, and you will feel the yank. When you battle true evil, you risk everything."

Madam began to cough, and I concluded the phone call so that she could catch her breath. Even the coughing attack seemed to hold sinister significance in my state of mind. I replaced the receiver and tried not to show how upset I was.

"What are we going to do?" Zelda asked.

"We have to unravel the past of Roswell House," I said. "And we have to do it now."

<hr />

Minnie Sayre was most helpful in finding a source for a history of Roswell House. She'd moved to Montgomery after her marriage, but she'd become friendly with many of the old families in town.

Minnie served us strawberry shortcake and coffee as she made a list of possible sources for us to talk to about Roswell House. "It's been empty for at least a decade," she said. "Maybe longer." Her face lit up. "Bernard West's the man to talk to. He knew the Roswells. He was a business associate of the Roswell who abandoned the estate and left. Maybe he can shed some light on this."

"Mother, people say Mr. West is not right. He's heavy on the sauce." Zelda frowned. "I remember him before he started drinking, but now . . ."

"I'm sure he'd welcome a visit from you," Minnie said. "He was that rare adult who didn't find you to be bold and abrasive."

Zelda laughed. "True enough. He enjoyed my 'attacks against the foolishness of peahens and gossiping cats,' as he said."

"Speak with him. Give him a chance," Minnie said. "Perhaps he's not right because he knows something. Did you ever think of that?"

This sounded hopeful, at least. "Where does Mr. West live?"

"On the outskirts of town. His circumstances have fallen considerably. He was once a lawyer, like his father and grandfather. I believe the West law practice handled Roswell House for the family for several generations."

"Could we call and make an appointment?" I asked Minnie.

"You can't call. He doesn't have a telephone. Take him a basket of food and a bottle of wine. You'll brighten his day."

I looked to Reginald.

"Ab-so-lute-ly," he said with a nod. "Now, if not sooner."

"I'll drive you over," Zelda said.

"Wonderful." Thank goodness we had Zelda to help us navigate.

We stood from the table, prepared to leave, when the front door opened and Judge Sayre returned home for lunch. His grave face stopped us in our tracks.

"What is it, Father?" Zelda asked. Her normally flip tone and languid behavior had vanished.

"They found the young girl who'd gone missing from Autaugaville."

Pamela DuMond. "She's dead, isn't she?" I hadn't meant to speak, but I remembered the apparition I'd seen in the bedroom.

"She is. She's been dead since the day she disappeared."

"What happened?" Minnie asked, preparing a glass of sweet tea for her husband.

"She was found in a ditch on the road to Tuscaloosa. She was wearing her best dress and shoes, and someone had made her up like a . . ."

He faded. "To look older than she was. She was strangled and dumped in the ditch."

"How tragic," Minnie said. "What a terrible thing. Her family must be distraught."

I thought of the young girl in the restaurant eating with the older, portly man. And the spirits who haunted the halls of the hotels. All were young women made up and dressed to look older, provocative.

"Another girl's missing, too." The judge drained his glass and looked longingly at the whiskey decanter on a sideboard. He was a serious man and didn't partake during the workday. "Virginia Ames. She goes by her mother's family name, Ritter. Ritter Ames."

"How long has she been missing?" Reginald asked.

"Since early this morning. She was walking to her cousin's house but never made it." Judge Sayre walked to the dining table and sat down. "It's been a long morning."

I hated to add to Judge Sayre's burdens, but I needed his long reach over to Tuscaloosa to discover if the sheriff there had found the men who'd run Reginald and me off the road. "Could you check on an accident—"

"Father, does the sheriff know who killed the young woman?" Zelda cut over me.

Beneath the table, Reginald tapped my toe with his: a signal not to discuss our accident. I understood. If Judge Sayre perceived that we were truly in danger, he would pull the plug on our investigation. Zelda would be sent packing to New York, and we would be dispatched back to Mobile.

The judge seemed not to hear his daughter's question. Or chose not to answer it.

"Let me get your lunch," Minnie said. "Althea made chicken salad, just the way you like it. Girls, Reginald, stay for some lunch?"

"That would be appreciated," Reginald said.

I hadn't realized it was time for another meal, but I found I was hungry. As soon as we finished eating, we'd head out for Bernard West's place. During lunch Judge Sayre revealed no more details on the missing girl, and Zelda was quieter than normal. We finished eating and piled into Zelda's car. Minnie stopped us in the driveway with a basket of homemade goodies, including chicken salad, bread, jam, and cooked bacon. "Tell Bernard I said hello," she said.

"Will do." Zelda took off, driving with more zest than caution as we tore through the neighborhood and took the road to downtown Montgomery. "I'm glad you didn't spill the beans about the wreck to Father," Zelda said.

"We'll have to follow through on that on our own," Reginald said. "Somehow it has to be connected to Camilla. I can't see how, but there's no other explanation."

"Unless it's about Bryce Hospital," I said. "Girls are disappearing from there. If someone thinks we're probing into what's happening to those young women . . ."

My thoughts remained unfinished. If we'd stumbled into a mystery at the mental institution, it hadn't been our intention. Our concern was Camilla, first and foremost. But I was also determined to find out what had happened to Connie Shelton.

We passed through a simmering downtown and beyond to a small country road, unpaved but thankfully dry, and into pastureland and hardwoods forests. The beauty of the area lulled me into complacency. It was hard to imagine something dark and dangerous as we drove through canopied stretches of road where the oaks met overhead and the shade offset the broiling sun.

It was another fifteen minutes before we turned into a drive in front of a clapboard house that had seen better days. The ruin of the house and the yard touched me like a veil of sadness. A rope swing hung from a tree, and I knew that it hadn't been used in years. The rope was frayed and rotted to the point that any weight would bring it crashing down.

The gray paint of the porch floor scaled into crisps that crunched as we walked to the door. Flower beds were filled with weeds and briars. This house had once been lovingly tended but now showed the decay of neglect.

Zelda knocked on the door, and we waited long moments until we heard some rustling and the door opened, releasing a cloud of stale air and cigarette smoke. Bernard West was a man who'd simply forgotten that he was already dead. Almost emaciated, he smiled at Zelda. "Little Miss Sayre," he said in a voice that still contained an educated inflection, "you've come to pay a visit."

He looked at Reginald and me and stepped back. "Come in. Who are your friends?"

Zelda made the introductions and told him only a partial lie—that I was interested in Roswell House for a potential story.

He led us into a front room with a shabby sofa and chairs while Zelda took the basket of food to the kitchen and put things away.

"Would you care for something to drink?" he asked.

"No, thank you, we just had lunch."

"So it's Roswell House you came to talk about."

"Yes," Reginald said. "Can you help us?"

"Mayhaps I can."

"We'd certainly appreciate it." Zelda had reentered the room. "Back when you were handling the Roswells' business, did they ever talk about how they came to own the property where the big house was built?"

Bernard lifted a hand to smooth back his hair, and I saw the tremors in his hand. "It's been a while since I put my mind to anything like this." He cleared his throat. "Roswell is just one part of a large tract of land that was sold shortly before Alabama became a state in 1819. The buyers were land speculators who saw an opportunity and hoped that they could influence the development of a city on a bend in the river that abutted their property. If that occurred, they would be sitting on valuable land."

"But Montgomery ended up being upriver instead." Zelda pretended to have no use for history, but she'd paid more attention to her studies than she let on.

"Yes, there was a natural inlet for the docks, and the consortium of developers who bought it hoped to locate the capital here. The moneyed interests who invested upriver won out, and Montgomery was situated in the bend of the river to the north. The tract where Roswell sits proved to be a bad investment, and the land was parceled out and sold off to various people. Ramsey Roswell bought some of the lower land, but it wasn't until years later that his grandson, Wick, bought the high ground where Roswell House is situated today."

"I heard stories that Wick didn't always walk on the right side of the law," Zelda said.

"True stories. He traded in illegal goods and dealt brutally with his adversaries, but always maintained a public persona of community goodwill. Donated to charities, attended church, hosted fund-raisers for good causes. Most folks knew what he was hiding behind the mask of pleasant propriety, but no one dared confront him."

"And Roswell House?"

"He built it for a wedding present for his bride-to-be. The story was that Wick had found a young woman he wanted to marry. Though he had a reputation for cuckolding half the men in the area, he decided it was time to settle down and have a family. So he built Roswell House for her, with plans to marry in the house."

The parallels with Camilla and David made me lean forward, eager to hear every word.

"Was that uncommon? To build a house for a bride-to-be?" I'd come of age in a period of pending war. I didn't travel in circles where men built mansions for their loves.

"Such a gesture was proof to the community that a man would—and could—take care of his wife and family. Wick liked to do things in a grand manner."

"Without a doubt." While the gesture was impressive, I'd been happy in my cottage with Alex. I wouldn't trade our brief time together for all the fine houses in the world.

Bernard continued, his body relaxing into the telling. "The house is a masterpiece of craftsmanship. The cupid crown molding was designed by a Scottish craftsman Wick had brought from Scotland just for that job. There are other details I've forgotten. It was said that if you stood between the two foyer mirrors, you could see your past in one and your future in the other." He laughed. "I tried it, but I saw only my sad, sorry present."

"I remember that tale," Zelda said. "Tallulah and I broke into the house one night with lanterns just so we could look."

"What happened?" Reginald asked.

"We saw two daring but very frightened girls with a sordid past and a dicey future." Her laughter made us all smile. "Like Mr. Bernard, we didn't see anything unusual. It's just one of the tall tales that grew up around Roswell, probably because it was empty."

"Wick did marry and move into the house. It was a showcase for Montgomery parties. So what exactly is it you want to know?"

CHAPTER TWENTY-ONE

The history of the house was part of what I needed to know, but I had specific questions in mind, and I was glad Bernard seemed open to them.

"Did any tragedies occur on the premises?" I asked, thinking of the little girls.

"There was a duel in 1876, just after the construction was complete. Wick and Johnson Little. Mr. Little claimed that Wick had seduced his wife. He issued the challenge; Wick accepted. It was rumored that Wick's mistress, Nina Campbell, was responsible for the duel, that she'd manipulated Johnson Little to challenge Wick's honor. Wick shot Johnson dead on the front lawn of Roswell House during a Fourth of July celebration."

Bernard reached for a glass on the side table that wasn't there. Zelda took pity and went to the kitchen to make him a drink.

"Was he prosecuted?" I asked.

Bernard shook his head slowly. "Wick had most of the authorities on his payroll. It was ruled justifiable homicide because Mr. Little accosted Wick on his own property."

"What happened to Little's wife?" Zelda asked as she handed Wick a healthy portion of wine.

"She was driven from town as an unfaithful woman who'd caused a good man's death. I heard she went to Saint Stephens and started over, but I didn't keep up with her. It was a kindness to let her go. She'd been ruined for polite society here, as a lot of people put the blame for her husband's death on her."

"Isn't that always the case?" I asked somewhat sharply. "The woman always gets the blame."

"Your suffragette sympathies are showing," Reginald whispered in my ear.

"I concur, Mrs. James," Bernard said. "Loretta Little was a victim, and she paid the price for her foolish behavior and her husband's temper. Only Wick escaped punishment. It was said that when he passed Loretta on the streets of Montgomery, he merely laughed at her."

What a devil he was. He'd participated in this woman's ruin, and then he was done with her. I kept my comments to myself. Nothing I said could change the past.

"Was the duel the only tragic death you know about at Roswell House?"

"There were illnesses, of course. Fevers claimed some lives. And accidents. One of Wick's girls died of a broken neck from a horse fall."

"You don't recall anything about twin girls who died . . . in a brutal way?"

"No, and I would have heard, I'm sure."

"How did David come to own it?" Reginald asked.

"He'd heard about the house when he first moved to Montgomery. It was rapidly going to ruin, abandoned and uncared for. Teenagers went there to make mischief." He cast a quick, amused look at Zelda. "David inquired and discovered that I had once been involved in handling affairs for the Roswell family. When he came to me, I told him about the latest owner, Oscar Roswell, a rancher out in California. He'd never been to see the Alabama property, and, as it turned out, he was eager to sell it and be done. I helped arrange the sale. It was the last official bit of business for me." His voice dropped. "Right before I gave up the law and took up the bottle."

He wasn't apologetic, only sad. He'd made a choice. Now I wondered if he would be able to change his mind even if he wanted to.

"What happened to the Roswells?" I asked.

"Wick was eventually shot. Gunned down on a backstreet in Montgomery. Likely up to no good. His wife was a local girl, but after Wick's death she moved to Chicago. It seems they were plagued by tragedy. Neither of the children, both girls, lived to be adults. A cousin named Herman Roswell came to live at Roswell House and maintained the property until he died."

"And he was the last to live there?" Reginald asked.

Bernard nodded. "After Herman died, the house was empty. I guess it's been close to fifteen years now. As I said, when David made an offer, the last remaining cousin, Oscar, was delighted to take it. No haggling over the price. Oscar had no interest in Alabama. In fact, I'd say he had only negative feelings for the state and the people here."

"Wick's wife . . . is her family still around?"

"No, she died young. Maybe some cousins remain. She was a Harlow. Priscilla Harlow. Minnie should know if the family's still in the area."

"Mother is like the telephone switchboard," Zelda said. "She keeps up with everyone in town. Partly because she works good deeds, and partly"—she arched her eyebrows and made Bernard laugh—"because she can't stand to be behind in the gossip."

"You always were a firecracker, Miss Zelda. I'm glad you found a man with a bigger life than Alabama. If you had to stay here, you'd blow this town apart."

"I'd make a bloody mess—you're right about that. I'm surprised Father hasn't sold me to the Gypsies just to be rid of my bad conduct."

"The Gypsies would bring you back and pay your mama to take you in." Bernard was having a good time. The shared affection between the two was enjoyable, but I still hadn't discovered why the spirits of twin girls remained at Roswell.

"Wick Roswell's daughters . . . they weren't twins, by chance, were they?"

Bernard shook his head.

"And they died more or less naturally?"

He nodded. "Before their time, but, no, they weren't murdered, if that's what you mean. The business with the horse was strange—I'll give you that. But neither girl was murdered." Bernard's smile slowly faded, and for the first time, he really scrutinized me. "Zelda said you're a writer. What kind of writer? You don't work for the newspaper, do you?"

"Not the paper. I'm a writer of sensational fiction. My first story will be published in October in the *Saturday Evening Post*."

"Congratulations. That's an accomplishment." He studied me a bit longer before he focused on Reginald. "What are you two really up to?" He held out his glass to Zelda, and she went to the kitchen to replenish his drink.

I was caught short. For a man devoted to the bottle, Bernard West still retained his wits.

"We're private investigators, and we've come to help Camilla Granger." Reginald told the truth, because he sensed, as I did, that Bernard would sniff out anything less.

Zelda handed Bernard a fresh drink. "Camilla's mother is going to have her brain sliced and stirred with some experimental surgery." She used her finger in a very graphic illustration. "I hired them"—she nodded at us—"to help figure out why Camilla went round the bend. It's serious, Bernard. Camilla is at Bryce."

Bernard's eyes widened. "I wouldn't wish that on my worst enemy. Well, maybe one or two people."

I had to smile despite the sad truth. "It's a tragic place. Camilla doesn't belong there."

"What happened with her?" Bernard asked, and it wasn't idle curiosity or a desire for gossip.

Zelda relayed the story of Camilla's attacks on her fiancé. And I added that we hoped that somehow Roswell House was influencing her.

"The house influencing her?" Bernard let his skepticism show. "How?"

"Reginald and I are private investigators, but we explore strange happenings, hauntings, cases where a supernatural element is involved. We believe Camilla is under the influence of something or someone at Roswell House."

Bernard was flabbergasted, and he didn't try to hide it. "You're serious?"

"We are. Camilla isn't crazy. She's . . . being controlled by something in that house."

"Surely—" He stopped himself. "You believe this?" he asked Zelda.

"I hired Raissa and Reginald. I do believe it. And time is running out for us to prove it. Mrs. Granger is going to have Camilla operated on. To make her docile. So she can marry David and bear his children."

"Dear God." He put his drink down. "Maude should never have been allowed to have children, much less raise them. She's never been able to put anyone ahead of herself and her own selfish desires and her misbegotten idea that somehow she was cheated in life." He clenched his fist. "I remember Camilla as a young girl in the church. She was in front of me and my wife, a perfectly behaved little girl. After an hour she began to squirm in her seat. I thought Maude would inflict permanent damage. I just remember Maude hissing, 'You sit still or you'll be sorry.' I believed Maude would punish the child. Poor Camilla had to jump a very high bar to rise to Maude's exacting expectations."

"Maude is a bitter, selfish, greedy lizard of a bitch." Zelda didn't mince words. "If we can't figure out what's happening to Camilla quickly, it will be too late."

"So you ask about Roswell House because you think there is a ghost or spirit or influence there from some past event?"

"Yes." I said it simply. "And I pray we're correct. Her behavior must be explained and stopped or she's going to submit to the surgery."

"I told you everything I know about the house," Bernard said. "But I will study the matter more—I promise. Zelda, would you bring me some of the food Minnie sent? If I'm going to poke around in the past of Roswell House," he told Reginald and me as Zelda went to the kitchen, "I'll need my strength."

"Thank you, Bernard."

While I knew the strange powers the dead sometimes had, this was the first time I'd seen a man who'd given up on life return to the land of the living. Bernard had an abiding love for Zelda and Camilla, it seemed. Or maybe he simply sought purpose.

"Don't thank me yet," he said.

"We appreciate your taking us seriously," Reginald said. "Seriously enough to offer to help us. That deserves thanks."

"I drink a lot. Sometimes I see things. Most folks would say it's the whiskey, but sometimes, on those rare occasions when I see something that gives me a bit of comfort, I want to believe it's not the liquor. For Camilla, I'll believe the same. She's a gentle girl whose fate so far has been cruel. Maude for a mother . . . I knew Maude's mother, who also felt that life had cheated her of things that were her due. Maybe Camilla's future can be better."

CHAPTER TWENTY-TWO

The hot sun drove us back to the Sayre home to wait for the midafternoon zenith to pass. As we parked beneath a shady tree, I had visions of my airy bedroom dancing in my head. I'd done nothing but ride and talk and eat, yet I was exhausted. A nap would be the perfect thing.

I'd barely put my feet on the grass when the front door burst open and Tallulah ran across the lawn, her long legs flashing in the bright sun. She waved something in her hand and almost bowled Zelda over as she hugged her.

"A telegram. From Camilla. It's marked urgent."

Dread almost made me grab the envelope from Zelda's hand, but Reginald put an arm around me. To support and to restrain me, I presumed.

Zelda tore open the note and drew out a single page. "She says her friend Joanne Pence has disappeared from Bryce. Camilla and Nurse Brady have searched everywhere, but there is no sign of the young woman. Camilla's distraught. She thinks her friend has been abducted. And she says Dr. Perkins is returning on Monday."

For a single sheet of paper, it had a lot of information packed in. I could feel Camilla's worry and dread.

Zelda looked from Reginald to me. "She asks if you've found Connie Shelton safely with her uncle."

I told the group about Connie Shelton, another of Perkins's patients who I was sure was dead. "I don't know what to do about Joanne. Zelda, maybe you could call Nurse Brady and ask."

"I can do that. Perhaps mention my father is looking into missing girls in the state."

"That's a good idea." Reginald paced the lawn, wiping sweat from his forehead. "We have to focus on Roswell House and what's happening to Camilla there, but since David is still out of town and he'd be most helpful, why don't we look up that uncle? James Patrickson, I believe his name is. I'll run by the sheriff's department and ask if they can call up to Decatur to be sure Connie is safely there. While I'm there, I'll ask them to call the Tuscaloosa authorities and find out if they have any leads on who ran us off the road."

Action was the cure for the heavy burden I carried. "I'll go to the courthouse here and research the land records for the Roswell property. I know that Camilla's problem and these missing girls are connected somehow. I don't understand how, but Camilla's the link. We need to take action on both fronts, though I fear we'll find only heartbreak about Connie."

Zelda motioned us toward the house. "Take the car, Reginald. I'll telephone Bryce from home. I want to spend some time with Mother and Tallulah before I have to return to New York. It'll go smoother for you in the courthouse if I'm not there." She grinned. "I'm not the probate judge's favorite person."

An understatement, no doubt. "Thanks, Zelda. It's best if we head on, because if I make it inside, the bed will call to me. Let's go, Reginald. No time like the present."

Reginald was a surprisingly smooth driver who seemed to have filed a road map of Montgomery in his head. He navigated the town without any difficulty. While Reginald went to the sheriff's office, where a man's inquiries would meet with more respect than a woman's, I perused the land records for the Roswell property. A very nice clerk helped me locate the legal description of Roswell House and put me in a stack of musty books that held recorded deeds.

As Bernard West had said, Oscar Roswell of Devondale, California, had sold the property to David Simpson a year ago. At one time the Roswell tract had been huge, but I found the deed with which Wick Roswell had purchased the high ground from a Tommy Peebles.

Camilla had told me most of this. I hadn't discovered anything earthshaking. But I had asked my helpful clerk about the Peebles family. She wasn't familiar with the history of the parcel, but she told me that often those with a yen for land and adventure would come in the first wave of settlers, buy up property, then sell it and move west.

"The pasture is always greener," she said. "It's an illness with some— that need to move on, to see what's beyond the horizon."

"Would there be any place to check if the Peebles family lived here after he sold the property?"

"I can check, but it'll take some time."

"It would be very helpful."

"Come back Friday," she said. "I'll see what I can find."

I didn't have high hopes, but at least I'd put the quest in motion. If there were answers in the past, I'd turn over every rock to find them. I thought of one of my mother's favorite sayings about a hard task: "You have to turn over a lot of rocks and pick up a lot of grubs to find what you most desire." That saying was usually coupled with: "You're short on patience and long on wants."

"Thank you." I wrote down the Sayres' address. "I'm staying with the Sayres this week. If you should turn up something sooner, would you call?"

She pushed the slip of paper back to me. "I know Judge Sayre. I'll get to this as quickly as I can."

"I do appreciate your help."

I stepped into the hallway, wondering how Reginald was faring at the sheriff's office. I wanted badly to join him, but I lingered in the cool hallway instead. Movement at the end of the corridor caught my eye. Someone was going upstairs to the courtroom. It looked like a young girl.

Because I had nothing better to do and time to kill, I decided to explore the courthouse myself. Above me I heard the slap, slap of leather soles on the floor. I climbed the stairs and stopped at a landing with an open window. A cooler breeze lifted the hair from around my face. As much as I loved the short bob, long hair was cooler in the summer because I could pull it back. A woman paid a terrible price for fashion, and I was determined to be a modern woman.

Staring out at the lethargic traffic of downtown Montgomery, I sat on the windowsill to access as much breeze as possible and thought about the story I'd been writing. I hadn't had as much time to pursue my literary interests as I'd hoped, but I couldn't shake the image of the slain twin girls at Roswell House. I wanted to tell their story, even if I had to fill in the details. What could have happened to those children? There'd been a number of Indian skirmishes in these parts; and also river outlaws, land pirates, and renegade soldiers from both armies. Brutality could arrive in many different guises.

My imagination could supply a number of reasons why the girls had died, and some would make a whooping story of bloody revenge, but I knew instinctively those details weren't right. Those girls had died brutally, and at the hands of someone without emotion. Or perhaps too much emotion. Their severed heads spoke of swift, unhesitating action.

In every fairy tale I'd ever read, the wicked stepmother was to blame. The female figure in the window of Roswell House, flies buzzing all around—had she murdered her stepchildren? Or her own children?

I allowed myself to drift back in time, back fifty years, when the isolation of rural homesteads was a permanent situation for all but a handful of families who'd gathered in towns. The settlers, primarily farmers, braved the wilderness and hacked out homesteads far removed from other white settlers.

I could see it clearly, the wood-frame house with smoke rising from a chimney made of baked clay bricks, the stumps of trees still scattered in the vegetable garden, waiting for fall when they'd be pulled out by a mule team. I watched those girls playing with their cloth dollies, mimicking the things their mother did as she cooked and ran the household. It was a hardscrabble life of toil, but the reward was a tract of land they owned, property that belonged to them, and the chance to build a better life.

And they had died at the hands of someone who should have loved them.

The story I'd woven was certainly grim. Shaking my head, I stood and descended the stairs. I was almost down to the first level when I heard a voice. It was so plaintive, so confused.

"I'll be good."

I stopped. I'd seen someone go upstairs, and it was one reason I'd stopped at the window. The courtroom was there, but court wasn't in session. I'd assumed whoever it was sought solitude, and I'd decided to wait until she came back down. Now, though, step-by-step, I climbed back up the stairs, passing the window and moving up to the courtroom door.

I touched the doorknob, and a chill penetrated my body. I forced the door open and stepped into the empty courtroom. In front of the judge's dais, the young woman I'd seen at Bryce Hospital, the elusive Connie Shelton, floated in the air on her back. Her hair fell in a tumble of curls; the skirt of her yellow dress hung low. She looked as if someone were carrying her in his arms, but there was no other person there. She was suspended in air.

"Connie?" She turned to me.

"I'll be good," she said with a sob.

But it was too late for that. She was dead. Whoever had checked her out of the hospital had done a terrible thing. They had taken her and killed her. "Who took you?" I asked.

"Put me down, please."

155

I had no clue to whom she was speaking, but foreboding set in. "Connie, who took you?"

She began to weep, her sobs broken by the phrases "I'll be good" and "I won't tell."

And then she was gone.

I turned, and Reginald stood in the doorway. "What did you see?" he asked.

"The girl from Bryce, Camilla's friend, the one you were checking on. She's dead."

"I suspected as much. I got in touch with the Decatur police. They knew James Patrickson. They went to his house to check. He denied having a niece or ever going to Bryce Hospital. Apparently, someone used his name. Patrickson is something of a recluse, so if we hadn't asked specifically, chances are no one would ever know the girl disappeared."

"It was all a lie. She didn't disappear. She was taken and killed. I'm worried sick about Joanne."

Reginald smoothed his mustache, a twitch he rarely gave in to. "Zelda spoke with Nurse Brady. There is no sign of Joanne. She's disappeared."

"Just like the young girl from Autaugaville. And now another girl is missing, too. The one Judge Sayre mentioned. And there are the others our driver mentioned, from Marthasville. Someone's abducting young women, little more than girls. And killing them. This is why they tried to kill us. Because they assumed we were investigating the girls."

Reginald frowned. "It might be worse than just killing."

"Worse?"

"These young country girls are fresh and unspoiled. They would be . . . sought after by certain types of men."

The young girl in the restaurant in Tuscaloosa came back to me. That she was a prostitute I didn't doubt. That she might have been forced into the work hadn't occurred to me. "I'm so naive."

"Never feel badly that your mind doesn't work in such ways. It's sickness. But I've seen it before. New Orleans is a city known to provide flesh for many appetites. Some mothers sell their children into the sex trade."

I was honestly too shocked to say anything. That a mother would do that—and then I thought of Maude Granger. She would do worse. She would mutilate her daughter for the prospect of a "good" marriage. Maude wouldn't risk that Camilla might maim or kill David in a "fit." The scandal would be too much for her to bear. But she was perfectly willing to risk her daughter's health to an experimental surgical procedure in the hopes of gaining control of Camilla and rendering her a tractable wife.

"What should we do?" I asked.

Reginald took my arm. "What can we do? Camilla has to be our focus. Then we can go to the authorities if we find any concrete evidence about the girls."

He was right. Camilla took priority. We had only a few days before Dr. Perkins returned, and I had no doubt he'd resume his surgery schedule immediately.

"I want to check the census records before we leave the courthouse." When I explained why, Reginald was eager to help me look. We went back to the 1840 census, but we could find no trace of twin girls belonging to any member of the Roswell family. Perhaps they'd been visiting neighbor children. It was a puzzle I couldn't resolve by looking at old deeds and records.

We left the courthouse and stepped into the sunshine, blinking like owls. The heat rose up from the paved road in waves. I longed for Caoin House, for the beauty and serenity that reigned there now that the criminal elements and the past had been put to rest. This case threatened to overwhelm me, and even though Reginald was stalwart, I knew he, too, felt the pressure. We needed to find Zelda and regroup, but the only path I saw before us would hold danger for everyone.

CHAPTER TWENTY-THREE

When we returned to Zelda's house, we found that Judge Sayre had left for work, Tallulah was gone, and Minnie was napping. Reginald, Zelda, and I gathered on the front porch amid the birdsong and heat. On the drive from the courthouse, Reginald and I had formulated a plan.

"We all agree that Camilla's in danger at Bryce, right?" I looked at Zelda, who nodded. "Dr. Perkins's patients are disappearing: one drowned and two missing or dead so far. And someone tried to kill Reginald and me."

"Agreed," Zelda said. "A thousand times agreed! But how can we spring a patient who refuses to leave under her own power?"

"We have only one option," I said. "Reginald?"

"We forge her release document."

I smiled—finally something that made Zelda's jaw drop.

Reginald shrugged with cool composure. "I grew up doing whatever I had to do to survive. I'm a fair hand at faking signatures."

"You'd do that?" For the first time since I'd met her, Zelda showed caution. "It's illegal." Then again, her father was a judge.

Reginald lit a cigarette, and the smoke curled slowly upward in the still July air. "We don't have a choice. If Camilla stays at Bryce, she'll have her head opened like a cantaloupe. That's *best* case. Worst case, she dies on the operating table or disappears like the other patients."

I nodded my agreement. "Reginald and I believe Roswell House itself is behind Camilla's violent outbursts, but we haven't figured out why. To do that, we need to take Camilla there, for a séance."

Zelda took the cigarette from Reginald's hand and inhaled deeply before she gave it back. "You're still forgetting the tough part—getting Camilla to go with you. But I'm all for it." She took the cigarette back again. "Tell you what. I'll hire Jason Kuddle to search for Joanne—that way you can at least tell Camilla we're doing our best to find her friend. Maybe it'll help encourage her to leave Bryce."

"That's brilliant." I sat forward. "Kuddle's already looking into missing girls himself." I thought for a moment. "Our driver told us about three girls disappearing at the same time from Marthasville. Maybe they're all connected."

"They might be." Reginald was grim. "And if there is a ring abducting young women, then the faster someone gets on it, the more chance of survival those girls will have. Kuddle can investigate while we help Camilla."

"Plus he has the law-enforcement connections to make something happen quickly if he finds any evidence." Zelda tossed the spent cigarette and nudged Reginald. "Butt me." She took the smoke he offered and ducked her head for a light. Reginald's gaze met mine above her head, and I knew instantly that, although he was collected and nonchalant about his offer to forge Maude Granger's signature, he was worried.

"How are we going to do this forgery thing?" I asked.

"I'm going over to the Granger house shortly," Reginald said. "While I'm speaking with Maude about my 'drug protocol' for Camilla, someone needs to search the house for the signature of either

Jefferson or Maude Granger. I suspect Jefferson signs whatever Maude tells him to."

Now we were adding trespassing to our list of illegal acts. "I'll do it."

"I'm a decent actress," Zelda said. "Tallulah is better but—"

"No, it can't be you or Tallulah. I'll do it."

"And if you're caught?" Zelda asked.

"I'll say I fell asleep in the car and came in to look for Reginald."

Zelda's amused laugh let me know it was a pathetic excuse. "That might work for you, but never for me."

I told her, "Which is why I'm going to be the one searching her house. Just be sure to get her away from the library or wherever Jefferson keeps his checkbook and legal things."

"Library desk, bottom drawer on the left. I've been in the room when Mr. Granger wrote a check for Camilla. I can draw an outline of the house with windows and doors where Raissa can enter."

"Where *is* Mr. Granger?" I asked. I'd never met the man.

"He hides out at a real estate office where he works as an accountant. He goes to work very early and comes home very late. And I understand why."

So did I. Ditch digging might be preferable to leisure time with Maude Granger. "Are we ready?" I asked, wiping my sweaty palms on my skirt. If I was going to be a true investigator, I had to get over my law-abiding ways.

"Take the car," Zelda said, offering the key yet again. "I'll call Kuddle. Daddy has his business card, I'm sure."

"We're off."

Zelda grasped my wrist and gave me an impromptu hug. "Thank you. I know this is not easy."

"Not easy but necessary." Saying the words made me realize the truth. I might not like entering someone's home uninvited, but I could see no other way.

Reginald drove and parked down the street beneath the branches of a maple tree that offered some shade. "Give me five minutes. Then get inside. I'll occupy her for twenty minutes, even if I have to pretend I'm having a heart attack. After that I can't guarantee that I can keep her busy. When you're finished, knock on the front door, okay?"

"Yes." I clutched the map and watched him walk toward the house. Reginald had left me his pocket watch to keep the time, and at exactly five minutes, I hurried down the sidewalk to the back of the house. As Zelda had said, a library window was open. Cursing my dress, I climbed in, went straight to the desk, and opened the bottom right-hand drawer. Several legal documents were there, and I looked through them until I found Camilla's commitment papers with both Mr. and Mrs. Granger's signatures on them. I tucked the papers into my brassiere, the hated garment coming in handy as a hiding place today.

We'd have to calculate a way to return the papers, but that was a problem for another day. I put everything else back in order, closed the drawer, and fled out the window. A moment later I was knocking on the front door.

"Is Mr. Proctor still here?" I asked the maid, who remained completely emotionless.

"Yes, ma'am. Please wait here on the porch, and I'll tell Mrs. Granger you're asking for him."

I took a seat in a white wicker chair and waited.

The front door opened, and Reginald stepped out. "I wish you'd reconsider, Mrs. Granger. I feel certain I could help Camilla."

"She's made her bed. Now she'll lie it in. Her surgery will be performed Wednesday. We'll put an end to her rebellion once and for all."

I stood up because I couldn't stop myself. "Are you aware what will really happen in this surgery? Dr. Perkins will cut her skull, remove a portion, and slice into her brain. There's no real way to tell where or how much tissue to destroy. Parts of the brain will be damaged. It could be the part that makes her Camilla. Never to be repaired."

Maude drew herself up. "You know nothing. Now get off my property. If I see you here again, I'll have you arrested, and I don't care what Judge Sayre has to say. If he were so wise and brilliant, he wouldn't have a hoodlum for a daughter."

Reginald grabbed my arm and assisted me to the steps. As we were leaving, Maude called after us. "I can tell how poorly you were raised, to come to my house and behave like the ill-bred creatures you are. My daughter will never behave in such a manner again."

Reginald kept a good hold of my arm, maneuvering me out of the yard and down the sidewalk.

"I hope you got what you went for, because we'll never be allowed back on that property."

"I got it." I shook free of his grip, turned around, and pulled the document from my underclothes. "How we put it back will be another story."

"I'm not worried about that." He studied the document. "Both signatures." A smile lifted the corners of his neat mustache. "Good job, Raissa. I can work with this."

Finding a typewriter was our next chore, and we ended up at David's bank, borrowing the machine his secretary used. I typed up the letter, per Reginald's whispered directions. It was clear, forceful, and to the point, directing Dr. Perkins and Bryce Hospital to release Camilla to the bearer of the letter, who was her appointed guardian for the return trip to Montgomery, where she would seek additional medical care.

Since neither Reginald nor I had ever written such a directive, we did the best we could, with coaching from Zelda, who'd obtained legal advice from Bernard West.

"We're on the verge of marrying trouble," Reginald said as we left the bank.

"Pos-i-lute-ly." I seldom indulged in modern slang, but my effort earned a smile from Reginald. "We don't have a choice."

"You're right about that."

We returned to the Sayre home in time for cocktails. The judge was one drink ahead of us, and he was clearly worried about something. Zelda gave us the eye and a wink to let us know she'd been successful in hiring Kuddle to investigate Joanne Pence's disappearance. Tomorrow, when we went to Bryce to retrieve Camilla, we could tell her someone was looking into her friend's disappearance. We could only hope that this fact, plus the mounting evidence of danger at Bryce Hospital, would convince Camilla to leave the facility with us.

Zelda broached the subject of the missing girls with her father, but he turned the conversation with deft finesse. "Yes, a troubling set of circumstances. I received a call today from Maude Granger. She claims that my houseguests assaulted her." He stared at Zelda, not us—a good thing because heat suffused my face.

"I'm sorry, sir," Reginald said. "I did speak to her, but I didn't assault her."

"Are you calling Maude a liar?" he asked. The room had grown deadly quiet.

"Yes, sir. I am."

He held his stern expression for a few seconds, and then the first true smile I'd ever seen broke across his face. "She's a vile creature. What is it you call her, Zelda?"

"The dragon." Zelda lit a cigarette, and I could see she'd been as tense as I was.

"She's worse. She claims you yelled at her and threatened to harm her."

"Not true." Reginald sipped his predinner drink. "Raissa described in detail the brain surgery she's arranging for Camilla to have. The dragon was unflinching in her resolve. No threats were made and no voices were raised, except when Mrs. Granger screamed at us, ordering us off her property."

"I thought as much. I told her I would ask. So I did." He looked at each of us in turn. "Most things that happen in the state, I hear about."

Guilt at the things we were planning—and the knowledge we would ultimately be found out—must have risen off me in waves, because Zelda only laughed. "You do have your network of spies, Father. So tell us about the missing girls. What is being done?"

"It's a troubling situation." Zelda's father eased back in his chair, his shoulders visibly relaxing. "I've spoken with the sheriffs in several counties, and there's a pattern of young women disappearing between Montgomery and Tuscaloosa. So far we've had reports of eleven missing females. Three of them have been found dead, including the DuMond girl."

"Were they—" Reginald broke off.

Judge Sayre stood. "Ladies, if you would excuse us."

Whatever he intended to reveal to Reginald, we would have to wait for a secondhand report. Judge Sayre was protecting our feminine sensibilities, I understood, but it chafed me nonetheless. I rose and left the library to reassemble in the sunroom.

"Father is so old-fashioned," Zelda whispered to me. "He acts like we don't know a thing about forced prostitution or the seamy side of life. He'd be shocked at what I've seen."

I finally laughed, because it was likely I'd be shocked, too. "Be glad someone loves you enough to protect you, even though the leash is sometimes too tight."

"I can see you're good with words. Tell us about your story. Scott was asking the last time I spoke with him. I need a report or else he'll come down here to fetch me."

My stories were one thing I was always eager to talk about, and I did so with gusto.

"I'd say you're the berries, but Mother would correct me on my language," Zelda said. "I clean up my act in Montgomery, unless I'm trying to poke the old wet blankets."

"Zelda!" Minnie's correction was more by rote than true disapproval. She indulged Zelda terribly.

"I've always wanted to write, but one short story doesn't make a career."

"Maybe Scottie can put in a word for you with his editor."

I was stunned by her generosity. "Really?"

She shrugged one shoulder and rolled her eyes. "If I ask nicely, and I can be nice when I want to."

"Which isn't often enough," Minnie said with a spark of Zelda's own verve.

"Thank you." I felt as if I'd won a Triple Crown ride on Man o' War.

Althea entered the room to tell us dinner was ready to be served. I'd have to wait until the meal was over to discover what dire details had been revealed to Reginald.

CHAPTER TWENTY-FOUR

Zelda and Reginald smoked silently on the front porch of the Sayre home. We'd made the best decisions we could, based on the shocking information Reginald revealed to us. All the young women who'd been found dead had been brutally abused. Reginald refused to give the most graphic details, but he said that even in the worst New Orleans brothels or the flesh trade on the streets, he'd not heard of such savagery.

"Do you think this is what happened to Camilla's friends at the hospital? Connie and Joanne?" Zelda was pale.

In Connie's case, although no body had been found, I had no doubt. Having gone under Dr. Perkins's scalpel, Connie had left the hospital completely docile. She'd failed to object to leaving the premises with a man who most likely was not a relative—a man she might have never seen before. She'd simply done as she was told. The Perkins's "cure" had rendered her incapable of defending herself. I couldn't speak to the fate of Joanne, but the odds were clearly against her.

"There's a connection between that asylum and *all* of these girls." I spoke what we were each thinking.

"I fear you're correct," Reginald said. He crushed out his cigarette and lit another. He seldom chain-smoked, a sure indication he was emotionally agitated. "I don't know what do to about it."

"Father says the police are investigating. And we've hired Mr. Kuddle to look for Joanne. He said he'd have another report soon."

Kuddle had told Zelda that it was Dr. Bentley who'd released Connie to her so-called uncle. Bentley was also the doctor who'd been in charge of Joanne Pence while Dr. Perkins was absent. Kuddle had set an appointment with Bentley for the next morning. He vowed to have some answers for us about the girls' whereabouts. He told Zelda he had a couple of promising leads on both Joanne and Connie. We could only hope that he'd find Joanne Pence in time.

Only *we* could save Camilla, and the time had come to plan our rescue.

A half hour later, we had put aside our many reservations and settled on the actions we needed to take. David Simpson would take Reginald's and my place in using our forged paperwork to retrieve Camilla from Bryce. I'd chosen this tactic for three reasons. First, because I believed that he had a better shot at convincing her to return to Montgomery than anyone else. Second, because the Bryce staff was far more likely to respond to his request for release than ours. And third, from a legal standpoint, while Maude Granger would have no problem prosecuting Reginald, Zelda, or me, she'd be less eager to file charges against David.

Once we removed Camilla from Bryce, we had to decide where to hide her.

"I can't ask Mother to allow Camilla to stay in our home," Zelda said. "She'd do it, because she cares for Camilla. But Maude Granger would want Mother's head on a platter. There could be legal repercussions, which I'm willing to confront. But I can't involve Mother or Father."

"I think a hotel room would be good." It would uncomplicate a lot of complications.

"Or perhaps the Montgomery hospital," Reginald suggested. "Dr. Abbott can put her under his care."

I shook my head. "Remember, we want to take her to Roswell House. If Dr. Abbott's in charge, he may disagree. And there is also the risk of gossip about her condition. Camilla is opposed to that. It could ruin her."

"Then hotel room it is," Zelda said. "I'll make arrangements at the Greystone. We'll tuck her away until we're ready to hold the séance at Roswell House."

We left it on that hopeful note and bade Zelda good night. When she'd gone inside, I turned to Reginald, who looked troubled.

"Uh-oh. What did we leave out?"

"We've failed to speak with one of the principals in this case. I want to meet with Jefferson Granger."

"Why?"

"The more we know about Camilla and her family, the better prepared we'll be for Roswell House. The house is inhabited by something dark and malevolent. Why has it chosen Camilla for its target? Jefferson might just enlighten us."

As far as I could tell, Maude ran the show, but Reginald had a point. "It's a long shot," I said.

Reginald nodded, then shrugged. "But he is Camilla's father. If he has a shred of love for her, maybe he'll help us."

"If there's a chance Jefferson can be won over, you're the man for the job. Maybe he'll give something away that helps us. While you're checking into Mr. Granger, I'll see if I can find out anything useful from Florence, the Grangers' maid."

In the breaking dawn of a hot July morning, Zelda, Reginald, and I met David at the train station to see him off for his trip to retrieve

Camilla—a plan we'd explained to him over numerous cups of coffee. Even in the heat he wore a freshly pressed suit, starched shirt, and vest. Having him serve as our proxy concerned me slightly—because I could still not rule him out as somehow involved in Camilla's strange behavior. Even so, Reginald and I agreed that the benefits outweighed the risk.

"Be careful," Reginald told David as he gave him the documents we'd forged requesting Camilla's release and return to Montgomery. "If you can study the files on the two missing girls, do it. I looked them over, but I didn't have time to explore them in depth. They might help us find the missing girls."

David nodded. "Banking hasn't prepared me for espionage, but I'll do my best."

"Camilla's future may depend on it."

We each hugged him in turn and watched the train pull out of the station. Zelda kicked rocks beside her car. "We've embarked on a dangerous path."

"That's true," I agreed. "But what option do we have?"

"None. Now, assuming he succeeds, what will you need for the séance, Raissa? Do I need to find supplies?"

"Sharpened pencils, paper, candles . . ." I couldn't think of anything else. "I'm not an expert at this. And I'm worried that the entity we're trying to contact won't behave like a regular ghost. I'm not experienced—"

"She'll do fine," Reginald assured Zelda. "We'll need you and David and Camilla to be in attendance. We'll use the energy of all four of us to find out what this spirit wants."

As Reginald had said before, we didn't have another option. I clung to that as David's train departed and we drove away from the train station. I dropped Reginald downtown, where he could ambush Jefferson Granger at his office when he showed up for work. Zelda was next at the Greystone Hotel, where she would make arrangements for Camilla's stay.

Because the trolley didn't run to my destination, I drove the car to the poorest part of town. The houses were little more than wooden shacks, and in some, daylight could be seen through the cracks in the walls. This was Biggerville, a section of town where only Negroes lived.

The rutted dirt roads hadn't seen a grader in months, and the smell made it evident that sewer lines hadn't been run to the house. Hand pumps in a few front yards told of the lack of running water. Though Biggerville bumped into downtown and two residential areas, it had none of the amenities of the white neighborhoods. No power or telephone lines ran to the unpainted houses with sloping porches and patched roofs.

There were similar neighborhoods in Savannah and Mobile. I knew about them, but I'd never paid such close attention. John Henry's death had awakened a moral conscience in me that had slumbered. I was aware of the inequality toward women, but the treatment of the Negro population had slid below my awareness. Now I saw the signs of "White Only." Some restaurants proclaimed "All White Waiters," and the division of labor with Negroes, who were allowed to cook the food and not allowed to serve it in fine restaurants, was clear. While Negroes had the legal right to vote, they often couldn't pay the poll tax or were afraid to register for fear of retribution. What good was the right to vote if Negroes were afraid to use it?

Following Althea's directions, I parked in front of Florence's house, aware of the eyes watching me from all down the quiet street. I'd arrived at her home without asking about her circumstances. Was she married? Did she have children? Like the other white people she served, I knew her only in the narrow capacity as maid to the Grangers. I'd not thought to ask more information, and I doubted Zelda could tell me. I should have asked Althea, the Sayres' maid, but that thought came too late. I needed to catch Florence before she left for work.

I rapped on the screen door, which was loosely latched. Florence unlatched it, and though she was normally stoic, she didn't bother to hide her surprise. "Mrs. James, come in."

She'd remembered my name. I hadn't bothered to ask for her last name. "Thank you, Florence." I stepped into the sparsely furnished house.

"I have to leave. I can't miss the trolley. Mrs. Granger don't tolerate no late."

That was likely an understatement. "I need to speak with you, and I'll give you a ride to work if that's okay."

She looked out at the car and back at me.

"I'm a good driver. I promise."

For the first time since I'd met her, she smiled. "Okay. Let me get my things." She picked up her purse and a sack with clean rags in it. I was hardly surprised that Maude would ask her to bring her own cleaning supplies.

"I'm trying to help Camilla," I explained as we walked to the car. When she stopped, unsure whether to get in the back or front, I opened the front door for her.

"Help her how?" Florence asked.

"Her mother wants Camilla to undergo a very dangerous procedure. I want to stop it."

"What does Miss Camilla say she wants?"

"She doesn't want to hurt anyone. Florence, do you know why Mrs. Granger is so determined to see her daughter surgically changed?"

I walked around the car and got behind the wheel before she answered. When the car was moving, Florence finally spoke. "Mrs. Granger, she hate Camilla. I never found out why."

"There must be a reason for a mother to hate her only child to the point of wanting to see her harmed."

"It's always been that way. That girl works to please her mama. No matter how much she does or tries, it's never good enough. Mrs. Granger'd get that look in her eye, and I'd know Miss Camilla was gonna suffer."

"Did she hit Camilla?"

"If what I say gets back to her, I'll never work in this town again. Not for anyone. I need my job."

"I only want to help Camilla. Whatever you tell me will never get back to the Grangers. Not a word. I swear it. But I need your help."

She considered as the scenery flashed past us. "No, Mrs. Granger never struck Camilla. She's not one to lift a hand. She sit all morning in her chair, ringing her bell for me to bring her tea or fluff her pillow or find her easy shoes. I bring her the phone, fetch her makeup, brush her hair. She's not much to move around. It's words she use to hurt Miss Camilla. Mrs. Granger's a hateful person. Filled with hate and ugliness. Miss Camilla is filled with light. Maybe that's why her mama hates her so much. Because no matter how hard Mrs. Granger works to tear Miss Camilla down, she can't. That girl has a natural light in her."

"And Mr. Granger?"

"That poor man barely alive. He's afraid to breathe too deep for fear she'll peck his head in."

"Would he stand up for Camilla?"

She pursed her lips and stared straight ahead as I drove onto a tree-shaded and well-maintained paved road. "He's got no backbone, but doin' nothin' is different than doin' somethin'. At least to some folks. They don't see doin' nothin' is just as bad."

CHAPTER TWENTY-FIVE

I let Florence out of the car at the bus stop so she wouldn't be seen in Zelda's car. Maude Granger could be malicious, and I didn't want to jeopardize Florence's employment. I stopped at the Greystone and sat down in the dining room with Zelda to wait for Reginald to conclude his talk with Jefferson Granger.

Zelda was quieter than I'd ever seen her. We were both concerned about the plan we'd set in action. We were tampering with Camilla's health and well-being, her future. A misstep on our part and the consequences could be dire. If we were taking a mentally ill person from a place where she felt secure and safe and exposing her to a house where she felt threatened, we could do irreparable damage.

"I'm going back to New York by Wednesday at the latest," Zelda said. "Either Camilla will be cured or she will be altered surgically to the point that I—" She picked up her coffee cup with trembling hands. "I can't bear to see her like that. Our plan has to work."

Reginald joined us before we ordered breakfast; his face was the only sign I needed to realize Jefferson Granger would do nothing to help his daughter. Florence had called it squarely. The man had no backbone.

"He says his wife has only Camilla's best interests at heart, and the surgery will return her to the loving daughter she once was." Reginald sipped the coffee the waiter put before him. "It's hopeless. There's no help from that quarter. That household is unsafe for Camilla to return to. Once this is over, she'll have to find other living arrangements."

"He's as spineless as a grub worm." Zelda's voice was quiet, but fury clipped her words. "How a man could be so . . . castrated, I'll never understand."

"I'd hate to walk in his shoes," Reginald said.

"Then we move forward with the séance." There wasn't another choice that I could see.

We had to put the Roswell House portion of our plan into action the moment David returned with Camilla. We had very little time before the Grangers would realize that Camilla was gone from Bryce. Once they knew she'd fled the hospital, it wouldn't take them long to figure out where she might be.

"I know this isn't what Camilla wants, but I'm going to talk to the minister and have him ready to perform a marriage ceremony." Zelda's thoughts paralleled mine—seal the marriage and protect David from charges of kidnapping, should Maude go completely bananas. If Camilla married, she would never have to return to her mother's supervision.

"I'd like to go to Roswell House now," I said. "See if I can learn more about the entity there. If I know what to expect, I can better prepare and protect Camilla."

"Is that really necessary?" Zelda appeared uneasy at the prospect. "It would seem the more often you attempt to draw this . . . entity out, the more dangerous it will be for you."

"I don't believe I'm in any danger at all. It's Camilla who will take the risks. It may save us time and effort this evening, and we may not have much time. Besides, the workmen are there."

Reginald didn't object, though he looked worried.

"Kuddle's due to make a report on his investigation into Joanne's disappearance," Zelda said. "He might be at the sheriff's office because he hangs out there all the time. One of us should go there. If he's found something, we can telephone David at Bryce and tell him. We need all the help we can get in convincing Camilla to leave with him."

"You'll make more headway with Kuddle," I told Reginald. "I promise I'll be safe. Nothing bad will happen in broad daylight." I glanced up and realized that a rainstorm had moved in, blocking the sunlight and coloring the day gray. At least it would cool the paved streets and sidewalks. Any remission from the humidity and heat would be welcome. "With the workmen there we'll be fine."

"Sure thing." Zelda sounded less than sure, but her set jaw told of her determination. "I'll drive."

We left Reginald in the lobby of the Greystone, which was a lovely and well-appointed hotel. We'd meet up at the Sayre home when we were done with our tasks. As Zelda and I crossed the lobby, I glanced back at Reginald, who looked perfectly at home reading a newspaper while a shoe-shine boy buffed up his wing tips. I borrowed an umbrella from the concierge of the hotel, promising to return it in a few hours, and we were off.

The pain pelted the hood and roof of the car, but the cooling aspect was so welcome, Zelda and I only laughed at the difficulty of actually seeing the road. We crawled along until the turnoff to Roswell House, the trees still so thick we almost missed it. The rain came down in buckets as we parked and ran across the yard, giggling as we shared the umbrella under the cool rain.

When we entered the house, I was instantly aware of the silence. The workmen had gone, leaving the house shut up and still. Zelda and I cracked windows to allow some ventilation.

"At least it's quiet," I said. I was more hopeful that an entity might show itself and reveal something of its nature. It wasn't that I sought connection to the dark force in the house, but I'd be much happier if we could spare Camilla a séance.

"Must we really subject Camilla to coming here with David?" Zelda asked, almost as if my concerns had rubbed off on her.

"If I can avoid it, I will, but I believe whatever is here at Roswell is connected to her. While I may feel or see it, I believe only Camilla can understand what it wants."

"Why Camilla?"

"I don't know." Zelda had asked the right question. "That's what we'll learn at the séance. Twice, this entity has taken control of her. No one was able to speak to it through her. That's what I'll do. With Reginald and David here to restrain Camilla, and with your help, we can keep her safe from harming herself or anyone else. If I can't draw out the spirit on my own, then I will need her to be there. I don't know any other way."

"What can I do to help?" Zelda asked.

"Move some chairs to the ballroom. And we need a table, but we may have to wait for David and Reginald to help us move that."

"Or we could use the parlor," Zelda suggested. "The dining table's there under a drop cloth. We can take out a few leaves to make it cozier."

"That makes more sense." If the entity was in the house, it could just as easily manifest in the parlor as the third-floor ballroom.

"What if you become possessed?" Zelda asked. "What should I do?"

I'd actually given that some thought. "Get it out of me. Whatever you have to do." I tried for a cocky smile, and I hoped it was effective. "Take me to Madam Petalungro in New Orleans. She isn't well enough to travel, but she'll help."

"Okay." Zelda looked a bit green.

"I'll be fine."

"I know," she said as she walked upstairs. The burden of her decisions and actions seemed to be heavy on her shoulders.

I went to the kitchen, where the knives had been returned to their place in the drawer. Still, I checked twice to make sure all the blades were there. They were—even the one that had been missing earlier. I removed them and put them in a trunk I'd seen in one of the bedrooms. The trunk had a lock and a key, and I turned the lock and pocketed the key. The wicked blades were safely tucked away, and I was the only one who could open the trunk. We'd search the rest of the house for weapons before the séance. Some of the workmen's tools could be lethal, and those would also have to be secured.

Much of Montgomery had electric power, and David was paying to have a line run to Roswell House. Camilla should arrive while we still had daylight, but I put candles around the parlor with matches beside them. If the séance went longer than I anticipated, I didn't want to break the mood to hunt for sources of light.

Once the candles were in place, I looked around the room. The fourteen-foot ceilings allowed the room to cool. Windows as tall as doors yielded onto the front gallery, and I opened a few to allow ventilation. The workmen had closed them to keep rain from blowing in, but the house would quickly grow stifling since the storm had passed. Rain was almost an everyday occurrence in July—and a welcome one—but the high heat and humidity made it difficult for the painters and plasterers to work.

I scanned the front yard as I unlocked the last set of windows. The yard crew had made progress. More and more of the once-landscaped lawn had been reclaimed. I could see the pattern of camellias, liberated now from vines and underbrush. A beautifully intricate gazebo had also been freed from the encroaching woods. There was an air of fantasy about it, as if it had been created for a fairy-tale princess. The dark memory of the woman in the upstairs window, the wicked stepmother who ruled the flies, forced its way into my mind. The entity was here, in the house. It was aware of me. Would it come forward and allow me to spare Camilla? Certainly not if that was what I requested. This was not a spirit seeking help or release. It sought control. I pushed my thoughts away and studied the gazebo.

Once it had been repainted and patched, it would make a lovely place for trysts for Camilla and David, or perhaps a playhouse for the children they might have. I focused on a happy future for Roswell House and the couple who would live here. I visualized a family, laughter in the halls, and the footsteps of children.

It took me a moment to realize the laughter I heard was not just in my mind. Someone was chuckling softly. The hair on my nape stood up. This was not the happy laughter of my imaginings. This was dark, cunning, cruel.

Movement on the front lawn caught my attention. The twins were there. "Run," they told me. "Run!"

And they did, into the underbrush, disappearing. I wanted to run, too, but I didn't. "Who are you?" I asked.

The knife drawer in the kitchen opened, then slammed with great force.

"You okay in there?" Zelda called.

"I'm fine." I didn't want her down on the first floor. I needed to communicate with the spirit if possible. "What do you want?" I asked quietly. "Show yourself."

A swarm of flies buzzed around me so suddenly that I let out a startled cry. They pelted my skin, driven mad by whatever force compelled them. They flew at my eyes and nose and mouth, blinding and choking me. Normally merely annoying, these flies were malevolent. I swatted and spun, finally losing my balance and falling against the wall beside one of the windows.

"What the hell?" Zelda came across the room at a dead run. She flapped her arms at the bombarding flies and then picked up a dust cloth from a chair and tried to swat them. As suddenly as they'd arrived, they fell to the floor. The wood around my feet was black with the still-buzzing and dying insects.

"Are you hurt?" she asked.

"Something really doesn't want us here," I said, shaking the dead flies from my blouse and hair.

"Why does it only happen to you?" she asked. "I don't see anything. Neither does Reginald. The minute we leave you alone, you're attacked."

I didn't have an answer, only a suspicion. "Maybe because I'm the person who can help Camilla. It wants to frighten me away." Saying the words out loud firmed my resolve to see this through.

"We should leave. We need Reginald and David here. I'm no believer that men are the answer to everything, but if we have to drag you out of the house, they could be useful."

She was right about that. "I've learned something here today. Tonight we have to be prepared for the worst. We need water, bandages, smelling salts." A weapon of any kind would be pointless and might be turned against us. "Dr. Abbott should be alerted that his services may be needed."

Whatever we faced at Roswell House, it was powerful. And determined. But not more so than I was. With each new thing I learned, it became more and more clear that Camilla's mental issues stemmed from Roswell House. Here was where it had to end.

"Who do you think is here?" Zelda asked quietly.

"I don't know. I saw the figure of a woman in the window, but Madam Petalungro warned me not to trust all spirits. Some are liars, just as some living people lie for their own purposes." A thought occurred. "May I borrow your car?"

"Of course. Why?"

"Who cooked and cleaned for the last Roswell who lived here?"

"I don't know, but Althea can tell us."

"Let's find out. If Herman Roswell's help is still alive, I need to speak with her."

"Brilliant idea. We can talk to Althea, and you can drop me at home. What if David needs to call us? One of us should be near the telephone. I'll call the sheriff's office and let Reginald know what's going on."

CHAPTER TWENTY-SIX

At last, luck crowned me from a clearing Alabama sky. Althea knew the back-porch truth—Doddie McCann, Herman Roswell's former household helper, had taken a job sitting with an elderly man on Mulberry Street. I held the address in my lap as I drove Zelda's coupe, searching out the landmarks Minnie had given me.

Doddie had been a young woman when Herman, a bachelor in his midfifties in poor health, lived on the Roswell property. She'd cooked and cleaned for Herman until he died. Althea had made a phone call, and Doddie had agreed to speak with me. Robert Wiles, her current employer, a former chemist who compounded drugs and who had an impeccable reputation, was confined to his bed. He slept most afternoons, lulled by medication, the heat, and the oscillating hum of several fans.

The connection between Doddie and the Roswells went back even further than her service to Herman, according to Althea. Doddie's mother and grandmother had worked for the Roswell family in a number of capacities, from cook to nanny to housekeeper. If anyone could help me, it would be Doddie.

When I arrived, Doddie was sitting on the front porch waiting. She put a finger to her lips. "Mr. Robert's restin', but it ain't peaceful. I'll leave the door open so I can hear if he needs me."

Doddie was still a relatively young woman, and a beautiful one, but caring for others had taken a toll on her. Gray had begun to claim her temples, and crow's-feet—I hoped from laughter—marked the corners of her eyes.

"How is Mr. Wiles?" I asked.

"He's leavin' us. A little bit each day. I think when he sleeps, he visits the folks and the places he loves, and he says his good-byes."

The remarkable calm she demonstrated told me a lot about Doddie's relationship with time and death. She wasn't afraid. She would travel with Mr. Wiles on that journey as far as she could go.

"I'm sorry to hear that."

"Sorry for me, but not for him. He's been waitin' a long time. Not too much longer to go. He won't last until the muscadines come ripe. He loved muscadine jelly and told me stories of how he'd make up a batch of wine every August. I'll just make his passin' as easy as I can."

It occurred to me that Doddie had seen more than her share of death. She'd worked for Herman when he died; now it was Robert. And who knew how many others she'd cared for in their final days? Althea said Doddie was the best person to hire to be with those who were old or ill. I'd lost many people, most tragically. None had had the benefit of a loving hand as they released this life and moved on to the next. I'd never had a chance to sit at a bedside and offer the comfort and strength Doddie gave so generously.

She noticed my sadness. "No need to be sad. Mr. Robert, he's ready to go. His wife passed on some years back. I was with her, too, and it was harder. She didn't want to leave him alone, but there wasn't any stoppin' what fate ordained. His children moved away and don't come home. Nothin' but his old hound dog LeRoy to hold him here, and I promised him I'd see LeRoy over the River Jordan, too. I love that dog as much as he does."

As if he heard his name, the dog, a big redbone hound, slipped out the screened door without a sound and came to settle at Doddie's feet.

"Seems like he loves you, too."

"Dogs know. He's been sayin' good-bye to Mr. Robert all this week. He goes in there, puts his head on the bed under Mr. Robert's hand, and just stands that way for an hour or more. He'd give his life for Mr. Robert, but not even LeRoy can stop the passage of time."

Her words brought tears up. My mother had bonded with a cat. After the accident that took her life, the cat had been inconsolable for weeks. He missed my mother, and, though he loved me, it was never the same. I blinked the moisture away. What kind of investigator cried in front of the person she was interviewing?

"Would you mind telling me about Mr. Herman Roswell and your time at Roswell House?"

"What information are you lookin' for?" She had light-brown eyes that didn't flinch.

"There's something in that house. Something . . . dark. I need to know what it is and how to get rid of it." Perhaps I should have beat around the bush and tried to trick Doddie into telling me what I needed to know, but time was running out for me. For Camilla. Either Doddie would tell me or not.

"What do you see there?"

She knew. There was no point lying. "Two little dead girls, twins. A dark image of a woman, standing in an upstairs window, watching. Always watching. She's surrounded by thousands of flies." I watched carefully for the skepticism or doubt that I expected. I saw none.

"My granny knew a woman like you. She had the gift of seein', too." LeRoy stood and put his head in Doddie's lap. She stroked his ears gently. "I'm not afraid of the living or the dead. Some go easy and some go hard, and I do what I can to make the passage without pain. I've had a few spirits come back to visit. I don't see them like you do. They come to me different, but I know who they are. There'll be the scent of vanilla, and I know old Paula Lamey is walkin' the floors, come to check to see what's what. Lord, that woman could make a buttermilk pound cake that would melt in your mouth. She was always baking for folks, always smelling like something warm and wonderful right out of the oven."

I envied her such pleasant visitations. "You were friends?"

"I worked for her for two years. Just before she died, she gave me her china cake plate. When she stops by, she'll move that plate around to let me know she was there." Doddie smiled at her memories. "Miss Paula loved to hear the gossip more than anything. I sat with her back around 1915, when her two boys signed up for the war. They never came back, and she let go of life, too. She fought it, but the will to live was gone. She just dried up until she hardly weighed nothin' at all. When she left, it was just a whisper on the summer wind."

"You're a strong woman."

"Not so strong. I just have a big belief that this life is part of a longer journey. Good folks continue down their path. Others, I can't say. I don't spend time worryin' about such things."

"Have you ever sensed any of the Roswells . . . staying behind?"

"Some chilly fall days, I smell the aftershave Mr. Herman wore. I'll get ready for work and step outside to walk to the trolley, and I'll catch that smell-good. I know he's sittin' on my porch. But he's there for company, not harm. Might be nice to see him and talk to him. I can't hear them either."

I had to be honest with her if she was going to help me. "Whatever is in Roswell House is not there for good. I promise you that."

"I know."

"What did Mr. Herman say about the house?"

She petted the dog until he settled again at her feet. "There were accidents there. All directed at the females. Never a male. That's what puzzled Mr. Herman. I don't remember the names or details all that clearly. Mama Glenn, my granny, told me stories, and so did my own mama. They're all mixed up with things Mr. Herman talked about."

"If you'd tell me what you remember, it might really help us."

She rocked a little as her eyes lost focus and she visited the past. "He told me about one of the Roswell daughters. Lorilie was her name, I believe. She loved horses, and they said she could ride like a Comanche. She'd ride across the fields, jumping fences and laughing with joy. Herman said the bond between her and the horse was amazing. But one day she was walking across the front lawn on a horse, and the horse went crazy. Herman was a little boy, and he saw it. He said it was like the devil grabbed hold of the horse's bridle. The horse tried to run, but it was trapped. It fought, screaming with fright, and the girl was thrown and fell under its hooves. The horse fell dead on top of her. They both died on the spot."

My heart pounded. That wasn't a riding accident. That was something else.

"What else?"

"One young woman named Tilly, I think she was a cousin, fell down those beautiful stairs. She was paralyzed from the waist down, and she died sayin' that someone pushed her. Pushed her hard."

"Are there more?"

"Oh, there were incidents galore. Trees suddenly fallin' and nearly killin' one Roswell bride. Carriage wheels that fell off in the front lawn just as folks were comin' or goin'. Fires. Lord, Roswell House nearly burned down twice. There were plenty of stories."

"But no other deaths?"

"Well, people sure died, but most were marked up to fevers or accidents. No matter how strange the circumstances, the doctor or the sheriff could find a way to get beyond the facts to sayin' it was accidental. No one in the Roswell family wanted the idea that there was a curse on the bloodline to get bandied about. That family had enough to overcome as it was. No need to put a hoodoo stain on it."

"What was it that the family had to overcome? I've heard they were wealthy and lucky."

"Money eases some troubles but not all. Death hovered over that family." A soft noise came from inside, and she stood up. "'Scuse me." She disappeared into the house, LeRoy right behind her.

I wondered if I'd been dismissed, but in a moment she returned with a tray and two pieces of pound cake. "I made this cake yesterday while Mrs. Paula was visitin' me. It's her recipe, and Mr. Robert loves this when he feels up to eatin'."

The cake was so moist it almost melted in my mouth. Doddie hadn't exaggerated. "Is he . . . okay?"

"Yes, ma'am. He's settled back to sleep. He needed a sip of water."

We ate our cake in silence, enjoying the buttery flavor. "This is wonderful."

"I'd make us some coffee to go with it, but the day is just too hot."

"I agree." I returned my empty saucer to the tray. "Thank you."

"If you're done with your questions, I'd better get to work. I've got clothes to iron while Mr. Robert is asleep."

"One more question. You never heard about any dead girls. Twins. They may have . . ." What was the polite way to say they'd had their heads removed? "They may have died violently."

"Never heard of any twins in the Roswell family." She thought for a minute. "If those girls were Roswells, maybe they died from the curse that was put on the house."

I sat up. "So there *was* a curse?"

"Happened back in my granny's day. She always said she was reluctant to go to work there because all the Negroes knew about the curse. Didn't harm a hair on the head of the menfolks, just the women. The Roswell women suffered plenty."

"Who cursed the house?" I thought of the man who'd died in a duel on the front lawn.

"The Roswell land wasn't bought all in one piece. It was bought up parcel by parcel by different family members. Now, Mr. Ramsey, he bought the most of it and built a nice house, but not like the big house Mr. Wick built."

"Why that land? What's so unique? There must've been land in every direction."

"It's that creek runs up behind the house. Tonka Creek. It's deep enough for bigger boats, and folks said Ramsey Roswell was tradin' in guns to both sides of the war, stealing food meant for the soldiers and selling it at high prices. He'd waylay the supply ships on the river and hide them away up Tonka Creek, kill the crews, resell the goods."

"This was before the actual house was built, right?"

She nodded. "It was Mr. Wick who finally bought that high ground where Roswell House is, and that's where the curse came about. That was just after the war ended. No one else had money, but he did. Mr. Wick wanted that high ground somethin' terrible, Mama Glenn said. He talked about the showplace he'd build his bride. One day the Peebles family was there; the next they were gone, and Mr. Wick was building his grand house. There were whispers Mr. Wick hurt the Peebles children to get the land." She stood and lifted the tray with our empty plates. "Only rumors, though. The family was gone, and no one looked for them to ask any questions."

"Were there ever stories or rumors about young women who were forced into prostitution associated with Roswell House?"

The plates on the tray rattled. "There was talk. Back when Mama Glenn left there. Said it was too far out of town for her to find a ride, but that wasn't the whole truth. She didn't like what was going on in that house."

"When was that?"

"Mr. Wick was a young man. There was talk he liked the young girls too much."

"That why your granny quit?"

She shook her head, but the china on the tray had quieted. "Mama Glenn never said. My mama refused to talk. She started goin' out there to help with parties, with the cleanin' and servin'. She was just a girl herself."

"The law never investigated?"

She scoffed. "Law? Like I said, up until Mr. Herman was left there alone, the law answered to the Roswells. Mr. Herman wasn't like that. He repented for the sins of his father."

"And what sins were those, exactly?" My gut had clenched. I was onto something. Something that bound past and present together.

"The sins of flesh and cruelty and oppression. Sometimes skin don't matter. A person can be a slave even if she's as white as the magnolia blossom. Now Mr. Robert needs me, and my chores are stackin' up."

"Thank you, Doddie." I left before I wore out my welcome. I had learned much of what I'd come to find out.

CHAPTER TWENTY-SEVEN

The afternoon heat had climbed to a climax, with the temperature sitting at one hundred degrees. The brick and paved roads were a luxury for the motor vehicles, but heat shimmered off the surface in waves. I drove through downtown Montgomery, which looked like a ghost town. Sane people retired from the summer heat and prayed for rain. Another storm front gathered to the west, and the clouds darkened as I drove. I prayed it might bring us a cool breeze.

I parked on the street and made my way to the Sayre house, a wilted flower of the South. My floral-print dress, sleeveless and cool, stuck to me in all the wrong places. I wanted a cool bath and a nap.

Zelda and Reginald were nowhere to be found, and I was happy to retire to my room and strip down for a bath. It was nice to be in a quiet, empty house so I could think about the coming events.

When I entered my bedroom, I found a letter on the bed addressed to me. I tore open the neatly written note from Uncle Brett and read that all was well at Caoin House. The wags about town were all talking about the superhot summer and the possibility of a big storm in the Gulf of Mexico. A hurricane. We'd had scares in Savannah from the storms that brewed along the Atlantic, but the Gulf storms were the most feared. While Uncle Brett's property was north of Mobile, the biggest storms could devastate Caoin House.

"I'm considering a trip to Alaska," Uncle Brett had written. "When you return, we'll discuss the possibility. It would not be a bad thing to spend the last of August and first of September in a cooler climate."

I could read between the lines enough to see that he was planning his trip to be sure I was safe. It wasn't a vacation Uncle Brett sought; he wanted to get me away from my investigations of ghosts and the dangers inherent in my work. It touched my heart and made me miss him.

I penned him a quick note, leaving out the dangerous encounter we'd had on the fish camp road. I kept it short and upbeat, noting that we had high hopes of helping Camilla within the next few days, and that soon we'd be traveling home. I also recapped my ride on the electric trolley car, something Uncle Brett would grill me about when I returned to Mobile.

I put the note on the side table beside the front door with the two cents for a first-class postage stamp and hurried to the bathroom for my long-anticipated bath. When I returned to my room, I was refreshed and ready for the work ahead.

The sound of Reginald's laughter, mingled with Zelda's excited voice, came to me. Though my hair was still damp, I went out to greet them. We gathered around the dining table to talk.

"You'll never guess what Reginald's been up to," Zelda said. "He saw that fine, fancy car of Jason Kuddle's parked in front of the Confederate Café and stopped for a chat. That's where he found my private investigator—wolfing down a huge plateful of food with two police officers. He was surprised to see Reginald, but he promised he was on his way to report to me as soon as he ate."

"Has he made any progress on the case?" I had my own news to share, but I wanted to hear Kuddle's report.

"Yes!" Zelda's eyes sparkled. "He has a lead," he said. "Joanne Pence left the hospital with relatives. He says she is safely home. I sent a telegram to the hospital for David. That will help him convince Camilla to come home with him."

"Excellent." I had my doubts that Kuddle's investigation had been thorough, but Zelda's happiness was contagious. Now to deal with Roswell House and the influence it exerted on Camilla. "We don't have a lot of time before David returns with Camilla. I—"

A knock on the front door interrupted them, and Zelda excused herself to answer. She returned with a telegram in her hand and tore it open. "Camilla is refusing to leave Bryce. She says that Joanne's still there, somewhere. She says her friend's in danger." Zelda looked at us, stricken. "Can't David make her understand that she can't do anything to help her friend from there?"

"It looks as if we'll have to try," Reginald said. "Pack a bag. We're going to Tuscaloosa. If there isn't another train, we'll have to drive."

It wasn't a prospect any of us looked forward to, but the road was open, and while there'd been some rain, it hadn't flooded or poured endlessly.

"Father always says I'm the most stubborn woman he's ever known," Zelda said. "I think Camilla has topped me." She swallowed. "I can't go with you. I can't. You can take the car."

I nodded my thanks. It wasn't the scenario I'd hoped for, but we could drive Camilla and David back with us. "We should leave immediately."

"No time like right now." Reginald took the key from the side table. "Stay out of Roswell House until we get back. We'll return as soon as we can. Could you telegraph David and ask him to wait for us at the same hotel Raissa and I stayed in? I can find him there."

"I will." Zelda's voice was barely a whisper. "I'm sorry I'm not going. There's something about that place that makes me think I'll suffocate and die on the spot."

"I understand." There was no point in heaping hot coals on the ashes of her fear. She was terrified. For whatever reason, she simply couldn't confront those fears.

"I'll call Mr. Kuddle and tell him what Camilla said," Zelda said. "If he has information that can prove that Joanne Pence is safe, I'll send another telegram."

"That would be very helpful," Reginald said. He, too, wanted to assuage her guilt at not going with us.

"Don't worry," I told Zelda as I put a comforting hand on her shoulder. "We'll bring her back."

I grabbed a change of clothes for Camilla and climbed into the front seat beside Reginald. He drove with confidence and care, and I relaxed into the seat and watched the scenery flash by. The storm that had threatened only an hour earlier had moved south and east, but the sun was still obscured by clouds, a blessing. We'd had no time to check road conditions, but the thoroughfare between the two cities was in constant use. Small towns, diners, and service stations had cropped up along the way. I realized that I'd never taken a car journey of this distance through such untamed land.

The trees were a rolling rush of green, from the dark evergreen of the pines to the lighter coloring of the oaks and the brilliant yellow-green of new leaves sprouting in the summer heat. On the outskirts of Montgomery, we passed pastures with cattle, mules, and horses, and fields of the dark-green foliage of cotton.

The road was paved in some of the larger towns, and we stopped for fuel and some sandwiches at a small place whose name escaped me. Then we were driving into the gloaming, intent on getting to Tuscaloosa and Bryce Hospital.

Along the way, I told Reginald what I'd learned from Doddie McCann.

He was thoughtful as we pressed on. "So Wick Roswell liked young women. Girls."

"Doddie said that Wick took what he wanted. And the curse that came down on the Roswell house involved only the females. All the males were spared."

"Don't you find that strange?" Reginald asked. "If it was a curse, why curse the females when it was the Roswell men who were up to no good?"

I saw his point clearly, but curses belonged to a voodoo culture I wasn't certain I believed in. Reginald, though, had lived in the city that was home to Marie Laveau, the famous voodoo high priestess. Though she'd died nearly forty years earlier, her reign as the queen of dark magic and voodoo curses remained prominent in the Crescent City.

"Curses don't always work the way they're intended."

"I see. But why would the Roswell curse apply to poor Camilla? She had nothing to do with the history of the property or the former owners." I'd never discussed curses and spells with Madam, but I'd been raised in a home where a bargain with Satan had a price—a single soul. And the Roswell family *had* suffered tremendous tragedy.

"I don't know," Reginald said. He slowed to take a sharp curve.

Had someone hated Wick Roswell and his predecessors enough to trade his or her soul for revenge? "Maybe the things Doddie told me were accidents."

He looked away from the road long enough to stare at me. "I'd say a horse spooking to the point that it died of fright is a little more than an unfortunate accident."

I couldn't explain that mystery, and I had another of my own. "Why would David Simpson buy a house with such a tragic past?" I asked. "Roswell House was beautiful, but any number of structures could have been renovated. Or a new home built."

"Maybe he didn't know about the stories. Zelda didn't. But that's something you'd best ask David," Reginald said. "And we can, as soon as we get to Tuscaloosa."

I nodded.

"What if Camilla won't come with us?" he asked.

"Then we've wasted our time and Zelda's money. If she won't work with us . . ." I shrugged. We'd never promised Zelda we'd be able to accomplish anything. "It's impossible to know what's in the heart of another person. Maybe Camilla wants to punish herself for something, and that is more important than marrying or being happy."

"You believe she may have aborted a child, despite Zelda's assurances she didn't."

"Perhaps Zelda doesn't know everything about Camilla that she thinks she does, or it's possible Zelda would like to protect her young friend. Someone has to ask David, and it should be you. Man-to-man. He won't take kindly to my asking that question."

"That's a lot of wisdom for a young woman not yet thirty," Reginald teased.

"Madness in the heart. There's no cure for it." I leaned back in the car seat. The last light was leaving the sky, and Tuscaloosa was still a distance away. On either side of the car, the dense black of the woods drew close to the road. Beyond that was the paler black of the sky with the stars just winking to life.

About fifty yards ahead, a young woman in a summer dress stepped out of the woods. She was barefoot, and her body had been lashed by branches and limbs where she'd run through the undergrowth. I sat forward and reached out a hand to force Reginald to stop the car, but I realized it was not a living girl, only the spirit of one departed.

Her long hair was tangled with vines and brambles, and she stepped toward the road as if she was dazed. When we were close to her, she faced me. "Don't leave me," she said in that peculiar ghost voice that could travel across time and distance as clear as a bell. "I'll be good. Don't leave me here alone."

"Who are you?" I whispered.

"What?" Reginald asked.

I didn't want to tell him about the spirit. Not now. He wanted so badly to see a ghost, and yet he couldn't. I didn't look back as we left the spirit behind. "Where are we?" I asked.

"On the outskirts of Dooneyville."

Up ahead the lights of a gasoline station drew us as surely as a flame compelled a moth. "Let's get some coffee," I suggested. The night was still hot and close and suffocating, but the dead girl on the side of the road had given me a chill.

"Sure thing. What did you see back there?" he asked, more observant than I credited him with being.

"There was another dead girl in the woods. A pretty brunette. She asked me not to leave her." I wasn't afraid; I was sad. Bone sad. "She's one of the lost girls."

"Maybe it's a good thing I don't see ghosts," Reginald said. "What I do see now, though, is that *you're* the connection, Raissa."

"What do you mean?"

"Of all the ghosts in Alabama, why are you seeing these poor girls? Something terrible is happening at the mental hospital. Somehow it's connected to Camilla. Maybe it's only that we're to save her from danger, but I think it's more. And you're the means of figuring it all out."

CHAPTER
TWENTY-EIGHT

We pulled into Bryce Hospital driveway just at midnight. Our late hour told me David had long left the premises—Bryce frowned upon visitors on the grounds after hours. I'd hoped to arrive sooner, but road conditions had interfered. So, without David, we would attempt, once more, to convince Camilla to come with us voluntarily. Failing that, we'd be forced to strong-arm her into the car and drive away with her. If that happened, then Camilla could charge us with kidnapping, but we were betting Zelda could convince her not to do that.

The storm that had threatened us for the whole drive had amassed on the western horizon. Wicked lightning forked across the sky and charged the air. High above the treetops, a half-moon glowed dimly, peeking in and out of the clouds. "Annabel Lee," Edgar Allan Poe's masterpiece of death and longing, came to me. I spoke a stanza of the poem.

"A wind blew out of a cloud, chilling

My beautiful Annabel Lee;
So that her highborn kinsman came
And bore her away from me,
To shut her up in a sepulcher
In this kingdom by the sea."

"That hospital does remind me of a tomb," Reginald said, picking up instantly on my mood. "Some of the patients there will never leave. A lot of them, I fear. No one wants them."

"Some have no family, and some are too ill to be on their own." I had to shake this malaise if I meant to do my job. "We can't fix this for everyone. Let's hope we can help Camilla."

"We'll leave the car here for the time being," Reginald said.

We'd parked at the very end of the driveway on a dark street. The hospital grounds were extensive, and the state hadn't maintained the road. There was no traffic, and the tree limbs drifting in the moonlight cast eerie shadows. He wiped a sheen of sweat from his forehead, and I knew the long-sleeve shirt, tie, and jacket were hot now that the car had ceased movement. My sleeveless dress was more comfortable, but still the night was extremely warm, and the impending storm was like a suffocating blanket thrown over the landscape.

"Let's do this." We'd driven a long way in the dark just for this opportunity—so that I might talk with Camilla uninterrupted by the nurses or, worse yet, a doctor. "Boost me into a window."

"In case you haven't noticed, there are bars on all the windows." Reginald was the observant one in our detective agency.

"Not on the front-office windows, only the patient rooms and dorms." This time I'd paid attention, too, wondering if Camilla's disappearing friends were slipping in and out without detection via windows. "David has the forged letter. He'll meet us first thing in the morning, if we don't pick him up at the hotel sooner. We'll be long gone before the hospital is able to contact the Grangers and discover our letter is a forgery. But I need to get in there now. I need time to convince her."

"And what will I do?"

"Find Joanne Pence. Camilla says she's still on the grounds, and I think Kuddle took the hospital's word that she was gone. He didn't check. Now's our best chance to search the outbuildings. There are barns and stables and chicken coops. Plenty of places for a clever girl to hide."

"I don't like you going into Bryce by yourself."

"I'm not alone. There are thousands of patients there—and nurses, doctors . . . ghosts." I gave him a smile that was more bravado than real. "They can't do anything to me. Charge me with trespassing, maybe. That's not so terrible. You know I'm in there. And you care. You'll find me. It's not like they can make me disappear."

"I wouldn't be so sure of that." Reginald's strained expression let me know he was truly worried that something would happen to me in the hospital.

"I'll signal from Camilla's window. If I'm in any kind of danger, I'll hang a scarf or pillowcase from the bars. Then you can call the police. You can say I'm being held prisoner or something to get them to take action. Call Judge Sayre. We do have a couple of big cards up our sleeve."

"I'm a gambling man, and this is too dangerous for my taste. What does that tell you?"

"I understand, but I have to try." I didn't see any other course of action. "Either you can help me, or I'll do it on my own."

"If anything happens to you, your uncle—"

"Won't blame you. He knows I'm an Airlie, just like him. Stubborn is bred in the bone." I didn't give him a chance to argue more. I ran down the long driveway, a shadow darting among the shifting patterns on the ground cast by the swaying tree limbs. Reginald followed close behind.

Again Poe's words seemed both to warn and hold me.

> For the moon never beams without bringing me
>   dreams
> Of the beautiful Annabel Lee;
> And the stars never rise but I feel the bright eyes
> Of the beautiful Annabel Lee;
> And so, all the night-tide, I lie down by the side
> Of my darling—my darling—my life and my
>   bride,
> In her sepulcher there by the sea,
> In her tomb by the sounding sea.

This hospital would not be Camilla's tomb—not while I still breathed.

I made for a ground-floor window of the reception office with Reginald at my side. None of the office windows were barred, and the young women working there had pushed this one open to let out some of the heat.

With Reginald's help, I managed to move the glass up enough for me to slide through. Reginald laced his fingers to make a stirrup and boosted me so I could slither over the edge. It wasn't the most graceful entrance I'd ever made into a building, but I managed to get inside without injury. Loss of a little dignity wouldn't kill me.

"I'll look around here for a bit. Please search for Joanne. If she's here, we'll take her with us, too."

It would be several hours before the day staff returned, and while I was in the business office, I decided to check on Joanne Pence's records, as well as Connie Shelton's. Connie's body hadn't been found, but I knew she was dead. Her spirit remained earthbound, free of her body. She was truly a ghost, and if I could help release her, I would. What

I needed to find out was how the mental hospital was classifying the disappearance of the young women.

I went to the office door and listened closely to be sure no one was near the business area. Nurses and orderlies remained in the wards and hallways all night and day, but I had to chance that the business offices weren't watched or guarded. I snapped on a light, knowing Reginald would be cursing me to the high heavens for my recklessness. I needed illumination to read, and I needed to work fast.

The patient files were listed alphabetically, and I checked Camilla's first to see if there had been an official diagnosis. Some of the handwriting was hard to decipher, but the majority of notes had been made by Dr. Perkins and included his diagnosis of a form of schizophrenia. One of his notes made my pulse thunder.

Dr. Perkins's final conclusion was that Camilla's brain was diseased and that rational thought and behavior would continue to decline—at an amazing pace, he had written—unless she received surgical intervention. He believed he could destroy the dying tissue and save a portion of her brain. In the margins to the right, he provided a thumbnail of the procedure he intended to use. Camilla's face and skull would remain unscarred, but the technique was horrific. A slender spike would be driven through the corners of each eye and into her brain. The surgery, it was noted, was completely experimental and had been tried only in Europe.

If I'd had any doubt about breaking into Bryce and removing Camilla, it vanished now. In the doctor's hand was another notation mentioning Camilla's pleasant and controlled behavior but also her fear of a violent outburst. He'd taken everything she'd said as supporting evidence of a diseased brain that could turn violent, a diagnosis I disavowed.

I returned her file to the cabinet and found Joanne Pence's. The patient was also seventeen and had been diagnosed as manic-depressive, with wild upswings of mania followed by plunging depression.

Dr. Bentley had consulted on the case, and his handwriting was a vast improvement over Dr. Perkins's.

Joanne had been brought to the hospital as a ward of the state because of her behavior at Saint Margaret's School for Girls, a place I vaguely knew about in Tuscaloosa. Runaways, orphans, and problem girls who defied parental authority were the inhabitants of the school, which trained the young women to be domestics, caregivers, and seamstresses.

The report from the school noted that Joanne had slapped a nun while receiving corporal punishment. A thousand different scenarios could be read into that single sentence. She could have been a total hellion, or she could have been defending herself—or any combination of the two. Her tenure at Bryce was court ordered, and there was no mention that relatives had taken her away. In fact, just reading her file, one would think she was still a patient. She was listed, by Dr. French's orders, for water therapy in the morning and exercise therapy in the afternoon. She'd received the same treatment yesterday, though Camilla said she was missing then. Another contradiction.

It was possible Camilla could be mistaken, but I didn't think so. Either Dr. French was unaware Joanne was gone, or he was deliberately covering it up, pretending that everything was normal. The hospital could be liable for losing a patient, I supposed. Maybe they were hoping they'd find her somewhere on the premises before her absence was documented. Or maybe there were other plans for her.

Connie Shelton's chart contained the same mania and depression diagnosis, mentioning pyromania and her "dangerous" symptoms. Surgery had been recommended and performed, with an optimistic charting of her improvement after the surgery. She'd been at Bryce for five months, an eternity if she'd been housed in one of the wards. A final notation showed she'd left Bryce with her uncle. But I knew that to be a falsehood—at least James Patrickson, the man listed as Connie's uncle, didn't know her and had never heard of her.

I flipped through until I came to Cheryl Lawrence, the young woman who'd drowned only a couple of days before. It seemed as though a year had passed since I'd stood on the riverbank watching them drag her body from the water.

Cheryl had come from the Lowndes County jail. She was a shoplifter and petty thief who'd attacked the jail warden and had been brutally beaten. She'd been diagnosed with brain trauma when she'd arrived at Bryce. They'd tried water treatment, solitary confinement, physical exertion. Nothing had helped control her rages.

Dr. Bentley, consulting with Dr. Perkins, had deduced that when the jailer had beaten her into submission, her brain had swollen, causing permanent damage. They'd decided to perform the brain surgery in an attempt to restore her to docility so that she could live a "normal" life.

The notes on Cheryl's chart were more extensive than the others I'd looked at. After the surgery, she'd been morose. She ran away from Bryce to be in the wooded areas, particularly along the river. When she was brought back to Bryce and admonished to stay away from the river, she told the orderlies that she had to go there. She said she was meeting someone there.

The doctor had noted that the flowing river water seemed to calm her, and she was often found sitting on the bank watching the current, waiting for her "friend," as she called the person she was to meet. She was docile and sweet tempered otherwise.

I thought of Nurse Brady's comment that she kept running away. To the river. I wondered if it was a clue to how she'd grown up, because she was listed as an orphan with no family. She'd had blood relatives once upon a time, but they'd simply abandoned her. Maybe her happy memories came from the river. There was little to go on and no family to check with.

In fact, none of the three—Connie, Joanne, or Cheryl—had close family. No one to check up on them. The surgery Dr. Perkins championed was experimental at best. It made sense he'd select patients who had no one to fight against it. I wondered how the male patients who'd been operated on had fared, but I didn't have any names to check, and the files were too extensive to start reading and hope I chanced across something.

I turned out the light and sat for a moment, allowing my eyes to adjust to the darkness. The sound of something clattering to the floor made me start out of the chair. Someone was inside the office with me.

"Who's there?" I asked softly. If it was a security guard, I didn't want to scare him and get shot for my trouble.

"Save me."

I inhaled slowly. The voice was feminine, tired, without hope. "Who are you?"

"Save me." She stepped into the moonlight filtering in through the open window where I'd gained entrance. She was young, the yellow dress covered in water and mud. Water puddled about her feet in their shiny black shoes with a single strap across the top.

"Who are you?" But I knew. It was Connie Shelton. I'd known she was dead, but I didn't know how. Now I believed she had drowned. We'd find her body in the river. She'd come to let me know.

"Save her." She'd changed the refrain.

"I will save Camilla. I will."

She nodded. "Beware."

"What happened to you?" I had to have some facts to take to the law. If she could help me with a detail of her death, I would have something real. The sheriff wouldn't come and search the river simply because I'd been visited by a ghost. "Who hurt you?"

"Save yourself," she said, her image wavering in the moonlight as if she were being blown about by a slight breeze. "Save yourself. He's coming." She started to cry, and the force of her emotions made her more corporeal. I could see the bruises on her throat, the swelling of one battered cheek. She'd been beaten before she died. "Save yourself!" Her words were a blast of chill air against my face.

And then I heard it.

Outside the office heavy footsteps echoed on the wooden floor of the lobby.

"He's coming," Connie said. She was across the room, pressing through the wall.

"Don't go." I had unanswered questions, and I might never get another chance. "Who's coming?"

"Save her." She beseeched me; there was no other word for it. Her voice broke on a watery sob. "Home. Oh, please, home."

The emotion she felt slammed into me, and I thought I'd break into tears myself. Homesickness, that wretched longing for a place out of reach, left my stomach roiling. I'd never shared emotions with a ghost, but Connie wanted her home, and I knew what that terrible desire was like. I let her memories flow over me and saw the rural clapboard house, unpainted, shaded by large oaks. The ground was bare but neatly raked. The front porch held planters of zinnias and variegated sweet williams, a swing, and two chairs.

A large tin pan filled with purple-hull crowder peas sat on the floor, waiting to be shelled for the night's supper. Beside the swing was a bucket of sweet corn, still in the shucks, also waiting to be cleaned. It was a small farm, isolated but lovingly maintained, somewhere in the South. This was the Shelton farm, I somehow knew. This was the home of Connie's birth father, not the stepfather who'd driven her to acts of violence. I jotted down some details and forced the image into memory so that I could examine it at a later date for clues to the place where I believed Connie had once experienced love. If I could, I would pay her grandparents a personal visit to tell them what I suspected, even if I couldn't prove it.

The cost of communicating the farm image to me had drained Connie's psychic energy and left her a mere shimmer. "I'll try to find it," I told her. "You should go home."

"Home," she said, the word sounding as if she were underwater.

"If I find your body, I'll take you home," I promised.

"Home," she agreed. She flared back, fully corporeal for just a moment. "Beware! He's here."

And then she was gone.

CHAPTER TWENTY-NINE

My body felt like a tuning fork, still vibrating from the charge of her warning. Footsteps came across the lobby floor. The same tread I'd heard earlier, coupled with additional steps and a strange, scrabbling noise. I ducked behind the desk, clutching my little notepad filled with the information I'd jotted down and my pen, and prayed that my heart slamming into my rib cage would not give me away.

Who was outside the office? Friend or foe? Alive or dead? Often the spirits I saw moved in a gliding motion or simply appeared closer or farther away. This was someone—several someones—walking with a solid tread, indicating they were alive. Truthfully, I'd rather face more ghosts than a security guard, nurse, or orderly of the hospital.

Cowering on my knees, I waited, afraid to breathe, running through the potential consequences. Uncle Brett would send bail money, hire a lawyer, and rush to my rescue, no questions asked. For his trouble, I would taint his name and ruin my own. Standing outside Bryce talking with Reginald about the potential price I'd pay, it had seemed negligible. Now I'd had a change of heart.

I was almost ready to stand up and confess my sins when the footsteps stopped. An eerie silence fell over Bryce. Even the breeze outside that had kicked up with the pending storm had stopped. After several minutes, I wondered if I'd imagined the footfalls. I was keyed up, afraid. Connie Shelton's warning may have excited my hearing, my expectations. I crept out from beneath the desk and eased over to the door, which was heavy wood with a frosted-glass top. I couldn't really see through it, but I could see vague images: the visitor chairs against the wall, two upright images that I figured to be pillars, the reception desk. The room was devoid of people or entities. I'd wasted valuable time hiding from my imagination.

I had to get to Camilla's room, and my time was running out. The day started early in Bryce, with inmates awakened for breakfast at five. I did not have long to convince Camilla. I couldn't hide out in the business office another minute.

My hand clutched the doorknob; then I heard a strange sobbing shuffle. It was so plaintive, so desperate that I froze. In the center of the frosted glass, I saw a blurry image in the center of the lobby. Two big men supported another person, who hung between them as if he or she were unconscious or injured. As they dragged the person, her feet made paddling movements. She tried to walk but couldn't make her legs work.

Through the cloudy glass, I couldn't tell who the people were, but they moved across the lobby at a funereal pace, and I realized they were not alive. I had to risk it. I cracked the door and peeked out. Two orderlies, lumps of men with no features, assisted Cheryl Lawrence. A trail of water dripped from her, and for a split second, a wild hope that she hadn't drowned, that she'd been revived and they were assisting her to her bed, fluttered in my chest. But I remembered her gray and bloated body coming out of the water, the grappling hook piercing her stomach and digging into her ribs as she was snared and dragged to the surface. She could not be alive. I was witnessing some scene from the past. Or something Cheryl Lawrence was trying to tell me, much in the way that Connie Shelton had.

She might be reenacting her murder, trying to show what had happened.

A cold, wet hand brushed my cheek from behind, and I whirled, barely stifling the scream that tried to tear from me. Dead Cheryl, water dripping, pale-blue eyes rolled up in her head, revealing the whites, reached out to touch my hair. "So pretty."

I didn't flinch, though every impulse in my body was to run. To run as far and fast as I could. Her hand patted my hair, water running from her flesh to mine.

"Pretty girl. The river brings her to me," she said.

"Who? Who does the river bring?" I croaked the words, but it was the best I could manage with her cold, dead hand stroking my hair.

"The good lady."

I realized that Cheryl's perception was childlike. Whether from drowning or her mental condition, I couldn't say. If I had to bet, it would be that the operation had done it.

"Where do you live?" I asked, my pen ready. If I could find her home, I could learn so much more about her.

"Beneath the water. She's waiting for me. I'll be a princess."

There were so many things to ask, but my throat clogged with emotion. This poor young woman's spirit was trapped in some watery fairy tale at the bottom of the river. Had she drowned trying to find a land where she would be a princess? The thought was unbearable. Would her mental condition condemn her forever to seek what could never be found?

Or, more sinister, had she been lured to her death deliberately?

Her wet hand moved through my hair again. "So pretty. Pretty as a princess. Do what he says and I won't be punished." Her features constricted. "Please don't hurt me."

"Who hurts you?"

She stepped back, and I realized she was weakening, much as Connie had after communicating her memories of home. What had been corporeal was now less dense. She was fading away.

"Where is Joanne Pence?" I asked. "Is she still here?"

"Tap, tap, tap." Cheryl reached out a bluish hand. "Tap, tap, tap." She tried to touch me, but I backed away. I didn't want to feel those lifeless, clammy fingertips against my skin again.

"Where's Joanne?"

Tap, tap, tap. Her fingers rapped against the wood of the desk.

"Hush," I said, worried that a guard or nurse might hear the commotion.

Tap, tap, tap. She came toward me, and her pale eyes stared at me. Tap, tap, tap.

I didn't understand what it meant or what she wanted. I only knew she was growing agitated at my lack of understanding. "Please, if Joanne is here, help me find her."

Tap, tap, tap. She reached out for me, her hand clawlike. "I heard it. Tap, tap, tap. And then . . ." She looked beyond me to the door. "Now I'm his."

"Who?" I didn't understand what she was saying.

"Go for a ride and never come back." Her words were echoey, unsubstantial, and then she was gone, and I was alone in the business office of the state mental institution. The only evidence she'd been there was a puddle of water on the lobby floor.

As I prepared to vacate the office, lightning struck so close the smell of ozone sparked the air, and a boom of thunder made the panes in the building rattle. The lights sputtered and went out, and a most unnatural sensation climbed up my spine. Cheryl had gone, but I was not alone.

CHAPTER THIRTY

The sensation that I'd sought at Roswell House and failed to find tingled the nape of my neck as I stepped into the lobby. The dead were near at hand. I couldn't see them, but I felt them. I'd noticed a candle on a shelf in the lobby, and I found it and struck a match beside it. The wick caught, and I turned slowly, aware of others around me. The dead filled the lobby with an overwhelming sense of loss and abandonment. The candle cast unsteady shadows against the walls and floor, hooded figures that loomed large and then shrank to hunched goblins as I walked.

I staggered under the weight of the dead as I reached the hallway and walked toward Camilla's room.

Bryce Hospital had seen many deaths. It was a place where patients were often critically ill and unable to express their needs or help themselves.

Most of the entities couldn't incarnate in a physical form but came through only as vague shadow and emotion. I'd simply not expected the weight of death to be so pressing. I'd been foolish to come into the hospital at night without Reginald. He helped balance me, kept me from being overwhelmed in this underworld of the dead.

My dream in the Tuscaloosa hotel came back to me. I'd journeyed to the tombs, the arched corridors of the spirits beneath the earth where Pluto ruled and the River Lethe brought forgetfulness. I remembered the figures, all clad in black hooded cloaks. The child who'd been featureless, unformed like the unborn. I hadn't understood the lack of individuality, but now I realized it was merely a transitory state.

These sad dead meant me no harm. At least none I could detect.

I kept walking.

Tap, tap, tap. The spirits crowded closer to me. They didn't speak—were incapable of language. They generated the noise of a hammer striking a nail. Not hard, delicately.

Tap, tap, tap, like a metallic woodpecker.

I traversed the halls, and all around me Bryce creaked and moaned as patients shifted in their bunks—mumbling, coughing, snoring, calling out for family. When I heard a door open, I ducked into a linen closet as someone hurriedly walked past me.

When the footsteps had died away, I stepped out into the hall and found myself confronting a half dozen young girls. The oppression of the multitude of spirits was gone. Now it was only the young women. I recognized Connie but none of the others. They wore dresses designed for evening wear, stockings, dark lipstick, and heavy kohl around their eyes that aged them. Several cut sidelong glances at me, their lips pulled up in a sneer. Others, like Connie, looked down, shy or ashamed—I couldn't tell which.

I recognized the two girls I'd seen in the hospital hallway earlier, and the two from the hotel corridor. They lounged against the wall as if they knew a secret, one that offered an advantage. Bad girls. They knew things, secret things. It was clear to see in their eyes. They clustered around the door of Camilla's room, forcing me to stand in the hallway or walk through them.

Why are you here? I asked without having to speak the words. And I knew. In my heart I knew. They'd been surgically traumatized here at

Bryce and then put on the street. Reginald had said the missing girls and Camilla had me in common. Yes. But it was more. We all had Bryce in common. They had experienced the horrors, and I had been brought here to expose what was happening. Something terrible was going on with the experimental brain surgeries and these young women.

The girls had no answers for me, at least none they were willing to share. They milled around the doorway.

"Stand aside, please. You have my word I'll try to help you."

They shifted back, and I felt relief and also curiosity that they'd obeyed me. I might feel pity for them, and I certainly wanted to help them, but Camilla was my first priority.

A breeze threatened to snuff out my candle, and I put up a hand to shield the flame. The entities around me drew back even more. A terrible odor rose up, overwhelming me. The young women began to decay in front of me. Wounds and bruises appeared, and some began to drip water. Their skin turned gray, and their bodies bloated, pressing through torn dresses. Others showed dark bruises on their necks—blood leaking from their scalps or eyes, leaking down their dresses and falling from their hems onto the floor, mingling with the water.

Tap, tap, tap. The sound was now sinister.

"What does it mean?" I tried to hold my breath to avoid the stench of decay that rose from them.

Tap, tap, tap, was the only answer.

"What does that mean?" I was beyond frustrated.

"Find us." One of the hotel girls stepped forward. "Find us."

The hallway was empty. My candle illumination showed only the silent hallway and the door of Camilla's room. I turned the knob to discover it was locked. I shouldn't have been surprised, but I was. I shook the knob. "Camilla?"

"Who is it?" She sounded groggy, and I wondered if they'd drugged her.

"Open the door. It's Raissa. I need to speak with you."

"I can't. They lock it."

I twisted the knob again, gauging how the bolt engaged. It was a simple mechanism, and one I might master with a hairpin. Thankfully the heat and humidity had prompted me to pin my hair back from my face. I removed the spiral pin and opened it, working as quickly as I could with the dim light from the candle on the floor.

In a moment the door opened. Camilla stood on the other side, fully dressed as if she'd been waiting for me to arrive.

"You have to come with me." I didn't intend to give her time to think. If we couldn't open the front door, we'd go out the window I'd entered. There was no time to waste. The dead had convinced me, by emotion if not words, that Camilla was in more danger than I'd suspected. We had to make our escape now. She was smaller than I was, and I could boost her up. I reached for her arm, but she stepped back.

"I'm not leaving."

My first reaction was to grab her and haul her down the corridor and then out the office window. I'd risked a lot to help her, a fact she seemed not to recognize. A little cooperation would be appreciated. "If Reginald and I can help you, it will happen at Roswell House." I forced civility and concern into my voice, burying the anger. "The house has a history, Camilla. Reginald and I have learned a lot about the property. It's possible something from the past, something lingering from the house's past, has . . . linked to you."

"You think I'm infected with some dark event that happened in that house?"

"I know it sounds improbable, even fantastical, but I've seen it happen. I've witnessed how unresolved issues from the past can corrupt a person." My actual experience was limited, but I'd read extensively and conversed with Madam Petalungro and Reginald, who'd seen far more than I had.

"How? How does it happen?"

She asked a question I couldn't answer, and certainly not as the clock ran down on my allotted time to convince her to leave Bryce. "I'll explain on the way to Montgomery. Reginald is outside, searching for Joanne Pence. If he finds her, we'll take her with us."

She sighed, and the stiffness of her shoulders relaxed. "I know you want to help me, that you've endangered yourself to break in here to talk to me. You're trying to help my friend, too. I thank you. It's just . . . I can't go anywhere with David. What if he's driving and I have another fit and try to harm him? I could cause a wreck and kill both of us."

Her fear was well founded and perfectly reasonable. I also had a solution. "Reginald has Zelda's car. You can ride with us. David can take the backseat. You'll be between me and Reginald. David will be safe."

"He wanted to stay here with me, but Nurse Brady made him leave. She said he'd upset me and that he wasn't allowed to visit again. She was going to call my mother. I convinced her not to, but she warned that if he came on the hospital property again, she'd have him arrested and call Mama. He should never have come here. It'll only make trouble for him and for me. I can't marry him. I can't do that, fearing I might turn on him again. His refusal to accept that only makes it worse for me." Her voice broke. "I couldn't live with myself if I hurt him. I love him."

"That's not going to happen, because Reginald and I are going to figure out what's going on at Roswell House."

"Do you think you really can?"

I saw the burning hope in her eyes. Camilla wanted a cure. She loved David enough to take whatever surgery brought—with the slim hope of coming through the operation with some part of herself left. "I do. I didn't know at first, but now I believe we can help. But you have to cooperate. Let's go before someone comes to check on you."

She stepped into the hallway. When she glanced over her shoulder, I knew she had decided to trust me. "What about my things?"

"We'll send for them. Or once this is all behind you, David will buy you new things."

"You're right."

For the first time since I'd met her, I saw a real smile, one that almost broke my heart. She'd been willing to sacrifice so much—without complaint. Now I saw what she might be like without the shadow of illness over her. Whatever doubts I'd had about the course of action I'd taken, they evaporated. Camilla's smile was worth all the risk.

"Let's go." I grabbed her hand, and we ran down the hall. In the areas where the dead slumped together, I ignored them. As we entered the office and closed the door, I heard them in the lobby.

The sound of their tapping came to me. Tap, tap, tap. I didn't know what it meant, and I had to get Camilla out the window and off the hospital grounds. "The car is at the end of the drive. I'm going to hand some things to you. Then run. Run as fast as you can to the car. Blink the lights four times. That's a signal to get Reginald back to the car."

"And you?"

"I'll be right behind you." I had one more thing to do. Something truly illegal. But it was now or never. "Just a minute and I'll help you out the window."

I turned on the office light once more to go through some files. As I moved to sit in the desk chair, I saw a long, slender needle with a beautifully crafted pearl-and-gold design on the end.

It was a hat pin, and a unique one. It hadn't been in the chair earlier when I'd been in the office. Someone had left it there for me. A sign or symbol I needed to know. I didn't have time to study it, so I stuck it through the placket of my dress and started pulling the files I needed.

When I had them stacked, I assisted Camilla up onto the window ledge. It wasn't much of a drop, but I held my breath as she slid over and hit the ground with a soft grunt. "Take these." I'd grabbed up the files on Connie Shelton, Joanne Pence, Cheryl Lawrence, and a few other young women whose names the young woman in the business office had mentioned when Reginald was charming her.

"You can't steal patient files." Camilla was horrified.

"If you want to find your friend Joanne, I have to. Take them." I pushed them through the window and into her arms. "Run! Don't look back. If you're caught, I'll take all the blame."

She cradled the files in her arms and began to run across the lawn. The clouds had thickened, and the lightning had moved on top of us. A jagged flash of a four-pronged bolt struck not far away. In the resulting explosion of light and crack of thunder, Camilla shied like a Thoroughbred, but she didn't scream and kept running. The dead girls lined the driveway, invisible to her eyes.

I clambered out the window and hit the ground running, my shoes in my hands. As the storm finally broke and an icy rain pelted me, I prayed that Reginald was in the car, ready to drive. We hadn't bothered with the fake release we'd forged. We'd abducted a mental patient—and patient records—from the hospital. I wondered if we'd be stopped at a roadblock on our way home. Anything was possible.

The lights of the car blinked on and off four times. Camilla had made it safely. I hoped Reginald had something to tell us about Joanne when he got back to the coupe, but we couldn't linger in Tuscaloosa.

As I neared the car, someone ran out of the trees that lined the driveway. I prepared for a fight, then realized it was Reginald. He intersected me and took my elbow to speed me along. "Hurry," he said. "There's no sign of the Pence girl, but Perkins is on the hospital grounds."

"How do you know?" I asked, thoroughly winded. "He's supposed to be on his way back from Vienna."

"He's here. I saw him and the other doctors in one of the outbuildings. They were in a heated conversation. He must have come back early—if he was ever gone at all."

CHAPTER THIRTY-ONE

Rain, mingled with hail, bounced off the car's roof and hood as we caught our breath inside. Reginald put the car in gear and coasted, lights out, away from the hospital. At any moment I expected an alarm to sound. Visions of police officers—pistols drawn, swarming the car—made me grip the door until my knuckles ached. I wanted to beg Reginald to press the gas pedal to the floor and get away, but he had the right approach. We needed to leave without drawing attention. In the rain and wind and storm, we were invisible if we didn't turn on the lights.

"Mama is going to be furious." Camilla's teeth chattered in the front seat between Reginald and me.

"You're almost eighteen," I told her. "You're entitled to your own life." If she didn't break free of Maude, she would be a prisoner in Montgomery far more than she was in Bryce.

"Yes. Too bad Mama doesn't feel that way." She clenched and unclenched her hands in her lap, the most unladylike expression of anxiety she would allow herself.

"If you love David, you owe it to him and yourself to fight for that love." Reginald turned on the car lights and drove faster, taking us east again down the long road that would be even more hazardous in the event of flooding. We were caught in a tunnel of rain and darkness, with only the puny headlights to illuminate our immediate path. After my experience with the dead in Bryce, it was discomfiting.

"What do you know about Roswell House?" I asked Camilla.

"Like all old houses, it's reputed to be haunted. I've told you what I know."

"Before you went with David, had you ever gone inside?"

She shook her head. "No. My friends and I only walked around the grounds, scaring ourselves silly. We didn't dare go inside."

"And did you see anything? Ghosts, shadows, impressions of something sinister?"

"I've thought about this a lot lately." She pushed her wet hair out of her face as the car's Kingston heater blew hot. Still, I shivered. It was strange to be cold in July, but the storm had brought icy rain, and we were wet in the moving vehicle. I thanked Scott Fitzgerald for adding the luxury of the heater to his vehicle. Camilla cleared her throat. "I have felt something there, something that tugs at me. But I only ever felt it when David took me. When I got out of the car, I had a sense we were being watched, and not by the workmen and carpenters." She stopped and looked at us. "I know . . . I must be going mad."

"Not at all," Reginald said. "Think back and tell us. Any small detail might help."

"Okay." She inhaled. "The beauty of the house captured my heart, but inside . . ."

We waited, letting her take her time.

"There's something sinister there. I didn't want to remember, but there are some things . . . the last time, when I was alone in the kitchen, there was this pressure on my chest, as if something were forcing its way beneath my ribs and sternum. It's the last thing I remember." She swallowed. "I know I have to go back there if you're to help me, but what if

I can't go inside? What if I simply can't make myself do it? I'm terrified that I'll lose who I am."

"No one will make you," I assured her. "You don't have to do anything you don't want. Just try. That's all we ask."

Reginald handed me his cigarette case. "Butt me," he requested.

I lit a cigarette for him and handed it over, and one for Camilla, too. She shook her head. "They make me cough. Zelda and Tallulah laugh at me. I'm pathetic at being a modern woman."

I inhaled and began to cough. I tossed the cigarette out the window into the muddy street. "I'm not very good at it either."

"Ladies, we need to make one stop." The rain had slackened and was now more mist than shower. Reginald pulled up in front of the hotel where we'd stayed last time we were there. It was three o'clock in the morning, and even the train station was dark and empty. "Wait here. I'll be back with David."

"He can't come with us." Camilla grew agitated. "I can't be with him."

"But he must," Reginald said calmly. "It will help us prove our theory. If you can ride with him and nothing happens, then it will help clarify the point that your affliction is tied to Roswell House. Remember, when he visited you at Bryce, you were just fine. Right?"

She nodded, wiping away tears. "I love him so much. I just—"

Reginald ran into the lobby. Five minutes later, he signaled from the door that David was on the way. Ten minutes later, David put his luggage in the back and climbed in the backseat.

"Thank God," he said, leaning forward to kiss Camilla's cheek. "Don't worry. Everything will be fine."

I couldn't make that promise, but I certainly hoped it was true. We set off into the wet night. The bulk of the storm had passed us, moving to the east. Lightning flashed in the distance as we drove toward it. I thought of the Mary Shelley story and the monster, brought to life by lightning, and his aching need to be loved. I'd read much more into Shelley's story than a simple monster tale. The desire for love was basic to humans, and the shame of it was that Camilla had become convinced she was monstrous—a danger to the man who loved her. We had to change that, or she would forever be doomed to live outside of love.

Two hours into the drive, Reginald pulled over to switch places. Camilla was asleep and didn't wake as David stretched his legs and talked quietly with Reginald while he smoked. I felt battered and abused, and paced beside the car to loosen my muscles. I got behind the wheel, and Reginald slipped into the passenger seat next to Camilla, allowing her to slump against him. She was so dead asleep she barely stirred.

I pulled onto the road, aware of the dangerous driving conditions. It wasn't long before the trip assumed a rhythm—Camilla's light breathing, David's soft snoring in the backseat, and Reginald's shifting about. I would drive until I grew too weary, and then we would switch up again.

Beside me, Camilla awoke. She sat up, and I could almost feel her blush at her sudden closeness to Reginald.

"How are you feeling?"

"Better. Stronger." She sat upright. "I can drive."

It was a tempting offer, but I declined. "You rest. We'll take care of the preparations. Tonight will be difficult for you, and you'll need all of your strength."

"Thank you for bringing me. For bringing David. Maybe it really is the house . . ."

"I firmly believe that's the case." Camilla was reluctant to enter Roswell, and so was I. Something powerful inhabited the place. I thought of the female form in the window, surrounded by buzzing and dying flies. Carrion, decay, waste, and death drew flies. This entity was not some lost spirit unsure of how to shift from the living to the spirit world. It was something that had managed to dig into Roswell

House and find a plump host. Ejecting it would require force and skill. "Thinking back, are you sure there's no family link or friendship with those who owned or lived on the property?"

She shook her head. "The last to live there was Mr. Herman, who was a friend of my mother's. He would stop at our house some afternoons to talk with Mama."

"I've been told he was a kind man. When did he visit?"

"I was very young. I remember because he would bring me a Squirrel Nut Zippers candy bar, or sometimes Hershey's Kisses. He would tell me to sit on the porch and enjoy the candy while he talked with my mother."

Camilla seemed totally unaware of the possible implications of her innocent memory. "What a wonderful treat for a little girl."

"He liked me. He said I was a special girl and that one day I would be a princess." She choked a little on the last word. "I didn't have a lot of dreams like that. Mama didn't believe in dreams, but he encouraged me to think of great things. He told me not to tell her. It was our secret."

Was it possible that Maude Granger and Herman Roswell, an old bachelor who lived alone in the splendor of Roswell House, had had an affair? A lot of sharp angles came into focus. "Did he ever mention the Roswell curse to you?" It was a long shot.

"No. But then he wouldn't have. He said children should live in joy and happiness, and that there was plenty of misery waiting for me when I grew up."

Herman Roswell sounded kind and smart, but as to why he had been so generous with Maude and Jefferson Granger's little girl . . . well, I had my suspicions. The question was whether to voice them.

"The curse supposedly follows the females of the Roswell family. Is it possible you're a Roswell?"

She inhaled sharply. "You think he's my father?"

"Is it possible?" I repeated.

She started to say no but thought better. "I can't say. I've often wondered if there was ever a time Mama loved my father. She is so cold and aloof around him."

I had begun to unravel what might be at the root of Camilla's problems. If she were a Roswell—

"Do you think I carry the Roswell curse?"

"I don't even know what the curse is, but Reginald and I will find out."

The road spun beneath us. As we put Tuscaloosa far behind, I started to relax a little. Perhaps we wouldn't be arrested at a roadblock. We might make it to Montgomery and be able to hide Camilla and our role in her abduction. Maybe. If our luck held.

The sky above the tree line lightened, and the first pink of dawn gave me renewed hope. We would resolve this. We would save Camilla, and she would have her Prince Charming and a fairy-tale ending. It hadn't happened for me, but it would salve my wound at the brutal loss of my soldier husband if I could help another.

"This presence you felt in the house," I began. "Did you get a sense of age or gender?" I was thinking of the dead twin girls and the fly woman. Were they the entities preying on Camilla? Were they the embodiment of the curse?

"I didn't."

"Did anyone ever mention the death of twin girls in the house?"

At first Camilla didn't answer, but then she began to make a strange gasping sound.

"Camilla? Are you okay?" I glanced at her, and she was clearly in distress, but I couldn't look away from the road for long.

"What is it?" Reginald was wide-awake now.

Camilla lifted a hand to point. "They've found us."

A long, dark sedan blocked the entire road. Two men stood beside it, staring into our headlights. Someone had learned of Camilla's escape and meant to stop us.

I thought I recognized one of the men, but as I wrenched the wheel, the headlight moved off him. Mud grabbed at the car tires as I attempted to move to the right of the sedan. The car careened into the soft shoulder on the right, and the dirt grabbed at the tires, trying to wrest the wheel out of my grip.

"Brake!" Reginald threw out an arm to brace Camilla.

I slammed on the brakes. David tumbled to the floor in the back, and the car slewed dangerously. I turned the wheel, trying to follow the wild spinning of the car. Just when I thought impact was unavoidable, we ran through the ditch on the right side, and the coupe managed to climb back onto the road. I'd smashed my chest against the steering wheel, and Reginald and Camilla had bounced about the front seat and dash. I could only hope David, on the floor in the back, was not seriously harmed.

"Faster!" Reginald said. He knelt on the seat and leaned back to check on David. "He's fine. Drive!"

I checked the rearview mirror, but the road behind us was dark. I wanted to stop and check the car, to see if I'd damaged it, but when I started to slow, Reginald touched my shoulder. "Keep going. As fast as you can. There's no time to stop."

"What if a tire's damaged?" I remembered all too well Uncle Brett's tragic accident that had almost killed Reginald and given our enemies the chance to take my uncle hostage. If we kept running hard on a damaged wheel, we ran the risk of a serious wreck. Our only advantage, though, was our limited lead and the fact that Zelda's sports coupe, if undamaged, might outrun the bigger, heavier sedan. Reginald was right. We had to press forward as quickly as possible.

I held the car in the middle of the road, but the mud tugged at my arms, and there were times I feared I might lose control. To drive so fast was madness, but to linger might prove more deadly.

"Who was that?" I asked.

"One of the men was Kern, an orderly from the hospital." Camilla's voice trembled. "They know I've run away."

"But how did they get ahead of us?" I asked. "We stopped only long enough to find David and buy gas. Not forty minutes in all, and no one saw us leave. There was no alarm."

"Maybe that's what they wanted us to think," Reginald said. "What if they meant to catch us on a dark and empty road?"

"But why?"

"Because Camilla knows something, and they're afraid she'll reveal it?"

"What could she know?" David asked.

"She was friends with two of the young women who went missing," I said.

"There's no other reason for an orderly from the hospital to be on a wet and dark road so far from the hospital," Reginald said. "Whether Camilla knows anything or not about those missing women, they think she does."

"And they know we're asking questions. Zelda hired Kuddle to probe the hospital. Maybe he's stirred a hornet's nest asking questions of the wrong people."

"I don't know anything," Camilla said. "If I did, I'd tell someone so they could find Joanne. I just know she hasn't left the hospital."

"How do you know that?" I'd been so intent on getting Camilla away from Bryce that I'd failed to ask that obvious question.

"I still have her earrings, those black jet earbobs she got from her brother. She asked me to hold them for her because they would be stolen in the ward. They were her prized possession. She'd never leave those behind, no matter what. She's still there at Bryce."

"One thing's for certain," Reginald said. "Bentley, French, and Perkins were all out in the barn in the middle of the night. Why?"

"A very good question," David said. "I don't like any of this. I can't thank you enough for getting Camilla out, for convincing us both that she wasn't safe there."

"Thank Zelda," I said. "We wouldn't be here without her and Tallulah's interference."

David put his hand over the seat and gently gripped Camilla's shoulder. "When this is over, and when Camilla and I have our wedding, I hope you can attend."

"I hope so, too." We weren't far out of Montgomery. All I had to do was concentrate on driving for a little longer.

CHAPTER THIRTY-TWO

Dawn illuminated the road and the outskirts of Montgomery. The road behind us remained empty, and I could only hope Kern and company had bogged in the wet shoulders of the road and required a farmer to come and pull them out with a tractor. We'd have a good head start.

The dense forest growth had given way to cleared pastures and gardens. David gave directions to back roads that would lead to his bachelor home near downtown, avoiding the main road where the police—or someone far more sinister—might be waiting. We'd have to find a safer place for Camilla, but this was our best option for the moment.

It was too risky to take Camilla to the Greystone Hotel, where she'd be exposed to public scrutiny, nor did we want to embroil the Sayres in our illegal scheme. The long car ride and her lack of aggression toward David had convinced her and us that she could stay at his place while he went to work.

Mud-spattered, but without mechanical issues that I could detect, the roadster cruised through the early-morning streets to stop before a lovely Victorian home with borders of the smooth-skinned crepe myrtles in vibrant pink hues in bloom. Inviting rockers with cowhide seats sat on a wide porch. David's gracious taste was in evidence, even in the smaller town house he'd selected for his temporary home.

When the workday was over and David was free of his duties at the bank, we'd gather at Roswell House. Until then, we had to keep out of sight because we were surely the prime suspects in Camilla's disappearance from the hospital.

"I'll stay with Camilla while David washes up for work," I said. "Reginald, can you check over Zelda's car? If it needs repairs, we should get that done." I opened the door and stepped out, more glad than I'd ever imagined to be standing on pavement. Reginald got out and assisted Camilla to the sidewalk, where David joined her.

"Take it to Turner's Garage over on Hamilton Street. I'll take care of the repairs," David said. "You did a magnificent job of driving, Raissa." He patted my shoulder. "Truly magnificent. I thought we were going to hit them dead center, but you managed to avoid them and get back on the road." He was almost gleeful.

"All by accident." I couldn't take credit when luck had been behind the wheel.

"Never disavow skill." David put an arm around Camilla. "I owe you both such a large debt. And, Camilla, I want to marry you today. At the courthouse. I'll arrange for a judge to meet us there at lunch. We'll make it legal. Then your mother no longer has any say in what happens to you. We don't have to stay here in Montgomery. We can live anywhere."

Camilla shook her head. "This must be settled. We have to figure out what is at Roswell House and why I'm susceptible to it. I won't marry you until that's resolved. Who's to say it won't follow me wherever I go?"

"I have some ideas," I said, eager to share them with Reginald when we were alone. "Reginald and I will check into some things. I hope to have more information later, and if I'm correct, we'll know what we're facing."

Camilla looked up at the pleasant white clapboard house. "I'll be fine here, Raissa. You don't have to mollycoddle me. Mama will never suspect that I'd actually stay at David's home. I've been too well trained."

"What she doesn't know . . ." I shrugged, but my offer to stay with Camilla had dual purposes. To watch over her and to obtain a little more detail, if I could get her to talk. "I'll stay anyway, and I'm sure our friends Zelda and Tallulah will be happy to spend some time with you. You won't be alone with David, so your reputation will be intact."

Camilla laughed. "A month ago, my precious reputation would have been a serious worry. I don't care anymore, but Mama will. What's important to me is that I don't try to kill my fiancé."

"Then we're agreed?" When everyone nodded, I signaled my partner. "Reginald, may I have a word before you leave?"

"We'll wait for you on the porch," David said, offering Camilla his arm.

We were a bedraggled group standing on the sidewalk as the sun came up, and the smart move was to hide the mud-spattered car and go inside. But I had to tell Reginald what I'd learned. When David and Camilla were out of earshot, I filled him in on my suspicions that Camilla might be a female descendant of the Roswell family and subject to the family curse.

"That would certainly explain a lot." He worried the car keys. "Be careful with her. I don't like leaving you alone. She seems perfectly rational, but—"

"I'll be fine," I said. "Once you've taken care of Zelda's car, would you bring Zelda to sit with her? We have to prepare for the séance tonight. We won't have another chance. Maude will get wind of the escape, and she'll come sniffing around David and Zelda."

"I'll be back within the hour." Reginald gave a cocky salute.

I watched him drive away with a strange sense of dread. We'd evaded the trap on the road, but by running, we'd failed to discover who had tried to waylay us. And there was still no explanation of how Kern and his partner had gotten ahead of us on the road home. That troubled me, and I wondered what they might attempt next.

When David had cleaned up, changed clothes, and gone for breakfast at the Greystone, which was his normal workday routine, I sat with Camilla in the quiet front parlor of David's home. The room was beautifully decorated, if a little sparse on personal items. There were only two photographs, one of his parents and one of Camilla, a beautiful portrait of her taken on her own front porch.

"I'm as nervous as a cat." Camilla paced the room, unable to settle.

"You had no aggressive action toward David. That should make you feel more confident."

"We weren't alone."

"I know you're worried, but you've spent endless hours together at functions, and many moments alone with him. Before you went to Roswell House, nothing untoward ever happened."

She eased onto a love seat. "You're right."

"I'm not in the business of false hope, but neither should you suffer from false fear. Tonight will tell the tale. And I promise you—Reginald and I will not let anything happen to David. I'm far more worried about you."

She made a derisive sound. "So I might become possessed by an accursed entity in the house my husband-to-be bought as a gift for me. Consider the alternative. Having part of my brain destroyed."

It felt good to release the pent-up tension, and for a long moment we simply laughed out loud. At last I heard a car stop out front. When I looked, I saw Zelda and Tallulah striding toward the front door. I didn't want to tell them anything until I'd checked some facts.

The young women came in, babbling brightly about dress lengths, the new swimsuits, and the trivia of a privileged lifestyle. They fought the darkness that hovered over Camilla with breezy gossip and inconsequential chatter. Zelda leaned over to whisper in my ear but loud enough for all to hear. "Do you think the bank is open for David yet?"

Camilla pretended offense, but we all laughed at the slang for sexual activity.

"Well, David is a banker. He should be very good at banking activities," Tallulah added, to more laughter.

It was good to see the friends united, and to see Camilla's cheeks pink from gentle teasing. "Where's Reginald?" I asked, knowing that he must have told them we were here.

"Since the car was running fine and Tallulah had her car for us to use, he said he had an errand. He asked us to apologize. He said he'd track you down later."

I didn't like the sound of that, but there was nothing I could do. And I had my own mission. I said my good-byes, assuring the women that events would fall into place and leaving without giving them any details. As I walked out the door, I heard Tallulah's throaty drawl. "You look a little pea-ked, Camilla, darling." Tallulah used the old pronunciation that I'd heard all my life. "If you'd let David tickle your fancy, you'd increase your health."

"Tease all you want," Camilla said. "I'm so happy to be here, to see you."

As I closed the front door on their chatter, I had no doubt we'd done the right thing taking Camilla away from Bryce. Now I had one immediate problem to handle. I went to the Greystone to find David and borrow his car—thank goodness Uncle Brett had insisted I learn to drive, and bless Travis, my uncle's gardener and estate manager, for his kind instruction. The trolley didn't run where I needed to go. Bernard West had not been completely truthful with me. Was he protecting

Herman Roswell or Maude Granger? I didn't care who or why—I just wanted answers.

When I turned down the neglected lane that went to Bernard's home, I slowed. The rope swing, the dead flower beds—nothing had changed, but I saw it all with different eyes. Hopefully wiser eyes. Bernard had taken to the bottle with gusto, and I wondered what was at the bottom of his desire to drink and forget. He'd once been a respected lawyer, a man with a loving family. What had driven him to abandon his life for an existence of solitary drinking? I intended to find out.

The screen wasn't even latched, and I knocked hard on it and called out his name.

"Go away," came from deep inside the house.

"I can't." I would get my answers.

"Zelda?" he called out, hope rising in his voice.

I opened the door and walked in. What was one more charge of breaking and entering in the long list of my growing illegal actions? The house was dark and musty smelling, but I continued toward the back. I found Bernard at the kitchen table. His hands were shaking so hard he'd knocked his glass of liquor onto the floor and couldn't get down to pick it up.

"Go away," he said.

I picked up the glass and the bottle, which still had an inch of corn whiskey in it. I found a clean glass and poured it for him, holding his hand to steady the drink to this mouth. I'd heard of the shakes that heavy drinkers suffered when they ran out of alcohol. "You need a doctor."

"You're wrong. I need a coffin. You don't know how much I look forward to the release of death."

Pity was too expensive at this moment. "Is Herman Roswell Camilla's father?" I asked him squarely.

His answer was a laugh that built until he almost choked. I steadied his hand for another swallow of liquor. "No, no, she isn't. I'd hoped that she might be mine, but that wasn't to be either."

"You mean . . . Maude was free with her favors to you *and* Herman?"

"The only person she shut the bank on was poor ol' Jefferson. He married her, thinking he got the prize. He hasn't had a moment of happiness since Camilla was born."

"You're positive she's Jefferson's daughter?"

"I am."

"How can you be so sure?" I wasn't keen on accepting a drunk's perception of something so important.

"Herman had been in an accident when Maude became pregnant, so he was out of the running. I was in New York."

"But you wanted her to be yours?"

"It's impossible to imagine, I know, but there was once a time when Maude was a beautiful young woman, alive and filled with mischief and laughter. She was born poor and with a great ambition to be a lady. It was that ambition that drove her to become what she is today."

"A bitter old peahen."

"You could have said a lot worse. When Maude realized Jefferson would never rise to the social heights she wanted, it twisted her. She'd trapped herself, but she blamed everyone, especially that little girl. Herman and I both tried to make it up to Camilla with little treats and pleasures that we could sneak past Maude. She seemed to begrudge that child a single moment of joy."

"I have to get to the bottom of what's happening to her at Roswell House. Camilla is in real danger, and you know Maude will do whatever it takes to control behavior that she doesn't approve of. She will eradicate Camilla's personality, if that's what it takes."

"You can't let this happen."

At last I had Bernard's complete attention. The blurry haze of alcohol he'd hidden behind was gone, burned away by my hard words.

"Then help me."

"How? What can I do?"

"What is Camilla's connection to Roswell House? If she isn't Herman Roswell's daughter, how is she tied to that house?"

His shoulders slumped. "It was all so long ago. Maude wanted that house. She always told me that she deserved to live there. When I was seeing her, we'd go there sometimes, in the woods where she could see the house when we made love. I thought I was getting something over on Herman, because we both wanted her. Now I know there was something else, some sickness in Maude. That's all I know. She said more than once that she should have lived there and that she'd been cheated out of it."

"Was she a Roswell? A bastard child?"

"I can't see how. Herman swore Camilla wasn't his. He was adamant that he'd never have children. If Camilla had been a Roswell, Maude would have seen that Herman provided for her. Maude was a Cooner, through and through, from the other side of the tracks. Her mother, Maybel Cooner, was a small-time grifter. The story I heard on Maude was that her mother attached herself to the powerful men in Montgomery. She had a yen for law officers, elected officials, wealthy businessmen. When the legislature was in session, she liked to party with the lawmakers. Stories around town were that Maude was the bastard daughter of a governor. If that was true, Maybel couldn't make the paternity stick or was afraid to try. Floozies who tried that trick sometimes died in mysterious ways. Anyway, all that rumor did was feed into Maude's sense of being cheated."

"So Maude could be a Roswell."

"Anything's possible, I guess, but I wouldn't lay money on it. I never heard of Maybel canoodling with any of the Roswells. I think trying to tie Camilla to the Roswell bloodline is barking up the wrong tree."

"Tell me about the Roswell curse. Who put it on the family and why?"

He finished his drink. "I need another bottle."

"I'll drive you to get one if you'll tell me." I felt like a heel bargaining with someone so desperate. "Do you know a place to buy whiskey?"

"I do. And I have the money, just not a car."

"Come on. You can tell me about the curse when we get the liquor."

CHAPTER THIRTY-THREE

Pulling up in front of the bootlegger's house, I had one thought: Uncle Brett would be very upset with me. Not because of the booze, but because the place looked like it might be inhabited by dangerous hillbillies. Some people, especially those making 'shine or involved in other illegal activities, didn't take kindly to a stranger driving up in their front yard. I'd had enough of a scare last night. I was wary of what might happen here on this isolated farm that showed only neglect.

Bernard told me to wait in the car, and I was glad to do so, especially when a mama sow and her shoats came around the corner of the house with a squeal of rage at Bernard.

He ran up the rickety steps to the porch with more speed than I thought he was capable of. He spoke to someone at the door. A few minutes later, a woman appeared with a jug of what I took to be moonshine. Money was exchanged, and Bernard came back to the car, one eye on the sow.

The woman in the doorway watched us. She would have been pretty had she not looked so tired and sad. Once Bernard was in the car, we drove away. He started to uncork the jug, but I put out a hand to stop him. "Tell me. You promised."

He cradled the jug in his arms. "Wick Roswell was a bad man. That's what I know. He married a fine young beauty, Priscilla Harlow, but she didn't live long. Died in her late thirties. She was from a respected family and gave Wick the social standing he craved. He built Roswell House, the finest house in the area at the time, but he was a ruthless man, and no one stood in the way of what he wanted."

"I know all this. How did the curse come to be?"

"Herman told me that Wick drove away the owners of the land where Roswell House sits. There were a lot of shenanigans involved in that property, starting out with old Ramsey Roswell. There was talk way back, and Herman confirmed it, that the original owners didn't want to sell the land. Ramsey ran them off. But the high ground that allowed a view down Tonka Creek was the piece of land Wick set his sights on. Problem was the Peebles lived there, a homesteader family. Peebles was a hardworking farmer with ambitions to use Tonka Creek for his own endeavors."

"There's no record of what happened to the Peebles. What's the truth?" I braced for what I knew would be unpleasant.

"Wick made them an offer, and when they refused it, he made it clear he'd have the land one way or the next. He warned them. About a week later, the eldest daughter was abducted and raped. She identified Wick as the man who hurt her. The Peebles made a report, but no action was taken."

"Why not? If the girl could positively identify him."

"Wick had the sheriff over a barrel, is what Herman said. Everybody has weaknesses, and Wick had a network of fancy women headed up by Nina Campbell, a woman as hard or harder than Wick. Those whores could dig a secret out of a man, and then he belonged to Wick."

"Blackmail."

"Wick called it persuasion." Bernard uncorked the jug and took a swallow. He gasped and his eyes watered, but he sighed. "That's better."

"So what happened to the Peebles?"

"When Mr. Peebles proved he was determined to hang on to that land despite Wick's threats, his twin daughters were murdered in a most brutal way. Their heads were almost severed from their bodies."

"Dammit, Bernard, you should have told me this." At least now I knew who the girls were. And how they'd died so brutally. Wick Roswell had committed acts so vile that they remained at Roswell House— not alive but not truly dead. The past hung over Roswell House like a shroud, and, somehow, Camilla was enmeshed in it.

"I should have. My memory comes and goes. When I'm drinking hard, the past is a jumble and the present doesn't exist. I don't put things together like I should. I hadn't thought about this for years until you stopped by with Zelda." His hand caressed the jug he held in his lap. "Herman was my friend. He suffered for the things his family had done. He could have married Maude when she was younger, but he said he couldn't risk having a child, carrying on the Roswell curse. I thought he'd begun losing his mind when he talked about the curse and the dead walking at Roswell House."

I did understand, but his failure to tell the truth may have put Camilla at greater risk. I had less time to prepare, and I knew that my intention to encounter the angry spirits at Roswell House depended on being ready to handle whatever they showed me. Still, I couldn't add more guilt to a man who'd buried himself in it.

"What happened to the rest of the homesteader family? Did Wick kill all of them?" I was thinking of the figure of the grown woman. Perhaps it was the mother.

"Peebles packed up what was left of his family and moved. No one knew where."

"You're positive Wick didn't kill them all."

"Herman said they left. Gone overnight."

"But there wasn't any record in the deed transfers."

"Are you really surprised by this? You're a smart young woman. What gets recorded is often what those in power want recorded."

Bernard was a cynic, but he had also worked the courthouse system as a lawyer. He knew how things worked in Montgomery, and probably everywhere else. "Did Wick kill those twin girls? I have to know the truth."

"I don't know." He took another nip from the bottle. "I never knew Wick, but I heard stories. He and Nina Campbell were the George 'Dutch' Andersons of Alabama. Folks were terrified of them because they did whatever was necessary. There was a brutality to them, an enjoyment of watching others suffer."

"They would murder children?" The Great War had awakened me to the atrocities man was capable of inflicting on man. But children? Young girls who'd barely begun to live, used as bargaining chips for a land deal? If that were true, Wick Roswell was a monster.

"They were capable of it. Did they do it? I can't say."

"This is the basis of the curse?"

"When Peebles left, he took nothing but his gun, his remaining children, and their clothes. He left furniture and everything else. Except for a note on the kitchen table, held in place by the butcher knife the killer had used to slice his children's throats."

"What did it say?"

"It's just family legend now, but Herman worried about it. He said the note promised that Wick's punishment would come when he least expected. That God knew his sins. Something to that effect. Wick burned the note, laughing as he did so. Herman always thought there might have been more to the note—a true curse, if you believe in that kind of thing."

"If Camilla isn't a Roswell, why is she suffering this way?"

"I don't know," Bernard said. He put the cork in the jug. "But I *will* help you find out. This time I promise. I can't come off the hooch all at once, but I can wean myself back. I've been working at it, and things are clearer. I remember more."

"What can you do to help?"

"There are some old papers left in a safe-deposit box. Herman gave me a key long ago. I pay rent on the box. It's in David's bank, so he could open it for us. We might find some answers there." He touched my shoulder so I would look at him. "I want to be there. I want to help Camilla overcome this. I should have stood up to Maude when I saw her crushing the girl, doing her best to break her sweet spirit, and I didn't. Let me help her now."

"Can you do it? Will you stay sober long enough to really help? We don't have time for you to fail." I didn't want to be cruel, but he'd said once before that he wanted to help and he'd only given me partial truths. Had he been capable of honesty with me then, I would be closer to finding the facts I needed.

"I can. For Camilla. For the life she should have had."

"Why don't you put that jug on the porch, and I'll drive you to the bank." I put a hand on his back, all too aware of the knobs of his spine. Bernard needed to gain a good fifty pounds. Maybe if he could truly pull back on his drinking, he could regain his life.

He got out of the car and put the moonshine on the porch. When he returned, he didn't look back. "Take me to the bank. I'll find out what's there. It may or may not help."

"I have to find my partner, too. I'm hoping he's with David."

We set off into the rapidly heating morning. Clouds amassing on the eastern horizon offered the promise of a cooling storm. The idea of Roswell House during a lightning storm didn't appeal to me. The energy there already crackled. I could only hope the storm would pass before we began the séance, and that I'd gathered all the information I needed to enter Roswell House armed.

When we arrived at the bank, David was more than surprised to see Bernard with me. I returned David's keys and asked him to help

Bernard with the safe-deposit box. Though I wanted to wait, I had pressing business. "Where did Reginald go? Is he at the Greystone Hotel waiting for me?"

David shook his head. "I haven't seen him. I thought you two were together."

"He said he had an errand." The sensation of dread I'd felt as Reginald drove away from David's town house hit me hard again. Where could he have gone? I didn't like the path my thoughts took. "Do you think he went to Roswell House?"

David replied, "He didn't ask for a key, and I've sent all the workmen away, so you could do whatever you needed. Shall I drive there with you?"

"No, help Bernard, please, but I will take a key to the house." David took it out of his pocket and put it in my hand. "Any word on our escape from Bryce?"

"I haven't heard anything, but—" He nodded toward the front of the bank, shock spreading over his features. "That's Jefferson Granger."

"He looks upset."

"I suspect he's going to share that feeling with me and the entire bank. You'd better take a runner out the office door. Best he doesn't see us together."

I hurried over to Bernard. "David will help you. When you're finished, go to the Greystone Hotel. Zelda has a tab, so if you need coffee or something to eat, order it. I'll be back for you as soon as I can."

There wasn't time for discussion. I hurried through the door David had indicated and stopped when I was out of view.

"Where is my daughter?" Jefferson Granger roared. He strode toward David. "What have you done? Maude is apoplectic. You've defied her and convinced Camilla to do the same. She won't have it. Maude will see you behind bars if you're involved in Camilla's disappearance. The hospital is frantic, and Dr. Perkins has called in the state authorities on this."

"I don't have a clue what you're talking about," David said calmly. "Now lower your voice and tell me what's wrong, or you'll be the one behind bars."

Thank goodness David kept his wits about him. He wouldn't give anything away no matter what Jefferson said.

As David ushered the red-faced Jefferson into his private office, I stepped out into a muddy parking lot. The heat made my head ache, but it was my fear that drove me. If Reginald had gone to Roswell House alone, he might be in trouble. There was something in that house. Something powerful and vindictive. And it meant to have its way.

CHAPTER THIRTY-FOUR

Before I went to Roswell, I stopped by David's town house to see if Reginald had returned. I also needed to let Zelda and company know that the Grangers had taken action, and that the state police were on the lookout for Camilla. Zelda and Tallulah had to be careful if anyone showed up at the door.

I was glad to see that Tallulah had moved her car away from the front of the house. I parked around the block and down an alley behind some houses and went on foot, the sidewalk heating up the leather soles of my shoes.

The intense heat shimmered off the brick road in waves that distorted the vista. I'd just turned the corner when a fancy teal-colored car stopped in front of the house. I stepped behind a thick shrub, my instincts kicking in before my brain. I sighed with relief when Jason Kuddle ran up the steps to the house. Still, I had to wonder why he was there. And what was the matter?

Kuddle knocked loudly and called out for Zelda. I came out of hiding and went to see him. "Mr. Kuddle, do you have news about Joanne Pence?" I stepped on the porch out of the glare of the sun.

"I do. Where's Mrs. Fitzgerald?"

"She's not available." I smiled. "I'll relay the information. I'm sure you know we're working together."

"Yes, I'm aware." He looked around. "Is she not here? Her mother said I'd find her at Mr. Simpson's address."

No matter that Kuddle was Zelda's employee; we could not risk anyone knowing Camilla was inside. "Zelda was here earlier, but she had business to attend to. And her presence here is strictly confidential. I'll be happy to relay any messages to her. What have you found about the missing young woman?"

"Joanne Pence isn't missing at all. I was misinformed that she'd left with relatives. She's still at Bryce." He gave me a knowing look. "But, strangely, Camilla Granger is gone."

News had traveled fast. "Camilla? Missing?" I reached deep for any shred of acting skill I might have. "How is that possible?"

"That's what everyone is asking about." He leaned against a post. "Folks are worried about her."

"Seems like the hospital misplaces a lot of patients. And they're all pretty young women. How did you hear about this? No one has informed me or Zelda."

"I'd left my card with one of the girls in the business office at Bryce. After I took her to lunch. She called me this morning to let me know what was happening."

"Well played, Mr. Kuddle."

Kuddle nodded. "The Pence girl was missing, but they found her hiding out in one of the outbuildings. Something had spooked her bad, but she's back in the ward and sedated, so she's safe. I have to agree, though, it's looking bad for the hospital. Folks take their loved ones there for treatment and care, and the hospital can't keep up with them. A girl like Pence doesn't have a family to raise a ruckus, but Camilla Granger is a different matter. Her mother is like a sledgehammer. The administration's very upset and has called the state police. This is considered an abduction, and whoever helped her escape is going to jail for kidnapping and a long list of other crimes."

"I would certainly hope so." Amazingly, I was calm enough to play my role. "Who would abduct a mentally ill young woman? And for what purpose?"

Kuddle leaned closer. "As an investigator, I'd have to finger her fiancé as my primary suspect, which is one reason I wanted to check his house if you'd let me in. He was up there at the hospital visiting her yesterday. Had some kind of paperwork saying he was in charge of Camilla. The hospital didn't buy it." A grin played across his face. "He got overly excited and demanded that she be released to him. Said he wouldn't allow her to have the necessary treatment to make her better. Makes him look mighty suspicious."

"I can see that. I know Mr. Simpson was concerned about the course of treatment proposed for Camilla." I frowned. "David is at the bank. Maybe you should talk to him."

"Oh, I will. But if you're going inside, maybe I could take a look around?"

"I thought you were hired to find Joanne Pence."

"That case is closed. But I'm willing to bet the Grangers will pay a nice finder's fee if I can figure out where their daughter is. Being a private investigator is always a hustle. Cases don't always walk in the door. Sometimes you have to seize an opportunity."

I smiled. "I'm sure Zelda will be very concerned over her missing friend, and just so you know, Mr. Fitzgerald's novel is a smashing success. He's said to be quite wealthy. If you hear anything about Camilla, I would bring the information to Zelda first. Better pay."

"A good point, Mrs. James. Thank you for the tip."

"One more thing: did you actually see Joanne Pence at Bryce?"

He looked at me, his gaze assessing and the friendliness gone from his eyes. "Are you questioning my word?"

"Of course not, but I have to wonder if the hospital is being totally truthful about another missing young woman. I'm curious to know if the hospital *told* you she was there or if you *saw* her in the flesh."

"I catch what you're saying. You make another good point." The anger disappeared. "There's no need to worry. Joanne Pence is there, at the hospital. Tell Mrs. Fitzgerald that when you run into her. And tell her I'm looking to make a final report and get my pay."

"Ah . . . you were also investigating Pamela DuMond's disappearance. Yes?"

"Yeah," he paused, shading his eyes from the sun's glare with his hand. "Poor kid. Someone worked her over good before they finished her off."

"What about that other missing girl—Ritter Ames? Have you found a connection between them?"

"Those girls were from different counties, different kinds of families. I don't see any similarities except that one's dead and the other's missing and probably dead. The sheriff's deputies had a witness who saw the Ames girl talking with a man in a big car. That was the last seen of her."

"There are other girls missing. Young women in their teens from Marthasville. Could there be a connection there?"

He stepped out of the sun and into the shade, closer to me. "I wish I could find something, but the truth is, girls like that get sick of working dawn to dusk on farms or being pushed to marry the local yokel. They hear about this glamorous city life where girls dress pretty and go to parties. They want to be a flapper, like my employer. She's put a lot of big dreams in the heads of girls who might as well think they can fly. They think they want to be Zelda Fitzgerald, the woman on the cover of all the magazines. They think all they gotta do is dress up, and the world will be at their feet. Most of them either give up or get hurt. The world is a hard place, especially for a young woman who doesn't have a clue of the dangers out there waiting for her."

"So absolutely no clue as to who's abducting and killing these young women?"

"Problem is, these girls are missing from different areas. Law enforcement doesn't talk to one another. If there is a link, no one sees it."

"But you're a professional. You could see it."

"If there was anything to see, you're right—I could put it together. I'm just not finding a connection."

"I'll let Mrs. Fitzgerald know that the young woman she was concerned about is safe. I'm sure she'll be in touch about Camilla. That gives me grave concern. Thank you for letting us know, Mr. Kuddle."

"When you see Judge Sayre, please give him my regards."

"Of course."

He walked to his car, a man in charge of his world, and yet I'd outfoxed him by diversion. He'd left without insisting that I let him into David's house.

I slipped in the front door to find Zelda and Camilla huddled up at the curtains, peeping out.

"That man is a terrible investigator." Camilla was about to hyperventilate. "I searched everywhere for Joanne, and she wasn't in the outbuildings. I know all of her hiding places."

"He never did say he saw her," I admitted, ruing the fact that I hadn't pressed him on the exact wording. Reginald would have made him say it.

"If the hospital is lying to Mr. Kuddle, they'll lie to anyone," Zelda said.

"Where's Tallulah?"

"She went to buy Camilla some toiletries. She needs a toothbrush, clean clothes, those things. Tallulah has an eye for clothes. Whatever she picks out will be a perfect fit."

"Where's Reginald?" I had hoped he might be in the kitchen or somewhere nearby.

"Haven't seen him since this morning." Zelda was instantly alert. "Is something wrong?"

"No." I needed a word alone with her, but I didn't want to make it so obvious. "Camilla, would you see what groceries we might need to pick up?"

"Of course."

If she knew I was trying to get rid of her, she was gracious enough not to let on.

CHAPTER THIRTY-FIVE

"What's going on?" Zelda asked as I maneuvered her to a corner in the parlor.

"The state police have been called in to find Camilla. They're calling it a kidnapping."

"At least you didn't take her across state lines. You'd be in real trouble then." Zelda lit a cigarette and blew a perfect smoke ring.

"David, Reginald, and I could go to prison."

She realized I was genuinely worried. "I swear to you this will be okay. Camilla has agreed that she *wanted* to leave Bryce. No matter what the dragon does or says, Camilla was a voluntary commitment. Camilla's word will count more than Maude's."

But we both knew Camilla was still a minor. Maude was in charge of her.

"Let's focus on clearing Roswell House and setting the manacles on David. As in marriage, not getting arrested," Zelda added.

I nodded. "I'm going there now to look for Reginald." Even saying the words made my stomach jittery. The things I'd learned about the history of the house, of the people who'd built and created it, left me with a deep concern. "If you see him, please tell him we need to talk."

"You're really worried about your partner." Zelda stubbed out the cigarette in a beautiful leaded-glass ashtray.

"I am. What if the men who tried to stop us last night have him? I mean, he is driving your car. They might have recognized it."

"I hadn't considered that." She began to pace. "I can call around. Where could he have gone?"

"Try the sheriff's office. He might have stopped in there." I spun through possibilities in my mind. "Probate office. Dr. Abbott."

"I'll take care of all of that."

"When you finish on the phone, you might want to take Camilla somewhere else. If Jason Kuddle's already sniffing around here, looking to make a buck off finding her, others will be here, too."

"I'll take her to the county club. I know the kitchen workers, and they'll hide us. No one will look there."

It was a brilliant plan. Never in a million years would Maude think to look among the servants for her daughter. Zelda had plenty of marbles, and she shot a mean game. "Perfect. If I don't call you or come by, meet me at Roswell House at five. David will be free then, and if I can rouse the spirits, it will be easier after dark. Camilla has to want this. It could be dangerous."

"We'll be there. As soon as Tallulah gets back, we'll make an escape from here." Zelda was energized by the danger. I wished for a moment that I had a tenth of her courage.

"Be careful." I started toward the door, then called out. "I'll see you in a bit, Camilla."

"Yes." She came out of the kitchen. "Are you done talking about me, then?"

Zelda laughed out loud. "We were planning your wedding, which will take place as soon as Roswell House is emptied of the spooks and haints. Tallulah, Raissa, and I will be your maid and matrons of honor, and Reginald will give you away."

"I'm more than ready." Camilla displayed a calm that I envied. "Be careful, though. I know you're risking a lot for me."

"I'll take care. Now I'm off." If Reginald wasn't at Roswell House, I didn't know what I would do. I had the key, and he didn't have one. It didn't make sense he would be there, but I had to check, on the off chance he'd gone there for something.

I felt as if I was spinning my wheels, rushing from one location to another, missing the important things in my haste to dash somewhere else. I wondered what Bernard and David had uncovered in the safe-deposit box. David would have no way to find me, even if the secret warranted such action. I had his car.

My plan was to check at Roswell House, then return David's car. Then I would either wait at the bank, the Greystone Hotel, or have someone drive me to the Sayre house, which was very near the country club. I could walk from there.

As I drove toward Roswell House, my foot eased from the gas of its own volition. I was afraid. There was no point denying it, especially not to myself. The house scared me. I'd been afraid of the entities in Caoin House, especially the anger of one particular ghost. But I'd never been afraid of the house. Roswell was different. It was as if the foundation of the house had been soaked in darkness and held it, embraced it into its wooden bones.

I pulled into the front yard, amazed by how much more of the lawn had been cleared. I was very aware that I was alone. The workmen were nowhere about, sent away in preparation for tonight's efforts. If something bad happened, there would be no one to rescue me. There was no sign of Zelda's car, and I was tempted to merely turn around and leave. But I thought to open the front door and call to Reginald—just to be sure he hadn't hidden the car and gone inside to search for something.

None of us knew if we'd been revealed as Camilla's liberators, and we all needed to use precautions, so it wasn't unreasonable that Reginald might have left Zelda's car beneath a good cover. I pulled David's car to the back, behind a hedge, and got out.

The sun was so hot and bright that my eyes failed to register any color in the landscape. Tints of brown spread before me, the lush lawn now a dead zone. I'd stepped into a sepia-tone photograph.

Or else the house was playing tricks on me.

The minute I thought it, I wished I hadn't. An electric current of fear shot through me, and I had a sense that the house suddenly pulsed. Something alive but not human pumped through its timbers. And it knew I was on the premises.

I'd neglected my writing while working this case in Montgomery, but I couldn't stop my mind from turning to Margaret Oliphant's marvelously creepy story "The Open Door." Roswell House was silent, unlike the servants' quarters in her tale. But the common denominator was the child who suffered from "brain fever." There was a striking resemblance to Camilla's troubles. She, too, had been diagnosed with a malady of the brain. But she had no loving father to protect and champion her. Camilla's father was spineless. If Camilla were to be saved, she had only her friends to do it.

I walked among the plants and shrubs with their brown leaves, knowing my sight played tricks on me. Another tale came to me, one far older than the Victorian stories I loved. In "Sleeping Beauty," a wicked witch generated an enchanted forest of brambles and thorny bushes around a castle to prevent the prince from getting inside and reaching his princess. Something similarly wicked was at work in Roswell House.

How was it possible that David had come here repeatedly to check on workmen—and that the workmen had come every day—and no one had sensed anything sinister? The truth was, I hadn't picked up on anything at first. I'd walked through the rooms, but I hadn't suspected the power of the residing entity. I understood why now. The house had played with us. It had hidden what it truly contained, waiting.

I slipped around the side of the house, feeling as if it watched my every move. My eyes ached from the bright glare of the sun. When I got to the front steps, I paused to gather my courage. I would not go inside. I would open the door and call to Reginald.

A soft creaking came to me, and I looked up to see a lantern hanging from the ceiling spinning madly. Before I could react, it fell, missing me by inches. Glass shattered, and a shard flew into my bare calf. I cried out and stumbled back, finally catching myself before I fell off the porch. Blood ran down my leg into my shoe, the jagged glass still stuck in my muscle. I gritted my teeth and pulled it out.

The wound wasn't deadly, but it hurt, and it was only the first skirmish. There would be more to come. Whatever controlled Roswell House would fight us. I grasped the key and walked to the door. Before I could touch it, the door inched open, creaking as if the hinges hadn't been oiled in a decade. I called out to Reginald. "Are you in there?"

He didn't answer, and I worried that the house had lured him inside, maybe had him trapped. The house was sentient. I believed it now more than ever. It was aware of me, and it wanted something from me. "Reginald! If you're in there, come out right now."

The house sighed. I felt it, the rush of expelled air. A soft scuffling sound came to me from inside. My worst fears rose to the surface. Was my partner inside, injured?

"Reginald!" Fear made my voice shrill. "Answer me!"

Scuttling turned to pounding, and I could imagine that someone bumped against a wall in an effort to get my attention. I listened, the door half-open as the sun burned into me. The blood on my leg had dried, the pain subsiding to a dull throb, but it was a reminder of what could happen. I didn't want to go inside.

"If you're in there, let me know or I'm leaving."

The thudding grew more frantic. Someone was in there and heard me. Whoever it was understood that I was going away and was frantic to stop me from leaving. The workmen had been sent away. Since I knew it wasn't David, I strongly suspected it was Reginald. The house had opened to him—the front door hadn't even been closed—and he'd stepped inside. And something had ambushed him.

I could drive back to town and get help—or I could find Reginald and save him. There wasn't a choice. If my partner was in the house, I couldn't leave without him. I had to go inside.

My foot inched toward the threshold, unwilling to obey my brain's command to move forward.

"*No.*"

The word came from behind me. I spun to find the twins standing in the middle of the front lawn. Their dresses were clean, freshly laundered, and free of any trace of blood or death. They were pretty girls in their Sunday best; the blue and green of their dresses and the matching bows in their curly hair were the only colors in the brown landscape.

"Don't go inside." They spoke with one voice, a fact that sent a chill spinning through me.

"I have to. My friend is in there." I put my hand on the doorjamb to steady myself. "I can't leave him."

The knocking—from where?—became louder now, more frantic than ever. What sounded like a muffled "Help" came from somewhere in the house.

"Don't go inside." They were suddenly closer. "She's a tricky one, she is."

I didn't want to enter the house. My legs demanded that I run, and I held my ground by sheer will. I couldn't risk leaving Reginald behind, injured and in need of my assistance. "I have to search for him. He's my friend. Who are you afraid of?"

They were suddenly in the doorway, blocking me. "She's a dark mistress. Don't go inside." They were so identical, I couldn't see a single difference. They were within touching distance, and a bone-chilling cold came off them. My fingers ached, and my breath frosted.

"After I find Reginald, I'll try to help you."

Their eyes rolled up in their heads, revealing only the whites. "Go away." Jagged red lines appeared at their throats. They widened into horrible gashes, and blood poured out. "Go . . ." Blood bubbled at their throats as they spoke.

"I'm going to find out who hurt you. I'll find out, and I'll do what I can to put you to rest."

I stepped through them and went into the house. The temperature dropped at least ten degrees, and the house was flooded with colors. The pale peach of the plastered hallway and the beautiful shadings of gold-and-amber oak from the polished floor glowed in the sunlight that filtered through newly hung lace drapes. A lovely Turkish rug had been spread in the parlor, and furniture in rich maroon tapestry had been put in place. A heavy sideboard contained a Chinese vase and two sculptures. Brocade pillows were cast about a sofa and two wing chairs. The workmen had been busy.

"Girls?" I turned back, but they hadn't followed. They'd disappeared. The thumping had stopped, and the house was eerily quiet.

"Reginald?" I sounded like a young girl. "Reginald! If you're in here, say or do something." My voice was slightly better, more forceful.

Only silence answered me.

I stepped into the foyer and stopped between the two mirrors that provided endless reflections of me. The story was that one could see the past in one mirror and the future in the other. I knew better than to look, but I couldn't resist.

The mirror to my left gave me only my own reflection: a white-faced young woman in a slim gray skirt, blouse, and cloche hat. My red lipstick looked startling against my pale skin. Dark curls peeked out from beneath my hat, and to my relief, when I reached up to tuck them back under my hat, my image did the same. I'd half expected my reflection to take on a life of its own. When it behaved normally, a soft chuckle of relief escaped.

Nothing moved in the house. Not a sound or a sigh or a whisper. If someone had been pounding earlier, he now was quiet. The young girls had vanished without a trace or any attempt to harm me. I had to accept that Reginald wasn't in the house. No one was. I'd spooked myself and had nothing to show for it except a sweat-stained blouse. Zelda and Tallulah would laugh at me for being such a goose. I bolstered my courage with such silly thoughts.

Movement in my periphery made me turn to look in the mirror to my right, and I froze. It was my image that gazed back, but a thin red line sliced across my throat. Blood trickled out, and then began to flow more freely, running into the white of my blouse. The mirror image made a gagging sound, and I couldn't breathe. My windpipe had been severed by a sharp blade.

"We told you so." The girls stood, one on either side of me. They, too, bled from identical wounds in their necks. I tried to push away from the mirror, but I couldn't move. The mirror held me in place, forcing me to watch as my image fell to her knees, blood soaking the front of the white blouse.

Behind me a swarm of flies drew near. I heard their buzzing, the angry hum of hunger. They'd come to feast upon the blood and bodies . . . to do their master's bidding. Even in my worst fears, I'd underestimated the entity that occupied Roswell House. And I'd grievously overestimated my ability to reason with it, or her, because the flies buzzed behind me, again assuming the shape of a woman in a dress with the longer cuirass bodice fitted over a whalebone corset that gave her the perfect figure. Her hair was upswept. Her face had no features, only a blank where nose, eyes, and mouth should be.

I took a step back, and a cloud of flies peeled away from the female form and came at my mirror image, diving into the open wound. They swarmed the raw edges and the blood, and I swatted frantically, hysteria swelling in my chest. It was as if they wanted to push into the wound, to buzz inside my throat and body. Suddenly, as quickly as they'd attacked, they left.

The smell of death and decay rose from the female form, and when at last I could breathe again, I thought I might vomit. She reached out a hand toward me, and I was helpless to avoid her touch.

"Run!" The twins pushed at me, hard enough to knock me off balance so that I stumbled away from the mirrors and toward the front door. When I escaped the mirror image, I could finally move.

"Run!" They scampered past me into the sunshine, and I was hot on their heels. I knew now that Reginald had never been in the house. The noises were a trap, designed to lure me inside. The girls had warned me. She was indeed a tricky one. And strong.

I rushed into the sunshine, the world once again a vibrant green with a blue sky and dark-purple clouds building on the horizon. Whatever spell had enchanted me, I was free of it. And I had learned something of great value. When I went back inside the house in the evening, I would be prepared.

But first I had to find Reginald.

CHAPTER THIRTY-SIX

David wasn't at the bank when I returned, and neither was Bernard. David's secretary, a stiff young man with spectacles, said he'd left in a rush with the older man in tow. While I was desperate to talk to David and find Reginald, I was relieved that he hadn't been arrested.

"Did they leave with anyone else?" I asked.

"No, ma'am. The two of them opened one of the safe-deposit boxes in his office. Ten minutes later, they left. Is something wrong? Mr. Simpson seemed upset."

"I can't say, but I have to find them. Did they mention where they were going?"

The neatly dressed young man cast a sidelong glance at me, and I knew he was wondering if I was one of those women who pursued eligible bachelors.

"I'm a friend of Camilla's."

He nodded a bit sheepishly. "Mr. Simpson didn't name his destination. He just seemed frantic, and about fifteen minutes ago, the sheriff was here asking for him. What's going on?"

"I'm not certain." And I wasn't about to say what I suspected. "Please tell David to check with Minnie Sayre as soon as he returns. And may I use the phone?"

I knew I had to be careful with what I said. The telephone switchboard was a place where secrets were too often shared, unbeknownst to the speaker. When the operator put me through to Minnie, I was as brief as I could be.

"If you speak with David or Reginald, please ask them to find me at the courthouse."

"Of course." Minnie was wise enough not to ask questions.

"Zelda and Tallulah are fine." I wanted to reassure her. "They're . . . planning a new production at the country club."

"I expect nothing less of those girls," Minnie said, playing along. She knew something was very wrong. I suspected Maude or Jefferson Granger had already paid her a call, hurling accusations about Zelda's involvement in Camilla's disappearance. Thank goodness Minnie could truthfully say that Zelda had been home all last night and couldn't possibly be involved. That worked to our advantage.

But where was Reginald? Now I was fearing the worst.

I left the keys to David's car with his assistant, and I walked to the courthouse. The heat was like a bludgeon, forcing me to seek any shade as I made my way the few short blocks to the courthouse. The Greystone Hotel was nearby, close enough that I could check there next. Zelda was also looking for Reginald, and perhaps she'd had more luck.

The sheriff's office was easy to find. I heard loud male voices and a chorus of laughter. It stopped instantly when I walked into the open doorway. Men in uniform disbanded and went to desks and work. A dreaded woman had invaded the inner sanctum of the male law officer.

"May I help you?" a uniformed man asked politely.

"Have you seen my friend Reginald Proctor?"

He nodded. "He was here a few hours ago. What a character." He grinned. "He sure can tell a story."

"He can indeed. Did he say what he wanted?"

"He was going on about some missing girls. Said they were somehow connected to the state mental hospital. That was news to us, and he didn't have any proof. We've had some girls go missing, but none of them had ever been sent to the crazy house." The amusement was gone from the man's face, though he still smiled.

Reginald was playing with fire. "He gets some wild ideas." I forced a chuckle. "Did he mention where he might be going?"

"Didn't say specifically. But he met up with a friend here, that private investigator Jason Kuddle. Used to be a top-notch copper before he got tied up with that doxy and went to work as a gumshoe. Kuddle was talking his ear off when they left. Looked like they were long-lost friends. Glad to see the backside of Kuddle, in here acting like he was the only one could find a missing girl. Lording it over us all that he makes his own time and does what he pleases."

"What's a doxy? Is that another word for a flapper?" Kuddle looked like the kind of man who'd have a flapper in every little town.

"Fancy woman." The deputy had the grace to be a little embarrassed. "Flapper had nothing to do with what his girlfriend was selling. More like the oldest profession in the world. And Jason was buying it on the clock. That's what got him fired."

"I see." My immediate reaction was to back away from a clearly improper topic. All the men watched to see if I would be offended, a delicate flower of the South who couldn't hear plain talk. Little did they know my real ambitions in life. "Does that woman have a name and a place I can find her?"

The officer laughed out loud, drawing looks from the others in the room. "Her name's Martha. And her place of employment is not any place you want to be seen. You'll ruin your reputation, and your daddy would be mad at me for sending you there."

"My daddy is dead, and so is my husband. War hero, if you want to know. Now I need to talk with Martha. I'll worry about my own reputation." I said it all softly, and while I clearly hadn't won any friends, I seemed to have gained a tiny measure of respect.

"Go to Big Buster's Bar. She works out of there. They won't let you in the door, but maybe she'll come out." He stepped back from the counter.

"Thank you. I appreciate your help."

"Hey, your friend dropped his car key." He reached below the counter and brought out the key to Zelda's car. "Give it to him for me?"

"Ab-so-lute-ly." I did my best to sound truly modern.

I found the car parked in the shade two blocks from the courthouse. The mud had been washed away, and, from what I could tell, there was no damage. But where was Reginald? I'd passed a diner, and I went back and ordered a sandwich and cup of coffee. It was past midday, and I had to eat or risk collapsing. I also thought a waitress might be more forthcoming with information than anyone else I could ask.

When the young woman put my food in front of me at the counter, I asked for directions to Big Buster's Bar.

"Not a place you should go," she said, busy setting flatware and napkins in front of me.

"I need to talk with someone. It's important."

She gave me the directions to the bar that specialized in women rented by the hour, gambling, and illegal rum. "They'll cut your throat as soon as look at you. The law don't mess with them because they're so vicious."

I'd wondered that a deputy knew about a local prostitution business and did nothing about it. But liquor was illegal, too, and no one lifted a finger. I was quickly learning that the activities wealthy men indulged in, illegal or not, were frequently overlooked by the law. "Thanks." I paid the check and left, the sandwich sitting like a lump in my stomach, much like my concern for my missing partner.

I found the tavern easily enough, and was stopped at the door and refused entrance. When I asked for Martha by name, the burly doorman said he would send her out. After ten minutes of broiling in the sun, the door opened, and I was ushered into a room so dark I stumbled into a chair.

"Over there." The stout man pointed toward a table in a corner, where a pretty woman wearing too much makeup waited.

She was in her forties, and she'd gone to great care to hide that fact. I'd expected her to wear a nightgown or some pretty lingerie, but she wore a plain skirt and blouse. I didn't have time for the niceties, so I jumped in. "I hear you're friends with Jason Kuddle. I need to find him."

"Jason can't be found unless he wants to be found." She wasn't contrary, just amused.

"He was with my friend, a tall, dark, good-looking man with a mustache, gray suit. They stopped by here." I made it a fact.

"Snappy dresser. Yeah, they came by here but left. That was hours ago. Said they had a lead on one of those missing girls. They were in a big hurry, headed across the river."

This was at least progress. "Was her name Ritter Ames?"

"Yeah, that's the name. That girl must have a hooch of gold, all her gentleman callers looking for her. What do you want with a missing girl?"

"Her mother wants her to come home. If I can find her, I hope to convince her to return to the farm. Thanks for your help. I need to move along."

"Everybody's in a rush these days. Flying around in cars, using telephones. Nothing gets finished any faster; folks just stay busier."

I felt the same way, but I had other fish to fry. "Did they say where Ritter Ames lives?"

"Somewhere on the road to Prattville. Lucky the weather's good, or crossing that river's a problem. The state's building a bridge, but it's not done. Gotta take the ferry."

"Can you remember anything more, a specific address?"

"Honey, you got it bad for one of those men. I'd say the cake-eater. He's a purdy thing, all right."

"Reginald is my friend. And my partner in a business. It's not about romance."

The humor left her face. "You got a business. A woman with a business other than selling her jelly roll." She studied me for a long moment. "Okay, let me think back to what was said."

The bartender brought us two neat shots of whiskey, and though I didn't particularly want to drink, I knocked mine back. I managed not to cough, but my eyes watered.

"You're a sport, aren't you?" She swallowed the alcohol without even flinching. "Apparently it's about a mile past the river, a dirt road called Canner's Fork on the left. Maybe another mile more, and a farm on the right. That's what Jason was saying anyway. But then again, he said they'd be back by now. Men. Never on time. Of course, the ferry might be out of commission, too. If they veer off course, they can run aground in the shallows, and no telling how long it would take to get them towed back in the channel."

"Thank you, Martha."

"No thanks necessary. Watch your back. Someone's killing young women. Just 'cause you own a business doesn't mean they won't hurt you." Her gaze was unfathomable as she knocked back another shot of whiskey.

Her point was well taken.

———◇———

The ferry crossing was almost more than I could complete. Driving Zelda's car onto the barge terrified me. Driving off the barge was easier, and I had recovered my nerve by the time I got to the farmhouse where I hoped the Ames family lived. I idled toward the homestead, taking in the details, trying to do what Reginald did so well. He could read a scene or a person effortlessly. I hoped I would soon be able to ask him face-to-face what he'd ascertained here.

The farmhouse was pleasant, freshly painted, set among rows of cotton that would soon be ready to harvest. When the bolls popped open, the long rows would be filled with workers, mostly black, stooped over, picking the cotton and stuffing it into the long canvas sacks that stretched behind each picker. It was hot, backbreaking work.

I parked in the shade of an elm and was met at the door by a pretty woman with deep-red hair. She'd obviously been crying.

"Mrs. Ames, I'm Raissa James. I'm helping with the search for your daughter."

She burst into tears and pulled up her apron to hide her face.

I felt tears start in my own eyes, but I kept my composure. "May I make you some coffee?" If I could invite myself inside and get busy, she might be more willing to talk.

She pushed the screen open, and I stepped into a front parlor lovingly maintained. Paintings of sun-burnished landscapes hung on the walls, along with treasured china plates. The smell of something baking came from the kitchen, a pound cake if my nose was accurate. I wasn't the best person in a kitchen, but the stove was stoked, and I put a kettle on for the coffee. Even I could work a coffeepot.

Mrs. Ames took a chair, elbows on the kitchen table, and hid her face in her hands. Tears leaked through her fingers onto the wood. I didn't know how Jason Kuddle did this kind of work every day—finding lost children, hunting for runaways, sitting with the victims of dastardly crimes.

"I know two men have been here today asking many of the same questions I need to ask. I apologize for putting you through this twice."

She looked up slowly. "No one has been here. Not since the police left two days ago when my daughter disappeared. John, my husband, has gone to town to see if there's been news. He doesn't think the law is trying very hard to find our girl. Other young women have gone missing, and nothing has been done. One was found dead." She fought to maintain control. "No one cares because we don't have money, but the law's supposed to protect everyone. Even the poor."

"Yes, ma'am." This had to be wrong. Martha had given me perfect directions to this farm, the Ames farm. This was the Ames farm, and this woman's daughter was missing. Yet she hadn't talked with Kuddle and Reginald.

"My associates would have been by maybe three hours earlier?"

"No one has been here."

The directions Martha had given me were dead accurate. She wouldn't know this unless Jason Kuddle had told her.

I tried once more. "Could you have missed them somehow?"

"I haven't left the house except to gather eggs in the chicken coop. I would have heard a vehicle."

I poured the hot water and brewed the coffee, puzzling over this strange turn of events. Kuddle and Reginald wouldn't have come all this way to embrace defeat.

"Can you tell me a little about your daughter?" I found a small pitcher of fresh cream in an icebox on the back porch and put it on the table. The wonders of electricity hadn't yet found their way to this farm. The sugar bowl was already in place.

"Ritter has a fanciful imagination. She liked to play in the shade of the mimosa grove right down the road. There aren't any other children around here, but she entertained herself."

"She's fifteen, right?"

"Yes, but still such a child. I think that comes from so much time alone, without brothers and sisters. John and I tried for more children, but we weren't blessed that way."

Even innocent fifteen-year-old girls knew about flappers and the dawning of the modern era. "She attends school?" Schoolgirls swapped tales of big-city wonders and delights. They fed the fever in one another. A mother might see innocence because that was what she wanted to see.

"She loves school, and she's a wonderful student. The teachers tell her she should be a teacher. That's what she wants."

"Did she ask to go to town? Maybe to visit with her school friends?"

Mrs. Ames considered the question as she stirred sugar and cream into the coffee I placed before her. "She didn't seem to care much about town. She was happy here, with me. That will change, I know, as she gets older and wants more of her own life. She'll want to be with young people. Young men. It's the natural way of life. But she wasn't interested. Not yet."

"Did she mention anyone strange or unusual around the farm?" I kept busy at the stove and sink. Mrs. Ames seemed to find it easier to talk when I wasn't staring at her.

"A few days ago a man in a fancy car came by and asked her questions. I told her not to talk to him, to run home if she saw him again. She promised she would, and my daughter never went back on her word, so I didn't worry." She started to cry. "I should have worried. I should have sent John to kill that devil. I know in my heart that's who took her."

"When did she see this man in a fancy car?"

"The morning she disappeared. She told me about him when she came back in for some breakfast. She ate and said she was going back out to play at her cousin's house down the road. She never came home." Mrs. Ames began to cry. "She's my baby."

I tried to bring her back, help her focus. "This is very important, ma'am. Did she describe the car?"

"She said it was fancy and a pretty green."

I reached across the table and patted her arm. "You've been very helpful. These details are so important. This is how we'll find the person who took your daughter. Is there anything else?"

My encouraging words seemed to help. Mrs. Ames wiped her face and looked at me, her eyes widening. I was a fright, I knew. I'd been up all night and most of the day, running on nerves. I hadn't had a chance to clean up or change clothes, but her reaction made me step back. "What is it?"

She pointed at my chest. "That pin. Where did you get it?"

I'd forgotten the pretty hat pin I'd found in the chair at Bryce. My fingers went to it instinctively, and I pulled it out of the placket.

She took it and examined it closely. "This was my mother's, a gift to her from the governor's wife. My mother was a cook in the Louisiana governor's mansion when she was young, before she married. She gave the pin to me, and I gave it to Ritter on her fifteenth birthday, so she would know she owned one beautiful thing, and that one day she'd have clothes and hats to wear it with."

I closed her fingers over the pin, absorbing the full implication of what this meant. "I'm glad I could return this." Ritter Ames had been at Bryce Hospital. Or else the person who abducted her had been there. I wanted to believe it was the young woman, and that she'd left the pin deliberately, a clue for someone to find her.

"Where did you get it?" Mrs. Ames asked again. She grasped my hand and held on.

What I said next would affect Mrs. Ames for the rest of her life, but I couldn't lie. Not to a mother. "At Bryce Hospital. I found it there."

"The mental hospital?" Fear followed her confusion. "How?"

"I don't know, but I promise you I'll hunt for your daughter."

The connection I'd long sought between the missing girls and the hospital was undeniably clear. Someone at Bryce was involved in these abductions. Were these young women, taken from rural places and people who couldn't afford to fight back, being used as experiments, then turned into prostitutes? There was no doubt that the dead girls who'd visited me were dressed to look provocative and alluring. Pamela DuMond had been assaulted and murdered and left dead, dressed like a flapper. Had her brain been damaged so she couldn't defend herself?

I thought of the poor drowned girl Cheryl, who was such a mental child that she believed in a magical kingdom under the water. What had driven her to the river? And had she truly drowned accidentally, or was she murdered because of what had been done to her?

"Do you have a telephone?" I asked. I had to get in touch with Zelda and Judge Sayre. If Ritter Ames and Joanne Pence were still at Bryce, still alive and undamaged, they had to be found immediately. Before Dr. Perkins could operate on them.

"No. The lines aren't up all the way out here. Not electric or telephone."

"I have to go."

"Tell me what you know." She clutched my hand. "Please."

"I promise you I'll do whatever I can to find your daughter. Do you have a photograph?"

She went to the mantel and picked up a framed picture. "It's the only one I have." She held the photograph of a smiling young woman with kind eyes and a generous smile.

I hated to take it, but it would be useful. "I'll return it."

She gave it to me, crying silently.

"I'll come back as soon as I know something."

"She's our only child. She's a good girl."

I'd come here hoping to learn when and how Ritter Ames had disappeared, but that didn't matter now. The only thing that mattered was finding her before she disappeared forever and became another one of the lost girls.

Grasping the photograph, I hurried to the car and headed back the way I'd come. The ferry crossing was as fearsome as it had been before, but I had another, larger fear pushing me back to Montgomery.

CHAPTER THIRTY-SEVEN

"Father called the Tuscaloosa sheriff's office." Zelda stubbed out her cigarette. "They're sending a dozen deputies to the mental hospital. If that girl's at Bryce, they'll find her. Nothing bad will happen to her."

I wasn't so sure about that, but the fact Judge Sayre was eyeing the circumstances around Ritter Ames's disappearance might be the one thing that offered her a bit of safety. Her abductors might be afraid to harm her. Kidnapping was one charge. Kidnapping plus murder was the death penalty. Ritter Ames might survive this, unless she knew too much.

Zelda, Camilla, and I sat in a back room of the kitchen of the Montgomery golf and country club. The world where the servants worked was far, far away from the starched-white tablecloths, glittering crystal, and airy dining room of the club, where ladies lunched while their husbands golfed. In the small, airless back room of the kitchen, I, at last, felt safe.

Tallulah had been called to Huntsville for a family emergency. She was still an enigma to me. She'd moved to New York at the age of sixteen, a wild girl who made no secret of her sexual escapades and excessive drinking, but she had strong bonds with her grandparents, who'd raised her following her mother's death. The red Alabama clay held her feet, despite her success on the London stage. She'd almost refused to go to Huntsville, but Zelda had convinced her that we could handle events in Montgomery.

"I know you're worried." Zelda lit another cigarette. When she was upset, she smoked almost as much as Tallulah.

"No one has seen Reginald or Kuddle since they were at Buster's Bar." My partner had vanished into thin air, along with the private investigator. Kuddle was a man I now viewed as potentially dangerous. A gumshoe who owned a fancy teal car, a color some would describe as green. They'd left for the Ames farm and never arrived, and I'd found no trace of their trip when I'd asked the ferrymen. Either Martha had lied to me—played me like a fine fiddle—or Kuddle had lied to Martha.

An elderly Negro brought a glass of iced tea and put it down in front of me. "Thank you," I whispered. Just as Zelda had predicted, the servants at the country club had united to hide Camilla. They adored Zelda and would do anything they could to help her.

"Law officers in five counties are looking for Kuddle and Reginald. That car is easy to spot. Father also hired a passel of off-duty deputies to search. They were headed back to the Ames farm and to talk with the ferry operators. I hate to say it, but the ferrymen might tell the lawmen things they wouldn't tell you."

She was right. My gender could be a drawback at times, an asset at others. Even if the lawmen found a lead, miles and miles of dirt roads snaked through deep Alabama woods. Plenty of creeks and rivers rushed toward the Alabama River. There were too many places to dump a body. Reginald might very well be dead, and we might never find his remains. I thought of the ghost girl stepping out of the woods on the drive to Bryce. Was her corpse buried somewhere near that spot? Was that what she was trying to tell me?

I had a sudden, almost overpowering urge to call Uncle Brett. But what could he do from hours away? I would only upset him and leave him helpless to take any action. I had to face this alone.

"What about tonight?" Zelda asked softly. Camilla was in the kitchen talking with Nan, one of the cooks, and helping her peel shrimp for a dinner, a fact that would have Maude Granger keeling over dead. Looking at Camilla, smiling as she worked, I saw the softness of a child in her features. She'd been through hard things but had managed to retain that innocence. She might be one of the lucky few who could stretch it through her entire life. I wanted that for her.

"Tonight we go forward." There was no other choice. We couldn't continue to hide Camilla, and she refused to marry David until she was free of the evil influence of Roswell House.

"And Reginald?"

I swallowed a sob. "He's smart. He'll stay alive, and Judge Sayre's agents will find him."

"Will you be able to handle whatever is in the house without him?" Zelda asked.

"I want you to find a priest. One who will help me if I get in trouble." I looked at her. "Just in case I need him." I wasn't sure that a priest could help, but it would be better to have a man of the cloth available than to need him and not be able to find him.

"What are we dealing with?" Zelda's eyes glittered with adrenaline. "You know, don't you?"

My last encounter with the entity had been enlightening—and terrifying. I hadn't had a chance to speak with anyone about what I'd experienced. "Not a ghost, but something from the other side. Something that has a great stake in Roswell House. It doesn't want to leave, and I think it's picked Camilla for its . . . host."

"Why Camilla?"

That was the question I hadn't answered. The most important question. And now time had run out. I either had to begin the séance or concede defeat without even trying. Camilla would be returned to Bryce and the brain surgery. We had to make an attempt, even if it was dangerous. Even if we failed.

"Camilla has a connection to that house. I don't know what it is, and we don't have time to search any longer. This thing, it's strong. If Reginald doesn't return . . ."

"We have David to help us."

I tried not to show my concern that Zelda and I couldn't stop a possessed Camilla from going after her fiancé. "He may be the target of this specter's anger. If that's true, he's in more danger than anyone. He bought Roswell House and is making changes. Maybe the renovations are what stirred this spirit up."

"Then I'll get Dr. Abbott to stand by, too. He'll help us."

I hoped she was right, but I didn't know if a man of science would willingly participate in a séance. "I'm going to speak with Madam Petalungro. I need her help, and she'll want to know about Reginald."

"You should go home and clean up. Use the phone there; then try to take a little nap."

"I need to return David's car."

"You keep it. He isn't at the bank. I don't know where he is, but I'll track him down and pick him up on the way to Roswell House. Do you need anything?"

"There's been no word from David either?"

"Not since this morning. But he couldn't be far. You have his car. I'm sure he'll turn up at the bank."

"He and Bernard found something, in a safe-deposit box." I couldn't help worrying.

"I'll find David and get the supplies. You make certain Roswell House is ready."

I made a list for her. Candles, holy water, religious texts—I had no idea what I might need. I'd never seen a ritual directed at an entity that might not be a ghost. My only experience came from the land of fiction, the stories of writers such as Doyle and Henry James.

Zelda took the list and gave me an impulsive hug. "I'll find David. And I'll bring a gun this evening. Just in case. Daddy has one in his bedside drawer."

"I'll meet you at Roswell in two hours." I wanted to argue against the firearm, but I didn't. The entity was powerful, and if it grabbed hold of any one of us, it might turn us to murder. The truth was I was petrified of what I was about to do. But I was more scared of doing nothing.

Sleep was out of the question, and though I was tempted to go straight to Minnie's house and phone Madam, I went to Bernard's instead. He was sitting on the front porch in the shade, a cup of coffee in his trembling hand. It appeared he was making an honest effort to slack off the hooch.

"Care for some coffee?" he asked.

"I'll get it." I walked inside and poured a cup without cream or sugar. I needed the jolt of black coffee. I went back outside and sat on the steps, where I could easily see Bernard. "Where's David?"

"He hired a car and sent me home. He said he had to find Martha."

"Martha the . . . prostitute?" I couldn't think of a nicer word.

"Yep. Had to do with the big secret in the safe-deposit box."

"What was the secret?" I forced my body not to fidget.

"Seems like Wick Roswell maybe didn't murder that homesteader family, after all."

His hand started to shake, and I reached for his coffee cup and steadied it. He had my attention. "Then who?"

"His girlfriend, Nina Campbell. According to the papers in the box, written by Wick himself, Nina hacked up those two girls and left word that the rest of the family would be butchered if the Peebles didn't leave the area. She said she'd live on the property with Wick, and no homesteaders were going to stop her. She threatened to kill the rest of the children, so the Peebles packed up and moved without leaving a trace of where they went."

"But Wick didn't marry Nina Campbell. He married a Harlow girl. Why would Nina Campbell kill for him if he was going to marry someone else?"

"Indeed, Wick did marry Priscilla in a huge ceremony in Roswell House. The work on the house had just been completed, and the wedding was the social event of the season."

"And what about Nina?"

"Up until the wedding, it seems Wick led Nina Campbell to believe she would be his wife and the mistress of the house."

"If she murdered for him . . ."

"Yes, well, she couldn't complain too loudly about being used and dumped, could she? Besides, she was from the wrong side of town. Everyone in Montgomery knew she was a violent whore. Even before Wick she had a reputation for cutting up the other girls . . . and some of their clients. Decent women crossed the street to avoid walking near her."

Nina was fine for Wick's bloody partner in crimes and sex, but when it came to marriage, he selected a fresh flower, a woman of good standing. Someone to bear his children and carry on the Roswell name. Old story. Nina didn't sound like the kind of woman to take being spurned without a fight. I had to wonder what she'd done to Wick to get even.

"This helps a lot, Bernard. Thank you. And you said David was seeking Martha, the woman at that bar."

"That's the one."

"Do you know why?"

"He didn't say, but he was troubled about something. He brought me home and took that jug of moonshine with him. I told him to. If it's here, I'll drink it."

"Is there someone who can sit with you?" I'd heard stories about people coming off booze. A doctor might be required.

"Lurleen from the bank said she'd stop by after work and bring me a plate of food. Put some meat on my bones." He sipped the coffee, his hand steadier. "There's still time for me to have a real life. I can put things back together, maybe practice civil law. David said he could use me at the bank."

I wanted that for him. In our brief encounters, Bernard's good heart had captured my affection. But I had to get moving. My partner was in grave danger, and David would hopefully soon be at Roswell House to help with the evening's activities. Now I had to speak to Madam Petalungro.

At the Sayre house, Althea let me in. Minnie was out; she'd gone to a meeting of women determined to expand educational opportunities in the county. Rural children were often left without schooling because the distance to travel to school was too far. I used the telephone in Judge Sayre's study. I kept the conversation short, and both Madam and I hung up more troubled than when the call began. She was worried about Reginald, and I was terrified that I wouldn't be able to control the events of the evening. But I had a plan, and it was all in or all out.

"Miss Raissa, you look like someone whupped you with a worry switch," Althea said. She set a plate with a chicken salad sandwich and a glass of sweet tea beside me. "I know you'll say you aren't hungry, but this will help."

I wasn't hungry. The sandwich I'd eaten for lunch seemed to still sit like a stone in my stomach. I ate anyway, and, remarkably, Althea was correct. I did feel better. The food and sweet, cold tea gave me the boost of energy I needed to force myself out the door and toward an encounter that literally made my lungs contract. And, as for Reginald, I knew I was helpless to find him. Judge Sayre had men, tracking dogs, and even federal officers in the search. There was nothing I could do to find my partner that wasn't being done by people far more experienced in such searches than I was.

I took a cool bath, dressed, and left the Sayre house before I had to explain why I looked like Count Dracula had drained the blood from my body. Zelda would have to make her own excuses, but I suspected that Minnie and the judge no longer attempted to keep up with her. She was ready to return to New York, and after tonight, she would be on the road at the first chance.

The sun was still unbearably hot as I drove to the isolated mansion. Turning down the drive beneath the trees, the air cooled. I wondered if it was the shade or something more sinister. I parked at the very edge of the front lawn, as far from the house as I could get. No one else had arrived, yet the front door stood open. The house taunted me.

Madam Petalungro had warned me that I was vulnerable to the entity and that it wanted to take possession of me. Camilla was the first choice, but, because of my sensitivity, I could also be manipulated. I could only hope Zelda showed up with a strong priest, Dr. Abbott, and a medical bag full of tranquilizers, should they be necessary. Though the heat and humidity made sweat run down my back, I waited in the car. I couldn't risk going inside alone. I knew better now.

I heard the sound of another car approaching, and I got out of the vehicle and stood in the shade of a sycamore tree. The white, barkless skin of the tree, peeling in places, reminded me of the dead skin of the drowned girl. I walked toward the car, which was being driven by Zelda. Camilla was in the passenger seat. I'd hoped some of the men would arrive first, but that hadn't turned out to be the case. We would wait outside.

I glanced at the house as I walked to greet the new arrivals, and I stopped. Someone stood at a third-floor window. The ballroom. The woman had an hourglass figure, carved by whalebone, no doubt. Her upswept hair crowned her head. She was tall, and if I was not mistaken, she held a long butcher knife.

CHAPTER THIRTY-EIGHT

"Raissa, is something wrong?" Zelda touched my shoulder, snapping me out of my trance. When I looked up again, the window was empty. Camilla had stepped away from us. She knelt at a flower bed, examining an exotic bloom that had been freed of overgrowth by the workmen.

"Did you find David?" I didn't want to tell her what I'd seen in the window.

"He's on his way with the priest and Dr. Abbott." She hesitated and got my full attention. "He was arrested and put in jail. That's where he's been."

I couldn't believe this. "For what?"

"Trespassing at the Granger home. After he took Bernard home, he went there to talk to Maude. It got very heated, and Maude actually had him arrested. She said he was threatening her and wouldn't leave. The world has gone crazy."

"Threatening her with what?" Had David found something in the safe-deposit box that might jeopardize Maude in some way?

"He said he'd tell us when he got here."

"Maude must know we took Camilla from Bryce."

"She suspects. Strongly. But David gave nothing away." Zelda's grin was impish. "Camilla is free of Maude now. She'll never forgive her mother for having David arrested, and I doubt David will forgive Maude either. Even if Camilla lives in Montgomery, Maude will no longer control her. This is the best thing that could have happened between them."

"Let's just hope that Maude's revenge isn't a surgical probe into Camilla's brain." I couldn't be happy the battle between mother and daughter was out in the open. Confrontation left little room for retreat, and the only thing I wanted was a safe and happy life for Camilla. She was not a modern girl like Zelda or Tallulah. I didn't believe she wanted to be forever estranged from her family.

"We won't let that happen. If this doesn't work, Camilla will leave with me in the morning for New York. We've agreed to it. If David loves her as he claims, he will marry her and move away from Alabama. His family owns banks in the city. They never have to come near Roswell House again."

That might be for the best. If the young couple packed up and left Roswell House right this minute, David could sell it. Or burn it. In a few months, Camilla would be eighteen. She would be married, and if she chose to visit family, she could come home on her own terms. The problem, as Camilla herself had pointed out, was that there was no guarantee whatever infected Roswell House would not follow her. That it hadn't happened yet was no guarantee that it couldn't. I'd read enough and learned enough from Madam to accept that spirits, entities, demons—call them what you will—were not bound by physical laws. Besides, there were other spirits imprisoned here. I couldn't abandon the twin girls who lived in terror. The malevolent thing that had attached to Camilla held sway over other spirits.

Another car pulled into the front yard, and David, a priest, and Dr. Abbott got out. The priest was transfixed by the house, as if he sensed the evil within. David introduced him as Father Gregory Montclair.

"Excuse me, Father," David said, motioning us all closer. "The safe-deposit box held the original deeds to Roswell House and a diary written by a Roswell cousin. She detailed some incidents that shocked Bernard as much as they did me. Bernard knew of the death of one of Wick's daughters in a horse accident, but the other also died in a tragic way. She was leaning out an upstairs window, and the glass shattered. A shard fell and severed an artery. She bled to death before anyone could help her."

"Bernard didn't know this?" I asked.

"Apparently rumors of the curse were already circulating. The family buried the details of Daisy Roswell's death to avoid more scandal. The diarist also believed the house was haunted."

Dr. Abbott glanced around at all of us, black bag in hand. "I don't like this."

"Neither do I." I squared my shoulders. "But it's the decision Camilla made. Not just for herself, but because it's the right thing to do. Let's get started."

"Raissa, I need to speak with you." David motioned me away from the group. "Be careful. There's more to Roswell House than you know."

I had no doubt he was correct. "What else did you find in the safe-deposit box?"

"It's Camilla's family. Maude is—"

The sound of piano music came from the house. I'd seen an old upright, covered with a heavy dust cloth, in the third-floor ballroom. I'd thought nothing of it until now. And in that moment, I realized that Camilla was missing. Dr. Abbott and the priest were talking, and she'd slipped away without anyone noticing.

I staggered back from David. "She's in there. We have to get to her. Now."

As he turned, stunned, Chopin's nocturnes came from the third floor, the fading day calling to the coming night, as if the house knew my thoughts and emotions.

Suddenly two windows on the third floor blew out, glass shattering and flying toward us as we ducked behind the cars some fifty yards away.

"She's in there by herself!" David turned toward the house.

"David, wait." I tried to grasp his coat, but he was already running toward the house. The thing I'd tried hard to avoid was happening. David and Camilla would be in the house alone.

"Wait! What's wrong with David?" Camilla stepped out from behind one of the cars. "We have to stop him."

I realized then that the house had tricked us. It had cut David from the herd, and I feared what it meant to do with him.

"Who's playing the piano?" Zelda asked.

I felt half-shocked to know that someone else could hear it, but there was no time to speculate. "Come with me." I strode toward the house, followed by Camilla, Zelda, Dr. Abbott, and Father Gregory, who didn't look happy to be part of the night's proceedings. Nonetheless, he might prove more valuable than anyone else attending. Madam's reading of the situation at Roswell House was that the entity came from the past. Without being on the premises, she couldn't be more specific, but she'd given me a series of questions to ask and rituals to perform. If Wick Roswell or Nina Campbell had killed with such viciousness that they'd warped the spirits of their victims, I would try to release them. If it was Wick or Nina in residence, then I intended to cast them out. And I might need Father Gregory to help me do that. But for now, we had to get to David.

I was surprised when we entered the house without problems. The piano music had stopped, and David sat on the stairs, a bit stunned but unharmed. The house, or the specter occupying it, had shown us the power it wielded. Now it was playing possum.

Camilla gave David some water as Zelda and I lit the candles, preparing the dining table for the séance. We had everything in order as the summer sun began to sink below the tops of the trees. A July storm had swiftly moved in, and lightning forked across the western sky, followed by thunder. My mother had told me to count the seconds between lightning and thunder, and it would tell me the distance of the storm from my location. Six miles. It would be upon us in a matter of minutes, and soon it would be full dark.

Roswell House was silent as we made our preparations, but I knew better than to trust it. It was waiting. She was in here. I'd seen her in the window, heard her fingers on the piano keys. She was a trickster, and she'd shown me how she could manipulate each of us. What if I lost control of the séance?

I thought of the kitchen knives, and I hurried there to make sure they had not been returned. They were still securely locked away, and the key remained in the pocket of my skirt. I gave it to Dr. Abbott without explanation, only asking him to hold on to it.

I desperately wanted Reginald to be here. In our short partnership, I'd come to rely on him to know when to intervene. I feared I might lose myself. Or that, if the entity overpowered me, I might try to harm Camilla or David. I kept those worries mostly to myself, telling David in a whisper that if I became aggressive, to render me unconscious with a tranquilizer or whatever it took. He understood my meaning.

Zelda went to the door and shut it as the sun dipped behind the treetops. There was still plenty of light, but it was the dying light of dusk, soon to be gone. Day yielding to night . . . I pushed those thoughts away. There was business to be done.

"Once we're seated, please don't get up. If I go into a trance, ask the questions you need to know, which is who fills this space and what does she or it want. I've written them down." I pushed the notes I'd made toward David. "Try to find out who's here."

"She?" the priest asked.

"I believe the entity is female, though I can't be certain. Some spirits, if this is a spirit, assume whatever form they need for trickery. If she attempts to take me over, please try to stop her."

My voice shook, and I couldn't help it.

The priest stood up. "I don't think I can be a part of this attempt to communicate with evil."

"Father," David said softly, "will you stay outside? In case we need you."

His request was so soft-spoken, so filled with desperation, that the priest nodded as he left the house. "I'll wait at the car."

No one else heard it at all, but I could have sworn the house giggled. I looked around, steeling myself for what was to come. "Join hands on top of the table."

I went through the ritual Madam recommended, purging the house of all spirits, of the past, of negativity. Zelda used sage smoke to cleanse the house, blowing the aromatic smoke from a smoldering bundle of leaves, into the corners of the first floor. She started toward the upstairs, and a burning ember dropped into the short skirt of her dress. In a moment, she was batting out flames.

It happened so quickly, I barely had time to stand up. David jumped up from his seat, threw his coat over Zelda, and smothered the fire before she was truly harmed, but it unnerved everyone at the table. Everyone except Zelda, who was spitting mad. "I loved this dress." She held out the charred skirt, which stank of smoke and fire. "You can't scare me away," she said to the house. "We will defeat you."

I wished yet again for her courage.

"Are you sure we should continue?" Camilla had sat silently at the table, but when I looked at her, truly looked, I could see she was in emotional distress.

"We must," Zelda said. "If this is to be ended, we must do it now." Lightning sizzled outside, and a clap of thunder so loud it made us all jump emphasized her determination.

I couldn't disagree, and we returned to the table, Zelda now seated beside Camilla. We joined hands. Before I could utter a word, the candles in the room were extinguished with a rancid gust of wind. Camilla gasped, and David urged her softly to remain calm.

"What is this?" Dr. Abbott demanded. "Some trick?"

"Be steady," David said. "Let Raissa work."

Without warning, she was with us. She stood not ten feet from the table. I saw her in the flash of lightning that illuminated her. And then I heard the buzzing of the flies. The rot of decay wafted over the table, and everyone began to gag. If Dr. Abbott had doubted me, he no longer did.

"What in the hell?" he muttered.

"Who are you?" I asked the creature.

She didn't speak, but I heard her answer. *The past is always alive.*

It was the best clue she'd given. "What do you want?"

Camilla gasped and struggled for breath. "It's pushing at me, trying to push into my chest again. Don't let it."

I now believed that whatever was pushing at Camilla was somehow part of her. Camilla *had* to be a Roswell.

Before I could pursue the matter, lightning struck in the front yard. Ozone filled the air, and I had a terrified thought for the priest. Had he been struck? Before I could even stand, the front door flew open.

Jason Kuddle entered the house, a gun in his hand. "Leaving a priest for a guard isn't so smart." He looked around. "Well, isn't this cozy?" He pointed with his pistol barrel. "Get up and move over to the wall. All of you." David, Dr. Abbott, Camilla, and I responded.

Zelda didn't move. "What the hell do you think you're doing?"

"What's necessary. Now move." He grasped her shoulder and dragged her up from her chair, thrusting her against the wall with the rest of us. "You couldn't let it go," he said. "You kept poking and poking and poking. You sent the law out to Bryce, and they found those two little bitches. I should've killed them."

"Joanne is safe?" Camilla asked.

"So what if she is? You won't see her again."

"And the Ames girl?" I asked. My question was sincere, but I also hoped to distract him. If we wanted to live, one of us was going to have to make a move. He'd left the front door open, and outside lightning exploded once again as the rain came down in a solid sheet.

"The cops took her. They won't get nothin' out of her, though."

I thought of Mrs. Ames, broken by her daughter's abduction, and I wanted to kill Kuddle. Zelda's hand caught mine, and she squeezed.

"Where's Reginald? He left with you. What did you do to him?" I had to know what happened to my partner.

"He ain't the pretty boy he used to be."

I pulled away from Zelda, fists clenched, but she pulled me back. She wasn't as tall as I was, but she was strong. "Stop," she whispered in my ear. "He'll kill you."

"He's going to kill us all. Don't you see? He's been a part of these abductions all along. He and Dr. Perkins are working together. They take these young girls, destroy their wills with that horrific surgery, and turn them out as prostitutes." There wasn't any point in pretending I hadn't figured it out. This was the connection to Camilla and the lost girls, to Bryce and the fate of rural young women whose families had no money to search for them. My efforts to help Camilla had led me to the lost girls. Had Zelda not hired Reginald and me to help Camilla, we would never have known what was happening.

"You're not as smart as you think," Kuddle said, but his cocky attitude had clearly taken a hit.

The storm crashed around the house, and the wind outside roared. A limb blew into the window behind us, and we all jumped. When I looked at the open door where the rain and shredded leaves blew into the house, I saw a sodden figure standing in the doorway. Soon it was joined by another. The house contained more than one spirit, and they came toward us. One held something in his hand. As they drew closer, I realized it was a tire tool.

No, not a spirit. Father Gregory had entered the house with a weapon.

He closed in on Kuddle, who remained unaware of his arrival. Father Gregory raised the tire iron and brought it down with enough force to drop Kuddle to his knees. The second man kicked him in the chest, sending him toppling to the floor. The gun skittered across the floor, and, in a split second, David had it in his hand.

"Reginald!" David said. "Thank God! You're alive!"

"Not because that bastard didn't try to kill me." It was indeed my partner, looking more like a miserable, drowned rat than my debonair friend. I ran to him and hugged him tightly. It was only when I stepped back and Zelda lit a candle that I realized Reginald was not just wet—he was bleeding. Blood soaked his clothes and the side of his head, face, and neck. He staggered but managed to stay on his feet, then toppled to the floor, unconscious.

CHAPTER THIRTY-NINE

The room was ablaze with candles. Jason Kuddle, still unconscious, lay on the floor by the wall, tied with cords from the heavy draperies. He wasn't going anywhere. Dr. Abbott expressed concern that he might have sustained a concussion, but Kuddle was at the bottom of my priority list.

Prior to examining Kuddle, Dr. Abbott had patched the gunshot wound in Reginald's shoulder and dressed his head wound, and we'd managed to seat him at the table. Reginald would require surgery to remove the bullet that Kuddle had put into him—leaving him to bleed out in the woods behind the bar where I'd met Martha. I'd been a hundred yards from Reginald and hadn't a clue he lay bleeding in the dirt. Martha had lied to me. She and Kuddle were in league together.

I sat in front of Reginald and put a hand to his forehead. At least the bleeding had stopped, and he was conscious and determined to finish our night's business. Even in his weakened state, he'd prevailed upon the priest to wield a tire iron and strike a man—a murdering criminal to be sure—because Reginald was too weak to hit him properly. Father Gregory had chosen wisely and saved all of us.

"I know the link between Camilla and Roswell House," Reginald said. We all drew close to listen to him. "I know why Camilla is being targeted."

"Tell us quickly." The temperature in the house shifted, and a chill swept over me. Camilla felt it, too, and rubbed her arms briskly, unaware what the wave of cold might signal. "Hurry, Reginald. Talk fast." We still had unfinished business in Roswell House. The storm had passed, but the hour was creeping toward midnight, and I had a sense that the house waited for that time between—the veil between the dead and the living was always thinnest in those hours or days where change, from day to night or season to season, occurred.

"Camilla is a descendant of Nina Campbell, Maybel Cooner's illegitimate child. Maude was Nina Campbell's child, though she's worked hard to hide it."

David stood abruptly. "That's what Maude didn't want me to find out. That's why she had me arrested. The letters in the safe-deposit box mentioned Buster's Bar. I went there, and that woman, Martha, told me Maude had terrible secrets that impacted Camilla, and if I wanted the truth, I should wring it out of her. So I went there, and she called the police on me."

"Wait," I said. "Nina and Wick Roswell had a child?"

"I can't say if Wick was the father, but Nina is definitely Camilla's grandmother." Reginald swallowed, and I handed him a glass of water.

"That can't be." Camilla stepped back as if she'd been struck. "Nina Campbell was a wicked woman. Cruel and malicious. I've heard stories about her all my life, how she ruined people's lives and committed robberies and shootings. I can't be related to her. She can't be my grandmother."

"But she is," Reginald said. His voice was weak, but his convictions made him sit up straighter. "You are her heir, and the presence in this house is between you and Nina. Before Kuddle shot me, Martha Campbell told me the truth. She's your aunt, Camilla. Martha and

Maude are sisters, though Maude has done everything in her power to hide that secret, even to the point of moving away as a very young girl, changing her name, and coming back. She's been paying Martha a stipend to keep her secret."

"The past is always alive." I repeated what I'd heard earlier, what the entity had told me.

"What does that mean?" Camilla asked. "I don't understand."

I wasn't certain I did either, but I had an inkling. "Do you believe that people return, that their spirits can reincarnate?"

"That's absolute foolishness," Father Gregory said. His impatience had been visibly growing. "You die and you ascend to heaven, or you're sentenced to hell or the limbo of purgatory. There is no coming back to live again."

I didn't want to dispute the man who'd saved our lives, but I had to. "I'm not an expert on religion, but what if a soul wanted to make amends, to come back as a good person instead of someone cruel and vile?"

"You think Camilla is confronting her past life as Nina Campbell." Reginald, even in his weakened state, understood. "She's reincarnated to make amends, but the past life never truly let go."

"No! No! That can't be." Camilla started toward the door, but David caught her.

"Think about it, Camilla," Reginald said. "Wick Roswell used Nina. Because Kuddle was going to kill me, Martha told me the whole story, how Wick promised Nina the moon. How he used her to do his dirtiest work. Together they murdered innocent children, took what they wanted, cheated, robbed, and intimidated. And then he abandoned Nina and married the society girl. He made Priscilla Harlow the lady of this house, the house Nina thought he was building for her."

It made perfect sense in a terrible way. "And this is the curse on the females of the Roswell line. Nina knew the surest way to mark the family." I put a hand on Camilla's shoulder. "You're here to balance the scales, Camilla. Your character, your compassion—these are things that offset the past. Where we come from doesn't dictate who we are."

"The problem is Nina has left a very strong remnant here, a past life. And she isn't ready to reform," Reginald added. "She wants her due. Roswell House. And she intends to take it, using you."

"This is nonsense." Father Gregory headed to the door. "I can't be part of this."

"I understand," I said. "But you saved us all from Jason Kuddle. We truly don't mean to offend you, and we thank you."

"I'll wait in the car."

When he was gone, I turned to Dr. Abbott. "If you'd like to leave, we understand."

"You think I'm leaving now? Not on a bet."

I motioned the others to give me a moment alone with Reginald. He was wan, but he would make it through the ritual. "What if we're wrong?" I asked.

"I'm not certain about the past life, but there is residual energy here. There's something from the past that is filled with darkness and cruelty. The priest might call it evil, but I don't know. I only understand that it's part of Camilla. Perhaps a part she left behind when she was Nina, or maybe a part she needs now to become her own woman." He touched my cheek softly. "Her own person. I believe that sometimes bits of us get scattered, and Nina Campbell was so terribly strong, all those cruel things were left behind."

"Maude is pretty awful, too. The apple didn't fall far from the tree."

Reginald snorted. "Truer words and all that. The problem is, Camilla disavows those aspects of who she is. I'm not certain she can accept them."

"If she doesn't?"

"They'll remain here, in the house."

"And if she does concede they are a necessary part of her, will it change her?"

"I can't honestly answer that. I've seen Madam integrate a past life once. The gentleman survived and went home, but who can say how it truly turned out? We never heard from him again."

"Then we at least have to try. I want this over."

I called everyone to the table. Reginald sat close beside me, his uninjured hand on my shoulder. He would guide me through this.

"Camilla," I said, "you have a choice. Do you want to try to accept this . . . shadow?" I avoided the term *past life* in deference to Dr. Abbott.

"Is it really a choice?" she asked.

"It is. You can leave Roswell House and Alabama. You can build a new life with David anywhere in the world, and I believe you'll be free. The entity seems attached to Roswell House."

"But she will always be here, waiting, wanting me to return—won't she?" Camilla brushed a tear from her cheek. "I'd rather face her now, with my friends, my fiancé, here to help me."

I nodded. She had made her choice. And I had learned that it wasn't up to me to choose. "Once again, hold hands." With the candles flickering and the moon, at last, lighting the lawn outside the house, I began. "Nina Campbell, we call upon you to appear before us."

Outside the window, I saw the twin girls. They watched us. And behind them others arrived. The lawn filled with the dead that Nina Campbell had harmed. I couldn't believe that gentle Camilla had anything to do with this woman who'd done such terrible things, seemingly without compunction. I had much to learn about the spirit world, though. My job now was to assist, not to understand.

"Nina Campbell," I said, my voice more forceful, "we *demand* you come forward."

I saw her then, just as everyone at the table gagged at the stench of death. She came forward, a tall, slender woman with luxuriant chestnut hair piled high on her head. When the candlelight touched her face, I inhaled sharply. Her amorphous features were like those of the child in my dream about the underworld. Nina Campbell belonged to neither the light nor the dark. Her time had come and gone, and she clung to a house that had never been hers.

"I name you, Nina Campbell. Spirit, ghost, demon, or lost soul, you will leave these premises and allow Camilla and David to live here happily."

"Milksop. I'll have no part of this." She had no mouth to speak, and the others clearly couldn't hear her.

"You will leave. I will cast you out."

"I will kill her." Nina shifted behind Camilla. She towered over her—a black, dense energy. Camilla winced as if in pain.

"There's pressure on my chest," she said, struggling to stand but unable to do so. "Please, I can't breathe. Make it stop."

Reginald's fingers pressed into my shoulder. "Keep going," he urged.

"Nina, you must leave this house. You are the past, and there is no place for you here."

A howl of wind burst through the room, guttering the candles. We gagged on the odor of decay, but no one left the table, and Camilla gulped in oxygen when the pain relented.

"I name you, Nina Campbell, and your sins. Judgment awaits you, and there is no more delay."

"I'll take the milksop with me," she said.

Camilla cried out and crumpled. I tried to rise, but Reginald held me in my seat. "Finish it," he commanded.

I'd memorized the words Madam had taught me. "You have no power here. You were unwanted here even by the man you killed for. You must leave. That life is over, and you must face your transgressions. Camilla has her own life, her own path. She has left you and your evil choices behind."

"I'm stronger than she is. I can inhabit her, control her, make her do my bidding. I made her cut her man, and I'll make her do worse." Nina spiraled into a dark cloud and disappeared into the top of Camilla's head.

Camilla sat up and shook free of David. Zelda attempted to restrain her, but she backhanded her friend. When she looked at me, I knew Nina was inside her. "Give me a knife," she said in a voice hoarse and unfamiliar.

I had merged the two, but I'd underestimated Nina's strength. She'd overpowered Camilla. Before my very eyes, the tender young woman I'd come to help disappeared. A harsh, cruel woman took her place, her mouth twisted into a victorious smile.

"What should I do?" I asked Reginald while the table was transfixed by Camilla's transformation. She seemed to grow taller, stouter. The soft planes of her face hardened, and lines formed on either side of her mouth.

"David, fight for Camilla," Reginald said. "Bring her back."

David gripped her hand and stood to face her. "I don't care who you are or why you're here, but you will get out of the woman I love."

Camilla's laugh was haughty. "I've bested better than you. I brought men to their knees, begging me to spare their children. I cut their throats ear to ear. I'm not afraid of you. Would you like to see what I can do to this person you love?"

"A physical change is not possible." Dr. Abbott's words lacked conviction.

Camilla cried out in pain, doubling over and sobbing. Zelda was instantly at her side, a frantic look on her face.

"Help her," Zelda begged.

"Stop it!" David said, panicking.

Nina laughed. "She is not a strong woman, is she? I will break her."

"Fight, David," Reginald said. "Her bond to you is stronger than Nina's power. Make her remember."

Dr. Abbott looked horrified, but he didn't move from the table.

David found a fresh wave of courage. "Camilla, you and I will raise our children in this house, in a loving family. But you have to fight. Push her back. Push her out. You are not controlled by this thing. Come back to me." He let go of her hand and grasped her shoulders, forcing her to look at him. "Remember, darling, we're going to lace the bannister on the stairs with passionflower vines and Confederate jasmine for our wedding. The blooms will fill the air with such sweetness."

Camilla's lovely face twisted into something unrecognizable. "She's mine. I'm in her now, and she'll never be your sweet Camilla again. She can't erase me. I'll have my due."

"Don't give up, Camilla." I encouraged her, though I saw no trace of the young woman remaining. Nina Campbell had completely taken over her body. But Nina was not simply a spirit from the past; she was something else. A shade of another life lived.

"Tell her she's good," I urged David. "Make her remember who she is now, in this life. Not the past."

"Camilla, I fell in love with you because of your gentle spirit. You are the kindest person I've ever known. But you're also strong. You make the world better, and I won't let you go. You are loved. And you deserve only joy. Don't let this angry apparition destroy our chance for happiness. Come back to me, to my love for you."

"Shut up, you fool." Camilla spat in his face.

Zelda gasped and stood. "Camilla! Stop it. Fight her." She grabbed Camilla's hand and defied the entity that now controlled Camilla. "I won't let you have her."

David wiped the spittle away. "Camilla, you and I will have everything Nina ever wanted. A love stronger than the two of us apart, a marriage we choose and that we'll honor each day we live together. A family of laughing children to run across the lawn. And we will live it here, in Roswell House."

"You'll never get her or the house." Camilla's body bent backward in a way I feared would snap her spine. "I will destroy her before I give up."

"You'll never have her." David captured Camilla in his arms. "I'll kill her and burn Roswell House to the ground. I swear it to you. She would not want to live with such a horror inside her. Let her go, or I'll damn us both to hell." His grip on Camilla's neck tightened, and she began to struggle to breathe. "Get out!"

Camilla's body contorted, then went limp.

"Lay her on the floor!" Dr. Abbott commanded. He checked her pulse at her throat. "We're losing her."

Something hard struck the wooden floor. Multicolored marbles rolled toward Camilla's prone body. They'd dropped out of thin air, it seemed, causing the others to gasp. Then I saw the girls. The twins came forward, marbles falling from their hands.

"I can't believe this," Dr. Abbott said as he knelt beside Camilla and stopped several of the marbles with his hand. "We have to get her to the hospital."

Beside the doctor, I saw Camilla's gentle spirit appear. She was the tender Camilla beloved by her friends, but I was terrified that she'd abandoned her body, that she'd quit fighting. "You can't be in this house," Camilla said to the girls, though no one other than me could see them.

"We belong. You have to leave. She will kill you."

Camilla's spirit solidified and grew stronger as she brushed her hand over one twin's hair. "I'll help you escape this place. I'll take care of you."

"No, Camilla, don't go!" I had to bring her back. She couldn't let Nina win. "David, call Camilla back. Tell her she has to accept the past, that she can reconcile all of it later. Tell her she can defeat Nina—because she's loving and kind. She can help the others trapped here. But she can't let Nina have her flesh."

David tenderly lifted Camilla's head. "I don't care what happened in the past. I know who you are now, and I love you. Together we'll sort this out, but you have to fight or I will lose you."

A swarm of flies dived at Camilla's body, and David and Dr. Abbott shielded her.

"Get out," the girls said. I joined in, motioning for Reginald and Dr. Abbott to join me. "Get out. Nina Campbell, get out. You don't belong here. You never did." We were a ragtag chorus that grew in strength as we chanted the same words over and over again.

"The past can't be undone," David said to Camilla, his lips close to her ear, "but it isn't who you are today. You learned and changed." As the flies dropped dead around them, David lifted her up. "Sit up and fight!"

Camilla's eyes focused, and she looked around.

No one else saw the dark mist that left her. No one living. The twins saw it, and together they chased it out of the house. When they were gone, the door slammed shut.

The house sighed. Everyone heard it and looked around.

"Could I please have some water?" Camilla asked.

"Whatever you need," Zelda said. "Whatever you need."

CHAPTER FORTY

Dr. Abbott drove Reginald to the hospital, where he would remove the bullet. Kuddle was conscious but restrained, and Dr. Abbott promised to send the police to retrieve him—as well as to pick up Martha Campbell and ascertain her role in Reginald's shooting and the abduction of the young girls. I believed Martha had helped turn out the stolen girls, but I had no proof. The sheriff would have to make his case in that regard. God willing, Martha, Kuddle, and the doctors involved would all face justice for using helpless young women for profit.

The storm had passed, but the rain seemed to have intensified the sweltering heat. Zelda and I sat outside Roswell House with Father Gregory. He was still upset with us, but he was thawing. As we told him the story of the missing girls, Jason Kuddle's role in what appeared to be a prostitution ring using young women stolen from rural areas, he dropped his anger at us for conversing with evil spirits. He was a good man at heart who'd been confronted with things he was unprepared to witness.

Per his promise, Dr. Abbott also called Judge Sayre and Minnie. They looked almost as frazzled as we felt when they arrived at Roswell House.

"The whole town's in an uproar," Judge Sayre told Zelda and me. "I have no doubt you two are at the bottom of it. Did you have anything to do with Camilla Granger's escape from Bryce Hospital?"

"Yes, sir," Zelda said. "We took her. She's here, and we want you to marry her and David. Right now. Before Maude gets wind of it."

Judge Sayre assessed his daughter for a long moment. "A good plan. Where are the bride and groom?"

"They're inside." I hadn't wanted to leave them there alone, but they had insisted. Camilla had to believe that whatever had lingered there to torment her was gone. She would never attempt to injure David again. And the only way to prove it to her was to allow her and David to wander Roswell House alone.

"Oh my," Minnie said. "Are you sure—but of course you are or you wouldn't be out here in this swampy heat."

"Father Gregory, would you serve as witness to the wedding?" Judge Sayre asked.

"Of course."

"Then let's get on with the ceremony. If Maude learns Camilla is here, she'll descend on us like a starving vulture."

I laughed out loud. Judge Sayre seldom expressed his true opinion, but he was on the money.

"What about Reginald?" Zelda asked.

"He'll understand. Time is our enemy."

We went inside and gathered at the base of the beautiful staircase, candles lit and glowing brightly, and Judge Sayre performed the ceremony that bound David and Camilla as man and wife and that transferred her care to her husband. Maude Granger no longer had any say-so in Camilla's future.

And not a moment too soon. Maude arrived just as the nuptials concluded. She brought with her two Montgomery police officers. We met them on the front lawn.

Maude charged toward us, hurling orders like cannonballs. "Charge that man with kidnapping. Detain both of those women. Where's the other man, the one with the mustache?"

Camilla's voice was a calm contrast. "Mama, I'm no longer your concern. David is my husband."

"Get in that car right now," Maude commanded.

Camilla took David's hand. "Go to hell."

I couldn't tell if Camilla had grown from her experience, or if perhaps she had absorbed a bit of Nina Campbell's power and strength. Only time would tell.

"How dare you?" Maude raised her hand as if to slap Camilla's face, but David grasped her wrist.

"Touch my wife, and I will snap your neck."

Minnie and Judge Sayre came through the open door to the lawn. "It's time for you to disappear, Maude Granger," Minnie said. "You've done everything in your power to destroy your own daughter's happiness. Now she's free of you. We all are."

David released Maude's wrist. "I know you now, Maude Campbell Granger. I know your mother's deeds and how you learned at her knee. None of that impacts Camilla. But you, you are another matter. Remove yourself from my property." David turned, and he and Camilla walked away, entering Roswell House and closing the door.

Judge Sayre took control. "Officers, there's a murderer tied up in the dining room. He needs to be transported to jail. Take him with you, and I advise you to get back to your duties."

Maude was left standing alone in the yard while everyone else went on about their lives. This was the fate she'd earned and deserved, the one thing she couldn't abide. Being ignored.

Two days later, we sat in the sunroom of Sayre House, the shade cast by the beautiful trees dancing fitfully in a welcome breeze. We sipped lemonade with a zip, laced with some bootlegged rum, and Zelda told her father and mother the whole story of Camilla's abduction and ultimate rescue. Zelda didn't have Tallulah's husky voice, but she was a natural-born storyteller. I listened with great appreciation as she added just enough embellishment into our great escape from Bryce and the near accident on the road when we'd almost been waylaid. Reginald had only one small detail to add, something he'd learned during his hours as Kuddle's prisoner. The crooked private investigator had arranged the posse that had attempted to block us on the road from Tuscaloosa, just as he'd paid the drivers of the car to run us off the road at the catfish camp. Kuddle had intended all along to get rid of Reginald and me and anyone else who might be asking the wrong questions.

Minnie put a hand over her heart. "Thank goodness. I had no idea what was truly going on."

"But we have the perfect ending for a wild story. Scott is going to love this. Maybe he'll even write it into a story. And you, too, Raissa. I can't wait to see what you make of the events."

I did have several ideas—and now that I would be returning to the solitude of Caoin House in the morning, I would have time to write. Nothing had ever sounded quite so lovely as the idea of long hours, sitting in my bedroom, staring out at the oak grove, and letting my imagination hold sway.

Reginald and Judge Sayre enjoyed a lively debate about the ongoing investigation into Bryce Hospital. I still wasn't certain I believed that the eminent Dr. Perkins was not involved in the prostitution ring and had never suspected that the pretty girls who conveniently showed up and "desperately needed" his surgery were kidnapped young women.

Somehow he'd convinced the police he wasn't involved, aided in part by his three-week hitch in Vienna. Dr. Bentley and Dr. French were another matter. Both doctors had admitted their part in the wretched operation. They'd been taken into custody.

Joanne Pence and Ritter Ames had been found, safe and unharmed. Nurse Brady, who had begun to suspect foul play, had helped the young women hide on the hospital premises. She'd been able to move them from place to place to avoid detection. Both had been returned to their families. I'd received a note from Mrs. Ames thanking me for my part in saving her daughter. I couldn't read it without crying.

Zelda plopped down beside me on the wicker sofa. "Come to New York. Both of you. I would adore introducing you to my set of friends. You're very proper, Raissa, but I sense that underneath you're dying to be modern."

"I would like that." The thought of a New York trip appealed to me. "Reginald would fit right in. He has the polish of a big-city man."

"He would. He's an enigma, isn't he?"

I wondered if Zelda sensed Reginald's secret. If she did, she wouldn't care. She and Tallulah were dedicated to living their own lives and allowing others to do the same. "Maybe we will. I'd love to see New York City when it's decorated for Christmas. Maybe this winter we can talk Uncle Brett into taking the train up. It would be such fun."

"We'll plan on that. Scott is very eager to read your story in the *Saturday Evening Post*. I'm sure you'll hear from him once it's published."

The generosity made me shake my head in disbelief. "That's wonderful."

"I'm leaving in the morning at five." She nudged me with her shoulder. "It's not too late to come with me. We can take turns driving, the three of us."

We heard a knock at the door, and Althea came to the sunroom holding an envelope. "It's for you, Mrs. James."

I took the heavy cream envelope, aware that everyone in the room was curious but too polite to ask. The postmark was from West Point, Mississippi. I opened the flap and withdrew a single note.

Dear Mrs. James and Mr. Proctor,

I turn to you with complete desperation. I've heard that you have been successful in solving mysteries that seem not to have a rational explanation. Can you please help me?

My husband and I, with our young daughter, have recently bought a home in West Point known as Waverley Mansion. It's a beautiful home on the Tombigbee River, with lovely grounds and a quiet history. We've been happy here, meeting our neighbors and settling into the life we always dreamed of living.

Recently, though, our happy home has been shattered by the strange behavior of our daughter, Amanda. She's eight years old and normally a sunny child who loves other children and playing. In the last four weeks, her personality has deteriorated, and I find her alone in the third-floor rotunda talking to an empty room. She has also begun sleepwalking.

She claims there is a child in the house, her playmate, Nan. But there is no other child here. No living child. Would you consider coming to Waverley Mansion to explore the phenomena? You'll be richly compensated, and my husband will pay all travel expenses.

Please say yes. My daughter's life may depend upon it.

Best,

Anne Sheridan

I gave the note to Reginald, who read it quickly and looked at me, one eyebrow cocked. "Another case? We seem to be in demand."

"I'd hoped for a break." I didn't really want to go to West Point, but Mrs. Sheridan sounded so desperate.

Reginald read the note out loud to the group.

"West Point's not too far beyond Tuscaloosa," Judge Sayre said. "It would be much easier to go there by train in the morning, and then you could take the Tombigbee River home in one of your uncle's riverboats. The downriver trip will go much faster."

"How exciting!" Zelda took the note from Reginald and read it out loud again. "A haunted child. That sounds delicious."

"Zelda!" Minnie reprimanded. "I can feel the mother's despair."

The problem was that I could, too. "I suppose we should check it out." I realized it didn't sound gracious, but I truly was tired.

"Indeed," Reginald said. "After this case, a haunted child should be a snap."

I didn't feel that at all, but it seemed I would at least find out the parameters of this new haunting.

"I'll change your accommodations on the steamship," Zelda said. "We can get you on the train first thing. I'd drive you but—"

"I believe your husband is waiting for you to return to him," I said. "The train will be fine."

"Then let's have dinner and another round of this delicious lemonade," Zelda said. "Tonight we play, for tomorrow is a day of labor." She turned to my partner. "Butt me, Reginald."

ACKNOWLEDGMENTS

Many, many thanks to the Amazon team, including Jessica Tribble, Ed Stackler, and Robin O'Dell. I turned in a pretty good yarn, and Jessica, Ed, Robin, and Jill Kramer made it sing. Editing is an art as unique and difficult as writing. It's such a privilege to work with such fine editors.

My writing career has marched side by side with my friendship with Marian Young, my agent. Thank you.

Many thanks to Rebecca Barrett and Susan Tanner, who were first readers on this manuscript. When I wanted to veer off the trail of the story and chase rabbits, they brought me to heel. Not an easy task.

Thank you to my readers, who are so willing to give my stories a try. I always ask my university students the first question: Do you want to write for yourself, or do you want an audience? I'm a storyteller. I need an audience, and I have to say I have the best audience in the business. I work hard to write a compelling story, and my readers give me their hearts and a willing suspension of disbelief as they enter the worlds I create. It's quite a relationship. I am privileged. As Raissa and Reginald delve into the world of 1920s spiritualism, I hope you'll continue to explore with me.

AUTHOR'S NOTE

Transorbital lobotomies were first medically documented in 1937, and I have played with the surgical timeline a little for the purposes of my story. The idea of opening the skull to eliminate mental illness dates back to the Neolithic era.

ABOUT THE AUTHOR

 Carolyn Haines is the *USA Today* best-selling author of more than seventy books, including the popular Sarah Booth Delaney Mississippi Delta mystery series and *The Book of Beloved*, the first novel in the Pluto's Snitch mystery series. A native of Mississippi, Haines writes in multiple genres. She's a recipient of the 2010 Harper Lee Award for Distinguished Writing and the 2009 Richard Wright Award for Literary Excellence. She has also been honored by *Suspense Magazine* and *Romantic Times* for best mystery series. An animal advocate, Haines founded a small 501c3 rescue, Good Fortune Farm Refuge. She cares for nine dogs, nine cats, and six horses.